CRITICAL ACCLAIM FOR *STOP DEAD*

'All the things a mystery should be, intriguing, enthralling, tense and utterly absorbing' – ***Best Crime Books***

'*Stop Dead* is taut and compelling, stylishly written with a deeply human voice' – **Peter James**

'A definite must read for crime thriller fans everywhere – 5*' – ***Newbooks Magazine***

'A well-written, a well-researched, and a well-constructed whodunnit. Highly recommended' – ***Mystery People***

'A whodunnit of the highest order. The tightly written plot kept me guessing all the way' – ***Crimesquad***

CRITICAL ACCLAIM FOR *DEATH BED*

'*Death Bed* is a marvellous entry in this highly acclaimed series' – ***Promoting Crime Fiction***

'An innovative and refreshing take on the psychological thriller' – ***Books Plus Food***

'A well-written, well-plotted crime novel with fantastic pace and lots of intrigue' – ***Bookersatz***

'*Death Bed* is her most exciting and well-written to date. And, as the others are superb, that is really saying something! 5*' – ***Euro Crime***

CRITICAL ACCLAIM FOR *DEAD END*

'All the ingredients combine to make a tense, clever police whodunnit' – **Marcel Berlins**, *Times*

'I could not put this book down' – ***Newbooks Magazine***

'A brilliant talent in the thriller field' – **Jeffery Deaver**

'An encounter that will take readers into the darkest recesses of the human psyche' – ***Crime Time***

'Well written and chock full of surprises, this hard-hitting, edge-of-the seat instalment is yet another treat… Geraldine Steel looks set to become a household name. Highly recommended' – ***Euro Crime***

'Good, old-fashioned, heart-hammering police thriller… a no-frills delivery of pure excitement' – ***SAGA Magazine***

'A macabre read, full of enthralling characters and gruesome details which kept me glued from first page to last' – *Crimesquad*

'*Dead End* was selected as a Best Fiction Book of 2012'
– *Miami Examiner*

CRITICAL ACCLAIM FOR *ROAD CLOSED*

'A well-written, soundly plotted, psychologically acute story'
– **Marcel Berlins, *Times***

'Well-written and absorbing right from the get-go... with an exhilarating climax that you don't see coming' – *Euro Crime*

'Leigh Russell does a good job of keeping her readers guessing. She also uses a deft hand developing her characters, especially the low-lifes... a good read' – *San Francisco Book Review*

'*Road Closed* is a gripping, fast-paced read, pulling you in from the very first tense page and keeping you captivated right to the end with its refreshingly compelling and original narrative'
– *New York Journal of Books*

CRITICAL ACCLAIM FOR *CUT SHORT*

'*Cut Short* is a stylish, top-of-the-line crime tale, a seamless blending of psychological sophistication and gritty police procedure. And you're just plain going to love DI Geraldine Steel' – **Jeffery Deaver**

'Russell paints a careful and intriguing portrait of a small British community while developing a compassionate and complex heroine who's sure to win fans' – *Publishers Weekly*

'An excellent debut' – *Crime Time*

'Simply awesome! This debut novel by Leigh Russell will take your breath away' – *Euro Crime*

'An excellent book...Truly a great start for new mystery author Leigh Russell' – *New York Journal of Books*

'A sure-fire hit – a taut, slick, easy-to-read thriller' – *Watford Observer*

'*Cut Short* is not a comfortable read, but it is a compelling and important one. Highly recommended' – *Mystery Women*

Titles by Leigh Russell

Geraldine Steel Mysteries

Cut Short
Road Closed
Dead End
Death Bed
Stop Dead
Fatal Act
Killer Plan
Murder Ring
Deadly Alibi

Ian Peterson Murder Investigations

Cold Sacrifice
Race to Death
Blood Axe

Lucy Hall Mystery

Journey to Death
Girl in Danger
The Wrong Suspect

LEIGH RUSSELL

DEAD END

A DI GERALDINE STEEL MYSTERY

NO EXIT PRESS

First published in 2011 by No Exit Press,

an imprint of Oldcastle Books Ltd,

PO Box 394,

Harpenden, Herts, AL5 1XJ

www.noexit.co.uk

ISBN

978-1-84243-356-0 (print)

978-1-84243-436-9 (epub)

978-1-84243-437-6 (pdf)

978-1-84243-504-5 (kindle)

4 6 8 10 9 7 5

Typeset in Times New Roman 11pt, by SunTec, India

Printed and bound in Denmark by Nørhaven, Viborg

Dedicated to

Michael, Jo & Phill

Acknowledgements

I would like to thank Dr Leonard Russell for his medical advice, all my contacts on the police force for their help, my editor Keshini Naidoo for her guidance, and Annette Crossland with all the team at No Exit Press.

'When you kill somebody you change the universe.'

Dr Gwen Adshead,
Consultant Forensic Psychotherapist, Broadmoor Hospital

Glossary of acronyms used in *Dead End*

DCI   -   Detective Chief Inspector (senior officer on case)

DI   -   Detective Inspector

DS   -   Detective Sergeant

DC   -   Detective Constable

SOCO -   Scene of Crime Officers (collect forensic evidence at scene)

PM   -   Post-Mortem or Autopsy (examination of dead body to establish cause of death)

GCSE -   General Certificate of Secondary Education (high school examinations)

CCTV -   Closed Circuit Television (security cameras)

PART 1

'When you are sorrowful look again in your heart, and you shall see that in truth you are weeping for that which has been your delight.'

Khalil Gibran

1

ABIGAIL

Abigail's head hurt. She was afraid something was wrong with her eyes. She couldn't see anything. A heavy weight was pressing down on her chest. She fought against a feeling of nausea, and tried to turn her head but couldn't.

'Hello,' she croaked. No answer. She was alone in the darkness.

It had been raining when she left the shopping centre. Her son, Ben, had been trying out for an under-fourteen football team at his new school and Abigail had promised to be there when he came home. She remembered hurrying along the street, away from the shops. Now she was lying in darkness, unable to move.

'Hello,' she called again. Her throat hurt and there was a strange smell. By now Abigail had realised she was in hospital, coming round from an operation. Nurses of all people should have known better than to leave her lying on her back. There was a risk she might choke to death if she were sick. She seemed to lie there for hours, drifting in and out of consciousness. 'Hello,' she called again. 'Is anyone there? Please?'

The light dazzled her.

'Am I in hospital?' she asked. Her voice sounded far away. 'Are you a doctor?'

'Hello, Mrs Kirby. Mrs Abigail Kirby.' The man smiled. 'How are you feeling?' He held up a syringe. Clear liquid glistened on the tip of the needle. The man leaned forward, his head framed by an aura of white light.

Abigail closed her eyes and drifted back into dreams. She woke up in darkness. 'Doctor?' she called. 'Hello? Are you there? Is anyone there?'

Silence.

2

WAITING

Matthew Kirby glanced irritably at the clock. It was half term but Abigail had gone out early as usual. She was obsessed with her work. Since her promotion to headmistress she barely seemed to spare a thought for her family. Matthew had long since forgiven her for neglecting him. He was making a life for himself, a life that didn't include his wife, but Lucy and Ben were another matter. That betrayal was unforgivable. Ben was doing well at his new school. He had settled in straight away. Lucy was a worry.

'It's her age,' Matthew's girlfriend, Charlotte, told him. He wasn't convinced. The upheaval of moving to the South of England when her mother changed job wasn't ideal for a socially awkward fourteen-year-old girl.

Matthew frowned and checked the sausages before shouting from the foot of the stairs. 'Lunch is ready!'

A moment later he heard Ben charging down the stairs. Ben's grin faded as he caught sight of his father turning from the hob with a frying pan of sausages. 'Where's mum? I want to tell her –' He stopped, registering the expression on his father's face. 'She's not here, is she? She promised –'

Matthew put down the frying pan. 'Where's Lucy?'

Ben shrugged. 'In her room. Where else?' He flung himself on a chair, long limbs awry. 'I'm starving.'

'We're waiting for Lucy.'

'If I heard you, she did. She'd be here if she was hungry.'

Matthew strode out into the hall. 'Lucy! Get down here now. Lunch is on the table!' He swept back into the kitchen and shuffled sausages and beans onto three plates. Behind him, toast popped up.

Lucy appeared, sullen, in the doorway. 'Aren't we going to wait for mum?'

'Your mother's not here.'

'I can see that.' Lucy made no move to join her father and brother at the table.

'Come and sit down,' Matthew said. 'Mummy's working today.'

'She's always bloody working,' Ben complained. 'It's Saturday.' His chair scraped on the floor as he pulled himself closer to the table. 'I wanted to tell her about football training.'

'You'll have to tell her tonight.'

'She doesn't want to come home. It's his fault.' Lucy glared at Matthew. 'Him and his friend.'

'Come and sit down,' Matthew repeated in an even tone.

'I'm not hungry.'

'Lucy –' he began but her feet were already pounding up the stairs.

'All the more for us, dad,' Ben grinned.

Matthew sat down and picked at his food while Ben shovelled beans into his mouth. After a few minutes, Matthew put down his fork. Ben listened to his father's footsteps on the landing above. He heard knocking at Lucy's door. Silence, followed by the muted buzz of voices. Ben stood up and helped himself to more sausages, picking out the ones that weren't charred. By the time his father came down, Ben was seated at the table again, wiping his plate clean.

'She never eats,' he told his father cheerfully. 'Any chance of seconds?' He jumped up and began scraping the last of the beans from the pan.

'Use a wooden spoon,' Matthew protested. 'You're scratching the saucepan.'

'I'm done.' Ben turned round. 'What did she mean, dad?'

'What?'

'About you and your friend. What was she talking about?'

'Nothing. You know your sister.' Matthew sighed. 'What does she do up there on her own in her room all the time?'

'She's on the internet.' Ben left the kitchen and raced up the stairs, two at a time. Matthew watched him go. Slim and lithe, Ben reminded Matthew of himself as a youngster. They had the same straight nose and blue eyes, an unexpected combination with their black hair. Matthew cleared the plates off the table and dumped them in the sink. Abigail could clear up when she came home or, more likely, leave it for the cleaning lady to do in the morning.

Matthew closed the kitchen door before phoning Charlotte. 'It's me. I'll be over later on this afternoon. You weren't planning on going out, were you?'

'What time will you be round?'

'Soon.'

'The sooner the better.'

Matthew grinned and rang off. He threw a glance at the dirty plates in the sink then went upstairs and tapped on Ben's door. No answer. He knocked more loudly.

'Come in.'

Matthew looked at the clutter of clothes and school books that littered the floor of Ben's bedroom. 'I'm going out.'

'OK.' Ben turned back to his computer game.

'I have to see someone from work.'

'OK.'

'I won't be back late but don't wait up,' Matthew added. Ben wasn't listening.

'Go away!' Lucy shouted out as soon as Matthew knocked on her door.

'Can I come in?'

'Are you deaf? I said, go away!'

Gingerly, Matthew pushed the door open. Lucy was sitting

at her computer, typing.

'Lucy –' he began.

Lucy minimised the screen and spun round, her face twisted in fury. 'Get out of my room! You've got no right to come in here without permission.'

'I just wanted to tell you I'm going out.'

'Good. Don't bother to come back.' She turned her back on him and sat waiting for him to leave.

Matthew closed the door softly. His daughter's resentment was just part of being adolescent, he told himself. He wasn't sure how Lucy had discovered he was seeing Charlotte. It wasn't necessarily a bad thing; his children had to find out sooner or later. In the long term he knew it wouldn't be a problem, because once they met Charlotte they were bound to like her. It would all work itself out in the end. Right now he was on his way to see her and life was good. He drove away from the house, whistling.

Abigail had moved South, taking the children with her, which meant Matthew had to go too. He had tried to explain to Charlotte that he couldn't split his family apart so soon. He felt responsible for the children whose mother was absent even though she came home every night. The only possible solution had been for Charlotte to follow him South. She had found a job in Faversham, on the understanding that Abigail would agree to a divorce as soon as she was established in her new post.

'Once she's busy with her new school, she won't worry about getting divorced. She'll be glad to be rid of me,' he assured Charlotte.

Only things hadn't worked out as Matthew had planned. When Abigail had been appointed headmistress of Harchester School in Kent, Matthew had been working for a partnership of surveyors in York. Several local firms had already folded with the collapse of the building trade, and he had the impression his colleagues were relieved when he resigned after nearly twenty years with the firm. Their reaction hardly made him feel valued. It didn't help when he had to settle for a tedious job in Faversham, where he spent most of the day biting his tongue, bored and depressed, taking instructions from a woman half his age. He wasn't the only one who had sacrificed a career. Charlotte had given up nursing to follow him. Matthew had suggested she apply for a transfer, but she seemed happy to leave nursing.

'I'm sick of working with blood and guts,' she had assured him. 'And I can earn more if I quit.'

But after all that, Abigail obstinately refused to agree to a divorce.

'I can't do it without her,' he told Charlotte miserably. 'She's threatened to turn the children against me. She'd do it, too. You don't know my wife.'

Charlotte was growing impatient. 'Tell her you insist. Just do it, Matthew. Go to a lawyer and get the papers drawn up. She can't force you to stay with her.'

Charlotte wondered whether to tell Matthew she'd received another letter from Ted, the third that week. After moving to Kent she'd thought she would finally be rid of him, but he still hadn't given up.

'You can't leave,' he had protested when she'd told him she was going. 'You belong here with me.'

'Ted, we went out once when we were still at school. That was years ago. There's nothing between us. There never was and there never will be. Get over it.' Seeing his stricken expression she had softened. 'We can still be friends. We don't have to fall out over this.'

'You're going away with him, aren't you?'

'He's got nothing to do with it,' she'd lied, annoyed again. 'Leave me alone, Ted. My life is none of your business.'

They hadn't spoken since that argument, but a week later the letters had begun. They would have made her uneasy if she hadn't known Ted so well, poor stupid Ted, too soft to harm a fly. She couldn't believe she'd ever agreed to go out with him but he'd worn her down with his persistence, and at fifteen she'd been foolishly flattered.

'He must really like you,' one of her school friends had said.

'He's a dork,' someone else added. It hadn't lasted long, was never a real relationship, just a few wet kisses and a hurried fumble on a park bench. Ted had been distraught when Charlotte finished it. The break up had been the source of much chatter at school. Charlotte's girlfriends had been unanimous in advising her to stand firm.

'It'll only get more difficult if you let it go on.'

'Just tell him plain and simple you don't want to go out with him.'

'He'll get over it.'

But Ted hadn't got over it. 'I'll wait for you,' he'd told her.

'You'll have a long wait.' She'd laughed at his intensity then relented and tried to be kind. 'You'll find someone else.'

'I don't want anyone else.'

Charlotte checked her appearance in the hall mirror as she passed it. With blonde curls and a snub nose, she looked younger than thirty-three. Twelve years older than her, with children of his own, Matthew didn't appreciate how urgently she needed a commitment from him. Several of her friends were already mothers.

'Just get yourself pregnant. That'll force his hand,' one of her friends had suggested.

'Or you'll end up a single mother,' another friend pointed out.

Charlotte carried on doing what she could to persuade Matthew to leave his wife. 'You're miserable with her. I'll make you happy. You deserve that much after all she's put you through.' She wisely avoided the subject of children. Matthew had already told her he didn't want a second family, but Charlotte was confident everything would be fine once they were married. Only first he had to leave Abigail. She was ruining everything.

Charlotte opened the door. Matthew burst into the flat and swept her off her feet in a whirling embrace. She laughed out loud, Ted and his plaintive letters forgotten in her excitement at seeing Matthew again.

'Has Abigail agreed?' She saw the answer in his face, the droop of his shoulders.

'Don't worry,' Matthew replied. His smile was forced. 'We'll be rid of her for good before too long. I promise.' Charlotte had been listening to his promises for years. Matthew was kissing her, pressing her up against the wall. 'It's cold out there,' he muttered. 'What are you going to do to warm me up?'

'I can make you a nice cup of tea?' she suggested, laughing, as he took her by the hand and led her into the bedroom.

3

DISCOVERY

The kite was one of Dave Whittaker's earliest memories. His dad had bought it for him when Dave was about eight. They must have been on holiday because Dave remembered flying it over the beach. He had never seen his dad looking so happy.

He felt a flutter of excitement now, watching his own son tearing the plastic cover off a new kite. The so-called recreation ground wasn't an ideal location, surrounded by woods, but it was the nearest open space to their home and they were both impatient to try it out.

Zac held it up in the air as high as he could while Dave backed away, playing out the flying line. 'Now!' Dave called out. 'Let go!' Zac threw the red diamond up in the air and groaned as it dived to the ground.

'What's wrong, dad? Why won't it fly?'

On their third attempt the breeze caught it. Zac squealed as the kite rose fluttering in the air.

'Don't go too near the trees,' Dave warned him, when he handed over the line.

'It's OK, dad. I'm not stupid.'

A gust of wind seized the kite. It flew up, scudding frantically while Zac chased after it, shrieking.

'Stand still and loosen the string,' Dave called to him. 'Give it some slack.'

Zac lost his footing and the line slipped from his grasp. The kite rose, a diminishing splash of scarlet against the grey sky. They watched it soar for a moment before it swooped gracefully downwards, heading for the branches.

'Dad! Do something.' Dave began to run towards the falling kite. It disappeared in the trees. 'Dad!' Zac wailed.

'You wait here,' Dave shouted. 'I'll get it.' Cursing, he thrust his way into the woods. The undergrowth scratched at his legs and he stumbled on the uneven ground. There seemed to be a sort of rough track. Someone had been there before him, snapping off protruding twigs on either side of a narrow pathway. He reached a small clearing and stopped abruptly. A woman lay flat on her back at the foot of a tree.

Dave hesitated. 'Are you all right?' He took a step closer and froze. Her eyes stared blankly. Below her nose was an oozing mess of black where her mouth and chin should have been. Dave stared at her unblinking eyes, unable to move. A light breeze rustled past, agitating a few dry leaves that hadn't yet fallen. Apart from that, the woods were silent. Dave held his breath and stared at the dead woman. There were bits of leaf mould in her dishevelled hair. It looked damp. Her jacket was stained black with dried blood. He wondered how long she had lain there, abandoned to the elements, as he stared in disgust at her face. At first he assumed her chin had been chewed off by a wild animal; a closer look revealed that her face was intact, but bloody.

Tearing his eyes away, he fumbled for his phone. 'Police, police, I've found a body. A dead body.' The phone shook in his grasp. His teeth were chattering so violently he could barely speak. He thought he might be sick and swallowed hard, concentrating.

'Can I have your name, caller?' The calm voice helped Dave to think. He spoke slowly and carefully. 'I'm in the woods beside the recreation ground. I'll go back and wait at the edge of the trees, to show you where she – it – she – is.'

He had a horrible feeling he wasn't alone, as if he were being watched. In a panic, he hurried back through the trees, calling Zac's name. He felt dizzy with relief when he heard an answering call as he emerged into the open.

Zac started forward. 'Dad! Dad! Did you find it, dad?'

Dave frowned, blinking in the sunlight. For a few seconds he didn't know what Zac was talking about. Then he remembered the kite and shook his head.

'Oh my God, Zac,' he said. 'My God.'

'Dad –' Zac began to whine. He looked up at his father and his expression changed. 'Don't worry, dad. It's not that important. We can get another kite. It doesn't matter, dad.'

Dave put his hand on Zac's shoulder. 'You need to be very grown up, now, Zac, and very sensible. Listen, I want you to go and sit in the car. There's – something's happened, son. The police are going to be here soon. Maybe an ambulance...' He paused.

'The police?' Zac burst out. His eyes were shining. 'Coming here? How do you know, dad?'

'I know because I called them. They need to see – something I found in the woods. Now let's go and open the car and you can wait for me. I need to show the police – something – and then we'll go home.'

Zac was jumping up and down. 'What is it? What's happened? Why are the police coming? Why, dad?'

Dave gazed at his son for an instant and made up his mind. He crouched down and stared into Zac's eyes. 'You remember grandad –' he began. A worried frown creased his brow. He didn't want to frighten his son.

Zac interrupted him. 'Is it a dead person, dad? Have you found a dead person in the woods?'

Dave nodded solemnly. 'The police will be here soon,' he said. 'And then we can go home and forget...'

'This is so cool,' Zac burst out. 'Who is it, dad? Can I see it, dad, can I? This is wicked, dad. Wait till I tell them at school. Did you get a picture? Please tell me you've got a picture!'

4

TEAM

Celia smiled. 'It's so nice to see you looking relaxed for once. I worry about you a lot, you know.' Geraldine didn't answer; she knew perfectly well what her sister meant. For nearly a year Celia had been struggling to come to terms with the unexpected death of their mother. Unlike Geraldine, Celia had been very close to their mother. Now she wanted Geraldine to fill the gap left by their mother's loss but, as a detective inspector on a Murder Investigation Team, Geraldine's free time was limited.

'I really don't understand why you have to work such long hours,' Celia went on. 'It's almost as though you don't want to see us. I sometimes feel I don't really know much about you at all. You know you're not an easy person to get close to, you keep yourself to yourself so much. Chloe's growing up so fast and I know she'd like to see more of you. She misses mum, you know. It won't be long until she's a teenager and then it'll be too late. She won't want to know any more.'

Geraldine felt a surge of relief when her work phone rang and interrupted her sister's recriminations. She was on her feet before the call ended. 'Sorry, Celia, I've got to go.'

'You've only just arrived! At least finish your tea before you go –' Celia remonstrated. 'Can't you even wait and say hello to Chloe? She'll be back soon and I know she'll be disappointed if she misses you.'

Geraldine gave an apologetic smile. 'I really can't wait. Tell her I'm sorry.'

'The busy life of a detective inspector on the Murder

Investigation Team.' Celia smiled but her voice was bitter. 'It's always the same with you, isn't it? Never mind your family. Never mind what we want. Work always has to take priority doesn't it, because without you we'd all be in danger of being murdered in our beds. Now what am I supposed to tell Chloe?'

'I'll make it up to her, I promise.'

'Well, you'd better. You're letting her down, you know. She was expecting to see you. But don't worry. We're used to it.'

Geraldine turned to Celia with a flash of impatience. 'I'll see you as soon as I can,' she promised as she took a hurried leave.

It would take Geraldine about half an hour to reach the station in Barton Chislet where the investigation headquarters was being set up. The first few hours in any investigation were crucial, before evidence could be contaminated. This was especially true when death occurred outdoors. She didn't yet know how long the body had been exposed to the elements before protective covering was erected. She drove fast through a steady drizzle, and arrived with ten minutes to spare before the initial briefing. Finding her way to the toilets, she did her best to smooth down the tangle of short dark hair sticking up on top of her head. Her eyes glowed with health above the slightly crooked nose that spoilt her looks.

'I'm afraid there's no room to give you a separate office. We're only a small station,' the duty sergeant apologised.

'No problem.' Geraldine actually preferred working in the hub of activity to the relative quiet of her own office space.

'That's your work station,' the duty sergeant added, nodding to a desk in the far corner. Geraldine thanked her and went to sit down. Looking round the room, she was pleased to catch sight of Detective Sergeant Ian Peterson. She turned to her computer screen and had just logged on when he interrupted her.

She liked and trusted Ian Peterson who was clearly pleased to be working with her again. Having worked closely together on their last two investigations, they occasionally met for a drink between cases.

'Morning, gov.'

'Hello Ian. How've you been?'

He nodded complacently. 'Can't complain. So, what's to know?'

Geraldine looked up. 'Difficult to say –' Before she could continue, Detective Chief Inspector Kathryn Gordon strode into the room. The buzz of conversation faded as everyone turned to face the incident board where she stood, waiting for silence. Geraldine exchanged a quick glance with Ian Peterson. They had worked with Kathryn Gordon on a previous case. To begin with Geraldine had found her intimidating but gradually she had come to appreciate her strict work ethic.

With Kathryn Gordon in charge this was not going to be a relaxed investigation and she launched in without any preamble. 'I'm your Senior Investigating Officer, DCI Kathryn Gordon. The body of a forty-eight-year-old woman, Abigail Kirby, was discovered at ten-thirty this morning beside the recreation ground known as The Meadows, two miles North of the town centre.' She turned to a photograph pinned on the board. Hazel eyes smiled at them from a square jawed face. It looked like a professional shot of a reasonably attractive, immaculately presented woman who had just stepped out of the hairdresser's. Geraldine unconsciously raised her hand to smooth down her own unruly hair.

Kathryn Gordon pointed at the photo with a hand that trembled, although she spoke calmly. She turned away from the incident board and glanced down at her notes. 'The body was discovered by a local resident, David Whittaker, when he was out flying a kite with his young son. The kite flew off into the trees and when Mr Whittaker tried to retrieve it, he found Abigail Kirby instead.' She pointed to a map of the recreation ground. To one side of the open land, an area had been circled in red ink. 'The medical examiner should be arriving any time so we'll know more soon. The victim looks robust, and there's no sign of a struggle. Did she know her attacker or was she taken by surprise? And what was she doing there? The remote location suggests she was meeting someone.'

'Do we know she was killed there? Or could she have been killed somewhere else and the body dumped there?' someone asked.

'How did she die?' another officer wanted to know.

'We don't have any details yet. We need to get down there and find out. We're waiting for a medical examination. A forensic medical examiner should be on the scene soon.'

'The woods around the recreation ground aren't used much, especially at this time of year,' a local sergeant chipped in, 'so we're hardly likely to find a witness.'

'It's possible someone saw her,' Kathryn Gordon replied. 'It depends what time she arrived – and if she was still alive when she got there. The more people there were around, the greater the chance someone saw her, and whoever was with her, but it may be she was taken there during the night. It might be that she was killed somewhere else and dumped there under cover of darkness. Now,' she went on, suddenly brisk, 'that's enough speculation. Let's see what the scene of crime officers can tell us, and then find out what we can about Abigail Kirby.'

'Oh my God, it's Mrs Kirby!' a female constable called out suddenly.

'What do you know about Abigail Kirby?' Kathryn Gordon asked.

'My son goes to Harchester School. Mrs Kirby is – was –

the headmistress there.'

'Not any more,' someone muttered.

'What do you know about her?' the detective chief inspector repeated.

'Not much, ma'am. I've never met her myself. I just heard her address the parents as a group. My boy's only been going to Harchester High since September.'

'Right. Was she popular? What sort of reputation did she have?'

The constable gave an apologetic shrug. 'I couldn't really say, ma'am. Like I said, my boy's new.'

'See what you can find out. What's the talk in the playground, at the school gates?'

'I've not heard anything, ma'am, except – '

'Yes?'

'She had a reputation as a strict disciplinarian. My boy was terrified of her.' She laughed apologetically.

'She was the head,' Kathryn Gordon pointed out, as though she approved of figures in authority being intimidating. 'If you can find out names of any gossips among the parents, and the staff, that would help. I'll have someone else interview them, keep you out of it as much as possible.'

'Thank you, ma'am.'

The detective chief inspector turned back to the Incident Board and tapped the picture of the victim with one finger. 'The post-mortem report should be ready later today. We know the victim's name, Abigail Kirby, we now know she was headmistress of Harchester School. Until we know more, let's not jump to conclusions. In the meantime, we need to start gathering information. Check your schedules with the duty sergeant and get started. Let's get cracking and wrap this one up quickly.'

5

SCENE OF CRIME

Geraldine and Ian chatted effortlessly as they drove past a modern shopping centre away from the centre of town.

'How's Bev?'

'She's great.'

Geraldine sighed. Somehow her own relationships never lasted. She envied the sergeant who seemed settled with his long term girlfriend. 'How long have you been together now?'

Peterson shrugged. 'Feels like a lifetime.'

They parked by the edge of the recreation ground, passed the police cordon and collected their protective suits and shoes from the forensic van in silence. Treading carefully to avoid disturbing anything, they walked in single file along a rough track through the trees, bending low to avoid overhanging branches. A protective tent had been erected at one edge of a small clearing in the trees. White suited scene of crime officers were busy photographing and measuring foot prints, scuffed earth, and disturbance in the bracken and grass under the trees around it in a painstaking process, scrutinising every centimetre of the area surrounding the body for microscopic shreds of evidence; even careless killers wore gloves these days.

A smart two-tone brown leather shoe lay on its side just outside the tent. It would have been more at home in the window of an expensive store. Brilliantly lit, the scene inside the forensic tent resembled a film set. Even the body on the ground looked like a prop. She lay beside a tree trunk, her legs outstretched, her chin a mess of congealed blood under the dazzling lights. Framed by short light-brown curls streaked with grey, her head was flung back. Hazel eyes stared blankly up at them, inches from a swirl of animal excrement. She was wearing a brown skirt dotted with tiny orange flecks, and a matching jacket heavily splattered with blood. Even damp, crumpled and soiled, the outfit looked expensive.

Gazing down, Geraldine felt a rush of adrenaline. There would be photographs, reports, statements, but only this one chance to view the victim at the scene of her death. She crouched down, bringing her face close to the dead woman's bloody head.

'She was probably killed somewhere else and dumped here,' a scene of crime officer said. 'It's a miserable place to end up, isn't it?'

'Was she carrying a bag?' Geraldine asked. The scene of crime officer shook his head. Geraldine straightened up. 'What did you find in her pockets?'

'A set of keys, a receipt for coffee bought at ten-twenty in a café in the shopping centre, a photo of two children, and fifteen pence in change.' He handed her an evidence bag.

'So that gives us an exact location and time for her in the morning,' Geraldine said, picking out a picture of a boy and girl, presumably the victim's children. The boy looked about twelve, the girl possibly a few years older. She had her mother's hazel eyes and light brown hair, while the boy was dark-haired, with blue eyes.

Geraldine replaced the photograph carefully in the bag and looked around.

The SOCO saw the direction of Geraldine's gaze. 'There's no indication of any struggle elsewhere.'

'You don't think she died here?' Geraldine nodded at the body.

'There's no disturbance on the ground. My guess is she

was already dead when she was brought here.'

'So we don't know where she was killed,' Peterson said.

'It's difficult to be sure,' the SOCO concurred. 'There's no sign of a struggle, but the evidence has been contaminated. It looks as if she was dragged along the ground either unconscious or dead, masking any footprints from the killer.' He indicated scuff marks and shallow tracks in the mud. 'We haven't found much blood on the ground, so she was probably killed before she was brought here, but it rained overnight, so the blood might have been washed away. We're checking every inch of the path but the man who reported the body made a mess of the place, trampling around. It looks as though he walked around while he was on the phone. It's a pity he arrived on the scene before we had a chance to examine it, although I suppose we should be thankful he found her when he did. She'd already been here overnight –' He shrugged. 'The ground here's full of droppings.'

'Are there any defence injuries?'

The white coated figure shook his head. 'There's nothing obvious but the medical examiner should be here soon to have a look. Looks like him now.'

A man entered the tent and straightened up, tall and slender. He approached the body with an air of authority and knelt down, shielding it from view.

Geraldine watched his swift movements. 'I don't think we've met.'

The kneeling figure swivelled his head round and looked up at her. Striking blue eyes stared at her from a lean face. 'Dr Paul Hilliard.' He had a bold, frank expression and spoke in a low, cultured voice. 'Are you the senior officer here?'

'Yes. I'm Detective Inspector Geraldine Steel. And this is Detective Sergeant Ian Peterson.'

Paul Hilliard nodded. 'Pleased to meet you. Shame about the circumstances.' He turned back to the body.

Geraldine stepped forward. 'What can you tell us?'

'Give me a minute.' Geraldine studied his back. There was a stillness about him as he worked. His hair was dark, almost black, but under the bright lights narrow streaks of grey were visible. After a few moments he looked round. 'I can of course confirm she's dead. It rained during the night but the ground beneath her is fairly dry which suggests the body's been lying here overnight. The uncertain weather conditions make it impossible to pinpoint an exact time of death but it must have been sometime yesterday afternoon.'

'How did she die?'

The pathologist looked at Geraldine again. 'I'll be able to tell you more after I've done the autopsy, but the apparent cause of death,' he paused, 'is blood loss.'

'Blood loss from a head injury?'

The kneeling figure held her gaze. 'Yes...' He shrugged. 'In a manner of speaking.'

'So that accounts for the blood on her clothes?'

'Yes.'

'Presumably it's not possible to be certain at this stage, but do you think we could be looking at murder? Until we have a full PM report I take it we won't know for certain this wasn't an accident?'

'She could have tripped over and hit her head,' Peterson suggested.

Paul Hilliard shook his head. 'There's no question of this being an accident. For a start, the body's been moved. She wasn't killed here.'

'Are you sure?' Peterson asked.

'Yes. There would be a lot more blood on the undergrowth because before she died her tongue was cut out, leaving only a stump. It would have bled profusely.'

'What?'

'The victim has no tongue, Inspector.'

6

SURFING

Lucy slammed her door. She wished she could lock it. It made her sick the way her parents thought they had the right to walk into her bedroom, unannounced, whenever they felt like it.

'Don't be ridiculous. You're up there by yourself,' her father replied when Lucy pointed out she might be having a private chat.

'Why don't you ask one of the girls from your new school over?' her mother had suggested. She was trying to be helpful, but she only made things worse. Lucy didn't answer. Her parents totally missed the point. They didn't understand anything. She couldn't just randomly invite some girl to her house and even if she did, no one would want to come. The other girls had all been friends for years and it was clear right from the very first day Lucy walked into the classroom in Harchester School that she wasn't going to be welcome in any of their groups. They spent all their time gossiping about the boys, and bitching about the other girls. Lucy didn't know any of them, and didn't want to either. She was pleased they treated her like an outcast. She hated her new school and didn't want to fit in with those stupid bitches. The boys were worse. While the girls ignored Lucy, the boys were openly rude. They called her 'four eyes' and 'skinny', and far worse names that hurt, and mocked her Northern accent. Lucy didn't like any of them, and wouldn't want to be friends with any of them even if they begged her.

Lucy had never exactly been popular, but she'd had her

own group of friends in York. They weren't cool, or clever, but they were her friends. She'd even had a best friend, Nina, who sometimes came to her house after school. Lucy's parents had accepted they should knock before they entered her bedroom when Nina was there.

'Everyone else's parents knock,' she had told them and, for once, they had listened to her.

Lucy was horrified when she learned they would be moving away from the area. Ben, who had lots of friends, didn't seem to mind so much. All he had to do was join some stupid football team and boys would be calling him up every day to go out and kick a ball around. It was harder for Lucy who was going to have to start all over again, making an effort to talk to strangers, pretending to be interested in their pathetic self-obsessed teenage lives. At first she had flatly refused to go to Kent with her family, but it was useless. Her mother had accepted the position as headmistress, her father was job hunting, their house was on the market and the date for the move was set. Lucy's parents were ruining her life and they didn't care.

'We've discussed this,' her mother said.

'I never agreed to go!' Lucy yelled. 'But I don't get a say in this, do I? It's only my life being ruined, that's all. You decide whatever you want to do, and we all have to go along with it, like so much baggage.'

'Don't be ridiculous,' her father interrupted. It was all he ever seemed to say to Lucy. 'Your mother has her career to think of.' He spoke sourly.

Lucy's mother turned on him. 'Matthew, don't you start. We've been over it so many times.' Lucy left them to it.

It was some comfort to Lucy when Nina burst into tears. 'You can't leave me,' she wailed. They promised to keep in touch, it was easy on Facebook. But everything changed when Lucy moved and, after a few weeks, Nina stopped answering her messages.

'You have to make an effort to find new friends,' her mother told her. 'These things take time, and they don't just happen by themselves. You'll soon get the hang of it. The first one's the hardest.'

'I've got friends,' Lucy answered. 'Leave me alone with your bloody clichés!'

Lucy couldn't sleep. Her mum would have been on at her by now to stop chatting online and 'do something useful,' but her mum wasn't home and her dad knew better than to interfere. He left her alone and that suited Lucy fine. She liked it best when he went out. She was fourteen, old enough to be left at home with her twelve-year-old brother. She didn't need her parents interfering in her life. They were always telling her what to do. Like they had a clue what was good for her. At least her mother listened to what Lucy said. Her father might as well have been a stranger. Lucy would have preferred it if he was.

She logged onto a Twilight chat room and stared at her screen for a few moments before typing furiously. 'My parents drive me nuts.'

Bunny answered straight away. 'Parents suck.' Several others joined in, complaining about their parents, insulting them and cracking pathetic jokes.

'LOL. Can't be as bad as mine,' Lucy typed. It passed the time.

The chat moved on to school. 'Everyone hates school. Why do we have to go?' Bunny asked.

'Waste of time,' Lucy agreed.

'Torture!'

'Crap!' someone else commented.

'Shit!'

They carried on chatting for a while.

'Are you Team Edward or Team Jacob?' Bunny asked.

'Team Edward!' Lucy wrote. She added a red heart.

Shortly after moving South, Lucy had met Zoe in the chat room. They soon discovered they had a lot in common and it wasn't long before they were exchanging private messages online.

'What about you, Zoe?' Bunny asked.

Zoe left without answering.

Next time she logged on, Lucy saw that Zoe had left her a private message. 'I love Edward Cullen!!' and three red hearts.

'Zoe, you there?'

'☺'

'You got a boyf?'

'No. Wish I had!'

'Who?'

'Can't say.'

'I won't tell.'

'Someone in my class.'

'Does he know you fancy him?'

'NO WAY!!!'

'!!!'

'You?'

'?'

'You got a boyf?'

'No. Not right now.' Lucy didn't add that she had never had a boyfriend. They chatted some more about boys and their past boyfriends. 'I loved him but he dumped me ☹,' Lucy lied. No one would ever know it wasn't true and she wanted to sound interesting. Zoe was the only real friend she had now.

'How old are you?' she asked Zoe.

'You say first.'

'I asked first.'

'You want to know.'

'Fourteen. You?'

'I'm nearly fourteen!!'

'What's going on, Zoe?'

'I hate school!!'

'Me too!!'

Lucy suggested they chat on instant messenger. 'More private. You can tell me about the boyf.'

'He's not my boyf!'

'Hate school, LOVE Edward Cullen!!' Lucy wrote.

Zoe sent her a red heart on instant messenger. 'Friends!'

'Friends!' Lucy agreed.

'Best friends!!'

'Forever friends!'

7

MORGUE

Abigail Kirby lay on the table like a waxwork model, her face cleaned-up to reveal her square chin. Geraldine approached and forced herself to look at the victim's open mouth: between even teeth the stump of her tongue looked surprisingly neat. Abigail Kirby stared back as though in silent protest at this scrutiny.

The pathologist looked up and Geraldine recognised the tall dark-haired medical examiner who had examined the body in the wood. 'Hello again Inspector. You'll forgive me if I don't shake hands.'

Geraldine glanced at his bloody gloves. 'Good morning, Dr Hilliard.'

'Please, call me Paul.' Geraldine smiled. The pathologist was about to speak to her again when Peterson entered.

'Shall we begin?' Geraldine said.

Paul Hilliard nodded. 'Abigail Kirby looked after herself. She was fit for her age, well nourished, with excellent muscle tone. She probably worked out, or at least took regular exercise. She'd recently had a manicure, and a pedicure as well I suspect, and her hair's well cut. She looks as though she lived in the public eye, or else she was a narcissist.'

Geraldine couldn't help laughing. 'You know she was a headmistress.'

Paul Hilliard smiled at her. 'That fits with a controlling profile. At any rate, she certainly took care of herself.' Geraldine squinted at her own nails, short and functional, and wondered if Abigail Kirby had been right to be so aware of the dignity of her position. Either way, it didn't matter now. 'The victim has several injuries. She was struck on the back of her head with a blunt instrument. The killer used considerable force, so her attacker was probably an adult male. The blow fractured the skull resulting in cerebral bleeding.'

'And the tongue?'

'That was removed subsequent to the blow on the back of the head.' He indicated bruising on the victim's upper arms. 'Whoever hit her on the back of the head grabbed her and lowered her onto her back, after which she was secured by her arms and legs.' He pointed to marks on her wrists and ankles.

'So he could get to her face easily,' Peterson said.

'The tongue was removed after the head trauma was sustained. The blood loss was considerable so she was still alive at the time it was removed. The stump bled quite profusely. She must have been unconscious, the gag reflex inoperative, and she was lying on her back. Blood flowed into the back of her mouth causing her to choke.' Paul Hilliard placed a hand gently on the victim's head. 'Abigail Kirby drowned in her own blood.'

There was silence for a few seconds.

The pathologist glanced at Geraldine before he continued. 'Head wounds are always serious. There's a very real danger of brain damage. In this case severe head trauma would probably have killed her, without immediate medical attention, possibly even with it. She would most likely have died from the knock on the head if she hadn't choked first.'

'He must have used a very sharp blade to cut her tongue out,' Geraldine said. 'It can't have been easy, can it?' Now that the victim's face had been cleaned, the stump of the victim's tongue was clearly visible. 'That cut really must have been tricky,' she repeated. 'I wouldn't have thought many people could have done that, not without taking their time. And I don't suppose the killer wanted to hang about.'

'This was carefully planned,' Paul agreed.

'By someone intelligent,' Peterson added.

'I hope not for your sake,' Paul replied.

'Why?'

'Because if this was a highly intelligent killer, he – or she – is unlikely to make any mistakes and is going to be more difficult to find.' There was a pause. 'What about the witness who found the body? Did he see anything?'

'We haven't interviewed him yet. The constable at the scene took a brief statement but the witness was in shock and he had his young son with him. We're going to speak to him later on and get a full statement. Have you got anything else for us? Any defence injuries?'

The pathologist shook his head. 'She was wearing gloves which have been sent off for examination, but I can't find any evidence of a struggle.'

'Where was she going?' Geraldine was talking to herself. 'Was she meeting someone she knew? Was she being followed? Or was her attacker a complete stranger?'

'In which case we could be looking at someone who kills for the sake of killing,' the sergeant added.

'A psychopath?' Paul Hilliard asked. 'Someone who's mentally disturbed?'

'Well whoever it was, they were certainly disturbed, even as the average murderer goes,' the sergeant replied. 'Not that any murderer is exactly sane, but most of them don't remove their victims' tongues while they're killing them.'

The pathologist gave a faint smile.

'We need to keep an open mind,' Geraldine said, returning Paul Hilliard's smile.

'Yes, we need to keep an open mind,' the pathologist agreed.

'So, anything else you can tell us?'

'She was about forty years old.'

'Forty-eight,' Peterson corrected him.

'Can you be precise about exactly how long was she dead before she was found?' Geraldine asked, turning back to the body.

'She was found at ten-thirty yesterday morning. I attended the scene at eleven-thirty and reported death had occurred some time on Saturday afternoon. It's difficult to be absolutely accurate as she was lying out in the rain overnight. When I carried out a preliminary examination I estimated she'd been dead for around nineteen to twenty-two hours, and you have to remember that's only an estimate.'

'She died between one pm and four pm on Saturday then,' Peterson said.

'Most likely, but there's no absolute certainty. Any number of factors can increase or delay the process of deterioration in a corpse, especially one that's left out in the open.'

'Do you think she was killed in the wood where she was found?' Geraldine asked.

'No. There was mud and leaves in her hair, all consistent with her lying on the ground but there's no sign of any disturbance there.'

'Well if that's all —'

'For now. You'll have my full report this afternoon.'

The sergeant couldn't leave the room quickly enough. Geraldine sympathised with his aversion for dead bodies, but she was fascinated by autopsies. As long as she could detach herself from the subjects as previously living people, they intrigued her. She thought Paul Hilliard must feel the same, and wondered what else she had in common with the slim blue-eyed doctor.

When Paul removed his gloves, Geraldine noticed he wasn't wearing a wedding ring. She glanced up from Abigail Kirby and saw he was watching her.

'I don't remember seeing you here before,' she ventured.

'I moved to the area quite recently. Have you lived here long?' Paul responded with a smile. She registered his friendly response to her tentative overture.

'I bought a flat near here recently. Just at the height of the market.'

Paul gave a sympathetic grimace. 'If you like –' he hesitated. Geraldine waited. 'I thought we might discuss the case. It's – an interesting challenge, isn't it? With the tongue being removed, I mean.' Something in his manner suggested that his interest might lie in her, rather than the case. 'If you have time, that is,' he added.

Geraldine scribbled down her private number before handing Paul her card. 'That would be nice.'

Paul smiled and pocketed the card.

'Is it me, or was there something a bit strange about that Hilliard bloke?' Peterson asked Geraldine as they left the morgue.

'Strange in what way?'

'It's just that he didn't flinch when he was talking about the victim's tongue. He looked like he was admiring the killer's handiwork.'

Geraldine shrugged. 'He cuts up corpses for a living. What's the odd tongue when you're carving up body parts all day long?'

'I suppose so,' Peterson agreed. 'God, I hate going to the morgue and seeing it all. I don't know how anyone can do that job.' He shuddered.

'Just as well not everyone's a big wuss like you,' Geraldine laughed.

8

FAMILY

There was no sign of Abigail when Matthew came home on Sunday morning, and when he knocked on her study door she didn't respond.

'Abi, are you there?' He tried the door but it was locked, which meant she wasn't working at home. He went upstairs and checked her bedroom. That was empty too. He peeped in on Ben and Lucy who were both still asleep. Matthew went downstairs, put the kettle on and ferreted in the cupboard for a packet of his favourite cereal before going outside to spend the morning in the garden. It was a bright day, and he was whistling as he went about his chores.

Abigail still hadn't come home by tea time. Ben was despondent, Lucy fractious, but there was nothing Matthew could do about it. He knew better than to try and contact his wife at work. That was for emergencies only.

'When will she be back, dad? I want to tell her about football,' Ben said.

'Shut up,' Lucy snapped. 'No one wants to know about your stupid football.'

When the doorbell rang, Matthew thought it must be Abigail. 'It's not like your mum to forget her key,' he said. He opened the door and was surprised to see a man and a woman standing in the porch.

'Matthew Kirby?' She held up an identity card and Matthew leaned forward to read it.

'Detective Inspector Steel,' she said. 'This is Detective Sergeant Peterson.'

Matthew nodded. 'My wife's not here,' he told them as he straightened up. 'I know it's Sunday, and half term, but she's been out at work all day. She's a headmistress.' He tried to suppress the bitterness out of his voice. 'I assume you want to see her about one of her pupils? You'll find her at Harchester School.' He began to close the door. 'I'm afraid I can't tell you anything.'

'It's you we want to speak to, Mr Kirby. Can we come in?'

'I'm just about to make tea,' he began. The two officers didn't budge and Matthew couldn't very well refuse to let them in.

Matthew Kirby led them into a kitchen where a boy of about twelve was leaning back in his chair, hands resting comfortably over his flat stomach, long legs stretched out under the table. With wavy dark hair and blue eyes like his father, he lounged in his chair in a crumpled t-shirt and faded jeans.

'I helped myself –' the youngster grinned holding up a huge slab of chocolate cake. 'Hello,' he added, catching sight of the two detectives.

'Hello, Ben,' Geraldine replied. She didn't return his smile. 'We'd like to have a word with your father. Where's Lucy?'

Ben sat up, his smile fading at her solemn tone. 'Dad, who's she?'

His father shook his head. 'I'll tell you in a minute, son. Just go to your room now.'

'But I want to know –' Ben faltered.

Matthew ignored him. 'My daughter's in her room. She spends most of her time up there on her own. She's a teenager,' he added, forcing a smile. 'Teenage girls, you know.'

'Dad, what's going on?'

'I've no idea.'

Geraldine glanced at Ben, before turning back to Matthew.

'Can we can have a few words with you alone please.'
Matthew nodded at Ben who looked at his father with a
puzzled shrug before sloping out of the room muttering
inaudibly.

'Gov –' the sergeant began but Geraldine shook her head.
A moment later they heard raised voices, followed by feet
thumping along the landing.

'I have some very bad news for you. Would you like to sit
down, Mr Kirby?

Matthew shook his head. 'Go on. Say what you've come
here to say.'

Geraldine watched him as she spoke. 'I'm afraid your
wife's been killed.'

Matthew Kirby spoke quietly. 'Abigail? Are you sure?'
Geraldine nodded. 'I don't understand. She was always such
a careful driver. What happened?'

'This wasn't a car accident, Mr Kirby. Your wife wasn't
driving. Your wife was assaulted yesterday.'

'Assaulted? Do you mean to tell me she was murdered?'

'Yes.' Geraldine paused to allow him to take in the
information. 'We don't know who's responsible, but we are
doing all we can to find out.' She looked straight at Matthew
Kirby.

'You're saying someone killed Abigail?' he repeated.
'You're telling me she was murdered?' He didn't sound
upset, more disbelieving. 'That's impossible. No, not Abigail.
There must be some mistake.' He looked from Geraldine to
Peterson and back again, dazed.

'Mr Kirby, for the purposes of elimination, can you tell
me where you were between about one and four yesterday
afternoon?'

Matthew Kirby looked flustered. 'Yesterday, between one
and four? Is that when it happened?' There was a very long
pause. 'I – I'm not sure. Saturday afternoon…' he tailed off,

at a loss. 'Oh yes, I gave the kids lunch. And after that I was out visiting a – friend. I came home – late.'

The door opened and a skinny pasty-faced girl burst in, followed by Ben. She looked about twelve and was wearing grey tracksuit trousers and a dull green jumper. Her dead mother's hazel eyes blinked short-sightedly at them from a sullen face half hidden by unwashed hair. Geraldine registered the girl's slovenly appearance, a stark contrast to her mother's expensive grooming. She was barely recognisable as the girl in the photograph Abigail Kirby had been carrying.

'Is this her then?' Lucy cried out when she saw Geraldine. 'What's she doing here? Get out!' Her voice rose in a sudden shriek. 'Get out of our house!' She took a step forward, caught sight of Peterson and stopped in surprise. 'Who's he then?'

When Geraldine introduced herself and the sergeant, Lucy subsided into a chair making no attempt to apologise for her outburst.

'What's going on, dad?' Ben asked. He looked worried.

'Kids,' Matthew said. His voice broke and he turned to Geraldine. 'Tell them. You tell them. I can't. I can't…'

'I'm afraid your mother's dead.'

Lucy yelped once, like an injured dog. Ben started forward, eyes wide with shock.

'Mr Kirby, we'll come back.'

'No.' He sounded very tired. 'I don't want you coming back here. Do what you have to do and let's get it over with.'

'Can anyone confirm your movements yesterday afternoon?' Geraldine asked.

'I just said – I was with a friend. Then I came home and the children were both here.'

'We'll need the name of this friend, and where we can contact him.'

'Her,' Lucy said.

'Geoff. He was playing bridge with his friend Geoff,' Ben

51

blurted out.

'That was Friday,' Matthew said. He seemed uneasy. 'I was visiting – a work colleague. She's been sick.' It was obvious he was lying. 'Her name is – Miss Jones. I – I've got her address somewhere. If you give me a minute, I can go and find it. I was there – we were working on a project – from about two o'clock, maybe closer to three. I didn't look at the time. I stayed there until – late. We had a lot to discuss.'

'He was with her,' Lucy sounded angry. Ben was sitting with his head in his hands, sobbing quietly. Neither Matthew nor Lucy made any move to comfort him.

Geraldine wasn't sure if he expected her to believe his story, or if he was lying for his children's sake. She wondered if it had been a mistake, questioning him in front of Lucy and Ben. 'One more thing, Mr Kirby,' she said. 'When did you notice your wife's absence? You didn't report her missing when she didn't come home last night.'

Matthew Kirby shrugged. 'She…' He frowned.

'Yes, Mr Kirby?'

'She hadn't come home last night by the time I went to bed, but that was nothing unusual. She often worked late. And she went out early this morning. Or that's what I thought. She often went into school early.'

'On a Sunday?' Peterson asked. 'Isn't the school closed for half term?'

'She was the headmistress of a large school, Inspector. She was worked off her feet. Weekends and holidays were her chance to catch up on paperwork. She had to keep records of everything. I daresay it's the same with you.' He gave Geraldine a nervous smile. 'When I woke up this morning, she wasn't here. I assumed she'd gone out early. It didn't occur to me she might not have come home last night.'

'Thank you, Mr Kirby,' Geraldine said. She glanced at the two children. Ben was gazing straight ahead, stunned. Lucy was staring at her father making no attempt to conceal her disgust. 'We'd like to ask Lucy and Ben a few questions, if that's all right.'

'Can't it wait? It's hardly appropriate –' Matthew Kirby protested. He threw a worried glance at Ben who was crying again. Lucy turned and ran from the room.

'We'll come back, Mr Kirby,' Geraldine promised and Matthew Kirby shrugged miserably.

'Not exactly what you'd call a happy family,' the sergeant remarked when the front door had closed behind them.

'They have just lost their wife and mother but I agree, something's not right. Is there something going on between father and daughter that's more than a normal teenage strop? She kept it up after the news about her mother, in fact that seemed to aggravate her resentment of her father.' Geraldine paused. 'She thinks he did it.'

'There's no accounting for teenage girls, and I should know.'

Geraldine laughingly pointed out that she had been a teenage girl herself once.

'Ah, but I've got three sisters. It's a miracle I wasn't put off women for life when you think about it. Oh yes, Lucy Kirby brought back memories, I can tell you. I could swear my sisters used to take it in turns to be stroppy.' He shook his head. 'Who'd have children?'

'You and Bev aren't planning a family then?'

'It's not something we've talked about really,' he replied, suddenly serious. 'I know she wants kids at some point. How about you? Could you see yourself having children?'

'I don't know. I wouldn't want to stop working. Talking of which, what did you make of Matthew Kirby?'

'He didn't seem surprised to hear about his wife's death.'

'That's what I thought. Like he knew what was coming and wanted to get it over with.'

Peterson checked his note book. 'Say what you've come here to say,' he read aloud. 'His expression didn't change, gov. I think he knew what you were going to say.'

'Let's not jump to conclusions. People take the news of the death of someone close in different ways.' She paused. She hadn't said the death of a loved one. 'What about Lucy? What did she say when she saw me? Read out what she said, Ian.'

Peterson flicked through his notebook. 'Here we go: "Is this her then? What's she doing here? Get out of our house!" She was furious with you about something, gov.'

'Not with me. "Is this her?"' Geraldine repeated thoughtfully. 'I think we'll pay Matthew Kirby another visit very soon, but before that I certainly wish there was a way to find out what Lucy had in mind. I don't know what your take on it is, Ian, but it's pretty obvious to me Matthew Kirby was seeing another woman. What do you think?'

'Do you think he wanted to get rid of his wife, gov?'

'We need more information,' Geraldine said when they were back in the car.

Peterson turned the key in the ignition and glanced in his rear mirror. 'Hold on, gov. That's her. She's going out. Looks like it might be our lucky day.' Lucy Kirby came into view scurrying down the front path. 'I wonder where she's off to?'

'Visiting friends?' They watched Lucy hurry along the road, head down, wearing a navy anorak over her baggy jogging pants. 'Let's see if we can catch up with her.'

They cruised slowly along the road and pulled into the kerb alongside Lucy who scowled as Geraldine's window slid down.

'Hello, Lucy.'

'Why are you following me?'

'We weren't following you, Lucy. We saw you walking by as we were about to leave and stopped to talk to you.'

She opened the car door and climbed out. 'I thought you might be able to help us.' Lucy stared at the pavement. 'I wondered if there was anything you wanted to tell us?' Lucy shook her head. 'I'll go then, Lucy. But here,' Geraldine held out her card. 'I'd like you to take this. If you think of anything that might help us find out who's responsible for your mother's death, call this number and speak to me. Now, is it a good idea for you to be out on the streets alone at a time like this? Can we give you a lift home?'

'Why would I want to go back there?'

'Don't you want to be with the rest of your family right now? With your father?'

Geraldine's suggestion sparked a response. 'Why would I want to be with him?' Lucy backed away from Geraldine, eyes suddenly blazing. 'If it wasn't for him, she wouldn't be dead. It would never have happened. Go away and leave me alone!' She spun on her heel and dashed away.

Geraldine sprinted after her. 'Lucy, where are you going?'

'It's none of your business,' the girl panted. She didn't slow down but Geraldine kept pace easily.

'Right now everything is my business, Lucy, including your safety. I can't let you wander the streets at a time like this without knowing you've got somewhere safe to go.'

Lucy stopped and turned to face Geraldine. Tears were streaming down her thin face. 'What about my mother's safety? You didn't care about that, did you? And now she's dead.'

'If I'd known your mother was in danger, I'd have done everything in my power to protect her –'

'He killed her, didn't he?' Lucy interrupted her.

'We're not sure how your mother died, Lucy. That's what we're trying to find out. Lucy, I'm really sorry about your mother. You know we're going to do everything we can to find out who's responsible.' The girl nodded, kicking at the ground with a dirty trainer. 'When you saw me in your kitchen, you said "Is this her? What's she doing here?" and then you yelled at me to get out of the house. What was that about?'

Lucy wiped her nose on the back of her glove. 'I thought you were someone else.'

'Who did you think I was?'

'I don't know.'

'Lucy, is your father seeing another woman? Is that it? Did you think I was your father's girlfriend?'

Lucy bowed her head. Geraldine had to lean forward to hear what she was saying. 'My mother knew. I heard them arguing about it. He said he wanted a divorce but she said she wouldn't give him up. She said she didn't care that he was seeing someone else but she was never going to let him go. I thought, why would my mum accuse him of seeing someone if it wasn't true? And he didn't deny it.' She looked up, her eyes burning. 'I'm never going to speak to him again. I hate him.'

'You could be mistaken.'

'I'm not. I asked my mum about it. We used to talk about things. She told me she followed him one evening and saw them together. Say what you like about her, she had balls, my mum. Nothing scared her. She told me she didn't care about him seeing someone else, but she wouldn't let him have a divorce. She didn't want to break up our family.' She let out a sob. 'He's a liar and a scumbag. I wish it was him who was dead, after what he's done.'

'What has he done, Lucy?'

'I just told you, he cheated on my mum and now she's dead. I wish he would go off and live with his other woman, and leave us alone. We don't want him.'

'Does Ben know your father's seeing someone else?'

'No, he doesn't know anything about it. You know what

boys are like.' Lucy raised a worried face to Geraldine. 'You won't tell him, will you? He's only twelve and he worships my dad, God knows why. I guess it's a boy thing. He'll have to find out one day but –' She covered her face with her hands and began to cry again. Her shoulders jerked with silent sobs.

'Lucy,' Geraldine broke the silence.

'What?'

'You know you have to go home.' Lucy didn't answer. 'Your father must be worried about you.'

Behind her hands, it sounded as though Lucy was laughing. 'He's probably with her right now. He won't notice I've gone. He never knew where mum was. Even when –' she broke off sobbing.

'Lucy, who is she?'

'She's called Charlotte.'

'Charlotte what?'

'How should I know? Charlotte. That's all I know.'

'Thank you, Lucy. That's very helpful. Now, we'll give you a lift home.'

'You won't tell Ben, will you?'

'I promise I'll only tell him if it's necessary.'

'How do I know I can believe you?'

Something about the girl's unkempt appearance touched Geraldine and she felt a rush of pity for her. 'You don't. But I hope you trust me, Lucy.'

At home that evening Geraldine thought about Lucy, motherless at such a young age, and sighed. At least Lucy had known her own mother. In her late thirties, Geraldine had only recently discovered she was adopted. The revelation had come shortly after the death of the woman she had believed was her mother. However benign the motive, the thought of the deception that had been practised on her was still too painful to contemplate. She had stuffed the paperwork relating to her birth and adoption to the back of her wardrobe behind a stack of towels, and tried not to think about what she had discovered. It helped that her work kept her occupied.

Making herself comfortable with a small glass of chilled white wine and a bowl of pasta, she made a conscious effort to focus on something more positive and settled on Paul Hilliard. He was undoubtedly attractive, and intelligent, and appeared to be single. She wondered if his invitation to meet up was motivated solely by a professional interest in the case.

9

SHOCK

In the quiet room where Abigail was laid out, Matthew Kirby cleared his throat nervously. 'Can I go over to her?' he asked, his face pale. Geraldine nodded. 'That's her. That's Abigail.' He leaned forward. 'She looks so peaceful. How did she die?'

Geraldine hesitated. 'She was hit on the back of the head,' she replied tersely.

'Can I touch her? I mean, I'd like to say goodbye.'

'Yes.'

Matthew reached out and touched his wife's hand. 'She's wearing her wedding ring,' he whispered. His voice broke into a sob. 'I'm sorry, it's such a shock. What's that?' He pointed to a line of bruising on the dead woman's wrist and his eyes widened. 'It looks as though she's been tied up.' Watching him closely, Geraldine was convinced his surprise was genuine. His voice broke as he asked if she had been interfered with in any way.

'There was no sexual assault,' Geraldine assured him and he broke down, sobbing.

'The bastard,' he kept repeating. 'Abi was a good woman, a good woman. Why would anyone do this to her? Find out who did this, please.'.

'We're doing everything we can, Mr Kirby.'

It was important to reserve judgement before gathering evidence, but Geraldine found it hard not to form an impression of Matthew Kirby. She took a deep breath and tried to clear her head as she drove home. It wasn't November yet, cold for the time of year. The sky had loomed white all day. The weather forecast was warning of snow in Scotland and there was a feeling that winter was on its way.

They had no idea whether the murder had been the result of careful planning or a chance encounter. If her killer was a random stranger, it might be impossible to trace him without any forensic evidence at the scene and apart from the bizarre removal of her tongue, Abigail Kirby's body hadn't been violated. Geraldine sighed. Every moron knew better now than to leave fingerprints behind at a murder scene and so far they didn't even know where Abigail Kirby had been killed. Sherlock Holmes might have lacked sophisticated forensic techniques, but at least his villains had left clues. Abigail Kirby's corpse had revealed nothing about her killer, although her mutilation posed many questions.

Arriving home, Geraldine kicked off her shoes and shuffled into the slippers waiting for her on the mat. She hung her jacket in the cupboard and gazed around her neat living room. In the kitchen she hesitated by the kettle. After the bustle of the police station, her flat felt silent and empty and she was lonely. There was no one she could call at such a late hour, just to hear the sound of another human voice. Too wound up to sleep, she flicked the radio on and poured herself a large glass of wine before opening the file on Abigail Kirby. She knew she wouldn't be able to sleep with so many questions buzzing in her mind.

Abigail Kirby was born in Yorkshire. Her first teaching appointment was at a school in one of the outlying villages. She stayed in the area and moved to a different school in York when she married Matthew, a local surveyor. They had a daughter, Lucy, followed two years later by a son, Ben. With no career break to raise her children, she had rapidly been promoted to deputy head of a local grammar school. A year before her death she had taken up an appointment as headmistress of Harchester School and moved with her family to Kent. Her husband, who had been a partner in a firm of surveyors, went with her.

Geraldine put down the file and tried to block out the memory of Lucy Kirby which was threatening to distract her from Abigail Kirby's history. The question remained. Who would have committed such a terrible atrocity against the mother of those two children, Lucy and her young brother? Perhaps she had been murdered by an ex-pupil who considered his own life blighted by some perceived injustice. It was hard enough to imagine hating someone enough to kill them, but to inflict such excruciating pain on another human being was incomprehensible. Maybe it was no coincidence that Abigail Kirby's death had occurred so soon after her promotion to headmistress, her killer an disgruntled or jealous colleague.

Geraldine's mouth was dry so she put the kettle on and made a mug of cocoa, still thinking about the dead headmistress. Everything about Abigail Kirby followed a logical progression in relation to her career but, after studying the file closely, Geraldine was no closer to understanding Abigail Kirby as a woman. Successful in her career, married with a son and a daughter, from the outside her life appeared ideal. Despite her premature and horrific death, Geraldine felt an irrational stab of envy as she got ready for bed. Alone.

Tired and sweaty she showered and ran dripping into the bedroom. As she pulled a towel from the top shelf of her wardrobe, a pile of them toppled down. She wrapped herself in a bathsheet and bent to pick up an armful of towels from the floor. Turning, she looked up at the shelf, empty apart from a battered old shoe box she had kept hidden there ever since her sister, Celia, had given it to her. They had been clearing out their mother's belongings a few weeks after her funeral.

'I thought you'd better have this,' Celia said. Geraldine squinted down at a faded grey box file and read her own name, handwritten on a peeling yellow label. 'I imagine she would've wanted you to have it.'

'What is it?'

'Your papers.' Celia lifted the box and thrust it at her sister.

'What papers? Celia, I don't know what you're talking about. What's in the box? What papers?'

'Your papers. Birth certificate, adoption papers...'

'You're telling me we're adopted?'

Celia's blonde head bobbed a nod but she didn't look up. 'Not us, you.'

Geraldine stood with an armful of towels and dithered. There weren't many situations that daunted her and she wasn't sure why she was holding back from looking inside the box. With sudden resolution she pulled it down and sat on the bed. The brittle elastic band holding the lid in place snapped when she tried to remove it. Her fingers trembled as she lifted the lid to see the box contained a single buff folder.

'You could have told me,' she whispered. 'I would have liked to have heard it from you.' It was shattering that she would never know why her adoptive mother had hidden the truth. Trembling she felt the sharp edge of the dusty cardboard with her fingers, but it was late and she was too tired to face it now.

It took her a long time to fall asleep and, when she finally dropped off, she dreamt about a young woman with dark brown hair and black eyes.

'You can't be my mother,' Geraldine protested. 'You're younger than me.' The young woman turned away, laughing. Geraldine wanted to reach out but she couldn't move or speak.

10

BRIEFING

'How did Matthew Kirby take the news of his wife's death?' Kathryn Gordon opened the meeting on Tuesday morning. The mutter of conversation died away and everyone turned to Geraldine.

She thought about her answer. 'He didn't appear to know what had happened. He thought we'd come to speak to his wife about one of her pupils. When we told him his wife was dead, his first thought was that she'd had a car accident. He told us she was a careful driver but he didn't seem exactly surprised to hear about his wife's murder, although I suppose that could have been shock. He claimed he was with a work colleague, talking about a work project, on Saturday afternoon and evening. He was obviously lying.'

Peterson looked at his notes. 'He said his colleague's name was Miss Jones and he had her address somewhere. It was all very vague. He claims they were working on a project from two or three in the afternoon until late, because they had a lot to discuss. He couldn't be sure what time he arrived at her home. The whole story wasn't exactly plausible even before we asked for the address and he couldn't find it.'

'We'll check once the switchboard opens but I doubt if we'll find this mystery colleague called Jones at his firm,' Geraldine said. 'It was a stupid, badly thought out alibi, but I think he was caught on the hop, covering up in front of his children.' She related what Lucy Kirby had told her. 'Lucy's convinced her father's having an affair. According to her, Abigail knew about it and refused to give him a divorce. That could be a motive – although a fourteen-year-old complaining about her father isn't necessarily reliable. She struck me as quite immature for her age, troubled and confused.'

'Hardly surprising, under the circumstances,' a constable said.

'She was probably exaggerating,' another colleague sighed. 'Girls that age generally feel aggrieved about something, especially if it's anything to do with their parents.' There was a murmur of agreement from some of the older officers.

'Maybe, but we have to follow it up,' the DCI said, 'and if Lucy's right then we need to talk to the woman Matthew Kirby was seeing.' She turned to Geraldine. 'What did Lucy tell you about her?'

'Only that her first name's Charlotte.'

'What else do we know about Matthew Kirby?'

Peterson slid off his perch on the edge of his desk and flipped open his notebook. 'We know that his wife took out a life insurance policy under a year ago. Including paying off the mortgage on their house, and a death-in-service lump sum, the whole package adds up to nearly a million. It all goes to her husband.'

The DCI raised her eyebrows. 'Let's hear more about what Lucy Kirby said.'

Geraldine checked her notes. 'I'm not sure if Matthew realises quite how much Lucy knows about his affair – if he's having one, although it looks pretty certain he is. Lucy told me she overheard her parents arguing, and asked her mother about it. I don't think she talks to her father any more than she has to. According to her, Ben doesn't know about his father's mistress. Lucy asked us not to say anything to her brother, who's close to his father.'

'And he's just lost his mother,' someone added. 'A twelve-year-old boy.'

'We need to speak to the man who found Abigail Kirby's

body,' the DCI said. 'Although he's unlikely to have anything useful to tell us. And we need to check Matthew Kirby's alibi for Saturday afternoon, and see if Abigail Kirby's colleagues at work can tell us anything relevant.'

They speculated about Matthew Kirby for a few minutes. As the victim's husband he was automatically under scrutiny if not yet a suspect. 'It sounds as though he was lying to conceal his affair from his children, but that doesn't mean he killed his wife,' Geraldine pointed out. 'He seemed genuinely shocked at seeing her body. According to Paul, her injuries were appalling.'

'Paul?'

'Paul Hilliard, the pathologist.'

'Yes, of course. Well in that case could we be looking at a crime of passion? If Matthew Kirby attacked his wife in some sort of frenzy he might well be shocked afterwards at the extent of the injuries he inflicted.'

'I think Matthew Kirby was angry with his wife for refusing to divorce him,' Geraldine conceded, 'but this doesn't look like a crime of passion. Matthew Kirby wanted to end the marriage. He didn't care about his wife any more but he didn't have to kill her, he could have just walked away. If he stayed because he loves his children then it hardly makes sense for him to go and kill their mother, and in so brutal a fashion too. At the very least he might have quietly poisoned her so she died in her sleep or something else relatively dull for the children's sake, not this vicious mutilation which is bound to be all over the papers. It's just the sort of thing they love, isn't it? And in any case, Abigail had been cleaned up by the time he saw her. I'm not sure it was the extent of her injuries that shocked him so much as the confirmation she was dead. I don't think he really believed it until he saw her.'

'Well, we've got no way of knowing what he did or didn't believe, or whether he killed her, so we'll start by checking

Matthew Kirby's movements closely. He might have been caught somewhere on CCTV on his way to see Charlotte, or maybe his car was parked on his drive all the time.' Kathryn Gordon tapped the picture of Matthew Kirby on the Incident Board. 'We know the victim's husband has two possible motives for wanting to be rid of his wife, money and her refusal to give him a divorce. We have to know if he also had the opportunity to kill her.'

'And mutilate her corpse,' Peterson added. There was silence for a few seconds as all eyes turned to the photograph of Abigail Kirby, gazing back at them from the Incident Board. Immaculate, commanding, she looked like a woman in control of her own destiny.

11

INTERVIEWS

Geraldine and Peterson's first task was to visit Harchester School. The gates were closed so they phoned the caretaker who glowered at them as he unlocked the gate. Despite his white hair and stooping shoulders, he gave the impression of physical power. 'You know we're on half term here. I hope this is important.'

The sergeant was blunt. 'We're investigating the suspicious death of Mrs Abigail Kirby.'

'Mrs Kirby?' The caretaker's demeanour changed at once. His jaw dropped and he fumbled with his keys. 'Mrs Kirby? The head? Dead? I saw her on Friday.'

He led them to a cramped hut stuffed with filing cabinets and cardboard boxes. One wall was covered with a board holding rows of keys, each on its own labelled key ring. Beside it, an electric kettle and a dirty mug stood on a metal tray on top of an old desk.

'Mrs Kirby's dead, you say?' he repeated, as though he couldn't believe he had heard right.

Briefly Geraldine told him that the headmistress's body had been discovered on Sunday morning in the woods beside the recreation ground, the victim of a fatal assault.

'So she's dead?' he repeated. 'But it's half term.' As though that made any difference. 'What happened?'

'That's what we're investigating.'

'She's got children of her own, you know. Who would do such a terrible thing?'

'We intend to find out.'

67

'When did it happen?'

'Sometime on Saturday.' Geraldine deliberately kept her responses vague. 'It would help our enquiries if you would answer a few questions.'

The caretaker nodded. 'You read about these things in the papers and see it on the telly. But you never think it will happen to someone you know.'

'How well did you know Abigail Kirby?' Peterson asked.

The caretaker considered. 'I knew her to speak to. She called me George. Everyone calls me George.' Geraldine and the sergeant exchanged a glance and waited. 'I wouldn't say I knew her personally. Although she's been here a year last September.' He sighed and rubbed his stubbly chin with one hand.

'Was she popular here?' Geraldine asked.

George hesitated before answering. 'Mr Hollins, the old head, he was here a long time. Everyone liked Mr Hollins. He was a hard act to follow, if you get my meaning. A real schoolmaster.' He paused. 'I don't like to speak ill of the dead, but it was a different story with Mrs Kirby.'

'You didn't like Mrs Kirby?'

'I'm not talking about myself, as such. I'm only the caretaker. I didn't have much to do with her, not really. She wanted lots of changes, and I had to shift a lot of furniture around – quite unnecessarily – a new broom sweeps clean and all that.'

Geraldine looked up at Peterson who was making notes. 'Did you have any disagreements with her about all the changes?'

The caretaker shook his head. 'She didn't discuss anything with me. She gave her orders through Mr Maloney, the deputy. He was the one who ran around making sure everything got done. Mrs Kirby didn't have time to talk to me, not like old Mr Hollins. She was busy meeting parents and governors, sitting in her smart office, issuing her orders for the rest of us.' He gave an apologetic shrug. 'It's not a bad job here but there's always plenty to do when a new head comes in. Now would you like a cup of tea?'

They sat patiently watching while the old man fussed around, going off to fetch a bottle of milk and clattering mugs onto a tray while the kettle came to the boil. Geraldine had the impression George was quietly very upset by Abigail Kirby's sudden death.

'Would you say Mrs Kirby had any enemies, Mr Ramsey?'

'Call me George. Everyone else does.'

'George, can you think of anyone who might have had a grudge against Mrs Kirby? Anyone who might have wanted her out of the way?' She paused. 'Perhaps someone with a temper?'

'Well, this is in confidence, isn't it? I mean, you won't go telling anyone you heard this from me, will you? Although I daresay you'll hear the same from anyone you speak to.' He leaned forward and Geraldine put her mug down on the table. 'Mrs Kirby wasn't popular with the staff. She's only been here since last September, just over a year, and there have already been a few – incidents. She's put a lot of people out. It's not so much the changes, which have meant more pressure for all the staff here, it's her manner that upsets people.' He hesitated. 'There's been talk. Some of the staff have been going around criticising her behind her back.'

'What sort of talk?'

'Some of them accused her of being incompetent – not to her face, of course – and they've all complained about extra duties they've been having to do since she came, that sort of thing. They called a meeting to discuss their grievances but nothing ever came of it. They won't do anything, that lot, they just sit around and whinge. I've never known people grumble as much as teachers. You wouldn't think it, would you?'

They thanked George Ramsey for the tea and asked who else was in school over half term. The secretaries, IT support and maintenance staff would be working, he told them, and the deputy head was due in shortly, but the rest of the teaching staff were unlikely to appear on site during the half-term break.

Geraldine wanted to see the headmistress's study. 'Please make sure no one enters the room. We'll put a constable on the door until a team has been in to make a thorough search, but I'd like to have a quick look round now, while I'm here.'

The caretaker led them across a concrete yard to the administrative building. They passed an unmanned reception desk, their footsteps echoing as they followed him down a corridor to a locked door. Once they were inside Abigail Kirby's carpeted office, they found everything easily accessible. Desk drawers were unlocked, unbolted filing cabinets held neatly labelled folders, the empty rubbish bin had a new plastic lining in place, waiting for the next day's detritus; everything in the room combined to give an impression of quiet efficiency.

Abigail Kirby had clearly been single-minded in her focus on work. There was nothing in the office that didn't relate directly to her professional life, no personal diary or notes, not even any photos of her family. They had almost finished flicking through the drawers and files when a man's head appeared round the door.

'Hello?' He strode into the room with an unmistakable air of authority. His lips pursed when Geraldine held out her warrant card but he introduced himself courteously enough as Derek Maloney, deputy head. 'How can I help, Inspector? What are you looking for? And shouldn't we wait for Abigail? This is her office.' He managed to look well turned out, even in casual clothes. Geraldine suspected his jeans had been ironed. Thinning hair slicked back across the top of his head failed to conceal the shiny bald pate beneath. The lenses of his glasses gleamed, masking his expression. 'What seems to be the problem, Inspector? I'm not sure where Abigail is, but we're on half term. If this can possibly wait until next week –'

'It can't.' Briefly, Geraldine outlined the reason for their visit.

Derek Maloney was visibly shaken. He sat on the headmistress's sofa and gazed helplessly round the room. 'She's dead? But – how? She was such a strong woman.'

Peterson described how Abigail Kirby's body had been discovered the previous afternoon.

'And you're certain this was murder? She couldn't have fallen and hit her head against something?'

'I'm afraid there can be no doubt she was killed, and the evidence suggests it wasn't accidental.'

'This is terrible.'

'Mr Maloney, it would assist our enquiries if you could tell us what you know about Abigail Kirby. Was she a popular head?'

'Well, how can I put this? I can't say she won't be a loss to the school, Inspector, but –'

'You didn't like her?'

Mr Maloney deliberated. When he finally spoke, it sounded as though he was rehearsing a speech. 'I had the utmost respect for Abigail Kirby both as a colleague and as a head...' He broke off and looked at Geraldine, stricken. 'She's wasn't a likeable woman, Inspector. She didn't go out of her way to make friends, but she was highly efficient and an excellent manager. The pupils regarded her with great respect, and discipline in the school improved enormously under her leadership. Her predecessor was hugely popular, but discipline had become somewhat lax with him at the helm.' He gave a weary smile. 'A school needs to be tough on discipline or things can rapidly get out of hand. Abigail had

71

her faults, as anyone will tell you. Not everyone will be sorry she's gone. But our whole school community will be united in deploring the circumstance of her departure.'

'What about the rest of the staff?' Geraldine asked. Mr Maloney didn't answer. 'Was she popular with the teachers?'

'You'd have to ask them,' he replied shortly. 'I can't speak for anyone else. But in my opinion her loss will prove to be a terrible blow for the school. A terrible blow.'

'Thank you, Mr Maloney. Please contact us if you remember anything that might assist us in our enquiries. And finally, can you think of anyone who might have had a grudge against Abigail Kirby?'

'A grudge?' he repeated in surprise, looking directly at her so the light played off his lenses, hiding his eyes. 'It would have to be some grudge for someone to kill her. You honestly think it might have been one of the staff who did that?' The deputy head sounded shocked. 'We're teachers, Inspector, not hitmen. We may not always see eye to eye with one another but we conduct ourselves in a civilised manner at all times, conscious that we are role models for the youngsters in our care.'

'Yes, sir,' Geraldine interrupted as he seemed to be straying into another speech, 'but someone's responsible for Abigail Kirby's death. We have to consider every possibility, however remote. Presumably you will be taking over now?'

'Yes, I'll be acting head until the governors can appoint a replacement.' Mr Maloney inclined his head. 'There won't be an internal appointment. They always appoint from outside. Always.'

On their way out, Geraldine and the sergeant spoke to the school secretary, a woman of about fifty who smiled glassily up at them from behind her desk. 'George told me.' She ran heavily ringed fingers across her greying hair. 'So it's true. Mrs Kirby – Abigail – she's really dead?'

'I'm afraid so.'

'What happened? She always looked so well.'

'We're investigating the circumstances,' Peterson told her.

'Investigating? Does that mean she was murdered?' Her eyes grew wide, fascinated rather than appalled.

'What makes you think that?' Geraldine asked.

The secretary shook her head. 'I don't know. You're here, aren't you. You wouldn't be here if –' Without warning she burst into noisy sobs. Spluttering an apology, she rummaged in her bag for a tissue and blew her nose noisily. 'I'm sorry. It must be the shock. It's not as if I even liked her, not really. I'm afraid she wasn't a very nice woman, Inspector. She wasn't well liked.' She blew her nose again.

Geraldine pulled over a chair and sat down. The sergeant closed the door to the secretary's office and took out his notebook.

'Why was she unpopular?'

The secretary frowned nervously. 'She had an unfortunate manner. She liked you to know who was boss. I mean, she wouldn't ask if you minded doing something for her, not like Mr Hollins, the old head. He was a real gentleman. He acted like you were doing him a favour, whenever he asked you to do something, however small. But not Mrs Kirby. Do you know, in a whole year, I don't think she once thanked me for anything I did. Bad manners, if you ask me. Not that I'd wish any trouble on her. She just wasn't a warm person. She was always working. She never had time to stop for a chat. Mr Hollins always had time.'

'Mrs Collins,' Geraldine spoke slowly. 'I want you to think carefully before you answer. I don't need to tell you how important this is.' The secretary nodded solemnly. 'We have reason to believe Mrs Kirby was murdered. Can you think of anyone who might have done this to her? Anyone with a grudge –'

The secretary interrupted her. 'Inspector, this is a school, not an institution for delinquents. If Mrs Kirby was murdered, I'm sure no one from Harchester School was involved.'

Geraldine sighed. She wished she could feel sure of anything. 'Would you say anyone on the staff has a temper?'

The secretary looked surprised. 'I expect they all do, but not so that I would see it.'

'Does anyone on the staff drink?'

The secretary laughed unexpectedly. 'They all do. All the young ones, that is. And most of the older ones too, I daresay. They're teachers.'

'We understand you wish to remain loyal to your colleagues, but if you know of anyone who might have had a grudge against Mrs Kirby, you have to let us know.'

'It's not a question of loyalty, Inspector. I'd help you if I could. Only if you want to know the names of staff who fell out with Mrs Kirby, well, it could be just about anyone. She had a knack of upsetting people, as I said. She was obsessed with bringing in new policies, and not everyone wants to change, do they? But I'm sure no one would have wished her to come to any harm.'

'Someone did,' Geraldine heard Peterson mutter under his breath.

12

WASTE

It perplexed him that people made such a disproportionate fuss about killing, because that was the easy part. Disposing of the body was trickier, but he managed it without a hitch. With meticulous preparation he couldn't go wrong, as long as no one saw him. If there had been a war on he would have been feted as a hero; as it was, he had to be discreet.

There had been no need to move the girl. After heaving her off the balcony it had been easy to slip away and establish his alibi. The headmistress had been more of a challenge because he had taken her home with him and needed to dump her somewhere away from his house. After scouting around he had chosen a clearing in the woods beside waste ground. It was suitably isolated, so perfect for the purpose that he half expected to stumble across another body while he was looking around.

But there were no dead bodies in sight as he skulked among the trees, only discarded beer bottles, cigarette packets and a few condoms. In the summer he might have come across youngsters shagging in the bushes, but at this time of year the woods were deserted. It was ideal. A wasteland for a wasted life.

No one had seen him return there late one night and find his way in the moonlight, lugging the headmistress through the trees to the long grass in the clearing. Afterwards he wasn't even sure exactly where he'd left her. It wasn't important. She meant nothing to him any more, even though he knew they were connected as irreversibly as if they had been parent and child, except they were joined by death not life.

He poured himself a glass of brandy. So far, so good. Everything had gone exactly as planned and there was nothing to stop him finishing the job. Most crimes were solved as a result of stupidity. Murderers were even known to disclose the whereabouts of their dead victims. He swilled the brandy in his glass and wondered why anyone would remember where they had disposed of a body. It puzzled him that people took the trouble to hide their victims. For his part, he really didn't care if the headmistress was found or left to rot among the trees beside the wasteland. No one could implicate him in her death, so whatever happened to her from now on was of no consequence to him. He had to focus on what did matter to him – covering his tracks – because he couldn't allow anyone to stop him before he'd finished.

Two down, two to go. He had dealt with the girl and the headmistress. Now, only the doctor remained and then he would be free to put an end to it all.

He knew where the doctor worked. It wouldn't be long now. He smiled. It was almost too easy.

13

MISTRESS

'Let's start with the obvious and ask Matthew for Charlotte's details,' Geraldine said. 'She's his alibi, so he should be keen to tell us where to find her, as long as we ask him when his children aren't around.'

'And if his alibi's a complete fabrication, he's had plenty of time to brief her on exactly what he wants her to say.' Peterson sounded irritated.

'That can't be helped and remember, he's not a suspect yet.'

At first Matthew Kirby was reluctant to give them his girlfriend's details. Peterson advised him that wasting police time was treated very seriously.

'It's not that I don't want to tell you where she lives,' Matthew Kirby rubbed the top of his head with the palm of one hand, ruffling his dark hair until it stood on end. 'The thing is, I don't want to drag Charlotte into all this. She had nothing to do with my wife. They never even met.'

'By naming Charlotte as your alibi, you've already dragged her into the enquiry,' Geraldine pointed out.

Charlotte Fox lived in a converted block of flats on the outskirts of town, off the main road.

'Fidelis Lodge,' Geraldine read the sign aloud. 'Ironic.' There was an entry phone. 'Charlotte Fox? This is the police. We'd like to have a word with you about Matthew Kirby.'

'Has something happened to Matthew?'

'No. But I expect you know his wife's dead.'

'Yes. Matthew told me. But that's nothing to do with me.'

'May we come in, Miss Fox?'

'How do I know you are who you say you are?'

'You can check our ID, or you can phone the local station. We'll wait.'

There was a pause. 'You'd better come on up. It's the second floor. Number twenty-two.'

Charlotte Fox opened her front door on the chain and studied Geraldine's warrant card. 'Alright,' she nodded, making no move to take the chain off the door. 'What's this about?'

'May we come in?'

Charlotte frowned. 'What do you want?'

'We need to ask you a few questions and it'll be more comfortable for all of us if we don't conduct the interview in the hallway. I don't suppose your neighbours want to hear this.'

Charlotte led them into a neatly furnished living room with a sloping ceiling, original attic accommodation for servants converted into a bijou flat. Geraldine studied Charlotte as they all sat down. She was slim, aged between twenty-five and thirty, with brittle blonde curls that moved when she turned as though her whole head had been carved in stone.

'Miss Fox,' Geraldine began. The other woman's eyes flitted nervously from Geraldine to Peterson and back again. 'How well do you know Matthew Kirby?'

Charlotte Fox hesitated. 'We're friends,' she said at last, her voice barely more than a whisper. 'We met in York.'

'How long have you known him?'

'Nearly five years.'

'How did you meet?'

'Matthew was a partner at a firm of surveyors in York. One of my friends worked there as a receptionist. I met her for a drink after work and Matthew was there and – well, that's how we met.'

'And you moved to Kent at about the same time as Mr Kirby and his family?'

'Yes. They moved here and I followed soon after.'

'Because of your relationship with Matthew Kirby?' Charlotte Fox nodded. 'Charlotte, we're interested in Matthew Kirby's movements on Saturday afternoon.'

'Was that when it – when she – when it happened?' She paused. 'When his wife died? How did it happen?' Geraldine and Peterson exchanged a glance before Geraldine answered.

'That's exactly what we're going to find out. Now, can you tell us what time you saw Matthew on Saturday afternoon?'

Charlotte Fox looked worried. 'I don't know,' she whispered. 'I was here. On my own. I was waiting for a call from Matthew.' She hesitated, crossed her slim legs and wrapped her arms around her body, staring at the carpet.

Geraldine prompted her. 'Did Matthew Kirby come here to see you on Saturday?'

Beneath her golden curls, Charlotte's blue eyes gazed at Geraldine, troubled and defiant. 'Yes, he came over – it's not a crime –' She sounded close to tears.

'Charlotte, your relationship with Matthew Kirby isn't our concern.' Geraldine allowed a hint of impatience to creep into her voice and Charlotte Fox responded to her brisk tone.

'Yes, we're seeing each other. He's good to me.' She fiddled with a gold chain at her neck. 'He wants to marry me.'

'Did you know his wife?'

'I've never met her. Or his children. Matthew didn't want his children to know about me. He told his wife because he wanted a divorce but she refused to give him one. That was typical of her. She didn't want him herself, but she wouldn't let him go.' She stopped suddenly and looked down, afraid she had been indiscreet.

'Charlotte, where were you on Saturday afternoon between one and four?'

She shook her head. 'I don't know. I was here.'

'Can anyone confirm that?'

'Matthew came round.'

'Did anyone else know you were here?'

Charlotte hesitated. 'I phoned my mother –' she said at last.

'Did you make the call from a landline?' Peterson asked.

'No. I've got free minutes on my mobile.'

'Did you leave your flat at all on Saturday?'

'Yes. I went to Tescos in the morning. I must have been gone for a couple of hours. After that I came home and did some chores, ironing and stuff. Matthew came round after lunch. We talked about him getting a divorce. We talk about it all the time. I'm worried about his daughter – she's only fourteen – but he says she'll come round. He says his daughter's sure to like me, and we'll get married as soon as his divorce goes through. I mean, we still will, only there won't be a divorce now.' She frowned and bit her lip. 'He's a widower, isn't he? I mean, we're free now, aren't we? Everything will be all right now, won't it?'

Geraldine gazed into the other woman's worried eyes. 'Charlotte, we believe Abigail Kirby was murdered. Now, let's start again. You say you were here in the afternoon, on your own, until Matthew Kirby turned up. What time did he arrive?'

Charlotte shrugged. 'I don't know. I didn't look. He just came round and we talked, that's all.'

'And what time did he leave?'

'I don't know. It was late. After midnight.'

'And he was here with you all that time? Think carefully, Charlotte, this could be important. Did Matthew Kirby leave you at all during the afternoon? Did either of you leave the flat for any reason that afternoon or evening?'

'No. I told you. He came round and he stayed here, with me, until late. Neither of us went out. I'm sure of it.'

Geraldine told Charlotte Fox not to leave the area without contacting the police first.

'Am I a suspect?' Charlotte whispered apprehensively.

'No, but we may need to ask you a few more questions.'

Geraldine and Peterson walked back to the car without talking for a few minutes, each absorbed in their own thoughts.

'She didn't confirm his alibi,' Geraldine broke the silence. 'But we may be able to establish her whereabouts from the mobile phone records.'

'She certainly gives him a motive,' Peterson replied. 'Abigail Kirby, late forties, interested only in her work, pays no attention to her husband but refuses to divorce him.' He glanced at Geraldine. 'Matthew wants to get rid of his wife because he's worried he's going to lose his young girlfriend if he can't marry her.'

'I agree so far it all points to Matthew Kirby,' Geraldine said. 'He wanted to be rid of Abigail all right. The question is, did he want it badly enough to kill her – and cut out her tongue? I don't believe it. He might have been in love with another woman but he didn't walk away from his marriage, he cares about his children, and he seems quite – ordinary.' She shook her head. 'I can't help feeling we're dealing with someone far more sinister than Matthew Kirby.'

ZOE

Lucy shut her door firmly. Her desk top was clear apart from her computer and a dirty mug that gave off a faint sickly sweet smell of chocolate. Lucy hated clutter and never put any school books on her desk, although that was what her parents had bought it for. She moved the mug out of sight before switching on her computer.

The screen flickered alight and she saw that Zoe was already online.

'Hey Zoe!'

'Hey you!' Zoe replied at once and Lucy smiled. 'What's new?' They chatted for a while. Grumbling about her brother, Lucy learned that Zoe had an older sister.

'You're so lucky!' Lucy told her. 'I wish I had a sister not a stupid useless brother.'

'It's not so great.'

'Do you share clothes?'

'Sometimes.'

'Lucky!'

'A brother's better. You get to meet all his friends.'

'He's 12! And he's a dick. Always poking his nose in where it's not wanted.'

'We ought to use a password when we log on then.'

'Why?' Lucy asked. 'Instant messenger's private. Isn't that the point?'

'If we're going to tell each other secrets we need to make sure no one else can read them!'

'OK.' A thought struck Lucy. 'We need to delete the

password every time.'

'Delete everything as soon as we've read it.'

'So what's it going to be?' Lucy asked.

'What?'

'What's the password?'

'Don't know. Any ideas?'

'Clueless.'

'Too obvious!'

Lucy shook her head. 'I wasn't suggesting it as a password! I meant I haven't got a clue! You got any ideas?'

'I'm thinking.'

'How about JLS?'

'Too common.'

'JLS aren't common!'

'No. JLS is too common for a password.'

Lucy tried again. 'What about schoolsucks?'

'OK. Memorise and delete!'

Engrossed in chatting, Lucy was startled when someone called her name. She minimised her screen and spun round to see her father silhouetted in the doorway. 'What do you want? Can't you see I'm busy?' What was the point of agreeing a password on a secure site if her dad was going to barge into her room, uninvited, and read her private messages over her shoulder? 'What are you doing in my room? How dare you come in without knocking?'

'I just wanted to tell you I'm going out –'

'Good. Don't hurry back.' Lucy turned to her screen and waited to hear the door close. After a few seconds she looked over her shoulder. Her father was hovering in the doorway. 'Are you still here?' she demanded crossly.

'I thought you might want some supper before I go out.'

'Well you thought wrong. And close the door behind you.'

'Lucy...'

'What do you want? Can't you leave me alone?' She heard

the door close and when she looked around, he had gone. With an angry smile she turned back to the screen.

Zoe had left three messages while Lucy was talking to her father.

'Sorry,' Lucy wrote. 'My dad came in.'

'Did he see what you were writing?'

'No.'

'Are you sure?'

'No worries. He was nowhere near my computer.' Zoe didn't answer. 'And I minimised the screen as soon as he opened the door.'

'Good.'

'No it bloody isn't. He can't just walk in without knocking.'

'You're right. It's your space.'

'I hate him!'

'Parents are a pain. Are you sure he didn't see what we've written?'

'I'm sure. The point is he's got no right to come in without permission. I could have been writing something private. He could've seen it.'

'But he didn't?'

'No. But he shouldn't come in like that. He's got no right.'

'No.'

'I hate my dad.'

'Parents are bloody annoying.'

'It's more than that. I HATE him.'

Lucy jumped when she heard her door open. She minimised her screen and leapt from her chair in a fury. 'What did I just say?' she yelled.

Her brother kicked a trainer across the room. 'I don't know,' he answered amiably. 'What did you just say?'

'What are you doing in here? Leave my shoes alone. And get lost.'

'That's friendly,' Ben grinned at her. He brushed his dark

fringe with the back of a hand but it flopped over his eyes again straightaway.

'Go away. I'm busy,' she said.

'You don't look busy.'

'Well that just shows how much you know.'

'More than you, because I came in to tell you something.' He made no move to leave.

'What is it then? And this had better be interesting.'

'Or what?'

'Or you've come barging in here for no reason, without my permission, and disturbed me when I was doing something very important.'

'Oh shut up, you're not in school now. I don't need your permission to speak. You're not my teacher.'

'You do need my permission to come in here. It's my room.'

'Well I don't need your permission to come in, obviously, because I'm here.'

'Well you can go away again. Right now.'

'Or what?'

'Or I'll tell mum –'

They stared at one another, shocked into silence.

'I only came in to tell you dad's gone out,' Ben mumbled. He didn't look at Lucy.

'Big deal. I hope he never comes back.'

Ben turned and left the room, banging the door behind him. 'You're a cow!' Lucy heard him shout as he stomped along the landing to his own room. 'A stupid bloody cow!'

'Oh fuck off,' she muttered under her breath. She turned back to her screen and was relieved to see that Zoe was still online.

'Are you there?' Zoe had written and, a moment later, 'Lucy?'

'Sorry,' Lucy typed. 'My idiot brother came in.'

'Did he see my messages?'

'No. He didn't see anything.'

'Are you sure?'

'Positive. I wouldn't let him anywhere near my computer! He's such a loser.'

'Bad as your dad?'

'No one could be as bad as my dad!'

'Why? What's wrong with him?'

'Can't tell you.' Lucy signed off abruptly. She couldn't even tell her best friend what her dad had done. She couldn't tell anyone that her father had killed her mother so he could get all her money and marry Charlotte.

The police were stupid. Even Ben didn't understand what had happened. She wondered whether to tell him but she was afraid he wouldn't believe her. He never took her seriously. No one did. Her mother was the only person who had ever cared about Lucy and now she was dead and it was all her father's fault. Lucy flung herself down on her bed and began to cry in earnest.

PART 2

'It is too rash, too unadvised, too sudden;
Too like the lightning, which doth cease to be
Ere one can say 'It lightens'...'

Shakespeare

15

VERNON

Vernon slipped his cuff back to check the time. In a few minutes Tim was going to lower the shutter over the entrance furthest from the tills.

'You doing anything tonight?' Susie asked. In his wildest fantasies Vernon might imagine she was coming on to him, but in reality he knew she had a boyfriend. She was never going to be interested in him anyway. She probably felt sorry for him. Susie was stunning, tall and willowy, with blonde hair and blue eyes; without a doubt the best-looking girl Vernon had ever met. He thought about her most of the time.

Tim had his back to them dealing with a customer, and Vernon relaxed. Tim wasn't bad as store managers went, but it wasn't a good idea to be seen standing idle these days. The fact that it hadn't been his fault when he had lost his last job only made him more wary. People were being laid off all the time, it was all over the news. Several of his mates were out of work and he had only managed to find a temporary replacement for his previous job. Once Christmas was over, the prospect of finding work was going to get worse.

'I might go for a few jars with a mate,' he answered vaguely. The truth was he would probably be spending the evening at home with his mum. 'How about you? Got anything nice planned? Wednesday night on the town, is it?'

Susie gave her easy laugh that made Vernon's breath catch in his throat. He wished he wasn't so awkward and sweaty. 'I'm seeing some of the girls from school. We might go to Wendovers. We'll probably go into town, you know.'

Vernon nodded. They watched Tim operate the shutter and wait while it slid silently down.

'Thank God for that,' Vernon muttered.

'Do you think Tim's gay?' Susie whispered conspiratorially, leaning forward so Vernon could smell the sweet scent of perfumed shampoo. The manager looked round and Susie's blonde hair swung as she turned away to busy herself at the nearest shelf, tidying the newspapers.

Susie was in the staffroom buttoning her coat when Vernon went up to collect his jacket. He followed her down the narrow back stairs and they left together. Although the outside doors stayed open until six, by five thirty the shopping centre was almost deserted. A few shoppers were wandering about carrying bags stuffed with early Christmas presents. Vernon and Susie passed a queue of people waiting to pay for their parking, and paused by a huge Christmas tree on display at the foot of the escalator. Beside it a sign advertising Santa's grotto was flanked by grinning life-sized plastic elves.

'They look like something out of a horror movie,' Vernon said and Susie laughed.

'You in a hurry to get off?' she asked. Vernon shook his head, suddenly self-conscious. 'Fancy a drink then?'

They went to the nearest pub. 'So nice to sit down,' Susie smiled as Vernon brought two halves over and they chatted about work, grumbling companionably.

'At least you've got the option,' Vernon said. 'I've got no idea what I'm going to be doing after Christmas.'

'You should see it as an opportunity.'

'An opportunity to be broke!' He stared glumly into his drink thinking how his mother would have told him off for wasting three quid, but it was his money.

'No, an opportunity to change your life. To do something new. You could do anything.' Vernon gazed into her eyes, bright with enthusiasm, and noticed funny little blotches of black in the corners where her make-up had smudged. He felt a shiver of excitement. Maybe Susie was right. He was only seventeen. 'You've got your whole life in front of you,' Susie was saying. 'You don't want to spend it stuck in some bloody shop counting the minutes till closing time.' Vernon nodded. He'd heard it all before from his mother, but somehow the words sounded different on Susie's lips. He gulped his beer then regretted drinking it so quickly. He wanted this conversation to last all evening.

Susie was talking about work again. Vernon watched the sheen on her lips as they moved, without really listening to what she was saying. 'So how was your day?' she asked.

'A funny thing happened, actually.'

'Yeah?' Susie yawned.

'I saw my old headmistress, Mrs Kirby, in the paper. You know, the woman that was found by the recreation ground, murdered.'

'Oh my God, she was your headmistress. You knew her!' Susie leaned forward. 'What was she like? It must have been dreadful, reading about it in the paper.'

'I didn't know her exactly. I don't think she ever spoke to me all the time I was at school. Not that I would've wanted to talk to her. She was a right old cow. Sorry, I shouldn't speak ill of the dead. She was only there for my last year anyway. But what was really weird was that I saw her in the shop on Saturday, the same day she was killed.'

'You saw her the day she was murdered!' Susie stared at him, fascinated, and Vernon felt his face redden as she leaned towards him. 'What happened? Tell me! Oh my God, this is huge.'

'There was this man.' He paused, trying to find words to explain what had happened.

Vernon had picked out his old headmistress, Mrs Kirby,

straightaway while she stood waiting to pay. As the queue shuffled forwards she had glanced around impatiently. Vernon hadn't heard what Mrs Kirby said to the man behind her in the queue, but he recognised the expression on the man's face after Mrs Kirby turned away. All the kids at school hated Mrs Kirby. If it hadn't been for her, Vernon might have stayed on, might even have tried for university in spite of his GCSEs. His dismal grades weren't entirely his fault. His mum had deteriorated so much when he was in Year 11 that she could barely get around without a wheelchair and although the council people sent in carers, Vernon had to help out with the shopping and the housework, not that he did much of that, but there was still the washing-up and the laundrette. Mrs Kirby didn't care about any of that. She had made it clear from the start that she had no time for pupils who had done badly in their GCSEs. The previous headmaster had been a decent guy, but Mrs Kirby had swept through the school like a cold blast.

The man behind Mrs Kirby in the queue was old, so Vernon was surprised to see an unmistakable expression of loathing on his face as he looked at Mrs Kirby. Vernon's own aversion to her was already fading. He didn't really care any more. But there was no mistaking the man's abhorrence as he stared at the back of Mrs Kirby's head.

Vernon struggled to describe the scene to Susie, aware that his anecdote sounded boring. It had made such a vivid impression on him at the time that he still remembered it as clearly as though it was taking place now, in front of his eyes, although nothing had actually happened. A stranger had seen Mrs Kirby and Vernon thought he'd looked disgusted. Big deal.

'The thing is,' he said, 'I saw her on Saturday morning, and it said in the paper that she was killed sometime on Saturday.'

Susie was really interested now. 'You might have been the last person to see her alive.' She bent forward again, lowering her voice. 'And the man you saw, he might have been the killer!'

Vernon gasped. The thought hadn't even crossed his mind. 'Do you really think so?'

Susie nodded, wide-eyed. 'You have to tell the police –' she began, but just then her phone rang. She stood up and slung her bag over her shoulder, still talking on the phone. Then, with a wave of her hand, she was gone.

Vernon stared disconsolately at a smear of lipstick on her glass. He almost wished he hadn't told her about seeing Mrs Kirby, because he knew she was right and he ought to tell the police. It was just possible he had seen Mrs Kirby's murderer. He closed his eyes and tried to remember what the man had looked like.

16

MATTHEW

On her way to the morning briefing Kathryn Gordon stopped Geraldine in the corridor. 'I had a word with a colleague last night.' Geraldine hesitated, uncertain where this was heading. 'A colleague on the Met.' Since the investigation had started Geraldine had barely given a thought to her proposed career move. The Met was having a recruitment drive and Geraldine had discussed her position with Kathryn Gordon who had agreed to support her application for a transfer to London; joining the Met would be equivalent to a promotion. The DCI had contacts in the Met and had even offered to put in a good word for Geraldine. Such assistance could make all the difference, but weeks had passed and she had heard nothing. 'I told him you couldn't possibly be released at the moment so I'm afraid any possibility of a transfer is on the back burner for now.'

'Of course.' Geraldine held open the door of the Incident Room. 'And thank you.'

'We have a warrant to search the Kirby property,' the DCI announced. 'Let's see if that throws up anything new. But first, what else have we found out?' She looked at Peterson who had been researching Matthew Kirby's affairs.

'Well, he's run up some debts since moving. He's been taking money out of the joint account he had with his wife, about thirty thousand pounds since he left York, plus he owes on two credit cards in his own name, that's another fifteen thousand pounds.'

'Did his wife know?' someone asked.

Kathryn Gordon thought for a moment. 'Funding Charlotte Fox's move?' she suggested.

'None of this gives him a motive for killing his wife, deliberately mutilating her body, and then disposing of her where she was only found by chance,' Geraldine pointed out, irritated that they were focusing all their attention on Matthew Kirby when she was impatient to explore other possibilities. 'Surely we're looking for someone more resolute and single-minded than a man who was too weak to leave his wife?'

The meeting broke up shortly afterwards and Geraldine and Peterson set off to question Matthew Kirby again.

'Charlotte Fox is a good looking woman,' Peterson commented as they drove.

'So assuming Matthew Kirby wanted to leave his wife for her, why didn't he just walk out?' Geraldine asked.

'There could be any number of reasons. For a start he was worried about the effect on his children. I don't think he wanted to feel responsible for breaking up his family. Lucy's at a vulnerable age and Ben's very close to Matthew.'

'So you're saying he killed his wife to keep his family together? Well I'm afraid I'm still missing something here, because that makes no sense to me at all.'

'Of course it doesn't make sense. Only a maniac would mutilate a corpse. You can't expect to make sense of it.'

'If he couldn't even bring himself to leave her, how could he have killed her?'

'You really don't believe he's our man, do you?'

'I've already said I don't think he did it.'

'Lucy Kirby's convinced it was him.'

'Lucy Kirby's a confused teenager.'

'What's your take on it all then, gov?'

'Let's start with what we actually know. Abigail Kirby was killed some time on Saturday afternoon, and her body was left by the recreation ground, hidden in the trees, presumably during the night. So far there's nothing to indicate the identity of the killer.'

'We know she wasn't killed at the recreation ground. Her body was just dumped there. If Mr Whittaker hadn't been out flying his kite on Sunday morning the body might not have been discovered for days, maybe even weeks.'

'But the killer had made no attempt to conceal the body. Sooner or later it was going to be found. Didn't he care?' Geraldine frowned. 'We don't really know anything about the circumstances of her death at all, do we? We don't even know where she was killed. What about motive?'

'She seems to have made enemies at school.'

'Some of the staff have been there for years. Some hostility to the changes she introduced were inevitable. But is a school teacher – or anyone else for that matter – going to kill and mutilate their new boss for making changes? We're agreed that our killer is insane, but isn't that pushing it a bit?'

'What sort of changes?'

'Does it matter? She was bound to be making changes that the staff resented, it goes with the territory, but how many people hate their boss? And how many people end up killing them? They go home and forget about it until the next day. They grumble and gossip, or look for other jobs, but it's hardly the sort of resentment that erupts in grisly murder. If everyone who didn't get on with their boss killed them, there'd be no one left! And this was hardly a straightforward killing, even as violent murders go.'

'We're looking for a monster then, not a man,' Peterson agreed.

'A monster walking the streets, looking as normal as anyone else.'

'A monster disguised as a man. We could be writing the front page for the tabloids!'

They drew up outside Matthew Kirby's house. 'Back to

the motive,' Peterson said as he switched off the engine. 'A husband forced to choose between his career and his children. He must have resented his wife for that, perhaps even hated her. And he was desperate for a divorce. Charlotte Fox must be getting on for thirty. How long was she going to wait for him?'

They fell silent as they approached the house.

Matthew Kirby looked surprised to see them when he opened the door, but soon recovered his composure. 'Inspector. To what do I owe the pleasure?' His blue eyes peered down at her from beneath enviably long lashes and she understood how Charlotte Fox might find him attractive. At the same time she was surprised by this relaxed and courteous greeting from a recently and violently bereaved husband.

'Mr Kirby we'd like to come in and take a look around here.' She held out the warrant. Matthew Kirby was no longer smiling but he stood aside to allow them to enter. 'Of course, Inspector. Feel free. It's not as if I can stop you, even if I wanted to. My wife has – had – her own office in the back,' he went on. 'I expect you'll want to look in there, but I'm afraid I don't have a key. She liked to keep her work private, even from me.'

Geraldine easily selected the key to Abigail Kirby's office from the bunch that had been found in the victim's jacket pocket. She stepped inside, followed by the sergeant who held up a hand when Matthew Kirby attempted to follow them in.

'We'll do this alone, Sir, if you don't mind,' Peterson said before he closed the door.

The room was tidy, the furniture and décor new and expensive: one wall was covered in polished wooden shelving protected by glass doors, a solid mahogany desk ran almost the entire width of the room in front of floor-length dark red velvet curtains, and a faint scent of polish hung in the air.

Every file was labelled, alphabetically arranged and colour-coded. Geraldine pictured Abigail Kirby scanning documents, signing letters and making decisions in the hushed sanctity of her personal space. The atmosphere was different from her public office at the school with its thin carpet and metal filing cabinets. This space belonged to Abigail Kirby; yet it remained impersonal.

Geraldine checked through the drawers of Abigail Kirby's desk. None were locked. A desk diary contained meetings and appointments all relating to her school, all neatly recorded in legible longhand. There were no coded messages, no inexplicable asterisks or isolated letters or symbols, no unidentified telephone numbers or email addresses. It appeared Abigail Kirby kept her room locked so that she could work uninterrupted, not to hide any dark secrets that might lead them to her killer. Geraldine felt a fleeting sympathy for the dead woman. She might have been unpopular, but she was undeniably dedicated to her work. Glancing up, Geraldine caught a glimpse of her face reflected in gleaming glass and wondered what her own work colleagues would say about her if she died unexpectedly and they went rummaging through her flat.

Peterson pulled a set of photo albums down from the book shelves and rifled through them.

'Found anything?' Geraldine asked, looking up.

'Some old school photos.' He gazed at picture after picture of Abigail Kirby seated in front of a whole school, or posing with different groups of pupils. At one stage in her career she had worked with girls and had been photographed standing with a group who looked like sixth formers, although it was impossible to tell these days. Several of them looked as though they were wearing make-up and gazed at the camera with knowing expressions, perhaps flirting with the photographer. A girl stood next to Abigail Kirby, her hair arranged in a long fringe. She would have been exceptionally pretty if it wasn't for a large angry birth mark disfiguring her left cheek.

'Nothing here,' Geraldine said, straightening up.

'Nor here.' Peterson replaced the albums on the shelf.

There was no sign of a sharp blade in the house, apart from the usual kitchen knives, all too blunt to have been used in Abigail Kirby's mutilation, and no wooden knife block with one blade missing. A cursory search of wardrobes, laundry baskets, washroom and rubbish bins, revealed no bloodstained clothes or discarded gloves. Matthew Kirby watched Geraldine with a puzzled frown as she rifled through the shirts in his bedroom.

'What are you looking for, exactly?' he asked. She didn't answer.

Ben Kirby was lying on his bed staring at the ceiling, his eyes bloodshot, as though he had been crying. He didn't notice them at first.

'Hello, Ben.'

'Have you found out what happened to mum? Who did it?' He sniffed loudly and wiped his nose noisily on his sleeve.

'We're still looking into it, Ben.'

'You will find out what happened, won't you?'

'Yes, Ben. We'll find out.'

'And you'll tell us, won't you? We want to know who…'. He turned his face to the wall.

'We'll tell you anything we can as soon as we know it, I promise you.' Geraldine left her sergeant to question the boy gently, while Matthew Kirby stood nervously watching.

They found Lucy, glued to her computer. 'Go away!' she yelled. She minimised her screen view without looking round.

'Lucy, it's the police,' Matthew said gently.

She spun around then. 'Have you come to arrest him?'

'We're pursuing our enquiries,' Geraldine told her.

'Pursue them with him then, because he's the one who did it, not me. I can't help you. If I'd seen him in a blood stained shirt, clutching a knife, I'd tell you, but he's too clever for that.' The girl folded her arms and glared at them, waiting for them to leave. As Matthew sighed and closed the door, Geraldine caught a glimpse of Lucy turning back to her computer.

That evening Geraldine thought about Lucy, isolated in her bedroom. Motherless. On a sudden impulse she knocked back the rest of her glass of wine and went to her bedroom. Fine dust made her sneeze as she lifted the buff folder out of its box. Slowly she slid an envelope from the folder, opened it and pulled out a yellowing birth certificate.

Place of Birth – Wexford Nursing Home Ashford Kent

Name and Surname – Erin Blake

Sex – Female

Name and Surname of Father – blank

Name Surname and Maiden Name of Mother – Millicent Blake

Occupation – Shop Assistant

Occupation of Father – blank

Where Registered – Ashford District

Geraldine stared at the document for a few seconds before she registered that the piece of paper in her hand was her own birth certificate.

Her name was Erin Blake.

'Why did you hide it from me all that time?' Geraldine asked out loud, knowing she would never hear the answer. But she had opened the box. There was no going back.

Her name was Erin Blake.

The box file contained a few faded baby photographs and a small brown envelope. She shook the envelope and a tiny discoloured baby tooth fell into her lap. Geraldine stared at it in surprise, touched that her adoptive mother had kept her first tooth. She realised that tears were slithering down her face, dripping into the box.

There were no papers about her adoption but she thought she would be able to trace the adoption agency that held her records. She had a name and an address: Wexford Nursing Home in Ashford. She ran into the living room and turned on her laptop. A quick search revealed a database of homes for mothers and babies. Wexford had closed down in 1984. That avenue was closed, but she would find another way to discover the truth. It was what she had trained to do. She located the agency that had arranged adoptions for Wexford Nursing Home and applied for access to her adoption file. Her finger poised over the key before she tapped it once. Send. There was nothing more she could do now at one o'clock in the morning.

'My name is Erin Blake,' she whispered to herself. 'My name is Erin Blake.' It didn't make her feel any better.

17

ARRANGEMENTS

Half way through the morning Geraldine received a response to the email she had sent to the adoption agency. She picked up the phone and paused before replacing it firmly on the cradle. She was crazy to even consider making the call from her desk in the Incident Room.

'I'm nipping out,' she told the duty sergeant who nodded and returned to the duty roster he was working on.

A chill breeze made Geraldine shiver as she wandered outside, unlocked her car and drove away from the centre of town in the direction of the recreation ground. She parked in a quiet side road and fumbled with her phone where she had saved the number of the adoption agency.

'Hello? I'd like – I'm calling to enquire about –' It hadn't occurred to her beforehand that a simple request for information might be so difficult to make. She took a deep breath. 'I was adopted and I want to find out about – it.' The words were out. With an overwhelming sense of relief Geraldine allowed the voice at the other end of the line to take control. The woman asking questions was kind but dispassionate. This was clearly a routine enquiry. Geraldine was suddenly aware of how cold she felt and was surprised to see her free hand trembling against the steering wheel.

She forced herself to speak slowly and calmly. 'Are you able to access my file now, or shall I call back?'

'I'm afraid we can't disclose any details over the phone.'

'What can I do then? I must know, whatever you have. I'm entitled to know what's on my file.'

'Of course you're entitled to that information, but you need to make an appointment to discuss your case with a social worker. I can book an appointment now.'

'I can't possibly come to the agency. I don't have time.' Geraldine knew she was being ridiculous. The woman was only doing her job. But having psyched herself up to make the call, Geraldine was swept up in a raging tide of impatience. She did her best to persuade the woman to fetch her file then and there, explaining that she was a detective inspector involved in a murder enquiry who couldn't be spared from the investigation. 'I just want to know why I was adopted,' she insisted, but the woman remained adamant. Adoption files were only discussed face to face.

'I'm sorry, Geraldine, but it's for your own protection. These situations can be very emotional so it's best to have appropriate support on-hand, just in case you feel you want to talk to someone. Many adoptees – most – are happy to discover their history, but sometimes the situation can be difficult or even upsetting.'

Rigid with disappointment, Geraldine made an appointment to discover her birth history, face to face with a stranger.

Ian Peterson glanced up as Geraldine returned to the Incident Room and she felt a sudden longing to escape to a new location where no one knew her, a busy city where she could be consumed by work and no one would know or care anything about her. She thought of the private office in Abigail Kirby's home and sighed.

'We off to see what we can find out then, gov?'

Geraldine nodded, thinking that she hadn't found out anything about why she had been adopted. Only a social worker in an adoption agency was privy to that information. A social worker and Geraldine's birth mother. If her birth mother was still alive.

'Come on, then, Ian. Let's see if David Whittaker can tell us anything we don't already know.' Neither of them expected the witness who had discovered Abigail Kirby's body to have any new information for them, but he had been too shocked to give a detailed statement at the scene and they had to go through the motions and question him. There was always a possibility he might remember something that would help them in their enquiries.

David Whittaker worked in a garage near the station. He thanked them for interviewing him at work. 'I don't want my wife to find out what happened. This way, no one needs to know. I know it's daft but the wife gets so nervous about, well, everything really. I suppose it's bound to come out. I've sworn Zac to secrecy,' he shrugged, 'but you know what kids are. She's going to find out sooner or later isn't she? Once she knows what happened, she'll give me hell. She thinks I let the kid take unnecessary risks, but it doesn't do any good, mollycoddling him like she does. And it wasn't my fault I happened on that dead woman, is it?'

'I can't see that you let your son take any unnecessary risk –'

'I didn't, but you try telling her that. She'll never let me take him to the rec ground again, and I've bought him a new kite. Where the hell else are we going to fly it? I mean, I'm taking him there and that's that, but there's no point stirring up a hornet's nest if I can possibly avoid it. I know she's only trying to protect the boy, but he can't stay in the house all the time, stuck in front of the telly. It's not healthy for a young kid. And it's not as if he saw anything. He was waiting on the grass when I went into the trees looking for the kite and that's when I found it. Her, I should say. It gave me quite a turn. I mean, you don't expect to find dead bodies lying around like that, do you?'

Shocked into taciturnity when he had stumbled on Abigail Kirby's corpse, David Whittaker had recovered from his alarm and was eager to talk. But for all his chatter, he had nothing new to tell them. 'All I wanted to do was get my boy home. I couldn't think about anything else.'

'We know the body had been lying there overnight when you found her,' Peterson said. 'But killers often wait around to watch what happens so it's possible you may have seen him. Can you remember anyone hanging around the area?'

'No. As far as I can remember, it was deserted, apart from me and Zac.'

'Did you notice any cars parked along the road when you arrived?' The mechanic shook his head. 'No cars at all?'

'There might've been, but I don't remember. I usually notice cars,' he waved his dirty rag at the one he was working on. 'But to be honest, I was more concerned about my boy. I'm sorry I can't be more help.'

They thanked David Whittaker and left, disappointed but not surprised.

'That was a waste of time,' Peterson blew out his cheeks and crossed his arms as he sat back irritably in his seat. Geraldine stared out of the window, thinking about David Whittaker and his son, excited about flying a kite together. She wondered who her own father was, and whether he was still alive. Perhaps even her birth mother didn't know his identity.

That evening, Geraldine assumed Paul Hilliard was calling to tell her the body had afforded some new piece of evidence. She wondered why he was phoning her on her private number.

'Have you found something?'

'No, nothing new – but I have a few ideas. The thing is, Geraldine, I find it hard not to think about cases like this when I'm involved, doing the autopsy I mean. I can't help wondering what could have possessed someone to do this. It's been playing on my mind.' He paused. Geraldine waited, uncertain what he was getting at. 'It must be the same for you. It must be hard to switch off.'

'Well yes,' Geraldine answered awkwardly. Usually she did tend to obsess over the victims in her cases, but she had allowed Abigail Kirby's fate to be overshadowed by her preoccupation with her own past – and by her interest in Paul Hilliard. 'Yes, it is.'

'But you've got your sergeant, and a whole team to talk it over with.'

Geraldine smiled, remembering the doctor's clear-cut features, and the way his eyes had held her gaze. 'It must be hard for you, wondering about it by yourself,' she ventured.

'Well, yes, I suppose, when you put it like that –'

'We could discuss your ideas, if you like?' She held her breath.

'That would be great. I'd really like to mull it over, if you have time. Perhaps we could meet up for a drink?'

Geraldine grinned but she kept her voice steady. 'Why not?' It never did any harm to see the evidence through another pair of eyes, and the doctor's views might help them start to find a lead to the killer.

'That's the only reason I agreed to meet him on Friday,' Geraldine explained to her friend, Hannah, when they spoke later.

'Oh yes, a date with a sexy doctor and you only want to talk about work,' Hannah laughed.

'It's not a date. We're meeting for a drink at lunch time to discuss the victim's injuries.'

'And you're hoping that isn't the only body he's interested in –'

'Hannah, stop it. That's ridiculous, and you know it. I've barely spoken to the guy. And we're not meeting in the evening. It's hardly a date.'

Hannah laughed again. 'Your eyes met across a bloody corpse…'

'A mutilated corpse, actually.'

'What?'

'Shit, I shouldn't have mentioned it. Look, this woman's tongue was cut out, I know it'll be all over the papers soon enough but, in the meantime, don't say anything to anyone.'

'Her tongue?'

'Please, Hannah, forget I mentioned it. Not a word. It's really important you don't tell anyone.'

'Of course I won't, if you say so.'

'I do. In fact, just forget about it, will you?'

'You think it's possible to forget something like that?'

'Welcome to my world, Hannah.'

18

BEN

Ben Kirby's life, which had always revolved around football and food, changed in one moment, with one terrible announcement. If he closed his eyes, he could picture the dark-haired detective who had brought the news that his mother was never coming back. Life would never be the same again.

Ben knew his father was trying to comfort him, but it didn't help. It was just words. 'We've got to be strong for each other,' his father said. 'Life goes on. Your mother would want you to be strong. Lucy's going to need your support.' He paused. 'I need your support, son.'

'I know, dad, but it's just so – so horrible.' His voice wobbled. He bit his lip trying to prevent it trembling but couldn't stop his eyes filling with tears.

'We have to look out for each other now.' Matthew glanced towards the door and Ben knew his father was thinking about Lucy. Ben was fed up with her hostility towards their father. They only had one parent now, but Lucy never let up.

His father was about to say something else when the doorbell rang and he went to see who it was. Through the open kitchen door, Ben saw the police standing in the porch. He held his breath and clenched his fists, waiting to hear they had found the sick bastard killer.

'Have you brought us any news?' Ben heard his dad ask. He invited them in but the two detectives hovered on the doorstep.

'We'd like to ask you a few more questions about your

movements on Saturday,' the woman said.

Something seemed to burst inside Ben's head and he leapt to his feet and raced up the hall. 'Leave him alone!' he yelled, feet pounding on the carpet. 'We've been through enough! He hasn't done anything wrong. Go away and leave us alone!' He was shaking with rage. Lucy came down the stairs to find out what all the commotion was about.

The woman detective looked at Ben sadly. 'I'm sorry, Ben, but we really do need to ask your father a few questions.'

'Ask him here,' Ben knew he was crying but he didn't care. 'Ask him right here, right now, and then go away. Go on. You said you only want to ask him a few questions. Ask him then. He's done nothing wrong.'

'Don't worry, son,' his father said. 'It's got to be done. The sooner we go through it, the sooner we can get this cleared up and they'll leave us alone so we can start trying to get through this together. Don't take on so. It's not their fault. They're only doing their job.'

'We all know whose fault it is,' Lucy snapped. 'Take him away. We don't want him here. You're welcome to him. You can lock him up and throw away the key as far as we're concerned.'

Ben knew Lucy was annoyed with their father, but he was shocked by her outburst. As for their father, he looked as though he was going to cry. He looked so pale and ill, Ben could have thumped Lucy for being so spiteful.

'I think you'd better come in,' Ben's dad told the police.

'We can interview you at the station if that's any easier.' The woman detective glanced at Ben who glared back at her.

Ben's father sighed. 'Yes, that might be better. But I'd like to give my sister a ring first, if that's all right. She's offered to come over.' He reached out and ruffled Ben's hair. 'Someone has to keep an eye on the place, and sort out washing and things. I think now would be a good time for her to come round. She can make supper, and... Well, I'll go and call her.' For a heady moment Ben thought his father might be planning to give the police the slip and escape through the back door, but the tall sergeant went with him. 'Aunty Evie will be here in about an hour, Ben, Lucy,' their father said when he reappeared a few moments later. He forced a smile. 'Take care of each other till then, and I'll see you later. With any luck I'll be back before Aunt Evie gets here.' Ben could tell his father was trying to sound cheerful. He remembered what his father had said earlier.

'Don't worry about us, dad,' he said, sniffing back his tears so violently that his nose hurt. 'We'll be fine. I'll take care of Lucy.'

As the front door closed Ben raced upstairs to his room feeling utterly abandoned and threw himself on his bed. Lucy followed him and knocked on his door. He didn't respond but she came in anyway. Lying on his back, one arm flung across his face, Ben didn't answer when she called his name but hiccupped and turned over on his side to face the wall. He felt the bed jolt as Lucy sat down.

'I'm glad he's gone,' she said firmly. 'We don't need him. It serves him right.' She paused. 'Ben,' he could feel her breath tickling his neck as she leaned forward. 'He killed mum.'

'That's crap.' His voice sounded muffled through his arm but she heard him all right.

'It's true. He wanted to get rid of her. He wanted a divorce and she refused. He wanted to marry someone else.'

'That's bullshit and you know it.'

'No, it's not. It's what I've been trying to tell you only you won't bloody listen.' Her voice rose, screechy with emotion. 'He was seeing someone else. A woman called Charlotte.'

Ben was interested in spite of himself. He propped himself up on one elbow and looked at his sister. 'What are you talking about, you freak?'

'That's why he wanted a divorce. So he could get married to Charlotte, whoever she is.'

'So how come you know all this?'

'I heard mum and dad arguing one night. He wanted a divorce and she said no, and that's why he killed her. So he could marry the other woman. I heard them talking about it.'

Ben flung himself back down on the bed and stared at the ceiling. 'That's a load of bollocks. You're making it up. I don't know why you hate him so much, but he's our dad and he's all we've got now, so if that's all you've got to say, then fuck off and leave me alone. Go on, get out of my room, freak.'

Lucy didn't budge. 'Why do you think I hate his guts?' she asked angrily. 'He killed mum.'

'Shut up, shut up! I don't believe a word of it.'

Lucy stood up. 'You're a complete pillock. You're an idiot!' She crossed the room, trampling on his clothes and magazines. 'I don't need him and I don't need you, and I don't need Aunty Evie poking her stupid nose around.' She went out, slamming the door behind her.

19

WITNESS

'There's a lad asking to see someone in charge of the Abigail Kirby investigation.' Geraldine was on her feet before the constable had finished speaking. They were all eager for a lead. As Geraldine entered the room, the boy looked up through a greasy black fringe that flopped sideways across his eyes. He looked about sixteen or seventeen. His pointy nose and chin gave him a gnome-like appearance as he dropped his gaze and sat twisting a chunky silver ring nervously on one finger.

Vernon Mitchell told her he was seventeen. 'I'm nearly eighteen,' he added earnestly, as though it was important.

'I understand you might have some information for us?' The boy hesitated. 'Something that could help us in our investigation into the death of Abigail Kirby?'

Vernon nodded uncertainly. 'She was my headmistress. I recognised her straightaway. I couldn't believe it when I read she was dead.'

'You read about her death?'

'Yes, I saw it in the paper. It was a shock, seeing it like that.'

Geraldine closed her notebook. 'You have my sympathies, Vernon. You knew Mrs Kirby and it's understandable for you to feel disturbed. It's hard to read about the death of someone you know, when they've been murdered.'

Vernon shook his head. 'I didn't exactly know her.' He turned sullen and all at once looked very young for his age. 'It's not like she showed me any respect.' He told Geraldine

114

that everyone at school was afraid of Mrs Kirby. If it hadn't been for her, Vernon might have applied to university. Mrs Kirby had joined Harchester School when Vernon was in his final GCSE year and she'd made it clear she had no time for pupils who weren't prepared to apply themselves in the hope of going on to further education. 'I'd have had to retake English and maths, for starters,' he explained. The previous headmaster had been decent, Vernon went on, but Mrs Kirby had been determined to weed out the less able pupils. 'All she cared about was the reputation of her precious school. She didn't care about us.'

Geraldine tried to hide her impatience. 'Vernon, your opinion of Mrs Kirby will help us to build a picture of her, but if you can't give us any information that might help us to find out who might have wanted to be rid of her...'

Vernon snorted. 'I can't think of many people who wouldn't have wanted her to go. I mean, like I said, she wasn't exactly popular – like, everyone hated her – but killing her is something else. No one would have wanted her dead. It freaks me out to think I might have seen her just a few minutes before she died.'

Geraldine sat forward, interested at last. 'What do you mean, Vernon?' His dark eyes flickered in alarm at the urgency in her voice and Geraldine sat back in her chair again. 'Vernon, take your time. What is it you came here to tell us?'

'I saw her,' he began and hesitated, twisting his ring again.

'Mrs Kirby?'

'Yes.'

'Go on.'

'I work in Smith's, in the shopping centre.' Geraldine nodded. The receipt in Abigail Kirby's pocket confirmed she had been there on Saturday morning.

'What did she say to you?'

'No, it was nothing like that. She didn't speak to me. I

doubt if she recognised me. But it was weird. There was this man.' He paused, struggling to find words to explain what had happened. He had spotted Mrs Kirby as she stood waiting to pay. As the queue shuffled forwards she had glanced around impatiently. Vernon hadn't noticed what Mrs Kirby said to the man behind her in the queue, but he saw the expression on the man's face when Mrs Kirby turned away.

'I mean, I've left school, she doesn't get under my skin any more. School's history. But this guy –' He shook his head and his long fringe lifted and flopped over his eyes again. 'It was funny, a grown man like that looking so worked up. I mean, he was old and he was shaking, he looked so mad. I thought he was going to hit her.'

'You thought he was going to hit Mrs Kirby?' The boy nodded. 'What time was this?'

'Before my morning break at eleven. Probably about ten, maybe ten-thirty.'

'Did you recognise the man?'

'No. I'd never seen him before in my life.'

'Can you describe him?'

Vernon's earlier reticence had vanished. 'He was tall, dark hair, in a dark jacket or coat. Mrs Kirby didn't seem to care. Maybe she didn't even notice because this man was behind her in the queue and soon after that they all moved forward and then it was Mrs Kirby's turn to pay and I didn't see her again. I was busy on another till.'

'Can you remember anything else about the man you saw?' Vernon shook his head. 'You said he was old. How old was he?'

The boy shrugged. 'Not old old. I mean he was maybe around forty. It's hard to say.'

Geraldine quizzed the boy for a few minutes about the incident, but Vernon wasn't able to tell her anything more about the man he had seen.

'You said,' Geraldine glanced down at her notes, 'you thought he looked so angry you felt he might hit Mrs Kirby. Why did you think that?'

Vernon shrugged. 'I don't know,' he replied. 'It was just something I thought.'

Back at her desk, Geraldine stared at her notes. A vague impression reported by a casual observer probably had no bearing on the case. 'What do you think? Time waster?' she asked Peterson. 'Let's take a look at the CCTV from Smith's. There's probably nothing there, but at least we'd better check.' As she stood up, she saw her own excitement reflected back at her in the sergeant's eyes.

Abigail Kirby was spotted on CCTV in the shopping centre at ten fifteen on Saturday morning going in to WH Smith's. She was picked up shortly afterwards on another camera, queuing in a coffee shop. At eleven ten she left the shopping centre, walked past the station, and vanished in the surrounding streets. In the throng of shoppers entering and leaving they picked out a tall man in a dark coat leaving the shopping centre immediately after Abigail Kirby. They were keen to trace him, but they had very little to go on.

An announcement was made over the local radio and sent to the local paper for inclusion in the following week's printed edition. It went online on their website straightaway.

'Police are keen to speak to a tall man wearing a dark coat who left the Harchester Shopping Centre at eleven ten on Saturday.' No one was surprised when they received no useful response.

'Just the usual nutters, ma'am.'

'There's a chance this man might be involved,' the DCI agreed. 'Geraldine, get a team of constables out to all the shops to see if anyone saw a man matching this description or, better still, if they can find him on their CCTV making a purchase by credit card before eleven ten. This is our best lead so far. Find him.'

'Yes ma'am.'

Geraldine co-ordinated the search. A bevy of constables asked in every shop and checked through film after film working solidly throughout the day, studying every tall figure in a dark coat or jacket they could find in an attempt to come up with a decent image of his face, and tracking Abigail Kirby's movements in case she encountered him anywhere else.

'Every other bloody man is tall, and half of those are wearing dark coats,' one of the constables complained and her colleague nodded. It was a hopeless task trying to identify a single shopper on the fuzzy shopping centre CCTV on a busy Saturday in November.

20

HANNAH

Geraldine slept badly on Wednesday night and awoke feeling tired and uneasy. The team were brought up to speed at the morning briefing, but the only new development was frustrating. On blurry CCTV film they could make out a tall man talking to Abigail Kirby for a second in the queue in WH Smith's, but was impossible to see him clearly. The woman wasn't even identifiable, but only one figure fitting Abigail Kirby's description appeared in the queue at the right time. Together with the eye-witness evidence from Vernon Mitchell, they were satisfied they had identified her correctly.

'Vernon Mitchell knew her by sight,' the DCI pointed out. That clinched it. They could see her, in the queue, talking to a man who could be her killer. But they had no idea who he was and his shadowy figure gave them very few clues. 'Right, we can estimate his height pretty closely,' the DCI went on. 'And we can be reasonably certain we're looking at a man. Either that or an unusually tall and masculine-looking woman.'

'Could be a tranny,' someone suggested quite seriously and there was a faint ripple of amusement around the room.

'They could be arguing,' the DCI went on. 'Let's see if we can trace anyone else who was in the queue at that time through the tills. Any customer who paid by credit card should be easy to find and most people pay by card these days –'

'In Smith's?' Peterson interjected. 'Buying newspapers and pens?'

Kathryn Gordon ignored the interruption. 'Mary,' she nodded at a constable, 'get onto it. We need to speak to anyone who witnessed the encounter in the queue.'

'Yes, ma'am.'

The atmosphere in the Incident Room was buzzing with muted excitement as they dispersed to check their duties for the day, but the mood rapidly deteriorated as witness reports from shoppers and shop assistants led nowhere. The image of the man in the queue was so vague that someone fitting the description had been sighted simultaneously in just about every store throughout the morning.

'One step forward, two steps back. This is a complete waste of time.' Peterson scowled. Geraldine was inclined to agree with him. They were wasting valuable man-hours chasing a shadow. 'Do you think the DCI's losing her edge, gov?' Geraldine didn't answer. Kathryn Gordon spent more and more time shut up in her office and when she was around she gave the impression that she was tired of the case. Or perhaps she was just tired. 'If you ask me, she never should have come back to work after she was ill,' the sergeant went on, referring to the DCI's period of convalescence earlier in the year after she had suffered a minor coronary.

'I didn't ask you,' Geraldine retorted, all the more sharply because she thought Peterson was right. As if it wasn't enough that her personal life was a mess, she now had to worry about whether her sergeant was losing his enthusiasm for the case. 'Coffee?' she asked, seeing her colleague's crestfallen expression.

'Don't worry,' she told him when they sat down. 'We'll get a result.' The sergeant grunted and stared into his cup. 'It's not like you to be so down.'

'It's not this.' He rolled his eyes around. 'Well, that too. But –' Geraldine waited. 'It's Bev.' They sipped their coffee in silence. 'I don't know what gets into her.'

'I thought you were an expert on women, with all your sisters.'

Peterson didn't smile. 'Something's up with Bev, I can tell. She's been really snappy lately.' Not for the first time, Geraldine was gratified he was confiding in her, but his fretting concerned her. He was usually so positive. 'Having problems with Bev on top of all this, it's just getting on top of me,' he explained. 'What if she wants to end it? I mean, I don't know what she wants any more.'

'You're just tired and stressed, Ian, that's why you're suspecting the worst. I expect everything's fine, but in any case it's better to know if there's a problem.' Geraldine thought about her own long-term partner Mark who had walked out on her after six years. Worse than his leaving had been the realisation that she hadn't even suspected he was seeing another woman. 'If you want my advice, sort it out with Bev as soon as you can. There's no point letting it drag on and if there is anything going on it's always better to know.'

'You're right, I'll talk to her. Thanks, Geraldine. I mean it, thank you. It's good to have someone to talk to. The lads here, they're good mates, but –'

'You don't want them to see your sensitive side?' She was pleased when he grinned. 'Come on then, back to work.'

At half past eleven Geraldine logged off and stood up.

'Where to, gov?' As usual, Peterson was eager to be away from his desk and the seemingly interminable paperwork.

'I'm going out.' Geraldine slung her bag over her shoulder. 'I'm meeting a friend, Ian,' she added, noticing his disappointed expression. 'I've got the afternoon off.' She hurried from the room.

Geraldine had arranged to meet her friend, Hannah, for lunch at midday. They had fixed the date several weeks earlier, before Geraldine had been assigned to the Abigail Kirby case. She didn't really want to spare the time, but she had put Hannah off so often that she was reluctant to let her down again. And she wanted to talk to her friend about Paul Hilliard.

They met for a pizza in Hannah's home town of Faversham.

'Are you all right?' Hannah asked. 'You look awful.'

'Thanks.'

'Seriously, you look really washed-out. 'Don't tell me, it's this case you're working on.' Geraldine nodded. 'Why didn't you say? We could've postponed getting together. You know I don't mind. Really, I'd hate to think you felt obligated –'

'What are you talking about, obligated?' Geraldine interrupted her. 'I wanted to see you. It's been too long already.'

'But –'

'But nothing. If I was too busy to meet, I'd have said.'

'Good. You know I'm always here.' Hannah smiled.

As they talked over olives and a glass of wine, Geraldine felt as though she had opened a door and glimpsed normality as her friend chattered about her husband's recent promotion, and her son's new teeth.

'Really?' Geraldine said and Hannah grinned. 'What's funny?'

'That's a crap pretence at showing interest if ever I saw one!'

'Sorry. I'm a bit preoccupied.'

'Work again? Don't tell me.'

'No, not work.'

'Must be a man then.' Hannah raised her eyebrows. 'Is this the one who cuts up dead bodies for a living?'

'Paul.'

'So? Tell me about Paul. How far have you got with him?' The waitress brought their food and they tucked in without talking for a few minutes. Hannah broke the silence. 'So? What's the latest? Have you seen him again?'

'No, I'm seeing him tomorrow.'

'Oh. Well, what do we know about him?'

Geraldine told her friend what little she knew. 'The thing is, I used to think I was a good judge of character but I just can't work out if he's interested in me. And if I can't understand anything about people, how can I even hope to do my job properly?'

'Listen to yourself.' Hannah put down her knife and fork. 'This has got nothing to do with your work. How can you possibly compare what's going on with this Paul with how well you do your job? In your work you're objective and that's what makes you so good at it. This is personal. It's all about your feelings. Obviously you're not going to be detached about it, especially if you fancy him.'

'I had a really weird dream about him.'

'Tell me about it and I'll interpret it.'

'Hannah, I'm being serious.'

'Go on then. I'm listening.'

'I can't remember exactly what happened, but Paul was there. He wasn't exactly threatening me, but I sensed he was going to hurt me. I was terrified, but I knew I couldn't show it. I had to get away from him but I knew if I left he'd follow me. And all the time I was talking to him and having to pretend everything was fine.'

'Well, it's obvious what that means. You know you're taking a risk and he might hurt you. But if you let the possibility of getting hurt put you off, you'll never have another relationship. If you like him, you just have to take that risk.'

'I do like him, I think.'

'Well, be careful not to get involved too quickly. You don't know that much about him yet. Do you even know if he's single?'

'Well, I don't know really. He wasn't wearing a wedding ring.'

'That doesn't mean anything. But if you think there's even a possibility you might get involved – I mean, you ought to find out before you start. Can't you just ask him?'

'I don't think he's with anyone. He seems to be on his own. That's the impression he gives.'

'You need to be more certain than that.'

Geraldine shrugged miserably. The thought that Paul might be with someone had crossed her mind. 'You're not helping, Hannah. I just feel ready.'

'For what?'

'For a relationship. It's six years since Mark and I split up. Time to move on.'

Hannah laughed. 'You mean you fancy this doctor of yours.'

'He's not mine. Not yet, anyway.'

'All I'm saying is, find out more about him before you go leaping in. You know what you're like.'

Geraldine nodded. With the best of intentions she never seemed able to make sensible choices where men were concerned.

'I just think Paul might be different.'

'Let's drink to that.'

21

AGENCY

'So how have you been coping since your mother died?' Hannah asked. 'She was a wonderful person. That chocolate cake she used to make when we were kids! I loved coming home with you after school.'

'Nothing to do with me, then?'

'No. Our friendship is based purely on chocolate cake.' They both laughed. 'Seriously, Geraldine, if you ever want to talk about her – well, it's OK to open up, you know. We've known each other since school, you can talk to me. It's not good for you to bottle everything up the way you do.'

Hannah was beginning to sound like Celia, voicing concern that was somehow demanding. By nature reticent to discuss her feelings, Geraldine was painfully aware of her emotional vulnerability but she couldn't explain it to Hannah. She wasn't even sure she understood why it was easier to talk about dead strangers than her own life. As she hesitated, the waitress came over with the bill and the moment passed. It was nearly a year since her mother had died, and soon after the funeral Geraldine had discovered the truth about her own birth. After so much time had elapsed it might be awkward now to reveal that the mother Hannah remembered had been an imposter.

'I'm fine, honestly, but I've really got to go.'

'That's OK. Work calls.'

Geraldine almost explained that she had an appointment at the adoption agency at two o'clock, but decided it was best to say nothing. Hannah might be upset that she hadn't been told about the adoption before.

The agency was located in the town hall, a Victorian building urgently in need of external renovation. Geraldine went up stone steps to a dingy reception area where she waited impatiently until a social worker came out to collect her.

'Hello. I'm Sandra. We spoke on the phone.' She led Geraldine along a draughty corridor.

An effort had clearly been made to make the interview room welcoming. The chairs looked new and a narrow-leaved plant drooped on the table beside a box of tissues. The social worker sat down holding a folder in her lap, and Geraldine perched anxiously opposite her.

'You applied for access to your adoption records?' Sandra asked. Geraldine nodded. 'I understand you have a copy of your original birth certificate?'

'Yes.' Geraldine's mouth felt dry. 'I was given it recently, when my mother – the woman who adopted me – died. Before I contact my birth mother, I'd like to know if there's an explanation in the file about why she gave me up for adoption.' The social worker hesitated and Geraldine felt a vague sense of unease that her mother was dead. 'Can I see the records please?'

'The sight of adoption records can be disappointing,' the social worker said. She patted the file. 'The explanation you've asked for is that your birth mother was only just sixteen when you were born. That's probably why she didn't name your father. He would almost certainly have been prosecuted for having sexual relations with an underage girl. As a sixteen-year-old single mother, she gave you up so you could have a better start in life.' The social worker looked at Geraldine. 'I'm afraid it wouldn't be appropriate for you to be in touch with her.'

'What do you mean?'

'There's a letter on file from your mother in which she says she doesn't want to have any contact with you.'

'Can I see it?' The social worker looked down at a piece of paper in her hand. 'I want to see it, please.' Geraldine was surprised. Her voice betrayed a desperation she hadn't been aware of feeling.

The social worker gave her a letter handwritten in a childish script.

Dear social worker
If my daughter ever tries to find me, tell her I don't want to see her. Please tell her it's not personal but I want to forget it ever happened. I hope she has a good life but I don't ever want to see her. You can give her my photo if she wants it but tell her not to try and find me.
I'll let you know if I ever change my mind but I won't. I have to put all this behind me now and I know she'll have a better life without me.
Thank you for your help
Milly

ps
Tell her I'm very sorry.

The social worker held out a small photo of a young girl's face. She looked about twelve. Geraldine stared at familiar features: dark eyes looked back at her from a face that would have been beautiful if it hadn't been spoiled by a slightly crooked nose. It could so easily have been a photo of Geraldine as a teenager.

'She wanted you to have it,' the social worker said gently. 'You know you look just like her.'

'She doesn't want to see me.'

'No, she doesn't want to see you. This kind of circumstance can be emotionally very difficult. If you'd like to talk to someone –'

Geraldine stood up abruptly. 'Thank you. I'm perfectly alright.' She gave a forced laugh. 'It's not as if I've been waiting all my life to meet her. I only recently discovered I was adopted, when my adoptive mother died.'

'Are you sure you're alright, Geraldine?'

'I'm fine,' she lied.

When she felt in her pocket for her car keys, Geraldine realised she was still clutching the photo. She regretted not having asked for a copy of her mother's letter, but she couldn't go back now she was crying. She climbed in the car and sat perfectly still staring at the small faded photograph in her hand. Her mother would be over fifty now – if she was still alive. Geraldine wondered how much she had changed from the thin, wide-eyed child in the picture. Perhaps her hair was turning grey. She'd probably had more children, and might have put on weight or been seriously ill. Geraldine didn't even know if she was still alive. One day she would find out, but she knew her mother might reject her all over again and she wasn't ready to take that risk yet.

It was just as well Geraldine was on duty that evening. It helped keep her mind off Milly Blake. Even so, her eyes looked puffy and red from crying.

'Are you all right?' Peterson asked when he passed her in the Incident Room.

'Fine.'

'You looked exhausted. Coffee?'

Geraldine shook her head. 'Too much to do,' she answered with a miserable smile, wishing he would leave her alone. His rocky relationship with Bev was a relatively simple situation to chat about. Her own problems were too complex to discuss over a quick coffee. But as the sergeant walked away Geraldine felt unexpectedly tearful and escaped to the toilet. Once again she had been betrayed by a mother who should have offered her unconditional support. Caught out by her outburst of emotion she pulled herself together with an effort, blew her nose and told herself it was pathetic for a woman of her age to break down like that. But she didn't trust herself to maintain her composure and scurried out to her car without looking around, like a criminal skulking in the dark.

The following morning they questioned Matthew Kirby again.

'You can't keep me here,' he protested. 'I've done nothing wrong. I've just lost my wife, for Christ's sake. Why are you doing this to me? I shouldn't be here.'

Despite his protestations, he was questioned at length.

'It would've made life easier if we could've told the papers he'd confessed,' the DCI said afterwards. Her shoulders were bowed and she looked tired, as though all the fight had gone out of her. 'We need a quick result. We've been on this for nearly a week now and we've come up with nothing.' She held up a newspaper. 'You've all seen the national papers?' A buzz went round the team. Geraldine had read the short article, largely accurate, on the front page of the Guardian.

HEADMISTRESS MURDERED

The body of Abigail Kirby, 48, headmistress of Harchester School, was discovered in woods beside a recreation ground on Sunday.

The police are treating the death as suspicious. 'We are following several leads,' Detective Chief Inspector Katherine Gordon said. The police are appealing to anyone who may have seen Mrs Kirby on Saturday to come forward. 'If you have any information about the victim's whereabouts at the weekend, please let us know,' the Detective Chief Inspector said.

Mrs Kirby leaves a husband and two children, a son and a daughter.

But for once the phones were silent. No one seemed to know anything about Abigail Kirby's whereabouts at the weekend. Even the usual nutters didn't bother picking up the phone to claim responsibility for a crime they hadn't committed.

22

CHARLOTTE

Charlotte gazed at the faded wallpaper in her living room, the dated armchairs and worn brown carpet. Although it was drab and depressing, she'd made no effort to brighten it up; that would be an admission that she planned on staying there, and she didn't intend to live alone in a one-bedroomed flat for long. She sighed, remembering her accommodation in York, light and bright, and just a short walk from the river and the centre of town. Her mother still lived in the semi-detached house where Charlotte had grown up in Heslington, a fifteen-minute bus ride from town. Her bedroom there had been pretty, with a view out over fields.

'I don't understand why you would want to spend all that money when you could stay here,' her mother had complained when Charlotte had announced she was moving out to live in the town.

'It's not as if I'm moving far. But I don't want to stay in Heslington all my life. There's nothing here.'

'What do you mean, nothing here? There's the university right on our doorstep. You used to like going up there with Karen.'

'Used to,' Charlotte echoed. 'But I'm twenty-five, mum. I've grown out of all that. The students are all younger than me and anyway, I don't fit in there.' And her friend, Karen, who was married with a baby, had lost interest in hanging around the student bars a long time ago.

The argument had dragged on for weeks until Charlotte left. 'I'll still come and visit, all the time,' she'd promised.

Her mother stood on the doorstep, stony-faced, watching her leave.

Then Charlotte had met Matthew.

'So when are you going to introduce your young man to me?' Mrs Fox had asked, her eyes bright with anticipation.

Charlotte had been uncertain how much to tell her. 'He's not exactly that young, mum. He's over thirty.' Forty, to be accurate.

'That's not so old. Your father's four years older than me –' She faltered. After seventeen years Charlotte's father had left her for a younger woman.

'And he's married,' Charlotte blurted out. She thought she might as well get it over with. Her mother would find out sooner or later. 'It's not as bad as it sounds,' she went on hurriedly, 'they're going to separate soon. He wants a divorce. He's already discussed it with his wife and –' Charlotte knew immediately that it had been a mistake to tell her mother Matthew was married.

'Just like your father,' her mother spat. 'I suppose his wife's older than you too.'

'It's not like that,' Charlotte insisted. 'His wife's only interested in her career. She doesn't love him.'

'Oh yes, the same old excuse.' Her mother, usually so stoical, burst into tears. 'I couldn't bear to see you hurt, Charlotte,' she sobbed. 'Leave this man, he'll be no good for you. You're a beautiful girl, find someone else. Not a married man.' Her voice rose in a wail. 'Not a married man. Why can't you find someone who won't make you miserable with all his lies and treachery.'

'He's never lied to me, mum. I knew he was married before we started seeing each other. He's always been totally honest with me.'

'More fool you then.'

Her mother had never been reconciled to the relationship,

and had steadfastly refused to meet Matthew. When she'd learned he was planning to move South, accompanying his wife after her promotion, she had done her best to persuade Charlotte it was for the best.

'He's been telling you for years that he's going to leave her and now, when he has the chance to let her go, what does he do? He's traipsing after her all the way to Kent. If that's not making his priorities clear, I don't know what is. He might as well be moving to another planet. You need to face the truth. It's over, Charlotte. It's time for you to move on and find someone who is prepared to devote himself to you properly as a man should, and make you happy.'

Charlotte laughed. 'It's not another planet, mum, and I'm going with him.' Her mother had been too flabbergasted to reply. 'It's all arranged. He's found me a flat down there – just until his divorce – and I've found a job.'

'A job?'

'As a kind of secretary.'

'A secretary? Why on earth would you want to give up your career like that? After all the training you did.'

'It's hardly a great career, stuck in theatre all day, handing over scalpels and mopping up blood.'

'But to go and work in an office –'

'It's my choice.'

Her mother had never forgiven her for quitting York to follow Matthew to Kent.

'She's an unforgiving woman,' Charlotte's father had said when she'd told him. 'Do you love this man?'

'I wouldn't be moving to the other end of the country to be with him if I didn't, would I? If his wife thinks she can take him away that easily, she doesn't know me.'

'And does he love you?'

'Yes.'

'Then marry him and be happy, Charlotte. You can't let

your mother hold you back from what you have to do.'

The brown suitcase had been far too small for her to take everything she wanted. Reminding herself she could return at any time to collect more belongings, her excitement had been dampened by the difficulty of packing. Even though she would have no use for it where she was going, at the last minute she had taken her nurse's uniform from its hanger and lain it, carefully folded, in the case. Matthew had carried the suitcase downstairs, past the disapproving glare of Charlotte's mother, who had watched them go without a word. In the car, Charlotte looked up as the engine started, but her mother had already shut the front door.

Matthew had done his best to make it as easy as possible for Charlotte to move, finding her a flat and taking on the rental agreement for her. All she had to do was move in. When she had first seen it she hadn't minded that the flat was pokey and ugly, because she hadn't expected to stay there for long. Although she knew it was wicked to feel glad his wife had been killed, the bitch had stood in their way for so long, it was a relief in the end to be rid of her. If Matthew's wife had still been alive, they still wouldn't have been in a position to discuss marriage. Her only regret was that now she would never know if he would ever have left his wife voluntarily to be with her.

Charlotte was taken aback when the police came round to question her again. Fireworks were popping loudly nearby as she opened the door, and she caught a smell of smoke from the street, although Guy Fawkes night was still a week away. Hiding her agitation as well as she could, she led them upstairs to her living room. It was typical of her mother to telephone just at that moment.

'I can't talk right now, mum. I'll call you back.'

'He's there, isn't he?'

'No, he's not here, but I can't talk now.'

'You mean you don't want to. I suppose his wife's –'

'I'll call you later.' She hung up.

'We'd like to go over your movements again on the afternoon of Saturday October 24th,' Inspector Steel said. Her face gave nothing away. She could have been talking about the weather.

'That's the day it happened, the day she died?'

'The day Abigail Kirby was murdered. We'd just like to go over your movements that afternoon once more.' The noise of fireworks outside interrupted the stillness, like rapid gunfire.

Charlotte repeated as much as she could recall of her Saturday afternoon and evening. It was horrible to think that someone had probably been killing his wife at the very time she had been in bed with Matthew. The police kept on at her with their questions, probing into every detail of her account, until she felt a prickle of fear. Surely they couldn't suspect her of being involved in the murder. It had briefly occurred to her that Matthew could have had something to do with his wife's death, but she had immediately dismissed that thought as ludicrous. If he hadn't been prepared to leave his wife for fear of upsetting his children, he was hardly likely to kill her. Charlotte wished the police would hurry up and sort out the mess, so she and Matthew could get on with their lives. They could finally start making plans to get married now his wife was out of the way.

She decided to be firm. 'I never met Abigail Kirby. I planned to. I wanted to talk to her, woman to woman, and beg her to agree to a divorce but – I didn't have the guts to approach her directly, and in any case it wouldn't have made any difference. Matthew told me not to bother. He said she wouldn't respond to any sort of emotional appeal, certainly not from me.' She forced a smile. 'I don't even know what she looks like!'

'Didn't you see her picture in the papers?'

'Well, yes.' Charlotte felt flustered. In attempting to distance herself from Abigail Kirby, she had allowed the police to catch her out in a lie. They might easily think she had told them other lies too. 'That's not the same, is it? I meant, I never saw her in the flesh.'

'But like it or not you were rivals for Matthew Kirby's affections.'

'It wasn't like that. We weren't exactly rivals. Matthew loves me and he stopped having feelings for his wife a long time ago. I'm not a marriage wrecker, Inspector. Their relationship was finished long before I met Matthew. They slept in different rooms, you know. They were as good as separated. There was no reason for her to keep on refusing to divorce him.'

'He could have left her anyway,' the sergeant pointed out.

'No he couldn't. You must know he was worried she'd turn his children against him. If it wasn't for them, he would have walked out on her years ago. We'd never have moved from York at all. It was all because of the children.'

'And Abigail Kirby. You certainly had real cause to hate her.'

Charlotte shook her head, fighting a sense of panic. 'I never met her. I didn't need to hate her. Matthew loves me. You can't say I was involved in her death.'

'Did I suggest that?' The inspector turned to the sergeant. 'Did you say that?' He shook his head.

Charlotte burst into tears. 'You're making it sound as though I loathed her and wanted her dead.'

'Did you?'

'No. I just wanted Matthew.' While she was wiping her eyes the phone shrilled and she lunged at the handset, hurling it to the floor. 'My bloody mother!' As she sank back in her chair there was a brief barrage of explosions from fireworks outside.

'Was that petulance at her mother's interference, or a display of real rage?' Peterson wondered when they were walking back to the car.

'I don't know, but in any case I don't think Abigail Kirby was attacked in a sudden fit of temper. If you ask me, her death was planned very carefully.'

23

WHITEWASH

He always locked the door before switching on the light. The darkness while he felt for the switch heightened his anticipation. As soon as the light came on, expectation exploded into reality. Finding a cracked basin with a functioning rusty tap in the corner, he had set to work washing the filthy cellar with sugar soap. First time around the water in the bucket had turned black every few minutes. He lugged the bucket over to the sink so frequently that in the end he had dispensed with it altogether and went backwards and forwards to the sink, sloshing water on the floor. It took weeks. When he was satisfied the room was clean, he had whitewashed the walls and ceiling. He had laid the floor lino himself too, working at night because he liked to conceal what he was doing, although no one else ever went down in the cellar. It was his territory.

Visitors to the house made him feel uncomfortable. The couple from the house next door had rung his bell one Sunday afternoon and introduced themselves a few days after he had moved in. If his wife had been there she would probably have invited them in. She liked to socialise.

'We're from number fifteen,' the woman said brightly. Her voice grated after the silence in which he had immersed himself. He liked sitting in silence. It helped to rest his mind. He wanted these people off his doorstep, off his property. 'We called to welcome you to the neighbourhood...' The voice petered out, the bright smile wavered on her painted lips. He nodded briefly but didn't speak. This was his house.

He didn't have to talk to anyone here. 'If there's anything you want to know –?' she tried again. He shook his head silently and closed the door.

To make the cellar secure he had fitted a deadlock on the door – the name made him smile. He had blisters from drilling into the hard wood but it was worth the effort. Only he had a key, which he kept with him all the time. The key to retribution.

Once the lights were on, the white room was dazzling. Halogen lamps hung from the ceiling. He sat down and gazed around, moved by the simplicity of the view, the purity of the white world he had created. He wrapped his arms around himself and rocked gently on his chair, nursing a raw rage. In the stillness his anger seemed more potent.

All at once he sprang to his feet and strode over to the sink. Donning a waterproof overall, he filled the sink and selected a hard bristled brush. He scrubbed vigorously at the floor before returning to his chair to look around and breathe in the white harmony of his secret chamber. It had taken him a long time to remove the blood stains left by the teacher's execution but at last the lino had returned to its original colour. The surface sheen had been completely rubbed away but there was no discolouration. Next he turned his attention to the wall, studying it closely. A few streaks had smeared when he'd tried to wipe them away, stark against the white setting, but he had scrubbed at them until he had reduced the soiling to a fainter pink though he hadn't been able to remove it without scraping away the paint until the brickwork showed through. Standing back to review the result of his efforts he frowned. Using a roller he painted over an entire section of wall until all the blemishes had vanished. Then he sat down again, exhausted but satisfied.

He had never worked so hard before. Success had come easily to him until, in a moment, everything had been snatched away. Soon even the loss would be over. Only one more death was necessary. The doctor had to die and then it would be his turn to find peace. The waiting made him uneasy. People who had near death experiences talked of seeing a white light before they died. He gazed around the white room and his shoulders slumped forward as his tension slipped away. Delivering death to others brought his own end closer and he would welcome it when the time came. Life held no meaning for him any more.

One more punishment and it would all be over. First the girl, then the teacher, now only the doctor remained. Why should the doctor live on surrounded by the dead? He belonged with them. Death was a fitting termination to his life's work.

24

DRINK

A ll through her preoccupation with the case and her visit to the adoption agency, Geraldine had been buoyed up at the prospect of seeing Paul Hilliard again. On her way to the adoption agency on Thursday she had nipped into Boots and hovered around the make-up counter, looking at different coloured eye shadows. She had tried a silvery blue powder on the inside of her wrist, resisted the temptation to buy a scarlet lipstick, settling instead for her usual neutral pinkish one, and lashed out on a new brown eye shadow. She had spent Thursday evening pampering herself, a routine that she normally reserved for the end of a case, plucking her eyebrows and blow drying her hair. It restored her equanimity after her futile attempt to persuade the social worker to put her in contact with her mother. Life went on regardless.

Throughout Friday morning she was distracted. 'It's only a casual drink,' she told herself fiercely, but it was a while since a man like Paul Hilliard had wanted to meet her alone. After Mark, her partner of six years, had unexpectedly left her for someone else it had taken her a while to trust another boyfriend. Eventually she'd met Craig but he too had left her because, like Mark, he had resented her putting work first.

Paul had suggested meeting at lunch time at The Gate, a wine bar in the town that Geraldine had seen as she drove past but had never been inside. She arrived just after one as they'd agreed, and was disappointed when she didn't see Paul Hilliard waiting for her at the bar. Glancing around she saw him seated in a corner bay, his face in shadow. She felt drawn by his air of remote vulnerability and pulled herself up short. There was no denying she fancied him, but he could be married for all she knew. Then again, he didn't wear a wedding ring, and he had chosen to meet her in the intimacy of a secluded alcove.

Geraldine sat down opposite Paul and smiled. He smiled back, but his hand trembled as he poured her a glass of wine. He was clearly jittery and Geraldine couldn't help wondering if his nervousness indicated he was interested in her.

'So,' Paul began, 'tell me about yourself. Why police work? Let me guess. It's the problem-solving that attracted you. The challenge.' Geraldine nodded and Paul went on. 'People talk a lot of bull about wanting to make the world a better place, don't they? I studied medicine because I found it interesting. I mean, I do my best to be a good person, useful. We all do that. But –' He shrugged. 'Being altruistic isn't enough, is it? I need the mental stimulation.' Geraldine smiled. She liked his honesty. 'So,' Paul repeated, 'what attracted you to your job?'

Geraldine put down her glass and summarised her advancement from constable to inspector. 'You're absolutely right,' she concluded. 'Maintaining social order is important. Vital. But I do like the problem solving.'

'What about this case you're working on? Abigail Kirby. How is that progressing?'

'Dull and frustrating,' she told him and launched into a detailed account of the investigation, aware all the time of his eyes gazing steadily at her. It was a relief to be able to speak freely. Usually she had to be circumspect in conversation with friends outside the force. Not only was her work confidential, but the details of murder enquiries were bound to put men off her, unless they were deranged or deviant. Talking about corpses was hardly conducive to romance. Discussing the case with Paul she realised for the first time how constrained she had felt in her past relationships, always having to guard what she said in case she was indiscreet, or described some detail they found disgusting. Dealing with appalling acts of inhumanity as part of her daily routine didn't make her macabre, just as cutting open dead bodies didn't mean Paul Hilliard was gruesome. As they faced one another across the table Geraldine felt a bond of mutual understanding she had never experienced with anyone outside the force before and realised her interest in Paul was more than simple physical attraction. She felt drawn to him and hoped he felt the same.

'So you think her husband killed her?' he asked when they had ordered something to eat. He had salmon, Geraldine a haloumi salad.

'He's a suspect, but I'm not convinced.'

'Oh? What else have you got to go on?'

'Not a lot.' She told Paul all about the witness who had reported seeing Abigail Kirby in WH Smith's.

Paul was dismissive. 'He would have been preoccupied with serving customers. You said there was a queue, so the shop was obviously busy.'

'Yes, I daresay it's nothing, but we have to follow up any lead. It's not as if we've got much else to go on. I don't want to bore you,' she added, aware that she was doing all the talking.

'No.' He gave a taut smile and leaned forward. 'I'm not bored at all. I want to know all about you.' Geraldine saw him look at her askance, as if gauging her reaction, and she lowered her eyes, reminding herself that she had proved a poor judge of men's intentions towards her in the past. Hesitantly she told him about her one long-term relationship.

'You loved him?' Paul asked gently while his eyes seemed to search hers.

Geraldine nodded and sipped her wine slowly. Both Celia and Hannah had accused her of never discussing her feelings with them, but Paul was easy to confide in. Perhaps it was the alcohol that led to her unexpected feeling of intimacy with him, but once she started talking she couldn't stop. She hoped she wasn't imagining the sympathy in his eyes, fantasising about recreating the relationship she'd enjoyed with Mark for six years.

'Tell me when I get boring.'

'No, you're not boring,' Paul assured her as he went to refill her glass.

She shook her head. One glass of wine was enough for her at lunch time when she was working. 'I'll better stick to water now.'

'Have you heard from Mark since he left you?'

'Not a word.'

'It's probably best that way.'

'I really believed it would work out with Mark but he said he felt my work was more important to me than he was, and maybe he was right. I've always been focused on work.'

'Sometimes things just go wrong.'

'I know.' Without meaning to, Geraldine started telling Paul about her own family history, what she knew of it.

'And you didn't find out you were adopted till you were in your thirties?' Paul sounded surprised. 'You had no idea while your mother was alive?'

'No idea at all. She never breathed a word. I don't think I'll ever forgive her. It's such a betrayal. My own mother! Only she's not my mother, is she?' Geraldine stopped, aware that she was feeling slightly drunk. She didn't want to sound bitter. 'She must have known I'd find out one day. My sister knew, and my father, and God knows who else knew. But not me.'

'And you don't know who your parents are? Your blood parents, I mean.' She shook her head. 'You could find out, if it's bothering you.'

'I went to the adoption agency yesterday. They said my birth mother has refused to have any contact with me.' She smiled, aware that she was slightly tipsy and feeling reckless. 'You're the only person I've told.'

'Maybe it was better for you not to know. Perhaps she wanted to protect you.'

'Everyone has a right to the truth, to know who they are.'

'You know who you are,' Paul said, firmly.

Geraldine felt light headed. 'Yes.' Their eyes met across the table and the thought that the two of them might become close hung between them, unspoken. Exhilarated at having shared something of her inner life, it felt like a breakthrough for Geraldine. She could never speak this freely, not even to her oldest friend, and certainly not to her adopted sister with whom she shared only a distant upbringing. But she held back from showing that she might be falling for Paul. It was too sudden, and she sensed that he too had been hurt. She would need to take things slowly although he could hardly be more guarded against intimacy than she was, and she had already opened up to him.

'What about you?' she asked. 'Have you – are you...' She felt herself stumbling but he didn't come to her rescue, even though her meaning must have been obvious. 'Have you ever been married?'

His face creased in a frown before he turned away. 'I don't like to talk about it.'

Geraldine immediately regretted her question but it was too late to recall it. 'I've really enjoyed meeting, Paul. Thank you. And I'm sorry if I intruded –'

'No,' he said, turning to her, his face relaxing into a strained smile. 'I'm the one who should be apologising for being so abrupt. I hope you can understand, Geraldine.' He paused. 'I suppose I'm a private kind of person. I don't like to rush into relationships.'

'Of course I understand.' She tried not to smile at the word on his lips. 'And there's no need to apologise. You've been hurt.'

'And threatened.'

'Threatened?'

'Yes, I had an unpleasant experience once, with a stalker, I suppose you'd call it.'

'A possessive woman?'

'No, actually it was nothing like that. It was someone who objected to the work I was doing. All that's in the past and I really don't want to discuss it, but it's made me more cautious with people. It's no excuse I know, but –' He shrugged apologetically.

'I'm sorry, I had no business asking about it.'

'No, it's my fault. I shouldn't have mentioned it. I've never told anyone, but you're so easy to talk to.' He smiled at her. 'We should do this again.'

Geraldine made no attempt to hide her relief. 'Yes, that would be nice.'

'Perhaps I can take you out for dinner?'

'Sounds even better.'

'I don't suppose you're free tomorrow evening?'

25

EVIE

Ben was hunched in a chair, channel hopping.
'Stop changing channels.' Lucy held out her hand for the remote.

'Let him be –' Aunt Evie began. She was doing her best to be patient with her niece. Matthew had warned her Lucy was being difficult at the moment, but Evie was shocked to discover how foul-mouthed her niece was these days. Lucy had never been an engaging child; as a teenager she had lost her earlier childish appeal and had become quite unattractive.

Ben interrupted her. 'Shit!'

Abigail's face was staring at them from the television screen next to a picture of her school.

'Abigail Kirby, headmistress of Harchester School in Kent, was the victim of a fatal knife attack last Sunday. She leaves a husband and two children.'

'That's us,' Ben said.

'Shut up, I'm listening.'

The picture switched to the deputy head of Harchester School standing beside the school sign. He spoke in a dreary monotone, blinking rapidly behind his glasses. 'I have worked closely with Abigail Kirby. Her death is a personal as well as a professional loss. We are all in a state of shock and extend our condolences to Abigail's family.'

'That's us,' Ben repeated.

'Thanks for nothing,' Lucy muttered. 'Smug git. He's probably after her job.'

'Where's dad?'

'He's gone to see her,' Lucy replied.

'Daddy had to go into work,' Auntie Evie said quickly.

Lucy turned on her aunt. 'Why do you lie to cover up for him all the time? And stop calling him "daddy". We're not fucking two-year-olds.'

Evie pressed her thin lips together and patted her grey hair nervously. 'Now Lucy,' she began and faltered. She had no idea what to say to her niece. She breathed in deeply and tried again. 'Your father has had to go into work. He's been off all week and felt he had to sort out a few things before the weekend. He's a conscientious man and deserves more respect –'

'He's a liar and a cheat,' Lucy snapped. 'You don't believe he's at work any more than we do.'

'I believe it,' Ben said. He was fed up with Lucy trying to make out he sided with her on everything. She had no right. And anyway, Auntie Evie wasn't nearly as bad as he had been expecting. She still had the horrible boney hands and pinched face that had led him and Lucy to think she was a witch when they were young, but she was there to support his dad, and she made great mash and gravy, and lots of it. She never stinted with his portion. If anything, she seemed to want him to eat more – not that he needed any encouragement – and she let him watch the football on the telly, when Lucy wasn't around shoving her oar in. He knew his aunt only pretended to follow the game, but he didn't mind. At least she was trying to be nice, which was more than he could say for his bitch of a sister.

'We don't need you here,' Lucy blurted out. 'We're fine without you.'

Auntie Evie smiled, her mouth stretched wide. 'I'm here for your father as well as to take care of you two. He needs my support. He needs all of our support right now, Lucy.'

'They're going to arrest him,' Lucy said.

'No, no. They just wanted to ask him a few questions, that's all.' Auntie Evie forced a smile which she hoped was reassuring.

'And stop grinning all the time. You don't fool anyone.' Lucy stood up and went to the door.

School started again on Monday but there was no way Lucy was going back there. Everyone would have heard about her mother. Seeing her face on the television, Lucy had made up her mind. They couldn't go on pretending that life would go on as before.

'Where are you going?' Auntie Evie asked.

'I'm going to my room.' She ran out before her aunt could ask any more questions. 'Mind your own bloody business, can't you?' Lucy added under her breath as she hurried up the stairs.

Alone in her room she sat on her bed trembling. The words rang in her head. '...the victim of a fatal attack... Abigail Kirby leaves a husband and two children...' Somehow her mother's loss hadn't truly hit her until she had seen it on the television, as though that made it official. Auntie Evie was the last straw. Lucy had to get away.

She went out onto the landing and listened. From downstairs she could hear the muffled buzz of the television. Ben and Auntie Evie must be watching, as though nothing had happened. Lucy went into the spare room where her mother used to sleep. It was hard to believe she wasn't busy at school now, and coming home late. Lucy felt a sudden desperation to feel close to her mother. She sat down on the bed and waited, perfectly still, but she could find nothing of her mother in the still atmosphere. The police had searched the room, strangers' fingers rifling through her mother's private belongings, seeing more than Lucy ever had. The thought of it made her feel physically sick.

She crept downstairs and slipped along the corridor to her mother's office. The door was locked. Even in death her mother kept her out. She hurried back to her own room, flung her rucksack on the bed, pulled a pile of t-shirts from her wardrobe and stacked six of them neatly beside it. With her underwear and jeans, she already had nearly enough clothes to fill the rucksack, and she would need to pack other belongings beside clothes. Rolling up her jeans as tightly as she could, she stuffed them into the bag and pushed them down as far as she could. The jeans filled half the space so she pulled them out and chucked them on the bed. She would have to do without a spare pair.

Her bed was covered in clothes and toiletries and she was trying to force her washbag into the rucksack when her door flew open.

'Piss off, Ben. You can't come in here. I'm busy.'

'Busy, busy,' he replied. 'You're always busy, but you never do anything –' He broke off, looking at her bed. 'What are you doing?'

Lucy glared at him, clutching her rucksack to her chest. 'Mind your own business.'

'Why are you packing?'

'What?'

'Your rucksack...'

Lucy dropped it on the bed. 'I'm having a clear out. Not something you'd understand. It's called being tidy. If it's any business of yours.'

Ben shrugged. 'Auntie Evie wants to know –'

'Tell her to mind her own business. And close the door behind you!' Lucy yelled. She ran across the room and slammed the door after him then sat down at her computer and switched on. Zoe was online.

'Hey, Zoe.'

'Hey you.'

'What you been doing?'

'Not a lot. You?'

'You mustn't tell.'

'You know I won't.'

Lucy paused before she went on. 'It's a secret!'

'Go on then.'

'I'm leaving home!'

'Because of your dad?'

'Yes.'

'What's he done?'

'Can't tell.' Zoe made a few obscene suggestions and Lucy grimaced. 'No!!' she typed as fast as she could. 'Nothing to do with me. WORSE than that.'

'Did he try it on with your sister?'

'Haven't got one.'

'With your brother?'

'No! Nothing like that.'

'Good.'

'No, not good. It's WORSE than that.'

'Worse?!'

'Much worse.'

'What??'

'Can't say.'

'You have to tell me now.'

'I can't tell anyone.'

'I'm your friend. You know you can trust me.'

'I can't tell.'

'I won't tell.'

'Promise?'

'Promise.'

Lucy hesitated. She glanced at the door. 'I hate my dad. I really hate him. I wish I could go away.'

She was relieved that Zoe couldn't see her face. She hadn't realised she was crying, but tears were spilling down her cheeks and she made no attempt to stop them.

'What about your mum?' Zoe asked. 'Don't you have a mum?'

Lucy was sobbing uncontrollably. 'My mum's dead.'

'OMG what happened?'

Lucy shook her head, logged-off and flung herself on her bed, still sobbing.

26

STALKER

Thursday was Susie's day off. Vernon hadn't appreciated how much he relied on seeing her during the day. He usually passed the time flitting around the shop floor, just in case he caught her as she went for a break, or came back from one. He watched out for her along the aisles, and hoped to see her on the till next to his, the monotony of his working day punctuated by their brief encounters. Sometimes they took their breaks at the same time and he would make a point of sitting next to her. Susie always had plenty to tell him about her social life. She had a boyfriend who didn't seem to be around much. Vernon didn't like to ask too many personal questions but, as far as he could make out, her boyfriend was away at university in Bristol and Susie spent most of her evenings going out with girlfriends, having a good time. 'It was a laugh,' was her favourite expression. Vernon struggled to make it sound as though he was equally busy. In reality he spent much of his free time looking after his invalid mother.

When Susie was away there was little to relieve the boredom of his working day, so he was pleased to see her walking along the shop floor towards him on Friday.

She caught his eye, paused, and smiled at him. 'Hey, Vernon.'

'Hey.'

'Got anything planned for tonight?'

He nodded. 'Seeing friends, you know. How about you?'

She grinned and started to tell him about an early firework party she had been to the previous evening. 'It was such a laugh,' she said, but just then the manager appeared from the other side of a display stand and she scurried away.

The manager pounced on Vernon. 'You don't look busy.' Vernon smiled back weakly but before he could think of anything to say the manager had launched into a catalogue of chores that needed to be done in the stock room. Vernon was only half listening. He was wondering when he would see Susie again. At last the manager finished and Vernon made his way miserably upstairs to start on his morning's tasks. He didn't expect to see Susie in the stock room and cheered up when he saw she was already there, stacking books into a plastic box.

'Oh, it's you,' she said, putting down the books she was holding. She sat down gingerly on the side of the crate. 'So? Tell me what happened. Did you go to the police?'

'Yeah, I did.'

'And? What happened?'

Vernon took a deep breath. He felt very clumsy standing in front of her. 'Tell you what, do you fancy going for a drink after work? Like we did last week?' She looked away. The gesture told him all he needed to know. She wasn't interested. 'Just a quick one?' he pleaded, hating himself for sounding so desperate. 'And I'll tell you all about it.'

'Tell me now. I really want to know. What did the police say?'

Vernon stared down at her glossy blonde hair and fought the temptation to make up an extravagant lie to make himself sound more interesting. 'Nothing really,' he admitted. 'I just told them what I'd seen, and they wrote it all down and made me sign it and – well, that was it, really.' He looked around the dusty room. 'Tim sent me up here to help with the book returns.'

Susie held out a list. 'Here you are then. Rather you than me.'

'I think we're supposed to be doing it together.'

'I know, but you don't mind, do you? It's hardly going to take two of us, is it?' She skipped out of the room and Vernon didn't see her again until it was five thirty and time for Tim to close the shutters and lock the door.

'At last!' Susie called out as she darted past.

'Have a good evening,' Vernon called after her but she didn't turn round. He didn't think she even heard him.

Vernon collected his jacket and left. He had the impression that someone walked out of the store immediately behind him, but when he turned his head to look the doorway was empty. He was in no particular hurry, so he decided to save the bus fare and walk home. The chances were he wouldn't get home much sooner if he waited for a bus anyway, because the next one wasn't due for a while, and he didn't think it was going to rain. As he left the shelter of the shopping centre, the fresh air made his eyes water. There was a faint acrid smell in the air and an occasional distant popping of fireworks. It was less than a week until November 5th. He wondered whether Susie would be going to another firework party and wished there was one he could invite her to, but there wasn't much chance of that. He turned off the main road and quickened his pace. It was growing chilly. Apart from an occasional car shooting past, the streets were deserted and dark.

A crackle of fireworks nearby startled him, making him jump, and at the same time a brilliant silver shower lit up the dark sky above the street lamps. In the sudden glare he noticed a movement behind him and looked back. Someone was moving slowly along the street towards him but, while he watched, the shadowy figure came to a halt. Vernon felt uneasy as it occurred to him that the person on the pavement hadn't stopped to look at the fireworks. On the contrary, whoever it was had been looking in the other direction away from the light, as though reluctant to be seen.

Vernon shivered and hurried on, telling himself not to be daft.

He knew that no one was following him, why on earth would they be? Nevertheless, when he reached the corner of his own road, he glanced warily over his shoulder and was reassured to see the street behind him was empty. A further burst of fireworks lit up the sky just as Vernon reached his gate. Raising his hand to close it he happened to glance up. A figure was standing motionless in the shadows on the opposite side of the road, watching him.

His mother was waiting for him. 'Is that you, Vernon?'

'Who else are you expecting?' He did his best to conceal his resentment, but it was hard. Most boys his age would be at the pub now, having a few pints on a Friday night, but Vernon's mother needed him at home.

'Carol was round. She brought a fish pie,' his mother smiled up at him as he went into the living room. Propped up against cushions she looked comfortable enough. 'It'll need to go in the oven for about forty minutes.'

'OK, mum.'

'Don't forget to heat the oven first.'

'I know what to do.' His mother smiled sadly at him. 'Fish pie sounds nice,' he lied, trying to sound cheerful. 'How was Carol?' His mother was always in a good mood after seeing her sister, Carol, one of her few visitors apart from the carers sent by the council. They were all kind and considerate, but strangers nonetheless. They hadn't known his mother when she'd still been able to walk. 'Did she take you out?'

'Yes, we went for a little turn in the park.'

'That's nice, mum.'

'How was your day?'

'It was fine. I'll go and put the oven on then, shall I?'

As he went into the kitchen, Vernon looked out of the window and saw a silhouette on the pavement across the road. As Vernon watched, the figure turned slowly and vanished into the darkness.

PART 3

'Do not fear death so much, but rather the inadequate life.'

Bertolt Brecht

27

MARRIAGE

Kathryn Gordon was adamant that they must do their best to force a confession from Matthew Kirby.

'Everything points to him,' she said. Geraldine's irritation was growing, not only because no one seemed to be listening to her doubts about Matthew Kirby's guilt, but even more because she had nothing to support her opinion, other than her intuition.

'He seemed pretty shocked at discovering she had been tied up,' she insisted. 'And he wanted to know if his wife had been raped.'

'If he killed her, he's hardly going to be giving the impression that he knew all about the manner of her death,' Peterson pointed out.

Geraldine frowned. It was true that, statistically, the murdered woman's husband was the most likely suspect. True, too, that his alibi was dodgy. His mistress's corroboration was hardly reliable. The rest of the team were in agreement about him, Geraldine alone insisting he was innocent. She wondered if she should reconsider. It was only Matthew Kirby's reaction to his wife's body that had convinced her he couldn't have murdered his wife, but perhaps she was relying too much on her gut feeling. Used to trusting her instincts about people, she felt a sudden wave of self doubt. She could be terribly wrong about Matthew Kirby.

Geraldine had to admit Matthew Kirby looked guilty as he sat down at the interview table. he was dishevelled and his eyes were swollen from lack of sleep as he slumped in a chair, unable to meet her gaze. His bottom lip trembled and he fiddled with the cuff on his left sleeve.

'This won't take long, will it?' he asked once the formalities were over. 'Only I'm worried about my boy –' his voice cracked.

'What about your daughter, Mr Kirby?' Peterson asked, leaning forward in his chair.

'And Lucy as well, of course. I was about to say –'

'Your daughter's had a few things of her own to say, Mr Kirby.' Peterson's voice held a quiet threat.

'My daughter's been... very upset... since her mother died... What... what has she been saying about me?'

The sergeant leaned back. 'We'll ask the questions, Mr Kirby.'

'I think –' Matthew turned to Geraldine. 'Look, do I need a lawyer? Am I being accused of... anything?' He waited but she didn't answer. 'Do you think I killed my wife?'

'Your daughter seems to think so,' Peterson answered.

Matthew Kirby's face fell into his hands and his shoulders shook. Peterson leaned forward but Geraldine shook her head. 'For the tape, the suspect is distressed. Would you like a moment to pull yourself together, Mr Kirby, before we continue?'

Matthew raised his head and turned aside, wiping his eyes on the back of his hand. 'No. I'm all right. It's just that Lucy's – well, she hates me. It all started long before her mother's death, before we moved from York. And it's not just the usual teenage father-daughter thing, it's worse than that. It's because she found out about Charlotte. She's never forgiven me. And now this... I do wonder what's going to happen to her. She seems so angry, all the time. Wouldn't you be worried about her, if she was your daughter?'

Geraldine thought about Lucy, reproachful and sullen. 'Yes,' she admitted. Peterson glanced round at her, and she hesitated. Caught out in a moment of sympathy for the suspect she realised that she still didn't believe Matthew Kirby was capable of killing his wife. She sat back and allowed her sergeant to question him.

'Lucy knows about your affair,' Peterson launched in. 'But that's not our concern. What's worrying us is her accusation that you are responsible for your wife's death.'

'I accept I'm at least partly to blame for the breakdown in my marriage. But not my wife's death. Come on, Sergeant, do you really think I'd kill her? It's a crazy idea. We'd been married for nearly sixteen years.'

'A marriage you wanted to end.'

'Yes, I've not made any secret of the fact that I wanted a divorce. I've been wanting a divorce for a long time. I was waiting until my children were old enough to be more independent and then I was going to leave Abigail, with or without her agreement. I fell in love with her, I married her, our marriage broke down, I met someone else. That's it. It's not a happy story, but it's nothing out of the ordinary. Relationships end all the time. It doesn't mean I killed her. Jesus,' his voice rose in indignation, 'if I was that desperate to leave, don't you think I'd have packed a case and walked out by now? But I stayed, because of the children. I love my children, and I wouldn't do anything that might harm them. Do you really think I would deprive them of their mother?' He paused before continuing in a more measured tone. 'Maybe I didn't love Abigail any more. Maybe I never really loved her. I don't know. But I know I wouldn't kill anyone. I couldn't. Why would I want to kill her when I could have left her at any time?'

Peterson stared at Matthew Kirby. 'You're a wealthy man now, Matthew. How much is it you stand to inherit from your wife? More than enough to pay off your debts, I'd say.'

'Oh please, Sergeant. That's ridiculous.'

Peterson went over Matthew Kirby's finances, then his movements on the previous Saturday and Matthew confirmed that after he had given his children lunch he had gone to visit Charlotte.

'Did you go straight there?'

'Yes.'

'What time did you arrive?'

'I can't remember exactly. I didn't look at my watch and make a note of the time, but I must have left home about one and it's only half an hour's drive.'

'Did you stay with Charlotte overnight?'

'No. I'm always home at nights. Because of the children.' He gave a helpless grimace. 'I didn't want them to know I was seeing someone else.'

'You've kept this from them for five years?'

'I thought I had. Is there anything remarkable in that? Plenty of couples carry on clandestine affairs for years. I'm not saying it's something I'm proud of, but it happens all the time.'

'Was your wife in the habit of staying out all night?'

'No.'

'But you didn't report her missing when she didn't come home on Saturday night, did you? You didn't even telephone the school to find out if she was there. Because you knew where she was, didn't you?'

Matthew shook his head. 'I must have got home around midnight, at a guess. Late, anyway. I assumed Abigail was in bed. When I got up on Sunday morning, there was no sign of her and I thought she'd gone out. She was always working, even in the school holidays.'

'Let's be clear on this. When you came home, you thought your wife was in bed. You didn't notice –'

Matthew interrupted the sergeant. 'We've had separate bedrooms since – since she found out about Charlotte.'

'Whose idea was it to sleep separately?'

'It was kind of mutual.' He gave a sheepish smile. 'We told the children it was because Abigail was sometimes phoned at night, and they knew she kept odd hours, often working till late … and there were my business meetings that kept me out late…'

The DCI was frustrated, but seemed hardly surprised, at the outcome of the interview with Matthew Kirby. 'He's got his story together,' Peterson concluded.

'I still don't think he did it, ma'am,' Geraldine added. 'Apart from anything else, his story's too vague. If he'd planned to kill his wife, surely he would have thought up a better alibi.'

'Perhaps it wasn't planned,' Peterson said. 'I don't trust him.'

Kathryn Gordon waved her hands in the air dismissively. 'What any of us think of the man is beside the point. As a husband with a clear motive, he remains a likely suspect. What we need now is hard evidence.'

28

TRUST

Matthew wasn't comfortable about lying to his sister but, as a single woman, Evie had no idea what a trial his marriage to Abigail had been and she tended to take the moral high ground, devoted as she was to the church and its teachings. So Matthew was in no hurry to tell her about Charlotte. Nearly ten years older than him, Evie had always stood by him when he was in trouble, but he knew she would lecture him interminably once she learned about his infidelity although he knew that, even if he kept quiet, Lucy was bound to blurt it out sooner or later.

'Adultery is a sin, Matthew,' Evie would tell him in hushed tones, adopting an expression of anger, or, more likely, sorrow. 'I will pray for your soul.'

He couldn't deal with her disappointment just yet, not with everything else that was going on, so he took the easy way out. 'I'm worried about work,' he told her. That much was true, anyway. 'I've hardly been in the office all week. I know it's Saturday, but I really should go in and check on a few things.'

'Of course you must go if you need to.' Evie turned to Ben. 'Your father has a very responsible job, and he's a conscientious man. I hope you follow his example.'

Over her shoulder, Matthew pulled a face at Ben who grinned. It was a relief to see the boy smiling again. Evie was good for him, feeding him and fussing over him like she did. It was a pity Lucy remained so hostile, rejecting all Evie's approaches and barely speaking to Matthew.

'I'll see you later then,' he said, relieved and ashamed to be leaving the house.

There wasn't much traffic and he was soon ringing Charlotte's bell, his guilt swept away in the anticipation of seeing her again. Nothing would ever convince him he was wrong to have fallen for her. How could it be a sin, when he had no choice, no control over his feelings?

Charlotte fell into his arms but didn't respond to his kiss. Matthew could feel her trembling and when he pulled away he saw she was in tears.

'What is it? What's up?' She shook her head, sobbing and hiccupping like a child. Matthew held her close and whispered soothing nonsense. 'Don't cry. It'll be all right. I'll take care of everything. No one's going to hurt you.' He didn't know what else to say. Her distress made him feel helpless. Even when Abigail had refused him a divorce, Charlotte had only been coldly angry. She had never given way like this.

At last she pulled herself together sufficiently to stop crying and drew back from his embrace. 'I'm sorry,' she snuffled. 'It's just all so awful. I can't bear it.' She began to cry again.

'What is it?' he asked, a touch of impatience in his voice. He softened it with an effort. He was the one who had lost his wife of sixteen years, after all. If anything, Charlotte should be offering to comfort him, if not discreetly rejoicing that they could finally be together. He had no idea what this emotional outburst was all about. 'What's wrong, my love?'

'I can't bear this waiting,' she wailed.

'Waiting?'

'Until they find out who did it – who killed her.'

'Does it matter?' She raised her eyes to meet his and frowned, at the same time withdrawing from his embrace. 'I mean, it doesn't make any difference to us, does it?' Matthew added. He could sense he had put his foot in it, but wasn't sure how. 'We love each other and now there's nothing to stop us being together. That's all that matters. We'll wait a few weeks – a few months – and then I'll introduce you to the children.' The thought of Lucy made him pause.

'Don't you want to know who killed your wife? Don't you want the police to find out who did it?'

'Of course, but I want to be with you more.' He took a step towards her but she stood rigid, staring at him.

'What if they don't find out who did it? What if they get the wrong person? It happens, Matthew. Miscarriages of justice. You read about it in the papers all the time. What if they think it was you? Don't they always suspect the husband? What if they arrest you – for murder?'

'Now you're being silly, Charlotte. You're overreacting and you know it. It's all been a terrible shock, but that's no reason to start panicking. Of course they won't suspect me. Why would they? I was with the children and then I came straight here on Saturday. When was I supposed to have – done it – done that?' Somehow, he couldn't bring himself to speak of Abigail's murder. 'In any case, they've already given me a grilling and they let me go.'

'The police were here again yesterday, questioning me. They asked me what time you arrived here last Saturday and I said – I said – I said I couldn't remember. I said I didn't know.'

Matthew gazed at her lovely face, now pale with terror, and understood why she was frightened. He took an involuntary step away from her. There was a certain irony in the way the woman he loved had destroyed his alibi. He could almost hear Evie's voice: 'Thou shalt not commit adultery... Whoever does so destroys himself.' And as if that wasn't bad enough, his own daughter had accused him of murdering Abigail. 'The sins of the fathers' and all that. He couldn't remember the rest of it although it had been drummed down his throat often enough when he was a child.

They had agreed to chat at ten that night and Zoe was already online when Lucy logged on at five to ten.

'Hi Zoe. You waiting for me?' Lucy waited a moment but Zoe didn't reply. 'Are you still there?'

'Yeah. You?'

'Yeah.'

There was another pause. 'What's going on? Are you OK?' Zoe asked at last.

'No. Not OK.' Tears began streaming down Lucy's face as she typed. 'I'm stuck in this bloody house. Have to get away. It's not safe for me here!!!'

'What's happened?'

'Can't tell you.'

'What are you going to do?'

Lucy glanced at her wardrobe. Her rucksack was packed. 'I'm leaving. Maybe tonight!!'

'OMG! Where are you going?'

'Don't care. I have to get away.'

'Come and stay at mine.'

Lucy stared at the screen for a second then she wiped her eyes and carried on typing. 'Are you sure? What about your parents?'

'They won't mind. They're cool.' Lucy thought about it. 'Are you still there, Lucy?'

'Yeah. I'm here. I have to think about it.'

'What's to think about?' Lucy didn't answer. 'Well, what do you say?'

'Dunno.'

'It'll be fun. I've got a huge room. It's the attic. No one comes up here! I'll put a mattress on the floor. Or you can have my bed.' Lucy's fingers were poised on the keys but she hesitated and Zoe sent another message. 'We can have a midnight feast!! and I'll get in some magazines and stuff. Bring your make-up!'

Lucy grinned. 'Are you sure?'

'Of course I'm sure. I wouldn't say it otherwise. Where do you live? Maybe me and my dad can come and get you.'

'I'm near Faversham. How do I find you?'

'No worries. Faversham's not that far. I'll get my dad to bring me over. We'll pick you up.'

'Are you sure?'

'No worries.'

'Hadn't you better ask him first?'

'I'll ask him. It'll be fine.'

'Don't tell him I'm running away from home!'

'As if!'

Lucy didn't want to give Zoe her address. 'You can't pick me up from here. Your dad mustn't know where I live! What if he finds out I've done a runner and tells my dad!!'

'Where shall we meet you then?'

'Can you pick me up at the station?'

'No. Someone might see! And there's cameras. If your dad tells the police you've run away, the police might hunt you down!!!'

'Good thinking. How about the corner of Belvedere Road and Western Lane?'

'OK.'

'Memorise it and delete the names.'

There was a pause. 'Got it.'

'Don't write it down whatever you do.'

'Don't worry. No one comes in here. Ever. Trust me.'

'I do.'

'We'll need a password so we know it's you.'

'How about fugitive!'

'What's that?'

'I think it means someone who's run away.'

'Nice one.'

'Ask your dad soon!'

'No worries.'

'And let me know!'

'Chat soon.' Zoe logged off.

Zoe was the only person who was genuinely interested in Lucy now, and when they met Lucy was going to tell her all about how her mother had died. It would be a relief to talk to someone she could trust. She sat at her desk thinking about her new friend who had offered her a lifeline and crossed her fingers, hoping Zoe wouldn't let her down. Since her mother's death, Lucy had grown to depend on Zoe more and more.

'I'm lucky to have a friend like you!' she typed before logging off. The message would be waiting for Zoe next time she went online.

29

ALARM

The investigation seemed to be grinding to a halt. Kathryn Gordon gazed round, waiting for silence. Once, the officers present would all have stopped talking the moment the DCI entered the room, but she seemed somehow to have lost her authority. Two of the young constables continued whispering together for a few minutes after the briefing began. Geraldine threw them an irritated glance, catching the eye of one of them, and they fell silent.

Kathryn Gordon didn't seem to notice the disruption. She sighed and looked around the room as though casting around for inspiration. 'Well? Has anyone come up with anything new? Any new evidence? Any theories?'

A number of officers chipped in with ideas but apart from a lot of talk, nothing useful transpired.

Geraldine wanted to discuss the possibility that Matthew Kirby and Charlotte Fox could have conspired to murder Abigail Kirby together. 'Or,' she concluded, 'if they hadn't planned the whole thing together, one of them might be covering for the other, ma'am. What if Matthew Kirby killed his wife, either in a premeditated murder or on the spur of the moment, in a sudden rage. Maybe he just snapped, couldn't put up with his wife's refusal to agree to a divorce any longer. Whatever the reason, the outcome's the same. After he killed her, he drove round to Charlotte's in a panic – probably speeding all the way – and told her what he'd done. Charlotte agreed to give him an alibi. Maybe it was her idea. Perhaps she felt he'd killed his wife as an act of love for her.'

'A crime of passion,' someone said.

'It would certainly put Matthew Kirby back in the frame,' the DCI agreed. 'But I thought you didn't believe he killed her?'

Geraldine shrugged. 'I'm not sure I do believe it, ma'am, but someone killed her. It's just a theory.'

'Could it have been the girlfriend, Charlotte?' Peterson asked.

'And where was he supposed to have done it? And how did he move the body?' someone asked. SOCOs had searched the Kirby household, and Matthew Kirby's car. There wasn't a shred of evidence that anyone had been killed, or a body stored or transported, anywhere.

'Back to square one,' Kathryn Gordon said sourly, as though the team were to blame. Everyone looked glum as they dispersed.

'We've hardly got going and the DCI already looks like she's had enough,' Peterson said to Geraldine as they walked across the room to her desk.

Geraldine tried to make light of it. 'I expect she's just disappointed. We were all just waiting for Matthew Kirby to confess. We all thought we had him.'

'You didn't.'

'I wasn't sure,' she admitted. 'But the wrong suspect is better than no suspect.'

The sergeant paused in his stride and looked at her in surprise. 'Hardly! You really think it doesn't matter if we get the wrong man as long as we nail someone?'

'No, that's not what I meant at all. It's just that when we were running round in circles chasing after Matthew Kirby, at least we had something to do as opposed to sitting around uselessly.'

Geraldine was about to go for lunch when a constable came over to tell her that Vernon Mitchell was in an interview room wanting to speak to her. Swallowing back a sudden rush of hope, Geraldine hurried along the corridor.

'Hello, Vernon,' she greeted him when they were both sitting down. 'Have you remembered something else about the man you saw talking to Abigail Kirby last Saturday?'

'No, it's not that.' He stared at the floor in silence.

'What is it, then, Vernon?' she prompted him after a moment.

'It's going to sound silly –' he broke off, red-faced. 'I don't know – I shouldn't be wasting your time – I wasn't sure whether to say anything only it's my day off so I thought as I was in town I might as well come and tell you about it.'

'Go on.'

'I think someone followed me home from work.'

'When was this?'

'Yesterday. Just after we closed up at five thirty. I decided to walk home because – well, it was a nice evening so I thought I might as well save on the bus fare. It's not even two miles. I can walk it in under half an hour and the bus often takes longer, if I've just missed one.'

'Who was it?'

He shrugged miserably, and his eyes flitted round the room. 'That's just it, I don't know. I'm not even a hundred per cent sure anyone was following me. I just had this feeling, you know. I mean, at the time I was sure, but now, looking back on it, I don't know if I can be sure about it. I just thought someone was following me.'

'Do you have any idea who it might have been?'

He shook his head. 'I only saw someone vaguely, in the shadows. But it was someone tall so it could've been the geezer I saw in the shop, the one who was talking to Mrs Kirby, just before she was killed. I think he could've been following me all this time. Do you think he has been? Following me and waiting.'

Geraldine looked down at her notebook, tempted to smile. 'Following you and waiting for what, Vernon?'

'I don't know. I mean, if he knew – if he'd seen me watching him talk to Mrs Kirby, he might think I could be a witness. I mean, I am a witness, aren't I? I told you about him. And he could be the killer.' He looked straight at her, and Geraldine saw fear in his eyes, heard his voice tremble.

'I don't think that's very likely, do you, really? He would have been focused on Mrs Kirby in the queue. The chances are she stepped backwards into him – he was behind her in the line, wasn't he?' Vernon nodded. 'In any case, even if the man you saw really did go on to kill her, how would he know you'd noticed him talking to her, there in the busy store?'

'He saw me watching,' Vernon replied. 'I could see it in his face. He gave me this horrible glare and I looked away. He was scary!' Geraldine smiled sympathetically. There was no doubt the boy was frightened. 'What now?' he asked.

'I'd like you to be extra careful for the next week or so, and if you see anything else that strikes you as unusual or threatening, come straight back here and tell me.' She stood up.

'Is that it? I mean, I could be in danger. Aren't you going to protect me?'

Geraldine sighed gently. 'I'm afraid our resources don't stretch that far.' He had come to her with a fanciful notion, born of stress. He must have been disturbed by the murder of someone he had known, a woman in a position of authority, her life snuffed out in a moment. 'Call me straightaway if you see this person following you again, Vernon.' She handed him a card. 'Here's my direct line. Call me at once if you see him, all right?'

'So do you think I'm in danger?'

'No, I really don't believe you're in any danger as a result of seeing Mrs Kirby in the queue in Smith's on Saturday.

There's no way the man she spoke to, if he is the murderer, could have known about your suspicions, even if he did notice you watching him for a few seconds. Why would he remember, or even notice? So I don't think he's following you as a result of that. But I'd like you to keep your phone with you, all the same, in case you recognise him out somewhere. If you do, I'd like you to call me straightaway so we can pick him up and ask him a few questions. I daresay he had nothing to do with Abigail Kirby's death, but he spoke to her shortly before she died, and we need to talk to him.'

Geraldine thanked Vernon for coming forward. It was a lead, of sorts, and right now anything was better than nothing.

30

DATE

Geraldine wore a clingy knee-length purple dress which she had bought specially for the occasion and Paul picked her up from her flat, held the car door open for her and drove them to the restaurant. As he handed his long black coat to the waiter Geraldine saw he was wearing dark trousers and matching jacket with a stylish open-necked shirt but it was impossible to be sure he had made an effort for the occasion because he was always well turned out.

Paul deftly peeled off a flake of salmon. 'I think I read something about the Kirby case in the paper.' He put down his knife and fork and raised his glass. 'It didn't say much, of course. How are you getting on? Any leads?' He listened intently and nodded as she told him how the case was progressing, or rather wasn't.

'I shouldn't go on about it,' she concluded, 'you must be bored, hearing all the details. It's just so frustrating. We seem to be getting nowhere, but the DCI thinks,' she lowered her voice, 'she's convinced it's him.'

'Really? Well, I suppose the husband's bound to be the most likely suspect from what you say, isn't he?'

'That doesn't mean he did it.'

'No, but the most likely suspect is probably the right one.' Paul smiled at her and filled up her glass. 'No point beating yourself up if you've got a result.' Geraldine slowly took a sip of her wine. 'So he'll be arrested?'

'It's not that simple.'

'It never is.'

'We've got no real evidence that points to him – or anyone else for that matter. We don't even know where she was killed.'

'You've presumably searched his house?'

'We've had a good look of course, but there's nothing there.'

'No hidden stash of bloodstained knives,' Paul grinned at her and she couldn't help smiling back, even though she felt slightly irritated by his light-hearted approach. But perhaps he was right and she was allowing her doubts about Matthew Kirby's guilt to get in the way.

'I suppose he may crack sooner or later,' she agreed. 'We just have to keep on at him.' The conversation drifted on and Geraldine found herself talking about her niece. A distant look appeared in Paul's eyes as though a shutter had come between them.

'Is everything all right?'

'Yes. Sorry. It's nothing.' He smiled apologetically. 'Now, what about you? Tell me to butt out if I'm prying, but have you managed to find out anything about your mother yet?' Geraldine told him about the devastating news she had received at the adoption agency. 'I expect your mother wanted to protect you,' Paul said.

'Which mother?'

'You only have one mother. Your real mother. The one who raised you. That other woman is nothing to you, really. She doesn't know you.' Geraldine nodded uncertainly. 'You never met her. You don't know her name –'

'I do know her name. I told you, I've got my original birth certificate. And the adoption agency gave me a photo of her – a photo of her at sixteen, anyway – and I read her letter.' A wave of emotion threatened her self-possession. 'I must be getting drunk,' she thought, putting her wine glass down. She took a deep breath.

'This is upsetting you,' Paul insisted. 'I can see how much it means to you and yet, apart from an accident of birth, she's nothing to you. She hasn't been a mother to you. It's easy for me to say, but why not do yourself a favour and forget all about the sorry circumstances of your birth. It hasn't been significant in your life, has it? You're a successful woman, probably far more successful than you would have been if you'd been brought up by a sixteen-year-old mother. She did you a favour, really, offering you the chance of a better life than she could give you herself.'

'That's what she said in her letter!'

'There you are then, she did care about you after all. She knew it would be better for you if she gave you up. That was a kind thing to do. Of course, it's not my place – or anyone else's come to that – to tell you what you should or shouldn't do, but I'd leave it at that, if I were you. Try and put it out of your mind.'

'You're right,' Geraldine said meekly. She resolved to forget about the picture of her mother, taken when she was not much older than Lucy Kirby. 'I think I've had enough to drink for one evening, but you're welcome to come back to mine for a coffee?' she said, on impulse, as they finished the bottle of wine.

'Why not come to my place?' he replied. 'It's only five minutes away.'

'Great.'

Paul drove to a detached house on a pleasant tree-lined residential avenue about three miles from the centre of town. Geraldine followed him through a large square kitchen into a small sitting room, sparsely but tastefully furnished. While Paul brewed coffee in the kitchen she studied the living room which was neat and orderly, suggesting he lived alone, but glancing over her shoulder she was dismayed to notice what appeared to be a recent family photograph. Paul had his arm around a striking woman. Between them a girl of about fifteen smiled at the camera. With her mother's blonde hair and wide mouth, and Paul's intense eyes, she could only be their daughter. If it hadn't been for a sizeable birthmark on her left cheek, she would have been stunning.

Paul came in with a cafetiere and a bottle of brandy, and put the tray down on the table. He sat opposite Geraldine and she wished she was sitting beside him on the sofa. He held up the bottle with a smile.

'I shouldn't really.'

'You can't let me drink alone, and I'll call you a cab to get home. I'm not driving myself after this. Was probably pushing it a bit when we left the restaurant. I guess I was relying on you to deflect the attentions of the local plod if we were stopped.'

Geraldine laughed. 'Go on then, just a small one.'

As she drained her glass, Geraldine made up her mind to tackle him about the photograph on the shelf behind her. 'Who is she? Who are they?'

Paul stiffened and she sensed his voice lose its warmth. 'My wife and... my wife and daughter.'

'You're married?'

'Not any more. We no longer see each other.'

'And your daughter?' He didn't answer. 'Do you want to talk about it, Paul?'

'No, I don't.' He stood up abruptly and remained on his feet, face averted, so after a few seconds Geraldine stood up too.

'Paul –' she ventured.

'I'll call that cab. They're only just around the corner, so they'll be here in a minute.' She trailed miserably after him into the hall desperately sorry she had mentioned the photograph, but at a loss how to retrieve the situation.

'I've had a lovely evening,' she thanked him lamely as they

waited for the cab.

'Look, Geraldine…'

'Yes?'

'I don't mean to be…'

'It's all right.' She was reassured by his concern. 'I'm sure you'll tell me when you're ready. These things can't be rushed.'

He heaved a loud sigh. 'Thank you for being so understanding.' He didn't look at her and she couldn't think of anything else to say.

'Call me,' she muttered as he closed the door and she hurried to the waiting taxi, cursing herself for her thoughtless curiosity.

31

HALLOWE'EN

One of his mates from school texted Vernon on Saturday afternoon.

'Party at Gary's tonight. Bring beer.'

'Who's going?' He knew he'd go along, he had nothing else to do, and if it sounded like a decent party he might even text Susie to ask if she wanted to go although she was bound to be busy.

'The old crowd. Jenny's going!' Vernon smiled. He'd got over Jenny a long time ago.

'What time?'

'Nine.'

He texted Susie and invited her. 'It's going to be brilliant,' he lied. 'Loads of booze. It's Hallowe'en.' He half hoped she would turn him down because the chances were it would just be his old mates getting wasted and mucking about while a few girls squealed and tottered about sloshed. He didn't want to be embarrassed in front of Susie, but he'd asked her now and it was too late. He didn't know whether to feel relieved or disappointed when she didn't reply.

On the bus to Gary's, Vernon felt in his pocket for his phone in case Susie called and realised he'd left it at home but he couldn't be bothered to go back for it. Susie wasn't going to get in touch with him tonight, and his mother would be alright. She could call him at Gary's if she needed him and it wasn't as if he was going to stay out late. He was glad he'd thought to leave her Gary's number before he left.

'Here you are, mum. In case I don't hear my mobile.'

'Oh don't you fret about me. You just go out and have a good time with your friends.'

'But what if – if you need me?'

'If I need someone, I'll call Carol or Moira next door. For goodness sake, go out and enjoy yourself, son. God knows you deserve to have a bit of fun once in a while. You worry too much and it's not necessary. I'll be fine here for a few hours. What can happen? It's not as though I'm not used to sitting by myself, and I'll have plenty to look at this evening, with all the fireworks going off outside.'

Vernon rarely went out in the evenings. His mother would never say so, but she liked him to sit with her and he felt guilty leaving her on her own. Sometimes a neighbour would pop in, or his aunt Carol would come round, but on the whole they left her alone in the evenings, knowing they could rely on Vernon to be there. It didn't do much for his social life but he fiercely suppressed any feeling of resentment. It wasn't his mother's fault she was confined to a wheelchair and he hardly had much of a social life to sacrifice, just a few drinks with his mates once in a while. It was worse for his mother, and she was certainly appreciative of his support.

'I don't know what I'd do without you,' she often told him.

He hadn't planned on telling anyone he thought he was being followed, wasn't even sure if he'd imagined the whole thing, but he had passed the police station that afternoon and had gone in on an impulse. He hadn't felt any better after telling the inspector about his misgivings. Leaving the police station he had noticed a black car parked across the street and had hurried round the corner, determined not to look round. The inspector was right. He was being ridiculous suspecting everyone he saw of stalking him. The car was nothing to do with him.

As it turned out, the party wasn't too bad. A few people were wearing masks, which was a laugh, and his old mates seemed pleased to see him. He drank loads of beer and felt on top of the world. Jenny arrived, her face plastered in make-up. They chatted for a while and he thought she still fancied him, but her giggling was irritating.

'I feel sick,' Jenny groaned after a while. Vernon turned away feeling slightly dizzy himself and at that moment a shout went up. Gary was about to set off some fireworks so they all trooped outside into the cold misty garden. After a rowdy build-up, most of the fireworks turned out to be damp, which was typical of Gary's parties. Some went off and everyone laughed and cheered, but most barely flickered before they fizzled out. It wasn't exactly a proper display but it was fun. Jenny was clutching onto Vernon's arm when she suddenly threw up all over the grass, narrowly missing his shoes. Stepping away, he wondered what he had ever seen in her when they were at school. Compared to Susie, he decided, she was hideous. She leaned over again and he left her to it. Shouting and laughing with his mates, he was enjoying himself for once. The cold night air was bracing and he felt glad to be alive. He had no idea where Jenny had disappeared to and he couldn't care less.

When all the fireworks were over a few people started to drift away. It was late, past midnight. 'Got to go,' Vernon mumbled, laughing. Suddenly it seemed hilarious that he could hardly find his way across the room which was swaying gently as though he was sailing away, free at last. 'Sailing away,' he said out loud. He began to sing.

As he made his way along the street, not quite sure where he was, he heard singing. 'I am sailing, I am sailing.' He hiccupped and the singing jerked. 'It's me!' he shouted in sudden realisation and carried on raucously as the road swayed from side to side. All at once he felt sick. He was aware of a dull ache in the small of his back, between his shoulder blades, and with every step he thought he might vomit. He thought of his mother. Was this what if felt like to be old and sick? He felt like crying.

He sat down on a low wall, shaking, with his head in his hands, and closed his eyes. After a few moments his head began to clear a little, and he sensed someone standing in front of him. Raising his head, Vernon thought he recognised the man looking down at him but it could have been a mask he'd seen earlier at Gary's. He blinked. The face was still there. A voice was talking to him, slow and silky. 'I hardly need to sedate you now, do I?' Vernon laughed uncertainly. He felt very confused. 'You've done the job for me.'

'Were you at Gary's?'

The face grinned. 'Yes. And now you're coming with me.'

Vernon shook his head and everything moved around unsteadily. 'No, sorry. See the thing is, I've got to get home to my mum. So I can't come with you, can I? I can't come with you because I've got to get home to my mum –'

A hand gripped hold of him, like a vice. Sharp pain shot down Vernon's arm and he opened his mouth to yell but something was forced against his mouth. He swung out with his left arm and it flailed uselessly in the air. 'I'm going to be sick,' Vernon tried to say, but no words came out.

'Just as well I've come prepared,' the voice purred by Vernon's ear and everything went black.

A face was floating above his head, bobbing about like a balloon. He knew it wasn't a balloon because the mouth was talking. Vernon tried to move but couldn't. He didn't mind. It was like being asleep while he was awake. With an effort he focused on a voice that seemed to be coming from the balloon face. He wondered if it was supposed to be a Hallowe'en mask.

'Soon you won't be able to see anything.' Huge white teeth grinned down at him, but the voice was very gentle. Vernon wanted to smile back at the friendly face. It was funny to be reassured by a balloon. He remembered his mother and tried to speak, to explain that he had to get back to her.

'Don't worry,' the grinning balloon said. 'It won't hurt. Not for long anyway. Soon you won't be able to feel anything.'

A black point hovered over Vernon's left eye. He barely felt the sharp blade slice into his flesh along the top of his cheek bone before burning pain overwhelmed him, but he couldn't move or cry out.

32

MISSING

The Incident Room was ominously quiet on Sunday morning. Computers hummed, voices kept up a muted muttering, and an occasional telephone shrilled, but they couldn't pretend anything was happening.

'No news is bad news,' Peterson grumbled as Geraldine passed his desk. The sergeant hated being stuck at the station, tidying up his paperwork. Geraldine walked on, past a couple of constables who were chatting as they worked.

'Did you see the bonfire night display down at the recreation ground?' one of them asked.

'I don't think they should've held it this year, so soon after that poor woman was found there.'

'But it had been planned for months. And anyway they always do, it's the only place really.'

A name caught Geraldine's attention as she crossed the room and walked past a constable talking on the telephone.

'What was that you said?' she asked when the constable hung up.

'What?'

'You said something about Vernon Mitchell?'

'That was his mother on the phone, ma'am. She's worried because he went out to a party and didn't come home last night. But a seventeen-year-old boy staying out all night is hardly headline news, is it? After all, it was Hallowe'en. I expect he went to a party and stayed over. That's what I told Mrs Mitchell anyway. She seemed quite upset though.'

Geraldine nodded and went to find Peterson. 'Vernon

Mitchell's the boy who saw a man arguing with Abigail Kirby just before she died.'

'Yes, I know who he is, gov. And?'

'And yesterday he came here to report that he thought someone was following him –'

'Which we both agreed was hardly likely.'

'I know. He was probably just feeling edgy because Abigail Kirby was murdered so soon after he saw her. But still –' She looked at the sergeant, a worried frown creasing her forehead. 'His mother just phoned in to report him missing.'

'Did she now.'

'It seems he went out to a party last night and never arrived home again.'

'Well, that sounds fair enough. He's a young lad, could be off anywhere.'

'But it's a coincidence all the same, isn't it? He thought he was followed home from work on Friday evening and the next day he disappeared. I think we should go and have a chat with the mother, see if she has any idea where he might be.'

The sergeant shrugged. 'If you think so, gov. But it can't be the first time he's been to an all night party.'

'It's the first time she's phoned in to report him missing,' Geraldine replied sharply. She was feeling decidedly uncomfortable about her dismissal of Vernon's worries the previous day and hoped she'd been right in assuming his concerns about being followed were unfounded. 'Come on, let's go.'

Mrs Mitchell lived in a row of well-kept terraced houses a couple of miles from the town centre. They were able to park right outside, and admired the neat tiny front garden as they approached the house along a short level path.

A voice called to them from the other side of the door. 'Who is it?'

'Mrs Mitchell, it's the police. You called the station to

report that your son may be missing. We'd like to talk to you if it's convenient.' The door was opened by a woman in a wheelchair. She had curly blonde hair and was wearing metal-rimmed glasses, which she took off to look up at them.

'Mrs Mitchell?'

'Yes.'

Geraldine introduced herself and her sergeant, and they followed Mrs Mitchell into a small living room. Geraldine saw a table and a couple of comfortable chairs, with a space between them large enough for the wheelchair to fit in, opposite a small flat screen television.

'It's my son, Vernon,' the invalid began when they were all settled. 'He went out last night to a friend's party and hasn't been home since. The thing is, officer, Vernon's not like other boys his age. He never stays out all night. He doesn't like to leave me on my own of an evening, in case – in case I need anything.' She gave an apologetic grimace and gestured to her wheelchair. 'I know he'd never stay out all night, not unless something was wrong.'

'Have you tried to contact him?'

'He left his phone at home last night. He didn't want to go out in case I needed anything, but I told him not to be daft. I'm fine on my own for a few hours and there are plenty of people I can call if I need help, which I don't. But he's been very protective of me since my illness. I had to insist he went out. He's a young boy, he should get out and enjoy himself. Only he hasn't come home and I think something's happened to him.' She pressed one hand against her mouth and stared at them wide-eyed with worry. 'Something's happened, hasn't it? That's why you're here, isn't it?'

'I'm sure whatever the explanation is will turn out to be perfectly simple, Mrs Mitchell.'

'Probably involving alcohol,' Peterson added with forced good cheer.

'Now, exactly when did you last see your son?' Geraldine asked.

'He was going to a Hallowe'en party. He left at about eight and – and I haven't seen him since.'

'Do you know where he went when he left yesterday evening?'

'Yes. He went to his friend Gary. Gary Morecombe. I don't know his address but Vernon left the number in case I needed him. I phoned Gary when Vernon hadn't come home this morning and he said he wasn't sure what time Vernon left his house but it was before midnight anyway. Vernon definitely hadn't spent the night there and Gary didn't think he'd – gone home with a girl. In any case,' she added quickly, 'Vernon would always have called to let me know he was fine, and to check I was all right. He'd never go off like that without getting in touch. I know he wouldn't.'

'We'll send a constable to speak to Gary Morecombe straightaway.' Geraldine nodded at Peterson who went out into the hall to make the call while Geraldine reassured Mrs Mitchell the police would do what they could to trace Vernon. She promised to call the fretting mother as soon as they found him. 'I expect he went home with a friend and got drunk,' Peterson reassured the anxious mother as he came back into the room. 'Seventeen-year-old boys can be very thoughtless like that.'

'Not Vernon,' Mrs Mitchell insisted. 'He's always worrying about me. I wish he wouldn't feel so responsible, but since my husband died it's just the two of us and, as you can see, I'm not fit.'

'What do you think, then, gov? If you ask me it's a case of a drunken lad who went out and got laid, or paralytic more like, and forgot all about his mother waiting for him at home.'

Geraldine hoped Peterson was right.

33

SCHOOL

Since her mother died, the teachers had stopped pestering her to work, but the other girls carried on taunting her as though nothing had happened. Lucy wasn't even sure if they knew about her mother's death. She certainly wasn't going to tell any of them about it. Debra was the worst, but they were all mean. It wasn't as if she'd done anything to provoke them. She was just a new girl who didn't fit in.

'Do you think she likes being so skinny?' Debra asked the other girls.

'She's so boney!'

'She thinks she looks like a supermodel.' They all laughed. Lucy shrugged and turned away, but they had backed her into a corner and were blocking the corridor.

'What do you want?'

'She thinks we want something. From her.' They sniggered again. 'Have you looked at your Facebook page lately, scarecrow?'

'I've closed my account. I never go on Facebook any more so you can say what you like about me. I don't care.' She knew they had written horrible things about her, calling her ugly and making up lies about what she did with any boy desperate enough to go near her.

'She's not on Facebook!'

'Saddo!'

Lucy made a sudden dash forward and caught the other girls off guard. They fell back allowing her to make a bolt for the toilets, while their jeering followed her along the hall. Lucy had never fitted in at school, and now it was just the same at home. Her dad didn't care about anyone but Charlotte, and Ben never stood up for her like brothers were supposed to do. He came barging into her room, poking his nose in where it wasn't wanted, as though she had no right to any privacy. As if that wasn't bad enough, now Aunty Evie had turned up and was sleeping in their mother's old room, and Lucy's father and brother didn't seem to mind at all. Lucy scowled. Auntie Evie hated her, and the feeling was entirely mutual. The only person who had ever cared about Lucy was her mother.

Someone rattled the door. Lucy drew her knees up to her chest and sat perfectly still on the toilet lid.

'Someone's in there,' she heard a voice say. Lucy held her breath but the speaker swore and moved on to another cubicle.

Cisterns flushed, the bell rang, and a voice called out. 'Come on, girls, the bell's gone.' Footsteps scurried past while Lucy perched on top of the lavatory, waiting for the commotion to die away. She couldn't face a geography lesson and considered going to the medical centre. Sister had told her she could go there whenever she felt the need for time alone. The school nurse wasn't normally so nice, but she was obviously being kind to Lucy because her mother was dead. Sister usually sent pupils straight back to lessons unless they were really sick and needed to go home, in which case she would phone their parents and insist on them being collected as quickly as possible. She was supposed to be the school nurse, but she never wanted to look after the children when they were sick. Adults were all like that. Fathers were supposed to take care of their children but Lucy's father was hardly ever even at home, and Aunty Evie said she'd come over to look after Lucy and Ben. That was a joke. Who wanted to be looked after by an old witch like her?

The final straw for Lucy was when Ben told her he liked

having Aunty Evie around.

'That old cow? You must be joking!'

'She's not that bad.' Ben sat on Lucy's bed. 'At least she can cook proper food.'

'Is that all you care about, stuffing your face? And you can get off my bed.'

Ben didn't move. 'I didn't say that was all I cared about. At least I don't go round looking like a skeleton. Aunty Evie thinks you're anorexic.'

'Well she doesn't know what she's talking about and you don't even know what anorexic means. And I thought I told you to get off my bed.'

'Of course I know what it means. I'm not an idiot, and I can sit here if I want.'

'No you can't. Get off my bed.'

'Stop telling me what to do. Just because you're older than me doesn't give you the right to boss me around all the time.' He lay back and stretched out on the bed.

'Get your filthy shoes off my bed!' Lucy shrieked. She leapt forward, seized him by the legs and pulled him as hard as she could. Ben grasped the duvet which slid across the bed beneath him. He was laughing so hard that he let go and landed on the floor with a thump, clutching his stomach. They heard Aunty Evie calling from downstairs. Ben clambered to his feet, still laughing, and left the room. Swearing furiously under her breath, Lucy replaced the duvet and brushed it down, although she couldn't see any mud from Ben's shoes on it. 'Filthy little shit, thinks he can come in here and do what he bloody well likes.'

She realised she was muttering to herself as she sat in the cubicle at school, clutching her knees to her chest, and fell silent, thinking, but as she tried to focus on making plans for the future, she heard Miss Abingdon calling her name.

'Lucy, are you in here?'

With a sigh, Lucy stood up and opened the door. 'Yes, Miss. I've got a headache.'

Miss Abingdon looked relieved to see her. 'As long as you're alright,' she said.

Lucy frowned. She had just told her teacher she had a headache. How was that alright? And her mother was dead. She'd been murdered. Was that alright? 'Yes, Miss.' There was no point talking to idiot teachers. They didn't understand anything.

'Shouldn't you be in geography now? Or do you want to go the medical centre and have a rest?' Miss Abingdon put on an air of fake concern, as though she cared about Lucy when the truth was she simply didn't want any bother. If Lucy had killed herself, there in the school toilets, it would have caused her tutor no end of trouble. Lucy lowered her gaze and stared at the grubby floor tiles wishing she'd done it, cut her wrists so Miss Abingdon would have walked in and seen the floor of the toilets swimming in blood. It would've served her right.

'Yes, Miss,' she said.

'What do you want to do, Lucy? Do you want to go and lie down? You look –' Miss Abingdon was keen to pass the responsibility for Lucy on to the school nurse. 'You don't look very well.' She didn't say Lucy looked as though she'd been crying and it might be best not to return to her class looking like shit.

'Yes, Miss. I'll go to the medical centre,' Lucy answered.

She glanced back over her shoulder before she turned a corner in the corridor. Miss Abingdon was watching her, a worried frown on her face. Lucy walked past the entrance to the medical centre and out through the side door into the school yard.

34

NEIGHBOURS

Geraldine and her sergeant went to interview the Kirbys'
neighbours to see if they could add to the picture the
police were building up about Matthew. The Kirbys lived in
a detached house towards one end of a wide avenue lined
with silver birch, a mixture of detached and semi-detached
properties. To one side of the Kirbys was a semi-detached
house and they tried there first.

The door rattled and a grey haired woman opened it slightly.
'Yes?' She peered suspiciously up at them, and they saw she
had the chain on.

Geraldine held out her warrant card and the woman
removed the chain and opened the door fully. She was short
and very thin, her shoulders bowed with age. Geraldine
thought she would probably scare children, with her sharp
eyes, pointed nose and chin.

'How can I help you, officer?' Briefly, Geraldine explained
the reason for their call. 'I thought it would be about the
woman next door. Shocking business, isn't it? Although I
suppose it's all in a day's work for you. Well, if you're hoping
I can help, I'm sorry to disappoint you but I can't really say
I knew them at all. To be honest, I hardly spoke to them. Not
that there was any bad feeling, but they were busy people and
I don't go out much these days. My daughter comes when
she can –'

'What about the children?' Geraldine interrupted her.

The old woman frowned. 'My grandchildren? Oh, they're
both away. Jessica's travelling. That's all she seems to want

to do. And Mark lives in Scotland –'

'I'm talking about the girl and boy who live next door. Did you see them very often?' Geraldine interrupted gently. The old woman shook her head. 'And Mr and Mrs Kirby – were you aware of any difficulties in the marriage? Did you ever hear them arguing?'

The woman's eyes lit up with sudden animation. 'Oh, do you think he did it? Was it him killed her then?' Unconsciously, she opened the door wider and leaned forward. 'Are you going to arrest him?'

'We've no idea yet who was responsible for her death –'

'It was terrible, wasn't it? A teacher.' The woman tutted loudly. 'Well, I hope you're going to lock him up soon. I don't want to live next door to a murderer.' She dropped her voice, as though afraid she might be overheard. 'Now, you'll come in for a cup of tea, won't you? And I've got some nice chocolate bourbons.'

Geraldine and the sergeant exchanged a regretful glance. 'That's very kind of you, but we need to get on. Here's a card. Please give me a call if you think of anything else.'

The Kirbys' neighbours on the other side were keen to help, but similarly short on information. A middle-aged man came to the door and looked enquiringly at them without speaking. Once again, Geraldine introduced herself and Detective Sergeant Peterson and outlined the reason for their call.

'Hmmm,' the man replied. 'They weren't exactly unfriendly –' He broke off as a plump, bright-eyed woman joined him on the doorstep.

'What's this, Brian?' she asked fussily. 'We're not –'

'It's the police, Maisie.' Her eyes opened wide in alarm. 'It's about the Kirby woman next door. You know, the one –'

'Yes, yes, I know,' she dismissed him and turned to Geraldine. 'Have you found out who killed her?'

'We're pursuing our investigation, but I'm afraid we can't

say any more than that at this point.'

'They want to know what they were like next door,' Brian explained to his wife. 'I was telling them they're not exactly friendly,' he went on.

Maisie turned to Geraldine. 'If you ask me, there's something not right about that family. I mean, she never seems to be there. He seems nice enough, doesn't he, Brian, but she's always off, out and about, till all hours, isn't she?' She appealed to her husband then continued without waiting for him to respond. 'Remember when they first moved in? We're not exactly demanding as neighbours. I mean, we don't like to intrude. But there's nothing wrong with being neighbourly, is there?'

'What happened?' Geraldine asked.

'We went to see if there was anything they needed and she came to the door and – well, she gave us our marching orders, as if we were making a nuisance of ourselves. He never said a word, just shrugged at us before she shut the door. Now that's not very friendly, is it?'

'I think she might just have been busy,' her husband interrupted. 'They had just moved in.'

'That was no reason to talk down to us like that, as though we were naughty children.'

'She spends all day talking to children –'

'Well, we're not children. She was hardly ever there, as far as we could tell. And as for him, I haven't spoken to him since that first night. Not that there's any bad feeling, we just don't see them.'

Her husband shook his head. 'Not everyone wants to chat over the garden fence. There's nothing wrong with keeping yourself to yourself.'

Maisie swivelled round to face him. 'There's friendly and there's neighbourly. Everyone has to make time for other people. It's only manners. We were only being good neighbours.' She turned back to Geraldine. 'Now I come to think of it, she was pretty rude, if you ask me. But I'm sorry about what happened to her. It's a terrible business.'

'And you say Mrs Kirby was hardly ever at home?'

'Yes, that's right,' Maisie replied. 'Like I said, he seems pleasant enough, but she's always off out somewhere – or she was, I should say. Those children are left to drag themselves up – and she's a head teacher. You wouldn't believe it, would you? That girl looks as though she could do with a good wash.'

'Yes, the girl's odd,' Brian agreed, 'but she's a teenager.' As though that explained it.

'I mean, you never hear any noise from them,' Maisie went on. 'Not that we're complaining, but that's not normal for teenagers, is it?'

Geraldine took a step back and handed Brian a card. 'Thank you both very much. If you think of anything else that might help us in our enquiries, please call this number.'

'What do you want to know?' Maisie asked.

'Of course we will, Inspector,' her husband replied at the same time. 'I told you, they want to know about Mr Kirby next door, to find out if he killed his wife,' he explained.

'Well, don't you go getting any ideas, Brian Fuller,' they heard her say as the door closed.

35

CAROL

'Carol Middleton's here and she's asking to speak to someone, gov.'

Geraldine looked up with a frown. 'Carol Middleton? Am I supposed to know who she is?'

'She's Vernon Mitchell's aunt.'

Geraldine slapped the file she was reading down on her desk. 'Has he turned up then?'

'I don't know, gov, but his aunt doesn't look very happy.' The constable pulled a face and Geraldine's spirits sank. Vernon was a healthy seventeen-year-old who had been missing for less than two days. Under normal circumstances the police wouldn't be concerned. If Vernon hadn't been to the station with his hazy account of a man talking to Abigail Kirby shortly before she was killed, the police wouldn't have paid much attention to his mother's anxieties. But Vernon Mitchell had disappeared soon after he had come forward with his statement, just one day after he had reported that he thought he was being followed. Something about his disappearance didn't feel right.

'OK, I'll see her now.'

A large red-faced woman was waiting in an interview room, a robust version of Mrs Mitchell. She had to be the invalid's sister. 'Mrs Carol Middleton?'

'I'd like you to tell me exactly what's going on,' Carol Middleton said before Geraldine had a chance to introduce herself. 'My sister reported her son missing twenty-four hours ago and she's not heard a word from you since then.'

'I'm sorry –'

'I don't think you have any idea what my poor sister is going through.' Carol went on without waiting for an answer. 'My sister is not a well woman, Inspector. She can't cope with the sort of stress you're subjecting her to.'

'I'm sorry about your sister, Mrs Middleton, but I'm not sure what more you expect us to do –'

'Find him, of course. Wherever Vernon is, you have to find him. My sister can't take much more of this. It's making her ill. Look, I'm not sure you quite understand the seriousness of the situation. I'd like to speak to a senior officer.' Geraldine introduced herself and Carol Middleton nodded when Geraldine said she was an inspector. 'Right. An inspector. Good. Now tell me exactly what you've done so far to try and find Vernon. I want to know exactly what's been happening.'

Geraldine began to explain that as much time as possible was being devoted to Vernon's disappearance but Carol Middleton interrupted her again.

'That's frankly not good enough, Inspector. You have to understand, this is not just any teenage boy who's run off. Vernon's mother is a very sick woman. He knows how much she depends on him and would never disappear like that, without a word.'

Geraldine looked directly at the other woman and kept her voice even. 'Mrs Middleton, has it occurred to you that Vernon might simply be taking some time off, taking some time for himself? Acting as a carer is difficult and demanding and Vernon's only seventeen –'

'He's nearly eighteen, and he isn't my sister's carer. She has carers who come in and look after her needs every day. But Vernon's her son, he's the only family she's got –'

'She's got you,' Geraldine pointed out.

Carol Middleton's naturally florid face turned a slightly darker shade of red with a flush that spread under her chin and down her throat. 'That's not the same thing. Vernon's her son. He lives with her.'

As Geraldine watched Vernon's aunt talking at her she tried to feel sympathy for the stout red-faced woman but she couldn't help thinking Carol Middleton's complaints were unfair. The police were doing their best. It was hardly their fault the boy had gone missing. Uniform had questioned people living on Vernon's route back home from the party. No one remembered seeing him and he hadn't been spotted on any CCTV on buses travelling the route that night. Everyone they interviewed who had attended Gary's party told them Vernon had spent the evening with a girl called Jennifer.

All they learned was that Vernon had left the party 'quite early' and alone. A lot of alcohol had been consumed at the party, but there had allegedly been no drugs. As much man power as could be spared had been diverted to the search but the DCI hadn't been able to draft in more personnel. The Superintendant thought it unlikely there would prove to be anything amiss in Vernon's disappearance but Geraldine couldn't shake off an uneasy feeling that she had been wrong to dismiss Vernon's request for protection so quickly. Although her response had been appropriate with the information available to her at the time, and was all detailed in her decision log where she had to record reasons for all her actions, her disquiet made it difficult for her to insist with any degree of confidence that the police were doing everything they could to find Vernon Mitchell.

'He's a young boy,' she told Carol Middleton. 'One day he's going to want to move out and live his own life. It's inevitable. He's going to want his own space and probably felt unable to demand it. It's not unusual for teenagers in his situation to run away from home like that and they almost always turn up, safe and sound. The chances of anything having happened to him are slight.' She realised her attempt to reassure Vernon's aunt had backfired as soon as Carol Middleton spoke.

'In other words you aren't taking this seriously and no one's doing anything to look for my nephew because you think he's run away from home. Are you really telling me you think Vernon's chosen to run off and leave my poor sister in a state of collapse, worrying about him? That's preposterous.'

Geraldine sat back in her chair and let the other woman talk for a while. It was a difficult interview. Carol Middleton insisted the police should be devoting all their resources to finding her nephew, on the grounds that his mother was an invalid. What made it worse was her refusal to listen to anything Geraldine said. By the time she managed to get away, Geraldine felt exhausted.

'You OK, gov?' Peterson asked when she returned to the Incident Room.

'I've just had a hammering from Vernon's aunt.'

Peterson smiled encouragingly. 'He'll turn up, gov. He's a seventeen-year-old boy. He's probably gone off with some girl. It'll be OK.' But he looked worried.

Carol Middleton's words niggled at Geraldine all the way home that evening. 'My sister... my sister...'

When Geraldine had eaten she picked up the phone. Celia sounded surprised to hear from her. 'Geraldine? What's up?'

'Nothing.' Geraldine felt a twinge of guilt that her sister had assumed something must be wrong for Geraldine to call her during the week. 'I thought I'd call because we haven't spoken for a week. I just rang to see how you are.'

Celia launched into her usual account of her daughter's news. 'Chloe got a commendation at school for a maths test. She's been seeing a fantastic tutor after school and -'

'What about you?' Geraldine interrupted.

'What?'

'Of course I want to hear all about Chloe, but I want to

hear about you as well. You never talk about what you've been doing.'

There was a pause. 'I had my hair cut,' Celia said uncertainly and Geraldine felt like crying. 'There isn't really much to say. What about you?'

It crossed Geraldine's mind that she ought to tell Celia about her visit to the adoption agency but she felt too tired to tackle the subject and was afraid she might become emotional. 'I'm fine. So – what were you saying about Chloe's maths? I thought she was struggling with it.'

Celia didn't need any more prompting than that. With a sigh, Geraldine sank back in her chair and listened. As Celia talked about her only child, Geraldine's thoughts drifted to Vernon's invalid mother. She wondered where the boy could be, and hoped he was still alive.

36

RELEASE

Matthew was checking through his post. 'Bugger!'

Evie glanced up at her brother, eyebrows raised. 'What is it?' She knew better than to comment on his language but her face expressed her disapproval. Ben continued eating his breakfast and Lucy picked at her disgusting scrambled egg, pushing it around her plate. Evie insisted they all sit down together for a cooked breakfast.

'I've got another bloody speeding fine,' Matthew mumbled.

'What?'

'I've got another speeding fine.'

'As if you haven't got enough to deal with right now,' Evie said. 'Can't they leave you alone? How much is it?'

'Oh God, don't ask.'

'Well I think it's outrageous!'

'Serves you right for speeding.' Lucy glared at her plate without looking up.

'Everyone speeds,' Ben told her.

'No they don't, not like him. He's always driving over the speed limit. It's totally irresponsible. He could kill someone –' She broke off, biting her lip, and scowled at her plate. 'They ought to take your licence away. Then you wouldn't be able to go and see her all the time.'

'That's enough,' Matthew warned her.

'So now I can't even open my mouth in my own home!' Lucy stood up, knocking her chair over. It fell to the floor with a crash as she dashed from the room.

There was an uncomfortable silence for a few seconds.

'Can't you say you were upset? Claim special consideration or something?' Evie asked at last. She turned to Ben with a bright smile. 'That's what I like to see, an empty plate. Can you manage some more?' He nodded and watched as she dolloped a spoonful of beans onto his plate. 'And another sausage to go with it?'

He nodded again. 'Thank you, Aunty Evie.'

She beamed at him before removing Lucy's plate from the table. 'I'll leave this. She might feel peckish later...'

Peterson stared in consternation. 'Speeding?' he repeated. 'Was it definitely Matthew Kirby?' The sergeant wasn't the only one to look dismayed. A mumble of irritable voices rose and fell silent again as the DCI resumed.

'Matthew Kirby's car was picked up on a speed camera at one ten on 24th October on the Maidstone road, just past the Tenterden bypass when, according to his statement, he was on his way to see Charlotte Fox – which means he couldn't have killed Abigail between one and four that afternoon, unless he left Charlotte again during the afternoon.'

'We don't know where she was killed,' Peterson pointed out. 'Could she have been in the car with him then?'

The DCI shook her head. 'The CCTV image is blurred, but there are no passengers in the car, and the driver looks like Matthew Kirby. There's no doubt it's him all right, driving his own car.'

'Could he have already killed her and stashed her in the boot of the car?'

Kathryn Gordon stated the obvious. 'SOCOs would have seen evidence. They've been over his car, inside and out, and found nothing. His tyres don't match any marks found near the recreation ground, and there's no record of his car being in that area on the 24th or 25th. So – could he have left Charlotte during the course of the afternoon, driven back to meet his wife somewhere, killed her and hidden the body, then dumped it by the recreation ground in the night?

Is that feasible?'

Geraldine flicked through Charlotte's statement. 'Charlotte said he was with her all Saturday afternoon and I don't think she was lying, ma'am. She didn't exactly have a story prepared, because she was very vague about the time he arrived. Here it is. She said, "He came round and he stayed here, with me, until late. Neither of us went out. I'm sure of it." She told us it was after midnight when he finally left.'

'Well now we know he must have arrived at around one twenty,' Kathryn Gordon said.

'Yes, ma'am. And apart from that, her statement's clear. She was adamant he was with her all afternoon and evening.'

'Damn!' Peterson burst out. 'I was sure we had him.'

'We can never be sure of anything until we have incontrovertible evidence in our hands. And even then we can be wrong...' Kathryn Gordon rubbed her forehead with the fingers of her left hand as though trying to erase the lines. 'You'd better go straight round there, Geraldine. Talk to him face to face and put him and his family out of their misery.'

'I'm sure they'll all be relieved, ma'am.' Except for Lucy.

Matthew was tempted to slam the door in her face when he saw the familiar features of Inspector Steel on his doorstep again. 'What is it now?' he could hear the agitation in his voice as he struggled to remain calm. 'It's one thing after another with you lot.'

'Mr Kirby, your car was picked up by a speed camera on the 24th October –'

'I know, I know, I've got the letter. It's not the first time.'

'Your car was picked up at ten past one on the Maidstone road, near the Tenterden bypass, indicating you arrived at Miss Fox's flat at around one twenty that Saturday afternoon. We believe your wife was killed between one and four that day. It's impossible to be exact about the time of death, so we will have to ask you not to leave the area without informing us of your whereabouts, but I'm here to inform you that you're no longer officially a suspect.'

'So you believe me now? That I didn't do it.'

'For the time being, Mr Kirby, but, as I said, please don't leave the area without telling us. If you do, it might look suspicious, and you don't want –'

'Oh everything looks bloody suspicious to you,' he replied, suddenly belligerent. 'If I hadn't been speeding, you lot would still have me top of your list of suspected murderers, is that it?'

The inspector's face didn't show any regret and he thought what a cold bitch she must be, carelessly ruining lives as though other people were so many pawns in a game she was paid to play. 'We're only doing our job, sir. I'm sure you're just as keen as we are to find out who killed your wife.'

Matthew shook his head, suddenly too tired to care any more. 'Frankly, Inspector, I don't give a damn about your investigation right now. All you've done is upset my kids even more, with your unfounded accusations, as if losing their mother hasn't been bad enough. And nothing you can do is going to bring her back, is it? All I want now is to be left alone to bring up my kids and –' He didn't add that he wanted to be with Charlotte.

'We wanted you to know as quickly as possible.' The inspector turned on her heel and walked away. He wasn't going to thank her anyway. 'Good riddance to bad rubbish,' he muttered under his breath before going inside to tell his family the good news.

'Lucy! Come down here!' he yelled up the stairs. 'I've got some news! Lucy!'

'Leave me alone!' she called back. Matthew hesitated then shrugged and hurried along to the kitchen where Ben and Evie were waiting anxiously.

37

TALK

The atmosphere in the Incident Room was dejected. At least while they had a suspect, there had been something positive to work on. Now it felt as though the investigation had lost direction, and they were casting about in thin air, desperate for a lead.

'What about Whittaker?' the DCI suggested. 'Is it a bit of a coincidence, his losing his kite in the trees near Abigail Kirby's body, the morning after she was left there?'

'Almost as though he knew where the body was –' someone added.

'And wanted us to find it?' another voice chipped in.

'He was more concerned about his son than anything to do with the victim,' Peterson said. 'He didn't even seem very curious about Abigail Kirby.'

'Because he knew all about her already?' a constable countered. The excitement in his voice was infectious. 'His preoccupation with his son could have been a deliberate distraction, to put us off the scent –'

The DCI cut in sharply. 'Let's not allow ourselves to get carried away with speculation. However, I think it's time we had another word with David Whittaker, Geraldine.'

'Yes, ma'am.'

Geraldine wasn't convinced by this new line of enquiry, but she was prepared to be open-minded about Whittaker, and anything was better than sitting at her desk pointlessly pushing bits of paper around.

'It's worse than the morgue in there,' Peterson said as

they drove off to the garage where David Whittaker worked. They agreed that Geraldine would question the witness while Peterson checked the garage records in case Abigail Kirby had taken her car there to be serviced.

'I wouldn't have put the two of them together,' Geraldine said, 'Abigail Kirby and David Whittaker –'

'Forming a liaison –' Peterson laughed at the idea. Geraldine was pleased to see he had regained his customary good humour. She guessed that things were going well with Bev but didn't ask for fear of setting him off again.

'You never know.'

'She might have brought her car here and met him. Fancied a bit of rough. And if he's lying about never seeing her before –'

'Let's not get ahead of ourselves,' Geraldine cut in. 'It's facts we need now.'

David Whittaker looked surprised to see them. 'Hello officers, have you solved the case then? I still haven't told the wife, you know.' He grinned sheepishly, wiping his oily hands ineffectively on a filthy rag. Geraldine hoped he wasn't expecting them to shake hands with him. 'She read about it in the papers. I was bricking it, thinking the boy would blurt it all out, but he held his tongue.' Geraldine and the sergeant exchanged a glance. 'You don't think I'm wrong do you, encouraging the boy to lie to his mother like that? It's not as if he had to actually tell a lie, he just had to say nothing. That's not the same as lying, is it?'

Geraldine smiled. 'You should have been a lawyer, Mr Whittaker.'

'Or a politician,' Peterson added under his breath as he went off to check the records.

Geraldine found it hard to believe that David Whittaker's friendly, chatty personality might be a front for a vicious murderer who had killed and mutilated his victim.

'Where does your son go to school, Mr Whittaker?'

Geraldine asked.

'St Gregory's. Do you know it? It seems a decent enough place, but at the end of the day you take what's on offer, don't you? He's happy there, anyway, and that's the main thing. He's a happy little chap, takes after me. People go bonkers over all this education lark, but what do they really teach the kids? It wasn't any different in my day. When all's said and done it all comes out in the wash. I can't remember too much of what they tried to teach me in school, and that's a fact.'

'Mr Whittaker,' Geraldine interrupted. He didn't strike her as nervous, he was just a man who liked to talk. She could easily imagine him spending hours with his mates, exchanging views and engaging in easy banter. 'Had you ever seen the victim, Abigail Kirby, before last Sunday morning?'

'Not as far as I know. She never brought a car in here that I can remember, so there's no way I would have come across her.'

Peterson joined them and nodded grimly at Geraldine. 'According to the records, Mrs Kirby brought her car here for a service and MOT back in August,' he announced.

The mechanic looked puzzled. 'Was she a customer then? Is that what you're saying? Well, if she was, I never met her. But I don't usually see the customers anyway. It's the girls in reception, or the manager if there's a problem. They're the ones who deal face to face with them when they bring their cars in. I just work on the vehicles.' He held up his greasy palms as if to prove his point.

'So you're positive you never met her while she was alive?' Geraldine pressed the point home.

'If I did, I don't remember. I already told you that. But tell you what, though,' he added, almost as an afterthought. 'If it was near the end of August when she brought her car in, I wouldn't have been here.'

'Because–?'

'We were on our holidays, me and the wife and the kid.'

'Can you remember where and when you went?' Peterson asked.

Whittaker threw the sergeant a puzzled glance. 'Can I remember? What that fortnight cost me, I'm not likely to forget! We went to the Costa del Sol to the Hotel Miramont, for the last two weeks in August. Lovely place. Two whole weeks, now that's the life for me!' He grinned. 'Beats working here.'

'Thank you, Mr Whittaker.'

'That's it then, is it?'

'For now, sir.'

Whittaker turned back to the engine he had been working on. He was whistling as they left.

'I suppose it's true he never met her,' Peterson commented as they reached the forecourt.

'She brought her car here, and two months later she's killed and he happens to find the body, concealed in the trees.' She shook her head. 'It's a bit odd, isn't it? But it's the coincidence that's odd, not the witness. He seemed to be on the level.'

'You believed him when he said he'd never met her?'

'Yes. Still, he can keep his mouth shut when he wants to,' Geraldine added. 'He didn't tell his wife he'd found a body at the recreation ground. We need to check out his alibi. Get onto it straightaway, will you?'

Geraldine knew it was rash to call Paul that evening, but she was impatient to know whether he wanted to see her again. If he gave her the brush off, at least then she would know where she stood. Nowhere. While things remained uncertain between them, she was unable to put him out of her mind. The last words he had said to her were that he would call. He hadn't said when. It could mean anything, or nothing.

'Geraldine, I was going to phone you this evening.' So far so good. She didn't believe him, but at least he sounded pleased to hear from her. 'How have you been?' It was an encouraging start. Paul made no reference to Saturday evening. Geraldine was nervous about making another gaffe so, after a brief and slightly stilted exchange about the weather, she steered the conversation round to the investigation. In any case, it was a relief to talk freely to someone who was involved in the case, yet not on the police investigation team. They had all been convinced Matthew Kirby was guilty; Geraldine alone had believed in his innocence all along.

Even Paul sounded surprised to hear that Matthew Kirby was no longer a suspect. 'I would've thought the husband was the most likely person to treat her like that. It had to be a crime of passion, surely. Whoever killed her must have been involved with her in some way. Cutting out her tongue in such a gruesome manner seems so specific, doesn't it? Unless the killer was completely insane.'

'Whoever it was could hardly be sane.'

'No. That's true. So if it wasn't the husband, was she seeing someone else?'

'As far as we can tell, she wasn't. She was only interested in her work and her children. I doubt if she'd have had time for another relationship and we've found nothing to suggest she was seeing anyone else.' Geraldine paused. Abigail Kirby and her husband had been sleeping in separate bedrooms. Matthew had told them it was because he was seeing another woman. The possibility that Abigail herself had been having an affair had never been raised. 'You know, we probably shouldn't rule it out, because we already have to assume there may be another man involved.'

'You just said you don't think she was seeing someone else, and now you're telling me there is another man involved?'

'No, not necessarily involved with her. I mean that whoever killed her was probably a man. You said that yourself. I didn't mean involved in the sense that she was having an affair.

At least, we never considered that as a possibility, although we probably should. We need to view this from every conceivable angle because we don't have anything else to go on right now.'

'What about the boy from the shop? Hasn't he been able to describe the man he saw?'

'No. And the CCTV footage is very blurred. But at the moment, that's the only lead we've got, insubstantial as it is. Only now the boy's disappeared.'

'Disappeared?'

'Yes.' Miserably Geraldine told Paul about Vernon Mitchell. 'And I can't help feeling responsible. I mean, if I'd taken him seriously when he told me he was being followed –'

'But there was no evidence to support that, was there? And a seventeen-year-old boy staying out overnight is hardly cause for alarm. I'm sure you'll find he went to stay with a girlfriend and didn't think to tell anyone.'

'Maybe. We also interviewed the man who discovered the body again, because we thought it might not have been a coincidence, his finding her the morning after she was hidden.'

'Yes,' Paul sounded thoughtful. 'That was a stroke of luck, wasn't it? But I suppose she'd have been found sooner or later. The body wasn't exactly carefully concealed, was it? A lot of people walk their dogs along there. It's almost as though the killer wanted her to be found.'

'Or was in too much of a hurry to stop and bury her.'

'Maybe he just didn't care enough to do anything but dump her and go. You said it yourself, the killer's got to be completely insane. It's impossible to imagine what he could have been thinking when he mutilated that poor woman.'

'We have to try,' Geraldine replied. 'We have to try and get inside his head.'

'Inside the head of a maniac who cut out someone's

tongue?'

'Yes.'

'Well, good luck with that.' He sounded sceptical.

'We'll find this killer,' she assured him. 'Someone somewhere must know something.'

'Well, all I can say is, I hope you find him soon. I've been wracking my brains to think of any clue the killer might have left on the body, beyond the obvious one of cutting out her tongue.' There was a pause. 'I wondered if you fancied meeting again for a drink one evening? I know I –' He hesitated.

'Yes, I'd like that very much.' Geraldine said quickly.

'Good. I'll call you.'

She hoped he would.

38

AGREEMENT

When Matthew went to see Charlotte after work on Wednesday he expected her to be overjoyed to learn he was no longer a suspect. Twenty-four hours after hearing the news, he was still ready to weep with relief when he thought about it. The idea that he might have had to abandon his motherless children to serve a prison sentence was unbearable. Even if a jury had acquitted him, he might have spent months in custody awaiting trial, leaving his children to the care of Evie. And Matthew was already tearing his hair out over Lucy. Her tutor had assured him Lucy was fine at school, but he wasn't sure he believed it.

'Of course she's distressed, but we're keeping a close eye on her. All the staff are aware of the situation, and Sister has told Lucy she can go to the medical centre if she ever feels she needs some space. It's bound to happen from time to time. It's only natural. And if she ever needs to come home, we'll contact you straightaway.'

'You've got my mobile number?' Matthew asked, although he knew he was probably the last person Lucy would want to see if she was feeling upset. She was better off with her friends at school.

To his amazement, Charlotte flew into a rage. 'You knew about this yesterday, and you've only just decided to tell me!' Her blue eyes glared wildly at him.

'I tried to phone you, several times, but you weren't answering your phone,' he protested.

'And it didn't occur to you to leave a message?'

'I wanted to tell you myself, not tell some answering machine that I'm a free man.'

'You could have come round.'

'It's not so easy now Evie's staying with us.'

'Why not?'

Matthew ran his hands through his hair in a gesture of helplessness. 'It just isn't. She doesn't know about you –'

'You mean you haven't told her.'

'Yes, obviously.'

'Well tell her. Go on. Phone her up now and tell her. Tell her where you are.'

'It's not that easy.'

'Why not? What could be more easy? Just pick up the phone and tell her: I'm seeing someone. She's called Charlotte and we're getting married.' She lunged forward, seized the telephone from its cradle and thrust it at him. 'Here. Phone her. Go on. Or would you rather I told her?' She began to press the keys wildly, her features twisted in anger.

Matthew wrenched the handset from her grasp. 'Stop it!' He clung on to the phone, staring at her face, which was glistening with tears. 'I can't tell her, not yet. Jesus, my wife's been dead for less than two weeks and you want to tell my family about us. I don't care about my sister so much – although God knows she'll be trouble enough – but my son has no idea what's going on with us. I can't just blurt it out.' He crossed the room and replaced the receiver on the cradle. 'You'll have to be patient, Charlotte.'

'Patient?' she shrieked. 'I've been patient for three fucking years! I've waited and waited for you because you said your wife refused to give you a divorce. And now she's not in the way any more, you're asking me to be patient all over again because your son doesn't know about us. Tell him, Matthew!'

'I will. But I have to give him time to get over what's happened. The boy's just lost his mother, for Christ's sake!

Show some consideration. You may not give a damn, but she was his mother!'

'So now I'm inconsiderate? Well, if I'm such a bitch, maybe you'd better not see me any more.'

'Don't be ridiculous.'

'What's ridiculous is that your wife's gone, and now you've suddenly come up with another reason why we can't be together, just like that. I left my home for you, I quit my job and left all my friends and my mother back in York to follow you down here, and it's all turning out to be a stupid wild goose chase, just like my mother said it would. I should have listened to her. I never should've let you talk me into this. And now where am I?'

It took Matthew some time to reassure her that her fears were unfounded. He wanted to marry her. The time just wasn't right yet. 'We won't have to wait much longer, I promise.'

'So you keep saying. But how long?' Her voice was jerky with sobs.

Matthew took a deep breath. 'Let's give it three months. That'll give us time to get through the funeral and for the children time to come to terms with what's happened. That's three months from now. How does that sound?'

'You want to get married in February?' Charlotte had stopped crying and was staring at him, listening intently.

'Yes, February. Why not? What's wrong with February?'

'No one gets married in February. It'll be freezing for a start.'

'Then we'll get married abroad – in Las Vegas. We'll get married in Las Vegas!'

A grin lit up Charlotte's tear stained face, smudged with black eye make-up. 'Really? Do you mean that? We're finally going to get married? In Las Vegas?' She laughed out loud.

'Of course we're going to get married. Isn't that what we both want?' She nodded. 'Time to kiss and make up?' She smiled and stepped towards him. 'I want to make up properly, with the future Mrs Matthew Kirby –' She flung her arms round his neck and kissed him. 'I've got to practise carrying you over the threshold,' he whispered as he lifted her up and carried her into the bedroom. Married, not married, it made no difference to him. He just wanted to please her.

'I must look awful,' she said, wiping her dripping nose on the back of her hand, as she lay down on the bed.

'You're the most beautiful woman in the world,' he replied. He wasn't looking at her face as he undid her shirt, and she giggled in anticipation. She knew that nothing could spoil her happiness now, not even the desperate letter she had received from Ted that morning.

'You won't stay with him, I know you won't. And when it's over, I'll be waiting for you.'

Matthew suddenly thought about his wife, lying in a cold drawer in the morgue, and blinked in an effort to dismiss the image from his mind. Abigail had been dead to him for a long time. His happiness depended on Charlotte now, warm and eager for his touch.

'A man's entitled to some happiness,' he told himself fiercely but, for the first time, he couldn't make love to her. Charlotte lay rigid on the bed beside him and refused to meet his gaze as he tried to explain to her.

'I'm just worn out with the stress of it all, I think,' he sighed. 'I'll soon be… it's nothing to do with you.'

He could imagine her thoughts: 'You see, you don't really want to marry me, do you? The idea's put you right off me.'

39

INTEREST

The following morning Geraldine's bell rang before she was even dressed. She opened the door and was surprised to see a boy holding a large bouquet of flowers.

'Geraldine Steel?'

'Yes.'

The message on the card said simply: 'To Geraldine, from Paul.' It was brief but it started her wondering if they might possibly have a future together and, if so, what would happen about her application for a transfer to London. She tried not to get excited at the idea that he might be interested in her as she hunted for a vase large enough to hold the flowers. In the end she put them in a plastic Pimms jug, the largest suitable container she could find.

Geraldine called Paul mid-morning to thank him and they arranged to meet up for a drink later on.

'I'm glad they arrived OK,' Paul said, 'and that you like them.'

'They're lovely.'

Geraldine didn't have time to go home and change, and scrutinised her face carefully in the mirror of the station toilets before leaving. She decided not to bother with eye shadow but applied her mascara carefully and put on some lip gloss before setting off. They were meeting at The Gate again. It was a pleasant place and convenient, with a public car park round the corner which was free after six-thirty.

This time Geraldine spotted Paul straightaway sitting in a corner bay waiting for her, an open bottle of Champagne on the table. It was Wednesday evening and the wine bar was packed with young men and women out for a drink after work. Geraldine was glad she didn't have to fight her way to the bar where people were waiting, three deep, to be served.

'Skulking in the corner again,' she said with a grin as she sat down. 'The flowers really were beautiful, Paul. Thank you again.'

He smiled and poured two glasses of Champagne. 'Do you know, I never even asked if you like Champagne. You might prefer a nice bottle of red. I assumed you'd like Champagne, I don't know why. Was that very remiss of me?'

'No, not at all, this is fine.' She took a sip. Flowers and Champagne. It could only mean one thing. 'It's perfect.'

'I owe you an apology –' Paul began.

'No, really, it's lovely.'

'I wasn't talking about the Champagne, Geraldine. I behaved very badly on Saturday –'

'Oh please, forget about it. I have. And I quite understand.'

'Do you?'

'Well, I'm not sure I do entirely, but it doesn't matter. You'll tell me if you want to. I really don't want to interfere. I shouldn't have let my curiosity run away with me like that.'

Paul gazed at her over the rim of his glass. 'You're very considerate.' Geraldine felt an unexpected rush of happiness. 'I wish I could tell you…'

'Please. There's no hurry.' Eager not to repeat her earlier faux pas, Geraldine changed the subject and began talking about the case. 'Sorry, I'm talking about work again. You must be bored of hearing about it.'

'Not at all. If I was you, I probably wouldn't be able to think about anything else right now. After all, a woman has died. You can't just put it out of your mind. So, the husband, Matthew Kirby, is genuinely out of the frame?'

'Yes. We're trying to think of other possibilities.'

'Have you come up with any new leads yet?'

'We've been investigating the garage mechanic who found the body.'

'You wouldn't think he'd want to be associated with finding the body if he'd killed her, but they say murderers always return to the scene of the crime. I don't know if that's true.'

'The witness claimed he'd never seen the dead woman before but it turns out Abigail Kirby took her car to the garage where he works,' Geraldine went on.

'Aha. So they had met and he lied about it!' Paul sat forward in his chair, interested.

'Well no, it turned out he was out of the country when she went to the garage so there's nothing to link them and no reason to suspect he's lying about anything. We're going over everything again, but so far we've not found anything.'

'Here's a question for you then. Do you think a woman could have murdered Abigail Kirby? Only if it wasn't the husband, maybe it was his girlfriend who killed her?'

Geraldine considered the suggestion. 'She was certainly desperate to marry him so I suppose that's a motive because Abigail Kirby had refused to agree to a divorce.'

'She couldn't stop him divorcing her.'

'No, but according to Matthew Kirby she'd threatened to take his children away, turn them against him, if he went ahead and left her. She saw it as breaking up the family.' Paul's fingers tightened around his glass and his face grew distant, inward looking. Geraldine held her breath. It was too late to recall her words. 'What do you think?' She threw the question back at him. 'You examined the body. Could those injuries have been inflicted by a woman?'

He nodded slowly, his attention returning to their discussion. 'It's possible of course.'

'But we're up against the same problem, because if Matthew Kirby didn't leave Charlotte alone, and they were together all the time on Saturday afternoon, she couldn't have done it either.'

'Unless they were in it together,' Paul suggested. Their eyes met across the table. It was possible.

'She was a theatre nurse before she moved to Kent, so she might have had access to surgical equipment,' Geraldine said.

'In that case she'd have known how to use it.'

'He could have arrived at Charlotte's flat –'

'At one twenty.'

'He picked her up and they drove back to Harchester together –'

'Keeping to side streets to avoid being spotted. Perhaps he even deliberately exceeded the limit as he drove past the speed camera on his way there, knowing his vehicle would be picked up –'

'To back up his alibi.'

'And they killed Abigail together. But where?' Paul shook his head and she went on. 'They concealed the body – we don't know where that was either – and that night before he went home, Matthew took her to the recreation ground.'

'Maybe the body was hidden in the boot of his car,' Paul said. 'He could have driven straight to the recreation ground when he left Charlotte.'

Geraldine shook her head. 'I don't think so. SOCOs have been over his car, and there would have been a lot of blood. No, we still don't know where she was killed or how she was moved. Or why her tongue was removed in that macabre way. In fact we don't really know anything.'

Paul still seemed genuinely interested in the idea. 'But the two of them could have been in it together. What about her car?'

'She doesn't have one.'

'She could have hired one?'

'It's possible, I suppose. We could check.' Geraldine

finished her glass of wine. 'I can't tell you how much I appreciate being able to talk to you like this, but do stop me if you're bored. I mean, I have to work on the case, but you're not responsible for finding out who killed Abigail Kirby –'

'No, but I do feel a responsibility towards the people I examine. I know they're just dead bodies now, but they were living people once, and someone has to care about what happened to them.'

'Yes,' Geraldine agreed. 'Someone has to care.' Their eyes met again across the table and he held her gaze for a few seconds. Paul looked away first. He raised the bottle and poured the last few drops. As he put it down on the table Geraldine noticed him glancing at his watch.

'I think I'd better be off soon,' she said quickly. 'I've got an early start tomorrow as usual.'

'We should do this again,' he replied.

'Yes. That would be nice.' They had suddenly become very formal. They said goodnight there at the table, and Geraldine left. When she looked back Paul was still sitting there, staring forlornly into his glass.

40

VISITOR

In the end Evie laid the table herself, grumbling all the while. 'Talk about spoilt.' Lucy and Ben ignored her and carried on watching the television. Now their father was home, they all knew there was no longer any pressing need for Evie to stay and her threat to tell their father had lost its clout; Matthew always sided with his children.

'Why are we eating in the dining room anyway?' Ben asked. 'Why can't we eat in the kitchen?'

'Mum used to let us eat in front of the telly,' Lucy added.

'Your father's bringing a friend home for supper.' Evie spoke sharply. 'Don't let him down.'

'What friend?' Lucy asked.

Evie shrugged. 'Someone from work, he said.'

'I bet it's her.'

'Shut up.' Ben kicked his sister.

'None of your squabbling in front of your father. I won't have you showing yourselves up in front of his work colleague.'

'Work colleague,' Lucy echoed sourly. Brother and sister glared at one another and Evie went to clatter around in the dining room, laying the table.

'Lucy, come and give me a hand,' they heard her call. Lucy turned up the volume on the television. After a while Evie came back in and sat with them.

None of them heard Matthew come in. 'Lucy, Ben, Evie!' Only Evie looked up. Lucy and Ben sat glued to the television. 'Lucy, Ben,' Matthew repeated, more loudly this time. 'I want you to meet Charlotte.' Matthew pushed the woman at his side further into the room so that she was standing slightly in front of him.

Ben heard Lucy's intake of breath and looked up. 'Hi dad –' He broke off and stared at the blonde woman hesitating in the doorway. She was pretty, he decided, but Lucy's words rattled around in his head. 'He's seeing someone else. A woman called Charlotte. That's why he wants a divorce. So he can marry Charlotte, whoever she is…' He glanced at Lucy who was sitting pressed against the back of her chair, her knees clutched to her chest, staring at the floor. Ben looked past the blonde woman to his dad who was gazing at him, eyes pleading. Ben felt his face flush with anger. His father had no right to look at him like that. What was he thinking of, bringing that woman into the house?

'Good evening.' Evie stood up with a smile and held out her hand. 'It's very nice to meet you, Charlotte.' Lucy coughed loudly and Ben stared at his feet. 'Supper's ready,' Evie went on brightly. 'This way. Come along, children.'

'We're not children,' Lucy muttered as she and Ben clambered to their feet and followed the adults into the dining room.

Evie had folded pink paper serviettes in five wine glasses beside five tumblers for water, and a small vase of pink flowers stood in the middle of the table.

'Why is it so posh?' Lucy asked loudly as they all sat down. 'What's all the fuss about?' No one answered. Ben squirmed uncomfortably on his seat. He wished Lucy would drop it, at least until their father's friend had gone.

'I've made fish,' Evie said. 'Salmon. I hope that's all right with you, Charlotte.'

'I hate fish,' Lucy said.

'That sounds lovely,' Charlotte said at the same time. Evie disappeared into the kitchen and no one spoke for a few seconds.

Matthew poured some wine for Charlotte. Lucy pushed her glass forward but her father ignored it.

'So, Charlotte,' Evie said when they were all settled with their food, 'you work with my brother?'

'Yes.' Charlotte smiled anxiously at Matthew.

'What is it you do exactly?'

'I'm –' Charlotte hesitated.

'Charlotte's a receptionist,' Matthew said.

'Can't she speak for herself?' Lucy asked.

'Lucy.' Evie frowned.

'I've known Charlotte for five years,' Matthew said. 'We met in York and –' His voice tailed off and he glanced at Charlotte who smiled encouragingly at him. 'Since your mother died –'

'Two weeks ago,' Lucy interrupted.

'Charlotte's been a good friend to me. At a time like this we all need support –' He stopped and put down his knife and fork. 'Lucy, Ben, I'd like you to get to know Charlotte. I know when you know her better –' Ben glared at him and Lucy scowled at her plate.

Evie stared at Matthew then she turned to Charlotte with a bright smile. 'Would you like some water?'

'Thank you. The salmon's lovely, Evie.'

The evening seemed to drag on interminably but at last Matthew offered to take Charlotte home.

'Will you be coming home tonight, dad?' Lucy asked loudly. Ben bit his lip and Evie glared at her niece. Matthew didn't answer but followed Charlotte who had hurried from the room.

As they drove off, Charlotte burst into tears.

'Oh lord, what's the matter now?' Matthew demanded. 'You've been nagging me to introduce you. What did you expect? I could hardly come straight out with it and tell them we're getting married, could I? February, that's what we agreed. Let's leave it until after Christmas to tell them. That gives them two months to get used to you. Then –'

'They hated me,' Charlotte burst out. 'They'll never accept me.' She blew her nose noisily. 'Did you see the way Lucy looked at me? She knows, doesn't she?' Matthew drove in silence, his face rigid. 'She knows about us.'

'They'll have to find out sooner or later. It'll all be all right, you'll see. Just give them some time.'

'It's never going to be all right, Matthew. They're never going to accept me.'

'They'll have to accept you when we're married,' Matthew replied grimly.

'You didn't have to be so mean,' Ben told Lucy after their father and Charlotte had made their awkward goodbyes and left. Auntie Evie was in the kitchen stacking the dishwasher.

'Now do you believe me? You saw the way she was looking at him,' Lucy hissed.

'Oh my God, don't you ever shut up?'

'If it wasn't for that bitch, mum might still be here.'

'What are you talking about?'

Auntie Evie came in. 'That's everything,' she said, sitting down with a sigh. Without a word Lucy stood up and left the room.

'Goodnight, Auntie Evie,' Ben said and scurried after his sister. He followed her into her room. Lucy was sitting on her bed, her legs stretched out in front of her, a bulging rucksack on her thighs.

'Get out,' she said amiably to Ben. He took her mild manner as an invitation to go in and slumped down on the floor leaning against the door.

'What's the rucksack for?'

'I'm leaving.'

'What do you mean, leaving?'

'Leaving. I'm leaving home.'

'Don't be silly. Where will you go?'

'I've got a friend.'

'What friend?'

'Just a friend. My best friend actually.'

'Who is it?'

'I can't say. I can't trust anyone else.'

'Thanks a lot.' Ben stood up. 'You're such a cow, Lucy.' He went out, slamming the door behind him.

41

CLEAN UP

He gazed around, a bloodied corpse beneath an oil cloth the only blot on the pure white world he had created. It was a shame about the dark streaks of blood staining the walls and floor, but it couldn't be helped. He remembered how he had scrubbed Abigail Kirby's blood from the walls until he had exposed the bare brick beneath the paint. Now he would have to do it all over again, but he didn't really mind; he was glad of the distraction. It was hard work, but he was nearing his goal and soon it would all be over.

The boy hadn't been part of the scheme but his death had been necessary. He had seen too much and had become a threat. If the boy had seen him around and recognised him, the plan could have been ruined. That was unthinkable. He had enough on his plate without wasting energy worrying about someone who got in the way. The boy had brought it on himself.

Cold anger began to swell in his chest because there was no getting away from the fact that it was a nuisance. It should have been the doctor on the table. Now he had another corpse, a boy who had nothing to do with him at all but had just interfered in something that was none of his business. Once he'd moved the body, he would fold the white oil cloth and put it back in the cupboard, and clean the walls and floor again. Only then would he be able to relax. It wasn't important where he left the body. It made no difference to anything. The room was perfect apart from the boy and the splashes of blood on the walls and floor making curious patterns like clumsy grafitti. Soon it would be clean again.

The basement was a large area. When he had finished laying the lino on the floor, there were the walls down the narrow stairs and the ceiling to paint as well as the walls of the cellar space itself, and after that the banisters down the stairs and the tall metal cupboard. It had looked beautiful when he'd finished, but it needed maintenance. Abigail Kirby had made a ghastly mess, and now the boy had blundered in with unfortunate consequences for them both: the boy had to die and as for him, he had to go to the trouble of cleaning up the cellar all over again.

This time he bought the paint in a different location. It was easy enough to find the right paint – white paint was white paint and he'd had the foresight to keep an empty tin in the cupboard so he could find a perfect match, and he knew its name: Brilliant White. He drove out of town to avoid being recognised in the store. As long as he was careful, there would be no problem.

'You doing your paintwork?' the cashier asked as he was fiddling with coins. It wasn't easy with gloves on. As if it was any of her business, he thought, but he knew better than to draw attention to himself so he returned her smile and nodded. A man buying white paint on a busy Saturday was nothing remarkable. She wouldn't remember him.

He bought extra cans of paint, enough to repaint the cellar twice over. He stored all but one of the tins in the cupboard and grinned. Here he could regain his sense of order in a world that had gone spinning out of control. Occasionally it crossed his mind that what he was doing was pointless because it wouldn't bring her back, but he had always been there for her. He couldn't stop now.

The doctor was responsible for two deaths so it was right that he should be executed. It would be soon.

PART 4

'What hands are here! Ha, they pluck out mine eyes.'

Shakespeare

42

GUY

Joe rolled over in bed but couldn't sleep. At the back of his mind he knew he had to get up soon or he'd be late for work. His boss had already been dropping hints about redundancies, regrettable but unavoidable.

'Joe!' Bethany called from the kitchen.

'What?'

'Get up!' She came in and yanked at the duvet.

'Oy, stop it!'

'It's nearly half past seven. You'll be late if you don't get up soon.'

He rolled lazily onto his back. 'You could join me.'

Bethany threw the duvet on him again. 'In your dreams.'

'Yes, there's always that.'

'Come on, I've made breakfast.'

'Now you're talking.' He hauled himself upright and groaned. He'd gone to bed far too late the previous night, completely wasted. He was surprised not to be suffering a worse hangover. Bethany hadn't wanted to watch the display at the recreation ground this year.

'Why not?'

'That woman.'

'What woman?'

'You know. They found some woman's body there in the trees a couple of weeks ago.'

'So? She won't still be there, will she? They don't leave bodies lying around for rats and foxes.'

'Shut up. That's disgusting.'

'Well, what do you suggest then? You want to set off a few damp rockets in the back yard? Like next door aren't going to complain.'

In the end they met their friends at the recreation ground as usual to watch the organised display, and drank far too much. It had been a good night. Bethany leaned over and kissed him but before he could grab hold of her she wriggled away and he soon heard her busy in the kitchen again. With a sigh he rolled out of bed.

'Someone's dumped a guy in the front garden,' Bethany said as Joe sat down. He watched her manoeuvre sausages out of the pan onto a plate.

'What?'

'Someone's left a guy in our front garden. Bloody cheek. You can see it out of the kitchen window.'

'What do you mean?' He gazed at her, bleary eyed.

'Just what I said. A guy – you know, a guy for a bonfire. Some kids have left one out the front.'

He shook his head and started chopping up his sausages. 'Why?'

'I don't know.' She sat down, cradling a mug of coffee in her red hands. 'I suppose they're going to pick it up later. It must be for a bonfire at the weekend.'

'I mean why leave it in our garden?'

'How the hell would I know? Perhaps it was on their way somewhere. I suppose they thought we wouldn't notice.'

Joe tucked into his breakfast. 'I'm going to move it,' he announced as he scraped the last of his ketchup off his plate with the edge of his knife.

'What?'

'That guy in the garden.'

'Where will you put it?'

'I don't know. What difference? I don't want a load of bloody kids tramping around in our garden. Why don't they keep it in their own garden? I'll put it on the pavement. They're lucky we're not having a bonfire of our own this year or I know exactly what I'd do with it.'

'Be careful,' Bethany warned him as she collected his plate.

'Why?'

'I saw a programme on the telly. Some arsehole parked a car on someone else's drive and buggered off on holiday and the people in the house were told if they moved it they'd have to pay for any damage.'

'That's bollocks.'

'I'm telling you, it's true. I saw it on the telly.'

'Well, this isn't a car, it's some kids' guy. And if they don't want it damaged, they shouldn't have left it in our garden. It's ours now, technically.'

'No, it's not. I told you –'

'Don't worry. I'm only going to put it on the pavement. But it's not staying in the garden. I don't want kids tramping around out there.'

Joe stepped outside, whistling. It was a lovely fresh morning. He saw the guy straightaway. Half concealed behind a shrub it was leaning against the fence, a hood pulled low over its face. It was quite lifelike, in proportion and everything. He walked over to grab it under the armpits and was surprised to find it stiff and surprisingly heavy.

'Bloody hell,' Joe gasped. 'What the hell are you made of?' He dropped it with a bump that dislodged the hood, revealing a horrific mask with gaping black holes for eyes. The rest of the face was very realistic, apart from the colouring, a kind of mottled grey, but as he leaned closer Joe saw the skin was pimpled and stubbly. He stepped back in surprise and caught sight of a grey hand, nails bitten to the quick.

'Oh my God!' He leaned forward and touched the guy on the cheek. There was no longer any doubt that he was looking at a dead body. He glanced at the empty eye sockets and looked away quickly, tears prickling at the corners of his own eyes. 'Jesus Christ!' He turned and ran into the street pulling his mobile phone from his pocket, fingers shaking as he punched the key three times. 'Police?'

'Hold on caller, I'm putting you through.'

'Police? I've – he's – there's a body in my garden. It's – he's a boy. He's dead. And someone's left it – him in my front garden. Oh God it's disgusting. Please, please come and take it away.' A dreadful thought struck him. 'Can you come and remove it before Bethany sees it? She'll go mental. She thought it was a guy for bonfire night.'

'What's your address, caller?' Joe gabbled the details. 'And your name, sir?'

'Joe Merton. I'm a plumber,' he added inconsequentially, desperate to cling on to something normal. The voice on the line assured him a patrol car was already on its way and as he hung up he heard a siren. He felt better at once. Now they would come and remove the body and he could forget about it. The dead boy was nothing to do with him, after all. Whoever had killed him had dumped him in Joe's garden, that was all. People probably left their rubbish in other gardens all the time.

Only most people didn't have dead bodies to dispose of.

43

GRIEF

Mrs Mitchell's poorly-dyed blonde hair cut in a loosely curling bob looked as though it hadn't been brushed for days. From a distance she could be mistaken for a much younger woman, with her turned up nose and large childlike eyes that gazed plaintively from beneath her fringe, but close up her face was lined, her eyes weary with age or sickness. She raised her head and looked anxiously from Geraldine to Peterson and back again. 'Have you found my boy?'

Geraldine hesitated. However many times she lived through this scene she knew she would never get used to it. Viewing the dead was harrowing but at least their suffering was over; for the living the anguish had only just begun. It didn't make it any easier, Mrs Mitchell being an invalid. She would find it hard to occupy her mind with other things.

'I'm so sorry, Mrs Mitchell –'

'You have to keep looking. You can't give up now. You have to find him. I've still not heard from him and it's nearly a week now since he went out to the party at Gary's and –'

'Mrs Mitchell,' Geraldine interrupted her. She imagined the distraught mother watching the clock, counting the hours since she had last seen her son.

'If he wants to go – break away, leave all this –' she gestured angrily at her wheelchair, 'tell him it's alright. I don't mind. He's young, he should be out there having a good time, having fun. I've told him so many times. A boy his age shouldn't be stuck at home with his mother every evening. He's got his own life to live. Tell him I can manage –' She broke off. 'Something's

239

happened to him hasn't it? Something's happened to Vernon.'

'Yes, Mrs Mitchell. I'm very sorry to have to tell you this, but Vernon won't be coming home again –'

'Don't talk nonsense. Of course he will. He doesn't have to live here, he doesn't need to feel responsible for me, but he has to come back. He has to come and see me. He has to –' She was crying too hard to speak.

'There's no easy way to tell you this. Vernon was found last night. I'm so sorry, Mrs Mitchell. Your son's dead.'

'No!'

Geraldine took a deep breath. 'His body was found early this morning. We have strong reason to suspect your son was murdered.'

Mrs Mitchell's eyes glittered. 'You can't be sure. A body could be anyone. Some drunk or more likely a drug addict. God knows there are enough of them –'

'It's Vernon, Mrs Mitchell.'

'Just because he hasn't come home this week. He could have had an accident. He might be off with some girl, or asleep. He probably drank too much on Saturday. You know what boys are.' She made a pathetic attempt to laugh. 'What you're suggesting, it's crazy.'

'Mrs Mitchell, please listen –'

'I'm telling you, it's not Vernon. This body you found, it's not Vernon, it can't be. I'd know if it was. You said this person was murdered. Well, there you are. Who would want to kill Vernon?' She shook her head. 'If you knew him, you'd realise what a stupid idea that is.' Geraldine let her talk, giving her time to take in the information about her son's death. 'The body hasn't even been identified, has it? Just because he didn't come home the other night. I wish I'd never reported him missing. Just because some mugger had Vernon's wallet on him you've gone jumping to conclusions –'

'He didn't have a wallet with him.'

'There you are then! It could be anyone. You can't come here telling me Vernon's dead. It's an outrageous idea. What makes you think it's him? How do you even know what he looks like? You show me this body of yours. Go on. Take me to it. Let's sort this out right now.' She was trembling with rage.

'Mrs Mitchell, I'm afraid we will have to ask you or a near relative formally to identify the body but you do need to prepare yourself. It's Vernon.'

'How can you say that, when you've never seen him?'

Geraldine and Peterson exchanged an uneasy glance. 'Mrs Mitchell, Vernon came to the police station recently on two occasions.'

'What?'

'I spoke to him myself.'

'Why? He wasn't in any sort of trouble. My Vernon was never involved in anything – like that. All he ever did was work and worry about me. Work and worry, that was all he ever knew.' Tears rolled down her cheeks.

'He came to see us to report an incident.'

'What incident?' Mrs Mitchell's eyes were puzzled now, suspicious. 'He never said anything to me about it.'

'I'm sorry, Mrs Vernon, but we can't discuss that with you yet. We're involved in an investigation.'

'So Vernon came to see you and instead of protecting him you let him go out on the streets and be killed? Why didn't you keep him safe? Why didn't you take care of him? Why didn't you tell me? Or let me look after him. He's my son.'

Geraldine hesitated.

'We receive a lot of information from the public –' Peterson began.

'He's my son!' The suspicion had vanished, swallowed up in that deep cry of anguish. 'My son!'

The front door slammed and a voice called out, 'Halloo! Anybody home!' The cheery greeting cut across the room like a slap. The door burst open and Carol Middleton entered.

Ruddy from the cold, her face fell when she saw her distraught sister and the police. 'Janice! What on earth's happened? You look terrible.'

Mrs Mitchell shook her head. 'Nothing, Carol. It's nothing. It's not Vernon. It's not Vernon.' She began to rock in her chair shaking her head violently from side to side. As she did so she gave vent to a long wail.

Carol turned to Geraldine. 'I'd like you to leave, now. My sister's not a well woman and mustn't be upset.'

Geraldine shook her head. 'I'm sorry, Mrs Middleton.'

'Oh my God.' Carol sat down in an armchair with a thump. 'What's happened to Vernon?' Mrs Mitchell's wailing increased in volume and Carol ran over and threw her arms around her sister's shoulders. 'Don't get in a state, Janice, we'll sort this out. Whatever trouble he's got himself into, I'll find him the best lawyer. The best. He's been under pressure. He's been led astray –'

'No.'

'He's a good boy,' Carol continued.

'No, it's no good – you can't –' Mrs Mitchell began to choke.

'Calm down, Janice. Come on, deep breaths. We'll get through this. I'm here. Now,' she turned to Geraldine, her eyes blazing. 'I'd like you to leave and in future you can deal with me. Leave my sister alone. She's not in a fit state to deal with stress, as you can see. Now Janice, whatever's happened, I'm sure we can sort it out. We'll get him the best legal –'

Geraldine made no move to leave. 'I'm very sorry to have to tell you Vernon's dead.'

'Dead? Vernon?' Carol fell back into her chair. 'Is it true?'

Geraldine inclined her head. 'I'm so sorry. Will Mrs Mitchell be all right? If you'd like me to call her doctor –'

'I'd like you and your sergeant to leave. Now!'

'Someone will have to come and identify the body. Perhaps you...'

'Yes. Yes, of course. Now please, leave us alone.'

'We would like to ask Mrs Mitchell a few questions when she feels ready.'

'Questions? Why?'

'We have reason to believe your nephew was murdered.'

Geraldine nodded at Peterson and they made their way to the door. Geraldine turned as she was leaving. 'I'm so sorry for your loss,' she mumbled miserably.

'Jesus,' Peterson grumbled as they walked to the car. 'Talk about shooting the messenger. I thought we were supposed to be the good guys.'

44

CORPSE

'An unusual corpse,' Paul Hilliard announced as they entered the room.

'What does a usual murder victim look like?' Kathryn Gordon asked. 'I thought –' She stopped abruptly, catching sight of the body lying on the stainless steel mortuary table. For a moment they all stood gazing down in silence.

'Oh my God,' Geraldine said.

Peterson spoke at the same time. 'Bloody hell. What have you done to the poor boy?'

'That's how he was found,' Paul replied quietly. 'The extent of the mutilation wasn't apparent until we'd cleaned him up but you can see for yourselves. Whoever killed him removed both eyes.'

Geraldine tried to connect the sightless figure in front of her with the boy who had been to see her at the police station. The body was pale, lying rigid on its back where it had been placed. While some corpses seemed relaxed in that position, almost as though they were sleeping, Vernon Mitchell looked tense and awkward. Her gaze travelled reluctantly to his face, the eye sockets pools of congealed blood.

Kathryn Gordon was the first to recover. 'Do you think this is the work of whoever killed Abigail Kirby?'

Above his mask, Paul frowned. 'It's hard to be sure but it looks like it. We have a similar set of injuries – a blow on the back of the head with a blunt instrument, sufficient to knock the victim out but not kill him instantly. If the cerebral bleed from the head wound hadn't killed him, he would in all likelihood have suffered irreparable brain damage. There are the similar patterns of bruising on the upper arms as we observed on Abigail Kirby's cadaver, and he was tied up, before he died.' He pointed to Vernon's wrists and ankles where fine darkish lines were clearly visible, like grim tattoos on the pale flesh.

'And what about this business with the eyes?' the DCI asked. 'What can you tell us about that?'

'The eyes were removed while the victim was still alive.'

Peterson let out an involuntary groan and hurried from the room. Geraldine registered the sergeant's distress but was too engrossed in what Paul was saying to pay him any attention. As she listened she stared at Vernon's face, thinking back to the boy who had been to see her at the station, anxious but alive, and his mother's accusation. Geraldine should have taken Vernon's fears seriously and offered him police protection. If she had made the right decision then, he would still be alive now.

'It must have been excruciating,' Kathryn Gordon said. 'This was not only murder, but torture.'

'Not necessarily,' the pathologist replied in an even tone. 'There are traces of a strong sedative in his blood. I'll be able to tell you more when the tox report's back, but the drug might have acted as an analgesic. Vernon might have suffered very little pain.'

'Oh, well that's all right then,' Peterson snapped as he rejoined them, pale and drawn. 'A considerate killer. We can all go to sleep happy now.'

Paul ignored the interruption. 'So in answer to your original question, yes, I think we're probably looking at the handiwork of the same killer. It's another neat job. The left eye was removed while the victim was still alive – there was a lot of bleeding. By the time the right eye was removed, the victim was dead. The cause of death was cerebral bleeding, and the shock of the blood loss probably speeded up the process.'

'Abigail Kirby had her tongue cut out as she lay dying. Vernon Mitchell's eyes were removed as he was dying. What the hell's going on here?' Peterson sounded agitated. 'This is –' He stopped, lost for words. 'It's hideous. It makes no sense.'

'We can't expect this to make sense as we know it,' Geraldine said, 'but we have to try and understand what's going on here, because there is a kind of logic to it. What is he thinking as he carries out this mutilation? And why is he doing it?' She didn't add the question uppermost in all their minds: what did the killer have in mind for his next victim?

'We haven't found the tongue, or the eyes,' Kathryn Gordon pointed out. 'Is he keeping them as trophies?'

'Jesus,' the sergeant turned away again.

'Perhaps we're looking for a modern Frankenstein, collecting body parts for a new creature,' Paul suggested lightly.

'Victor Frankenstein robbed graves, and gathered human material from corpses. He didn't go around killing people for their body parts.' Geraldine said sharply.

'Let's stick to the point, shall we?' Kathryn Gordon said. 'This isn't a seminar on Gothic literature.' She turned to Paul. 'What was the time of death?'

'Sometime around midnight on Thursday night, between eleven and one. I can't be more specific than that.'

'Which makes it around seven hours before he was found,' the DCI said.

'And almost a week after the party at Gary's where he was last seen alive,' Geraldine added.

The DCI turned to Paul, suddenly brisk. 'You'll let us have a full report as soon as you can.' She was ready to leave.

He inclined his head. 'And the tox report when it comes through.'

'So there's no sign of a struggle?' Peterson asked. 'Seems odd, doesn't it, with a young male victim.'

The pathologist shook his head. 'He was tied up,' he pointed out.

'But before that?'

'He could have been knocked out before he had a chance to fight back. He'd certainly consumed a lot of alcohol and, unless he was a hardened drinker, he would have been virtually incapable of walking, let alone placing a punch.'

'Is it possible he was sedated?' Peterson asked.

'With something like chloroform, you mean?' Geraldine said.

Paul considered. 'It's possible, but any trace would have evaporated by the time he was found. Remember, he was found hours later, in the open air.'

'Enough speculation,' Kathryn Gordon said. 'We'll discuss the possibilities again when we have the report.'

As soon as they arrived back at the police station, Kathryn Gordon held a meeting to bring the rest of the team up to speed.

'Is it a coincidence that Vernon Mitchell was killed – possibly by the same person that killed Abigail Kirby – shortly after he gave evidence pertaining to Abigail Kirby's murder? Evidence that, so far, hasn't given us any useful leads. It's too much of a stretch to think his death was a coincidence. All of this suggests the murderer knew that Vernon had been to the police.'

'He was killed to stop him from identifying the murderer. It all points to the figure we can't identify on the CCTV tape,' Peterson said excitedly. 'We have to track that figure down.' A couple of constables exchanged a glance. They had been painstakingly checking all the CCTV footage from the shopping centre, while a team had been out on foot, questioning shoppers and staff. No one had been able to recognise the shadowy figure in grey.

'His eyes were removed because of what he'd seen,' Geraldine was thinking aloud. 'Was Abigail Kirby's tongue cut out because of something she'd said?'

'That's stupid,' someone replied.

'Insane, yes, but not stupid. It's perfectly logical. Don't forget we're dealing with someone insane enough not only to kill but to mutilate his – or her – victims. A killer who cuts out a woman's tongue, or a boy's eyes, while they're dying, isn't following any normal rules.'

'Are we saying that whoever killed Vernon Mitchell knew he'd been here to talk to us?' Kathryn Gordon asked. There was a change in the atmosphere now they had something positive to work on. Everyone Vernon might have spoken to would be interviewed again. Geraldine and Peterson discussed the possibilities over a coffee as they waited for the duty sergeant to post a schedule for the day.

Peterson was worried. 'Vernon might have talked to any number of people, gov. And he could have been overheard talking about it to his mates or his colleagues at work.'

'Yes, he might've told anyone.'

Neither of them raised the only other possibility, that the killer hadn't found out about Vernon's visits to the police station through anything Vernon had said. If that was the case it meant they were looking for someone who was working alongside them on the murder team.

45

STORE

The shopping centre was deserted as Geraldine and Peterson walked through it early on Saturday morning.

'It must be so boring, working here,' the sergeant muttered.

'I suppose it's better later on, when it gets busier. It's only nine o'clock.'

'Yes, the great unwashed are all at home sleeping off their hangovers. Lucky sods.'

A balding man in a WH Smith's uniform came up to them and introduced himself as Tim Morris, the store manager. 'You must be the police inspector who phoned. Thank you for coming in so early. It can get a bit manic here later on.' He glanced around the shop floor. 'You can never tell. A lot depends on the weather. Who wants to be stuck indoors on a lovely sunny day? But when it rains they all troop in.'

'I expect it helps to pass the time, when you're busy,' Peterson said.

The manager gave him a quick, nervous smile. 'I've managed to get cover for today. One of my regular staff is coming in and taking a weekday off in lieu. I can't be short staffed on a Saturday, not if I can help it anyway. We're already understaffed as it is.'

Geraldine cut in. 'We'd like to speak to everyone who worked with Vernon, individually.'

The manager's face fell. 'Poor Vernon. What a terrible thing to happen. It was murder, you said?'

'I'm afraid there's little doubt about that, but we don't have any details as yet.'

'He was such a nice, unassuming, young man. Of course we're all happy to talk to you, if you think there's any chance we could say something that might help your investigation. I've put my little office at your disposal. It's not very grand, I'm afraid, but it's private. If you'd like to come this way.'

He led them up two narrow flights of stairs to a small whitewashed room with several slightly battered office chairs and a desk with a computer humming on it.

'Were any of your staff particularly close to Vernon?' Geraldine asked as she sat down. 'Did he have any particular friends here?'

The manager considered before shaking his head. 'I've got to say we all genuinely work well together, that's our ethos here. We're a strong team.'

'Were you aware of any concerns he had recently? We're particularly interested in the two weeks before he died. Did he mention anything that was worrying him?'

'No. He seemed perfectly fine.'

'And you're sure there's no one here he might have confided in?'

'Well, everyone here gets on pretty well, by and large. Most of my staff have been here for several years. Of course Vernon was relatively new, and not on the permanent staff.'

'He had no particular friends then?'

'No. But I'm sure if he'd been worried about anything he'd have spoken to me. I'm the manager.'

To begin with, talking to the other members of staff proved heavy going. They started by interviewing Bobby, the other young male shop assistant who seemed the most likely to have struck up a friendship with Vernon. The only other male shop assistant, Simon, was in his forties, like the manager. Bobby didn't appear particularly upset by his colleague's death and was almost too intimidated to answer when Geraldine asked him about Vernon.

'He was all right.'

'Were you friendly with him?'

'He was all right,' he repeated.

'Were you mates?' Peterson pressed the point.

'What, me and Vernon?'

'Yes.'

Bobby deliberated for a moment. 'No.'

The next interviewee, Jill, was more forthcoming. 'Vernon fancied Susie,' she told them before they had even posed their first question.

'Susie?'

'Susie Downes. She works here. Vernon was mad about her. If anyone knows anything about Vernon, it's Susie. I mean, there was nothing going on between them, not like that, he's hardly her type. Or he wasn't, I should say. But they used to chat a lot. Wherever she was, he'd pop up sooner or later. Poor Vernon. He wasn't a bad sort, a bit quiet, not very confident, but decent enough. He wasn't the sort you'd expect to be caught up in anything like this.'

'Like what?'

'Tim said Vernon was murdered.' She gazed at them, wide-eyed. 'Do you think – I mean, it could have been any of us, couldn't it? Do you think someone's out to get us?'

'No. This was personal, Jill.' Geraldine paused. 'Did you know that Vernon had been to see us?'

'No. What's going on?'

'I'm afraid we can't give you that information as yet. It's still a live investigation.'

'Wow!'

'I'm sorry?'

'I'll go and get Susie, shall I?'

'Thank you. And if you do think of anything about Vernon that might help us in our enquiries, please call this number. Ask for me, Detective Inspector Steel.'

Susie was a platinum blonde girl with knowing eyes. She must have been waiting just outside because she came in straightaway. She sized the sergeant up as soon as she walked in and directed most of her answers his way, regardless of which of the two police officers had asked the question.

'Susie, we understand you were friendly with Vernon Mitchell?'

'Poor Vernon. Jill told me. It was murder, wasn't it? Who would want to kill Vernon? He was harmless.' She sat down, crossed her legs and glanced up at Peterson under her long eyelashes. 'He had a bit of a thing for me – a lot of boys do for some reason – but he was a really sweet boy. He didn't deserve to be killed.'

'No one does,' Geraldine replied bluntly. Susie continued to stare at Peterson who looked at the floor. 'Susie, did Vernon talk about anything that was worrying him recently? Only he came to see us –'

'About that bloke he saw in the queue, having a bit of a barney with his old headmistress, was it? Good. I told him to tell you lot, because I could see he was worried –' She broke off suddenly and slapped her palms against her cheeks. 'Oh my God, he was killed because of that, wasn't he? And it's all my fault!'

'Your fault?'

'Yes, don't you get it? He only came to see you because I told him to. He never would have told you about that man otherwise. And that's why he was killed. It's all my fault.' She dabbed at her eyes, checking the black smudges on her tissue. 'It's my fault, isn't it? What shall I do?' The sergeant didn't answer.

Geraldine handed Susie a card. 'If you can think of anything else that might help us please talk to one of our constables.'

Susie nodded her thanks. She was crying in earnest now, genuinely upset, as if the truth of the death was only now finally striking her. 'He was a nice guy – just a nice guy.'

It didn't take long to interview the rest of the staff. None of them had spent much time with Vernon, but they all agreed he was a decent lad, sweet on Susie.

'You can't blame him for that, mind,' Tim added. 'If I was twenty-one I'd have a go at her myself. She's a good-looking girl.'

'You know, gov, when Susie asked me what she should do, it was on the tip of my tongue to tell her to grow up,' Peterson said as they left the store.

Geraldine laughed. 'She wasn't that bad, just young and enjoying the effect of her good looks. And she was the only one who seemed actually upset about Vernon's death. Shame she's an unreliable witness. I'm not sure we can take what she says at face value.'

46

IMPATIENCE

Lucy opened her eyes and strained to see her watch in the darkness. It was nearly half past one in the morning but she had distinctly heard footsteps on the stairs. She lay on her back, rigid, listening. A door was opening very slowly. Someone was walking around, and they were trying to be quiet. That could only mean one thing. There was a burglar in the house. Suddenly she couldn't stand it any longer, waiting in ignorance in pitch black. If the intruder saw her light was on he would probably leave her alone and, if she was going to be attacked, at least her assailant wouldn't have the benefit of surprise. With the light on she felt less vulnerable but she glanced repeatedly at the door as she rummaged in her bag for her phone. It wasn't there. She remembered she had received a call earlier on, some idiot from school calling her names, and she had switched it off and flung it across the room.

As she stared at the door she thought the handle moved. She waited, holding her breath, but nothing happened. A memory of her mother flashed into her mind. She wouldn't have crouched by the bed, trembling with fear. She would have been more likely to go out there and give the burglar what for. Lucy took a step forward, and looked around for a weapon. Seizing her hockey stick she crossed the room and opened the door as quietly as she could. The landing was empty. She took a few steps along the landing, brandishing the hockey stick in front of her face. Her eyes fell on her watch and she realised she'd misread the time in her panic. It wasn't half past one but nearly ten past six. She paused. It seemed a funny time for a burglar to break into the house, when the residents might be waking up. Some people were early risers. From behind her father's door came the unmistakable sound of a toilet flushing in his en suite. Lucy scowled, vexed that he had been out all night with his woman friend, but relieved at the same time. Before she turned to go back to her own room his door flew open and her father peered out. He was in his pyjamas. Behind him she could see the duvet lying smooth on his bed.

'Lucy!' He whispered. He was smiling but she could tell he was surprised. 'What are you doing up?'

'I was just going to the toilet.'

'With your hockey stick?'

'Oh, I have to do exercises, to strengthen my arms...' The worst of it was that he didn't even stop to consider how weird that was. He just nodded and went back in his room.

Lucy went back to her room and leant her stupid hockey stick against the wall. She hated hockey but the school made them play so her mother had bought her a stick of her own. She climbed back into bed but couldn't sleep. She had been awake since six, which was really annoying because the weekend was the only time she didn't have to get up early. It was all her stupid father's fault.

She couldn't sleep so she got up at seven and logged on but Zoe wasn't online. She hesitated before checking her Facebook page but it was only more mean comments from girls at school. 'Sorry about your accident' when she hadn't had one, and some really horrible anonymous messages. She had thought of going to the police at one point, or at least telling her mother, but while she had been worrying about what to do Zoe had come along and advised her to just ignore it.

'They'll soon lose interest,' her friend had told her. 'If you don't take any notice they'll stop bothering you, but the more you react, the more they'll pester you. Close your account and forget about it. No one looks at other people's Facebook pages anyway.' It was sound advice. She had told those idiots at school that she'd closed her account but that wasn't true. She couldn't resist reading the comments, like picking at a scab. At least she and Zoe had arranged to meet up on instant messenger. Having just one good friend made everything bearable.

Lucy's week at school had been horrible again. She had done her best to keep away from the worst of the bullies but she couldn't avoid them in all her lessons where they tripped her up, moved her bag, jacketed her pens and books and flicked hard little balls of chewed up paper at her face.

'Who threw that?' the teacher would snap but no one ever owned up. Occasionally someone called out Lucy's name and Lucy would deny having thrown anything. As the teacher continued the lesson a low chant would break out at the back of the class, 'Lucy, Lucy, teacher's pet.' Break times were the worst, when they surrounded her with jeers and insults.

They had laid off her for a few days.

'Leave the freak alone, can't you? She lost her mother.'

'Yeah, her mother's dead. Lay off.'

It was only two weeks since her mother's death and Lucy had only been back at school for a week but they had already resumed their teasing. By the end of the week even the school nurse was less sympathetic.

'You need to try and settle back into your lessons, Lucy. I know it sounds harsh, but it's for your own good. Now, let's see you making an effort to get back to normal next week. I know it's going to take time, and of course you can come up here if you need to, but it's really best if you try to carry on with your lessons if you possibly can. Otherwise you're going to have work to catch up with on top of everything else, and the last thing you want now is more stress in your life.'

'Yes, sister,' Lucy agreed. As if she gave a toss about her school work, with her mother murdered and her father shagging some stranger.

She had nothing else to do, so she unpacked and repacked her rucksack again. It was still only half past seven. She went downstairs, made herself some breakfast, and took it up to her room and stuffed herself until Zoe came online.

'At last!' she typed.

'Been waiting?'

'Yes. I have to get away.'

'You can come this weekend!'

'Yay!'

Someone banged on her door. 'Go away!' she yelled. The door flew open and Ben entered. 'I told you not to come in here.'

'You told me not to come in without knocking. I knocked.'

'Get out!'

'Aunty Evie wants to know if you're coming down for breakfast. I only came in to ask.'

'Well I'm not. So now you know you can get out! And don't come back!' she shouted at his retreating back.

She returned to her screen. 'Sorry, my stupid brother came in.'

'Has he gone?'

'Yes. So?'

'I just spoke to my dad. He's cool to drive me over tomorrow afternoon.'

'Are you sure?'

'It's not that far.'

'Great! I'm packed. What time?'

'Six.'

'It'll be dark.'

'That's OK.'

'I'll be at the corner of Belvedere Road and Western Lane

at six. How will I know it's you?'

'We'll be in a battered old black van – and don't forget the password!'

'No worries.'

'See you tomorrow.'

'Can't wait!' Lucy logged off instant messenger, closed her account, and shut down her computer. This had to work.

47

IDENTIFICATION

Vernon's aunt bustled into the entry hall, red faced and strident.

'Ah, there you are,' she hailed Geraldine, as though she had just spent hours searching for her. 'Come on, then, let's get this over with. I'm sure it's all some dreadful mistake. There's no way Vernon would have got himself involved in anything – anything like this.'

'Mrs Middleton, you need to prepare yourself. I'm afraid you're about to view your nephew's body –'

'Now let's not start jumping to conclusions,' the stout woman's voice boomed across the hallway. 'Whoever it is you have in here hasn't been identified yet. You can't possibly be sure it's Vernon.'

'I met your nephew twice, and I'm afraid there's no doubt. It's him.'

'Hmmph. Well, come on then, show me.' She glared as though challenging Geraldine to do her worst.

'I have to warn you, this was not an accidental death and it wasn't a simple murder. He's been damaged.'

Carol Middleton stared, her eyes wide, her voice suddenly low. 'You mean – someone interfered with him?'

'Not sexually. But his face has been altered.'

'What?' Carol frowned, uncomprehending. 'What are you talking about?'

'The killer mutilated his body. He removed his eyes. Vernon wouldn't have felt anything,' Geraldine added quickly, regardless of the truth, 'but you need to be prepared for what you're about to see. And you'll have to decide if you want the body returned to you in its present state for burial – if your sister should see him as he is. His eyelids can be reconstructed, of course, but if the papers get hold of this… '

'Oh my God,' Carol's face had lost its ruddy glow. 'Can we get this over with, please?' She followed Geraldine submissively into the viewing room and gazed at Vernon's eyeless face, her countenance almost as pale as his.

'Mrs Middleton, can you confirm this is your nephew, Vernon Mitchell?'

Carol whimpered and her bulky frame shook. 'It's him, oh God, it's him. What am I going to say to Janice?' She buried her face in her hands and her voice came out muffled. 'Take it away, please, take it away.'

Geraldine covered Vernon's face and steered the crying woman back into the hall. 'I'm so sorry, Mrs Middleton. We're doing everything we can to find out who committed this terrible crime.'

'Why?' Carol dropped her hands and stared at Geraldine in bewilderment. 'Why would anyone do that? Why kill him? And – Why? He was a nice boy. He was so good with my sister. God knows she hasn't got much in her life. What's going to happen to her now? Oh God.' She broke down in tears.

Geraldine led her to a chair. 'Sit down, Mrs Middleton and take your time. You're in shock. It's only natural.'

'How was it?' Peterson asked.

'Carol Middleton identified him. She took it badly, but that's understandable. He's not a pretty sight.'

'I thought they did a good job on him, considering.'

'But he was her nephew, and he was only a kid.'

'How about you, gov?'

'Me?'

'Are you OK?'

Geraldine shrugged. 'Some seem worse than others, that's all. But it's the same job to be done, so what's next?'

Vernon's colleague Susie was in the station waiting to be interviewed again. There was a possibility she might be able to give them more information.

'That's one for you, gov,' the sergeant said, his expression uneasy.

Geraldine smiled. 'I would have thought you'd be up for this one. She's an attractive girl. And more to the point, she seemed to like you. Don't you think she might open up to you?'

'Spin me a line, more like. No gov, take it from me, if a girl like that is going to talk sense – which I doubt – it's going to be to another woman.'

Susie was looking at the door, her lips arranged in a pout, when Geraldine entered the interview room.

Her face fell but she recovered quickly and greeted Geraldine brightly. 'Hello. Is the sergeant coming too?'

'No, it's just me, I'm afraid.'

'That's OK.' Geraldine was relieved that Susie didn't seem put out. She leaned forward. 'Just girls together, eh?'

Geraldine smiled thinly. 'Yes. I want you to think very carefully, Susie. What you have to tell us could make a crucial difference to our investigation into Vernon's murder.'

'It was definitely murder then?'

'Yes. There's no question about it.'

'How horrible. He was a really sweet boy, you know, and he had this thing about me.' Tears sparkled at the corner of her eyes.

Geraldine handed her a tissue. 'You know Vernon came to see us.' Susie nodded and blew her nose loudly. 'You know he was worried. He confided in you, didn't he?' Susie nodded again, with slightly less certainty. 'Did Vernon ever mention anyone, or say anything about anyone he thought might be threatening him?' She waited. 'Was he scared of anyone in particular?'

'Yes. He said he saw a man arguing with that woman who was murdered and then he said someone followed him home. He was scared, proper scared, so I told him to go to the police. I mean, I didn't know who was following him. I told him to see you lot. You're the ones who should've helped him. What was I supposed to do about it?'

'Susie, listen to me. No one's accusing you of not doing everything you could to help Vernon. You were a good friend to him – probably his only friend. As far as we knew, you were the only person he talked to about this.'

'I told you, he had a thing about me. I would've helped him if I could. He was a sweet boy. But what could I do?'

'Susie, this is important. Did Vernon tell you who was frightening him? Did he say anything about the man he saw in the queue? Was that the man he thought followed him home?'

Susie thought for a moment, chewing her thumb. 'I don't know.'

'Are you sure there's nothing else Vernon told you?'

'Yes.'

'This is very important now, Susie.'

'Everything's bloody important to you,' Susie grumbled.

'Just one more question. Did you tell anyone about your conversations with Vernon? About what was worrying him?' Susie shook her head at once. 'Are you sure, Susie? You didn't tell anyone?'

'Only Jill at work. It's not as if it was a big secret. We even had a laugh about it,' she added wretchedly, 'about Vernon and his stupid ideas. Honestly, we just thought he was being daft. I mean, who'd want to stalk him?'

'Someone did.'

48

ARGUMENT

Ian sometimes felt he was in the wrong job. Far from objecting to viewing bodies at a crime scene, he found that aspect of the job intriguing and wildly exciting because there was always the possibility he might spot a vital clue that would lead to an arrest. Preoccupied with scanning the ground for clues about what had happened, the presence of death almost passed him by, although that was the reason he was there.

Visits to the morgue, on the other hand, made him physically nauseous. After so many cases, he didn't think he would ever become immune to the horror of witnessing an autopsy against a brightly lit backdrop, everything focused on cadavers and body parts, as gloved hands deliberately lacerated human flesh while his senses reeled from the stench of antiseptic and death. More experienced officers had reassured him that he would grow accustomed to it, and the horror of his first visit would fade to a dim recollection. Ian never admitted to reliving that horror every time he entered the morgue. As he left, he struggled to shake off the image of Vernon Mitchell's empty eye sockets which had seemed to be staring straight at him, a physical symbol of the sightless dead. With sickening certainty, Ian knew he would have nightmares about it but he couldn't tell anyone. He knew what Bev's response would be.

He felt a huge sense of relief as he drove away from the station to spend a quiet evening with his girl. Hopefully he could forget all about Vernon Mitchell for a few hours.

'Come on,' Bev burst out, as soon as he stepped into the hall.

'What?'

'I don't want to be late. It's embarrassing. Everyone's going to be there.'

Ian groaned as he remembered their plans to meet up with friends that evening. He stared at her in dismay, registering her neatly brushed short cropped blonde hair, and carefully made up face. 'Just give me a moment to get changed –'

'Ian, there's no time. I've been waiting for half an hour. Where have you been?'

'I'll only be a second.' He ran past her up the stairs, barely trusting himself not to break out in a rage. While she'd been at home seeing to her hair, painting her nails and deciding which blouse to wear, he'd been investigating the murder of a boy whose eyes had been cut out. Not for the first time he wondered what the hell he was doing, with Bev, with his job, with his life. By the time he'd showered and changed he had come to the conclusion that it was a very good thing they were going out. It would help to take his mind off Vernon Mitchell. He hurried downstairs, kissed Bev lightly on the lips, and followed her out of the house. She was still grumbling about being late, but he could tell she didn't really mind.

'We're always late.'

'Can I help it if your boyfriend has such an important job?' he teased her and she turned away, smiling. It occurred to Ian that she was proud of what he did and an unexpected burst of happiness swept through him. Suddenly he no longer cared about the sightless boy, he felt so full of life and joy.

The row on their way home came from nowhere. By the time they reached the bedroom, Bev was refusing to speak to him but he knew an outburst wasn't far off. He saw her lower lip trembling. With cold determination he suppressed any impulse to be sympathetic. He was damned if he was going to allow her to manipulate him with her tears this time and besides, it wasn't his fault.

'Why don't you run off back to your precious inspector?'

'This has nothing to do with Geraldine.'

'Oh, it's Geraldine now, is it?'

'So you're throwing a tantrum because my boss has a name?' He knew she'd seize on the word but he was reckless in his misery.

'Tantrum? I'm not a bloody child!'

'Stop behaving like one then.'

She turned to him, her face contorted in rage. 'Me? You've got the gall to stand there and accuse me of being childish?'

'It was your word.' His calmness provoked her, as he knew it would.

'Take a look at yourself! You're nothing but a spoilt brat. Everything always has to go your way, doesn't it? It's always about you and what you want. I ask you one little favour, to be home on time, and do you do it?' Ian shrugged and made for the door. 'Don't you walk out on me!' she shrieked, beside herself with fury.

It struck Ian that he could do just that, walk out and never come back to her mood swings and her unreasonable demands. He spun round to face her. 'You think I wouldn't do just that?'

'Do what?'

'Walk out!'

'Don't be ridiculous.' Ian slammed the door on his way out. 'And don't slam the door,' she yelled after him.

As he went downstairs, Ian ignored the sound of her crying. She was putting it on for his benefit. Why else would her tears be audible through the closed door? 'Not interested,' he said aloud. 'Cry all you want. At least you've got eyes left to cry with.' In a sudden rage he shouted out loud. 'It's over, you sad bitch. I'm leaving and I won't be back!'

He drove aimlessly for a while, then parked the car and

walked, fast. It began to rain but he kept walking as though to put some distance between himself and Bev, and the blinded boy lying in a drawer in the morgue.

It was late when Ian returned home. If she was asleep, he vowed he'd leave her for good but Bev was waiting up for him. He barely had time to take in her eyes, swollen with tears, her face blotchy from crying, before she launched herself at him, shuddering in his arms in a paroxysm of sobbing. 'I'm sorry,' she mumbled and hiccuped, over and over again. 'I'm sorry for everything.'

'You don't know the half of it,' he thought as he held her close and kissed her hair, breathing in the comfort of her familiar scent. 'I'll never leave you, you know that,' he whispered.

'And I'll never leave you,' she replied.

Ian shivered as he gently kissed her inflamed eyelids.

49

SECRETS

There was a time when they had kept secrets together: the wooden chest hidden away in the garden shed, the hole in the trunk of the old willow tree at the bottom of the garden... Now he had a new secret. It was her secret too, even though she was no longer there to share it. People made a fuss about death but what difference would it make if he added three more bodies to the legions of the dead?

Everything was approaching its logical conclusion: his own death. Life held no hope of happiness, only the bleak satisfaction of knowing he had settled the score. After the girl had been punished, it had been the turn of the teacher. Only the doctor remained, the doctor who should be using his skill to save life, not waste it. Then it would all be over; the avenger could find peace.

He'd made sure the deaths couldn't be traced back to him and if his identity was ever discovered it wouldn't matter because he would already be dead. Nevertheless he wouldn't cut corners. Most killers gave themselves away with foolish oversights, avoidable lapses in concentration, but he was too clever for that. He'd always been superior to everyone around him when it came to intelligence, and that was what counted because you could work out how to achieve anything if you were smart enough. Tracking down his quarry had taken time but he had been patient. First the girl, then the teacher. Now only the doctor was left. But not for long.

After sitting motionless for a moment in his white cellar, lost in memories, he sprang over to the tall white cupboard, unlocked it, pulled open a drawer and selected a photograph. The eyes of the dead stared back at him, heedless. She looked so young it made his eyes water.

'It won't be long now,' he whispered. 'They'll all be punished for what they did. All of them.' She would have been pleased. The young had a strong sense of justice. With a sigh he replaced the photograph gently in the drawer of the white cupboard.

White for a bride. White for a shroud.

50

DISSATISFACTION

'So if Susie told her colleague, Jill, who seems to be a bit of a gossip, we can assume the staff all knew about Vernon's suspicions,' Geraldine told Peterson when they met for a quick lunch in the police station canteen on Sunday.

'Either Susie or Jill were bound to have told them. You know how rumours spread at work.'

'Vernon saw Abigail Kirby in the queue at WH Smith's on Saturday the twenty-fourth of October. Anyone could have spoken to any of the staff between then and the fifth November when he was killed, and found out Vernon had seen her talking to someone just before she was killed. If her killer knew that, and thought Vernon could identify him –'

'And found out Vernon had talked to us –'

'That's nearly two weeks for the staff to have chattered among themselves and we don't know who else they might have talked to.' Geraldine took a gulp of coffee. 'Let's assume for a moment the killer was the man Vernon saw in the queue. He could have talked to staff in the shop and found out he'd been seen talking to his victim shortly before he killed her.'

Peterson nodded. 'It's such a pity we can't get a better image from the CCTV. It's useless really.'

'Useless,' Geraldine agreed. 'A tall figure in a dark jacket. And of course the security guard didn't see anything.'

The sergeant nodded and shovelled a mouthful of beans into his mouth. 'And there's still the other possibility,' he added after washing his beans down with a swig of tea. He glanced around before meeting Geraldine's gaze and lowering his voice. 'Hasn't it occurred to you that one of our colleagues could be the killer?'

'You don't really believe that?'

'No, of course I don't. But you always say we have to keep an open mind, and consider every possibility, and all I'm saying is it's possible.'

They returned to the incident room and Geraldine made her way to her desk to sort through her paperwork before leaving for the afternoon. In some ways she wasn't sorry to be going out. Everyone was irritable. The investigation had been going on for two weeks, but it felt more like two months; not only were they no closer to making an arrest, with their main suspect cleared, but now a witness had been killed. The case couldn't be going much worse and all they had to go on was a shadowy figure on a CCTV film who might have nothing to do with Abigail Kirby's murder at all. He could have been a stranger standing next to her in a queue, cross at being jostled. In any case, their only eye witness was now dead. It seemed hopeless.

Geraldine had arranged to take her niece out that afternoon but being involved in a case wasn't a good time. She phoned her sister and tried to convince her it might be best to postpone the visit.

'It'll probably be fine,' she capitulated under pressure from her sister, 'but if I get called, I'll have to go.'

'Surely a few hours won't make any difference to anything.'

'It could do. It really is important to view a crime scene promptly before it can be contaminated, and witnesses have to be interviewed as soon as possible, while they can still remember something of what they've seen. I know it sounds very melodramatic, but time really is of the essence.'

'It's not exactly a matter of life and death,' Celia argued. 'I mean, with your work the victim's are already dead before you start, aren't they?'

'But it can make the difference between making an arrest and putting a murderer safely behind bars, or letting him slip away, free to walk the streets.'

'Yes, yes, I know. Spare me the lecture. If it wasn't for you we'd all be at risk of being murdered in our beds. Honestly, Geraldine, I don't know how you can do it, looking at all those dead people all the time. I mean, it's one thing watching murder stories on the telly when it's all made up, but what you do – well, I don't know how you can do it. But I don't want to argue. The point is, Chloe's expecting to see you. You can't let her down again.'

Celia's efforts to forge a relationship between Geraldine and her niece had intensified since the death of their mother. Geraldine realised she was being leaned on to fill that gap but couldn't really blame her sister. It was fair enough for Celia to look after her daughter's interests and it was important for Chloe to build strong bonds with adults other than her parents, but Geraldine could have done without that additional pressure on her time right now.

'Good,' Celia beamed when she opened the door. 'We've got you all to ourselves for an afternoon.'

Geraldine nodded warily. 'Celia, I can't switch my phone off –'

'What do you mean? You agreed –'

'Look, it's very unlikely I'll be called. They'll only contact me if there's another death, in which case I'll have to go. I'll need to be able to contact you, in the unlikely event that something happens, so if you go out, can you make sure you take your mobile?'

'I've got a hair appointment –' Celia protested.

'Fine. Where and what time? If there's an emergency I can drop Chloe off at the hairdresser's.'

'Oh for goodness sake, do you have to make a drama out of everything?'

Chloe caught sight of Geraldine standing on the doorstep and her face lit up. She ran up past her mother and flung her arms around her aunt. 'Aunty Geraldine. I knew you'd come. Mummy said you'd cancel, but I knew you'd be here.'

'Now tell me, where would you like to go this afternoon? I'm guessing the cinema, or shopping. Which is it to be?'

Chloe considered. 'It's too hard to choose,' she said at last. 'Can't we do both?'

Geraldine laughed. 'So it's the cinema and shopping?'

Chloe clapped her hands. 'Or we could just go shopping. Are you feeling rich today, Aunty Geraldine?'

'Yes. I'm feeling quite rich and in the mood for shopping.'

'Me too. I'm in the mood for shopping too!'

'Let's go shopping then.' She turned to her sister. 'What time do you want me to bring her back?'

'Shall we say six-thirty? Seven the latest.' Celia smiled. 'You look more relaxed already, Geraldine. Just enjoy the afternoon. You know you work far too hard.'

Geraldine nodded. Celia was right. She owed it to her niece to make the afternoon fun, and it would certainly do her good to have a break from the pressures of the investigation. But as she strode into the shopping centre with Chloe at her side, Geraldine couldn't help thinking about a young man killed and mutilated because of what he'd witnessed in another shopping centre not far away.

51

LEAVING

A black van came rattling along the street, battered, scratched and filthy. Lucy yanked her rucksack off her back and cradled it in her arms, suddenly nervous as the van slowed down and drew into the kerb. She bent forwards to look inside, her smile fading as her eyes met those of a thin dark-haired middle-aged man. She looked past him to the empty passenger seat and peered into the back but there was no one else in the van.

The driver's window slid down. 'Are you Lucy?' She nodded. 'Get in, then.'

'Where's Zoe?'

The man shrugged, raised his eyebrows, and lifted his hands off the steering wheel in a gesture of helplessness. 'Zoe's still up in her room, getting it ready for you. I told her it was time to leave but she insisted she wanted to finish rearranging her room. Don't ask me what she's doing up there, I'm not allowed in, but I couldn't drag her away. She's so excited about your visit, she wanted to decorate it up there. If you ask me she'd do better to tidy it. Anyway she asked me very particularly to give you a message.' He paused, frowning, and scratched at the grey stubble on his chin. 'Fugitive.' He said at last. 'That was it. Fugitive. It makes no sense to me but Zoe said you'd understand. Some sort of code is it?'

Lucy grinned. 'Something like that,' she replied as she walked around the front of the van and opened the passenger door. The man took her rucksack from her and chucked it in the back of the van.

'Off we go then,' he said as she climbed in, and the van shot forward.

'Excuse me,' Lucy shouted over the whine of the engine, 'can you slow down? I haven't got my seat belt on.' The man didn't seem to hear her. She fumbled with the buckle on her belt as the van gathered speed. 'I can't find where it goes.' The driver didn't answer but continued to accelerate. 'Why are we going so fast?'

'Don't worry about it,' he called out, his eyes fixed on the road ahead. Lucy sank back in her seat, faintly excited. Her own parents would never have allowed her to travel without a seatbelt, but where had living sensibly got her mother? Lucy's parents were pathetic, always worried about speed limits and playing it safe when travelling fast was much more fun. It would make the journey shorter too. She smiled at the streets whizzing past as they left Harchester and zoomed along a fast wide road.

'I brought Zoe a present. Do you think she'll like it?' She twisted round but couldn't reach her rucksack to show him.

'Yes, I'm sure she will.'

'I haven't told you what it is yet.'

'What is it then?'

'It's a book about an actor she's crazy about. You probably won't know who he is but she absolutely adores him. We both do.'

'Zoe's got a surprise for you too,' he told her.

'What is it?'

He didn't answer but stared straight ahead, grinning.

They passed a huge road sign and Lucy saw they were heading towards the coast. 'Where are we going?' She began to feel uneasy. 'Don't you think I should put my seat belt on?' She gazed out of the window at the fields whizzing past and told herself everything was going to plan. 'How much further is it?'

He didn't answer. They were travelling at over seventy miles an hour and she noticed he was clutching the steering wheel so tightly his knuckles had gone white

'Excuse me, but I haven't got my seatbelt on.'

The driver turned to her, his voice raised in exasperation. 'Stop fussing, will you? You're making me nervous and I need to think. It's not far now and we've got to get this right.'

Lucy slumped in her chair, taken aback by his hostility. For the first time it crossed her mind to question what she was doing sitting in a van beside a complete stranger. He could be anyone. Fear of the man sitting at her side seized her and she sat, rooted to the seat, as he drove her further and further away from home.

'Where are we going?' she whispered at last. He didn't answer.

After speeding along fast roads, they slowed down at a roundabout and drove past a row of new houses. Lucy read the name Chaucer Business Park on their right. They had been learning about Geoffrey Chaucer at school, although she couldn't remember much about him apart from his name. They took the road past Seasalter, reached Whitstable and descended a steep hill, past a fire station on their left and then she had a confused impression of shops, pubs, restaurants, houses and old people on the pavements. After a brief pause at a red traffic light they went under a railway bridge and turned right off the main road into a side street. The houses here were older and the van jogged along slowly, swerving and grinding over speed bumps as the road narrowed.

'Nearly there,' Zoe's father told her. He glanced at her, his face pale and sweaty, his eyes bright. Lucy nodded, telling herself there was nothing to worry about. The man knew the secret code word. He must be Zoe's father. But he looked weird and she wished Zoe was with them. They turned left past a plumbers suppliers on their right, and a builders yard, both of which looked closed. Lucy stared at wire fencing that made the builders yard look like a prison. They turned right into a narrow street then left and left again into a dead end. Lucy gave a silent sigh of relief. This had to be it. They drew up in a parking bay outside a disused lockup garage, a big blue plastic sack on the driveway in front of it.

'Wait here,' Zoe's father said. His voice sounded husky and he was sweating a lot. He wiped his forehead with the back of his hand and climbed out of the van.

'Can't I come with you?' Lucy asked, but he slammed the door without hearing her. A faint odour of sweat lingered in the van. She pushed the handle of her door, but he had put the child proof lock on and it wouldn't open.

Lucy looked around impatiently wondering where Zoe lived. In front of her was a blank brick side wall of a house. Beyond that, to the left, the road continued a short way past the house to a paved area in front of a high fence, the end of someone's back garden in the next road. There was a large For Sale sign outside the last house on the other side of the road, opposite the van. It looked empty, so she didn't think it could be Zoe's house. She couldn't see anything of the house in front of her, apart from the windowless wall. Next to it was a wooden slatted shed and then the lock up garage where Zoe's father had parked. It had a white pointed roof, like a little house, a peeling white up and over door, and red brick walls. Lucy couldn't see Zoe's father anywhere but she noticed the blue sack had gone. Perhaps they had only stopped here to collect his building materials, and Zoe didn't live in this road after all.

As Lucy watched, Zoe's father reappeared in front of the garage and unlocked the door. It rose smoothly. He strode energetically around the front of the van, opened the door and grasped her by the arm. 'Come with me. I want to show you something.' The urgency in his voice startled her.

'What is it? And where's Zoe?'

'This is it,' he replied, pushing her towards the lockup with the flat of one hand while the other kept tight hold of her arm. 'It's a surprise from Zoe, a little something she's been planning for you. Come and see if you like it.'

They were in front of the open garage now, and he was gripping her arm so tightly it hurt. 'Please let go, you're hurting me. I don't want to see it,' she replied. 'I'd rather go and see Zoe, please.' Without warning, Zoe's father gave her a vigorous shove, pushing her over the threshold into the garage. He switched on a light, at the same time slamming the door shut behind them. 'Stop it! Let me go! Where's Zoe –' He slapped her hard across the mouth and shoved her violently again. Lucy panicked, lost her footing and crashed down on the concrete floor, hitting her knee and jarring her elbow. She screamed in pain.

Zoe's father dragged her to her feet. Crying and shivering, she felt him pull a rough salty cloth across her mouth, before he tied her wrists together. Lucy fought to control her sobbing but it was useless. All at once, she wet herself, the hot pee turning instantly chilly against her bare legs.

'Don't worry,' Zoe's father said, 'I'll soon get you cleaned up. There's nothing to cry about. Don't you understand? I'm going to look after you from now on. I don't want you to worry about anything ever again. You're safe in here. No one's ever going to hurt you again.' Lucy was trembling so hard she could barely stand and she thought she was going to be sick. 'I'll be very good to you, Lucy. You'll see. I won't let your father hurt you again. He touched you, didn't he?' Lucy shook her head violently. 'This is what you wanted, isn't it? You wanted someone to come and rescue you from your family and keep you safe. And that's what I've done. So, are we friends again?' Lucy nodded warily. 'Can I take your gag off now?' She nodded again and tried to speak, making only muffled sounds like a dog in pain. 'There's no use calling out, I've soundproofed the lockup. I've thought of everything you see. So you can trust me. I know what I'm doing and I'm going to keep you safe.' He removed her gag and Lucy grimaced at the dirty taste in her mouth.

'What about my hands?' she asked. Her tongue felt thick and strange after being pressed down so hard by the gag. For answer, Zoe's father picked another length of rope from a shelf. He pushed her roughly onto a wooden chair and, standing behind her, wound the rope deftly around her waist while she tried her best to kick the chair over, sobbing all the while. 'You can't keep me here forever and when I get out, I'm going to tell Zoe. She's going to know all about you.'

The man laughed out loud. 'Don't you get it, Lucy? There is no Zoe.' He came round and stood in front of her, out of reach of her kicking legs. In a black coat, the collar turned up against his gaunt cheeks, he formed a stark silhouette against the white wall.

Laughter grated in her ears as Lucy bent double and threw up. At least some of her sick hit his shoes, she thought with grim satisfaction, although it made no difference. She was still a prisoner.

'My parents aren't rich, so you might as well just let me go because there's no point asking for a ransom' she told him with a sudden rush of anger, 'and anyway my father wouldn't pay and my mother's –' A wave of emotion shook her so hard she couldn't continue.

'I don't want money,' the man told her. He sounded surprised. 'It's you I want, Lucy. I thought you'd have worked that out by now. I want to help you. You asked for my help, didn't you? And now you've got it.'

'I wanted – Zoe – to help me – It was – supposed to be – Zoe.' She was crying uncontrollably, and trembling with shock.

'Forget Zoe,' he told her. 'There is no Zoe. There never was. It was only ever me and you, best friends forever.'

PART 5

'Nothing is more sad than the death of an illusion.'

Arthur Koestler

52

DAUGHTER

'I've been doing some research, gov.' Ian Peterson hesitated. Used to speaking freely to the DI, he was suddenly unsure what to say.

'Good.'

'The thing is –'

'Yes? What is it?' She glanced up impatiently.

'I discovered Paul Hilliard comes from York.'

'So?'

'Well –' Ian hesitated again, a sinking feeling in the pit of his stomach. 'It seems – I think –'

'Yes?' She leaned back in her chair with exaggerated patience and stared directly at him.

'His daughter went to the same school that Abigail Kirby taught at.'

The DI shuffled the expenses claim she had been filling out and looked up at him again, faintly belligerent. 'So?' she repeated. They both knew she was being defensive. It wasn't a good sign.

Ian took a deep breath and ploughed on. 'Paul Hilliard's daughter was at the school at the same time as Abigail Kirby, so Paul Hilliard must have known her.' He had said it and he took an involuntary step back, watching the DI's reaction warily.

'Let's not go jumping to conclusions, Sergeant.'

'But –'

'Paul Hilliard is a busy Home Office pathologist. He couldn't have met all the teachers at his daughter's school and obviously he never met Abigail Kirby himself. If he had, don't you think he would have remembered? In which case he would have told us, and he certainly wouldn't have carried out the post-mortem if he'd had anything more than a passing acquaintance with her.'

'Unless –' Ian didn't finish the sentence. Geraldine waited. They could both see where this was heading.

Geraldine broke the silence. 'Are you suggesting a Home Office pathologist concealed his connection with a victim, and conducted an autopsy on her? You realise what you're saying?'

'Yes.'

'This kind of guesswork isn't helpful. First of all we have no grounds for supposing they knew one another. Abigail Kirby happened to teach in the school Paul's daughter attended. But do we know that Abigail Kirby taught the daughter? Or that they even knew one another? And to leap from that to suggesting that Paul knew Abigail Kirby – it's –' She shrugged. 'Do you have any evidence to back up this – speculation?'

Ian shook his head. 'Only that they were at the same school, at the same time… Do you think we at least ought to tell the DCI?'

'Not yet. I'll question him first.'

'I think the DCI should –'

Geraldine stood up. 'I said I'll speak to him.'

'Is it a good idea, your questioning Dr Hilliard?'

'What?'

'It's just that your relationship with him –'

'What relationship?' She glared at him. 'Are you challenging my decision?' They both knew he was, but he backed down under the force of her anger. 'I'll question him. On my own.'

'Yes, gov.

'And don't challenge my judgement again, Sergeant.'

Peterson inclined his head but privately he decided he couldn't let this drop. It was possible Paul Hilliard had met Abigail Kirby while they were both living in York and Ian wasn't convinced the DI was being objective. It put him in an awkward position, but he knew what to do. He would get nowhere with the DI by voicing vague suspicions, so he would only raise the matter again if he could find evidence to back up his allegation. That meant he had more legwork to do. It might all be for nothing but he had to see it through.

Geraldine's fury abated as she drove to the morgue. She understood exactly what was happening. She had seen it before. Ian had allowed his judgement to be clouded by the frustration of waiting, and casting about for inspiration had lighted on Paul Hilliard. The flimsiest of reasons could appear to take on disproportionate significance in the absence of any genuine leads.

Paul looked surprised when she walked in but she thought he seemed pleased to see her. 'Geraldine, what brings you here?' He pushed back his chair and stood up.

'I need to ask you a few questions.'

'Here? Or –' He glanced at his watch. 'Can I take you out for lunch?' She hesitated. 'A drink?'

'I'm on duty.'

'How about coffee then?'

'Yes, that would be fine.'

'Coffee it is then. You're a difficult woman to please.' He smiled.

'Not always.' Unintentionally Geraldine had begun flirting. She bit her lip and followed him in silence, wondering how to question him without alienating him.

'There's a little bistro round the corner. Are you sure I can't tempt you to a quick bite? I'm starving.'

She caved in. 'So am I.'

While they were waiting for their order, Geraldine plunged in. 'There's something I need to ask you.'

'This sounds serious.' He smiled uneasily.

'It is. That is, I'm sure it's nothing, but I am here in an official capacity.' Paul raised an eyebrow and she regretted having agreed to question him in a restaurant. It was hardly an appropriate setting. 'I have to ask you about your daughter.'

'I don't see that my daughter is any business of yours.'

Ignoring his dismissive tone she ploughed on. 'We know your daughter attended a school where Abigail Kirby was teaching.'

'Really? Are you sure? Well, I don't suppose they were there at the same time –'

'That's the point, Paul. They were.'

Their food arrived and they fell silent while the waitress placed their dishes on the table.

Paul picked up his knife and fork and began cutting neatly into his meat. He seemed perfectly composed. 'I can see it might look odd, their being at school together, but I assure you I had no idea. I might have read in the paper that Abigail Kirby came from York, now you come to mention it – I seem to recall registering the coincidence – but I had no idea they were at the same school. It's a large school and to be honest,' he drew a hand across his brow, creased now with a frown, 'I left all that – parents' evenings and so on – to my wife. Not that I wouldn't have liked to be more involved, but I was busy at work. You know how it is. So can we drop this please?'

'Paul, I need to clear this up. Are you sure you never met Abigail Kirby in York?'

'Of course I'm sure. Obviously I would have recognised her if I had, and I would've told you what I knew about her. I might not even have carried out the autopsy, depending on how often we'd met. I don't understand. Why the questions all of a sudden?'

'We've only just discovered the connection between Abigail Kirby and your daughter.'

'Was there a connection, as you put it? Did Abigail Kirby teach my daughter? I didn't recognise the name and I read all of my daughter's school reports.' He put his knife and fork down, suddenly vexed. 'What are you trying to say, Geraldine? I thought you of all people could at least be straight with me. Am I under some sort of suspicion?'

'No, of course not. But we have to eliminate you from the enquiry. It's routine procedure. You know that.' Geraldine gazed miserably at her plate. He was clearly angry with her. They passed the rest of the meal in virtual silence. Paul ate very quickly, called for the bill as soon as he had finished and slapped some cash on the table.

'Not a great feeling,' he mumbled as he stood up, 'knowing someone you trust suspects you of – what? What exactly am I being accused of?'

'Nothing. You're not being accused of anything, really. Like I said, it was just routine. We had to ask –'

'If you say so. Well, I've got to get back to work.' He turned and left without another word.

It was raining outside, a cold steady drizzle, as Geraldine drove back to the station. Her mood didn't improve when she saw Peterson.

'Well?'

'Well what?' she snapped.

'Did you speak to Paul Hilliard?'

'Yes.'

'And?'

'You can see my report – on second thoughts it hardly warrants any paperwork, or are we going to report every conversation we have now? You'd better write your report on me then. And the DCI.'

The sergeant opened his mouth to reply but thought better of it.

53

PANIC

Ben eyed the fat sausages, his mouth watering. There were definite advantages to having Auntie Evie staying with them. 'Shall I call Lucy?' he asked.

'She knows it's time for breakfast,' his aunt replied a trifle sharply. 'She'd be down here if she was hungry.' They ate in silence, Auntie Evie watching complacently as Ben wolfed down his breakfast.

'Those sausages are great, Auntie Evie. Are there any more?' She stood up without a word to fetch the pan. At last Ben scraped his plate clean with his knife, sighed, and stood up to leave.

'Where is that girl?' Evie said. 'She'd better not still be asleep.'

'I'll go and call her. I've got to go up and get my school bag.' Ben trotted upstairs and knocked on Lucy's door. There was no answer. 'Lucy,' he called. 'Lucy! You're going to be late for school.' He paused. 'It's eight o'clock. I'm leaving.' He pushed her door open and peered inside. The curtains were drawn but he could see her bed was empty, the duvet neatly in place, the pillow smooth. Ben stepped inside. 'Lucy?' he repeated, although he could see she wasn't there. 'Lucy?' He left the room and knocked on her bathroom door. 'Lucy?' The door swung open. There was no one inside.

Ben raced downstairs in a sudden panic and ran into the kitchen where Auntie Evie was bent over the dishwasher. 'Auntie Evie, Lucy's gone.'

His aunt turned round. 'And so should you if you don't

want to be late. Where's your bag? I thought you went up to get it.'

'Auntie Evie, I don't think Lucy's gone to school.'

'Well I can't imagine where else she would have gone at this time in the morning. Now hurry up or you'll be late. You'll probably catch up with her on the way.'

'Do you think so?' Auntie Evie turned to the sink and began to run the tap. 'I thought – I thought –' Ben stopped. He'd been about to say he suspected Lucy had run away from home but Auntie Evie seemed so calm and everything in the kitchen looked so ordinary, he thought it would sound silly. Lucy had made idiotic threats before but she never carried them out. Auntie Evie was right, it was just more of Lucy's attention seeking behaviour. He ran upstairs, grabbed his bag and rushed out of the house. He had to hurry or he'd be late for school.

Ben forgot about Lucy until lunch time. Glancing around the dining room he couldn't see his sister in the melee but the canteen was so crowded it was hardly surprising. He wanted to ask one of her friends where she was but realised he didn't actually know who her friends were. She'd never mentioned anyone's name. After lunch he was making his way to the field where the boys were having an informal game of football, when he passed a couple of girls who looked about Lucy's age.

'Do you know Lucy Kirby?'

The two girls stopped and stared at him, chewing gum. 'Who wants to know?'

'I'm her brother.'

'Poor you.' They exchanged a glance and sniggered.

'What?' Losing interest, the girls turned away. 'I wanted to know if you've seen her today,' Ben said but the two girls walked off, arm in arm, without answering.

'Come on, Ben,' one of the boys yelled, and they raced

each other to the field.

Ben didn't think about Lucy again until he reached home. His father was out and Auntie Evie was in the kitchen, putting a large dish in the oven. Ben grinned in anticipation, called out to her to let his aunt know he was home, and went upstairs to his room. He dumped his bag on his bed and wandered along the corridor to speak to Lucy, but her room was still empty. Ben sat down heavily on her bed. He was genuinely worried now. He tried her mobile number but she didn't answer.

'Lucy,' he said aloud. 'Where are you?' After a few minutes he ran downstairs and burst into the kitchen where Auntie Evie was laying the table. 'Auntie Evie, Lucy's not in her room. I haven't seen her all day. I can't find her. I think she's run away from home.'

'Don't be ridiculous. What would she want to do that for?' She wiped her hands on a tea towel and set a plate of wet potatoes on the table beside a saucepan full of water. 'Supper will be ready at six so you've got plenty of time to do your homework. Are you going to do it in your room or do you want to sit at the table in the dining room?' She sat down and began peeling potatoes.

'Where's dad?'

'Your father's not home and he said he won't be here for supper.' Evie pressed her lips together, looking vexed. 'He's gone to see his friend.'

'Charlotte, you mean?' His aunt pulled a disapproving face but didn't answer. 'I'm worried about Lucy,' he went on.

'Yes, dear, we're all worried about Lucy. But it's nothing you need concern yourself about. You're not responsible for your sister. You should be concentrating on your school work. Lucy'll soon settle down. It's just a phase she's going through.'

'I think she's run away.'

His aunt frowned and shook her head, dropping a peeled

potato into the saucepan of water. 'Not now, Ben. I'm tired, and I'm sure you are too. Now, homework –'

Ben sat in his room staring at his school books but he couldn't settle. Now that he was alone in a quiet room, with no distractions, he kept thinking about his sister and he knew something was wrong. He'd tried talking to his aunt but she hadn't taken him seriously. He picked up his phone and dialled his father's number but there was no answer. It was all well and good Auntie Evie saying he wasn't responsible for his sister, but no one else seemed to know – or even care – where she was. He jumped up and ran downstairs.

'I need to speak to dad.'

Auntie Evie looked up from her magazine. She was obviously irritated at the interruption but she spoke gently. 'He's not here, Ben. He won't be home till – late.'

'I have to speak to him. I tried to call him but he's not answering his phone.'

'I expect he's busy. Now shouldn't you be doing your homework?' She looked down at her magazine.

'You don't understand –'

'I'm sure it's nothing that can't wait –' She flicked over the pages of her magazine and began to read.

'But Auntie –'

'Run along now. Whatever it is can wait.'

'What if it can't wait? If it's urgent, I mean? I don't know. It's Lucy – she's not come home.'

Engrossed in her magazine, Auntie Evie answered without looking up from her magazine. 'Don't worry about Lucy. She'll come home when she's ready.'

Ben went out into the hall. He was going to go back up to his room, and his homework, but he suddenly reached a decision. 'I'm going out,' he shouted. He heard his aunt's voice but not what she said as he yanked his jacket off its peg and ran out, slamming the front door behind him.

'There's a young boy here,' a constable told Geraldine.

'What does he want?'

'I don't know, but the thing is, he's Abigail Kirby's son, so I thought you might want to see him yourself.'

'Is he accompanied?'

'No, he's by himself but he insists he wants to talk to someone. He's very agitated, ma'am.'

Geraldine stood up. 'Is there a children's officer with him?'

'DC Everton's there. She's trained to interview underage witnesses. That's the best we can do for now, but the boy's very insistent he wants to speak to someone urgently.'

Geraldine hurried to the interview room where Ben Kirby was sitting on the edge of his chair, biting his nails. Detective Constable Christine Everton, a plump woman of about forty, was sitting quietly at his side. He looked up when Geraldine entered, his eyes wide, pupils dilated, his breathing fast. 'It's my sister,' he said, straightaway.

'Lucy?'

'Yes.'

'What about her?'

'She's run away from home.' To Geraldine's consternation he burst into tears. Not quite sure of her ground dealing with a distraught child, Geraldine was glad Christine Everton was in the room with them.

'Ben,' Geraldine said gently. 'If you know anything about where she is, you must tell me. You do understand that, don't you?'

Ben looked up at her tearfully, wiping his nose on his sleeve. The constable handed him a tissue. 'She said she was going to stay with a friend.'

'What friend?' Geraldine asked. He shook his head and began snivelling again. 'What friend, Ben?'

'I don't know. I don't know.'

'Can you tell me the names of all Lucy's friends?' He shook

his head again. 'Any names you know.'

'Lucy didn't have any friends.' He covered his face with his hands again and wept noisily.

54

NAME

The mood at the emergency briefing was tense. Not only were they no closer to discovering who was responsible for Abigail Kirby's death but now her daughter had been reported missing.

'We need to question both her father and her aunt,' Kathryn Gordon said. 'So far we have just the brother's account and he's only twelve. Is he still here?'

'DC Everton has taken him home, ma'am.'

'Good.'

Geraldine went to see Matthew Kirby and his sister, accompanied by a SOCO who had attended a basic computer interrogation course, as both Matthew and Ben had mentioned that Lucy spent hours on her computer.

Matthew Kirby's sister opened the door. Her eyes roamed past them and her face fell. 'You haven't found her then?' She sounded irritated rather than worried.

'We'd like to ask you a few questions about Lucy,' Geraldine replied.

'There's no point asking me. I'm lucky if my niece gives me the time of day. It's her age,' she added defensively.

'Is Mr Kirby here?'

'No.' The answer came too quickly.

'We'd like to take a look at Lucy's room. It might help us to find her.'

'She'll turn up when she feels like it, that one,' Evie replied but she stood aside so Geraldine could enter, followed by the SOCO.

Ben appeared on the landing as they went upstairs, looking pale and drawn and older than his twelve years. His puffy eyes searched Geraldine's face anxiously.

'Is Lucy here?'

'Not yet. Can you think of anything else that might help us find her?'

'Only what I already told you.'

'And you can't remember who the friend was that she was going to stay with?'

'She never said any name.' He looked so earnest and concerned that Geraldine was sure he was telling the truth. 'You will find her, won't you?'

'Poor kid,' the SOCO muttered under his breath.

'Of course we'll do everything we can to find her quickly. We're going to take a look in Lucy's room. Do you know if she kept a diary?'

'Check her computer. She's always on there. And –' He broke off.

'Yes?'

'She told me –'Ben hesitated then spoke in a rush, 'she thinks our dad killed our mother.'

Evie was listening from half way up the stairs. 'Ben!' she burst out.

'It's only what Lucy said.'

'You don't believe such wicked lies.'

'No. Of course I don't. It's just what Lucy told me. I don't believe it. I don't.'

Evie pushed past the two detectives and put her arm round the sobbing boy. 'Come on downstairs with me, Ben. You haven't eaten yet. I'll make us some supper and I expect there's something nice on the telly. Let's leave the police to do their job. The quicker they get on with it the sooner they'll find Lucy and bring her home, safe and sound. And I'm going to call your father. He should be here.'

Ben clomped downstairs behind his aunt, sniffling, and Geraldine went into Lucy's room. The bedroom was tidy. There was nothing on the carpet apart from a pair of pink fluffy slippers and an empty wicker bin. The duvet had been neatly placed on the bed with a pillow exactly parallel to it. No pictures or posters were displayed on the walls which were an unrelieved pale pink broken up only by grey curtains and a small square wall mirror opposite the door. A large desk was bare apart from a laptop computer, and one dirty mug which looked out of place in the otherwise orderly room. Like mother like daughter, Geraldine thought.

Lucy had told her brother she was going to stay with a friend. The SOCO sat down at the desk and booted up Lucy's computer. It was vital they find out who had been in contact with her. It didn't take Geraldine long to search the room while her colleague tapped at the keyboard, but she went through the motions without finding anything useful. If Lucy kept a diary she had taken it with her. Her desk drawers contained a random collection of pens and pencils, rubbers and rulers, tissues and paper clips, nothing personal it seemed.

They heard the front door slam and voices downstairs and a moment later Matthew Kirby entered the room.

'Where's Lucy?' he demanded.

'That's what we're here trying to find out,' Geraldine answered. 'Ben reported her missing.' Matthew flinched at the implicit accusation. 'Lucy told him she was going to stay with a friend. Can you tell us who that might be?'

Matthew shook his head and ran one hand through his hair, eyes wide in alarm. 'Lucy isn't a sociable girl. She struggles to make friends. To be honest, she hasn't coped with the move here very well, and I don't think she's settled into her new school yet. And then her mother – they were very close –' His expression changed suddenly. 'Oh my God.'

'Mr Kirby, do you have any idea where Lucy might be?'

'This is all my fault.'

'What do you mean? Mr Kirby, if you have any information that might help us –'

'This is my fault,' he repeated, staring past her with troubled eyes. 'I think someone's getting at me through my family. I should've said something sooner – oh my God, not Lucy too.'

'What do you mean someone's getting at you?'

'It's Charlotte. There's this man she knows who keeps writing to her and we thought – I thought it was a bit of a joke –'

'Writing?'

'Yes. Letters.'

'Threatening letters?'

'No, no. Nothing like that. Not exactly. He sends her slushy love letters all the time. She told me he's harmless, but –'

'Who is he?'

'I don't know. All I know is his name, Ted. Charlotte can tell you who he is. She's known him for years. I think they were at school together. She'll tell you.'

'Charlotte never mentioned these letters to us.'

'We never thought anything of it – she didn't think it was important.'

'It seems odd he would free you from your wife if he wanted Charlotte back, but we'll find him and get to the bottom of this.' She nodded at Peterson who was already on the phone. 'It looks as though Lucy's gone to stay with a friend,' Geraldine turned to Matthew Kirby again. 'That's what she told Ben, and that means it's unlikely she's come to any harm. Now, can you tell us if anything's missing? If we know what she's taken with her, it might give us a better idea of her plans.'

The SOCO continued tapping at the keyboard while Geraldine and Matthew looked in the wardrobe. Matthew thought some of Lucy's t-shirts and her jacket were missing, but he was vague about whether she had taken any other items of clothing with her. 'Abigail dealt with all that sort of thing,' he explained with an awkward shrug.

'If you can tell us what you think might be missing –' Geraldine prompted him but he shook his head helplessly.

Ben came up to tell his father supper was ready, and was no more help than his father. 'She always wears jeans when she's not at school,' he said, as though that summed up Lucy's entire wardrobe.

'Have you found anything?' Geraldine asked her colleague when Matthew and Ben had gone downstairs.

'There are plenty of nasty comments on her Facebook page.'

'What sort of comments?'

'Four eyes, skinny, pinhead, slag – there's loads, gov. It's just kids' stuff but there's lots of it from a variety of sources. It's a pretty concerted campaign of bullying if you ask me – there are even jibes about her mother.' He glanced at Geraldine, a frown creasing his young forehead. 'She's such a cow she drove her mother to kill herself,' he read aloud. 'That's terrible. And it goes on.'

'Who was posting these comments?'

'I can probably find out where they came from, but it looks like a gang who knew each other.'

'Kids from her school?'

'Most probably. Our best bet will be to send the hard drive to Lambeth Labs and let them do the necessary.'

'Is there anything on her Facebook page that might help us trace the friend she went to stay with?'

The SOCO shook his head. 'There's nothing friendly here, gov. I've checked her emails and there's nothing there. She's been on instant messenger but the messages have been deleted. We'll need to restore them. I can't do that, it's too advanced for me, I'm afraid. We'll have to send the hard drive to Lambeth.'

Geraldine nodded. 'We'll take the laptop with us. I'll check the bathroom while you're sorting it out.'

'Yes, ma'am.'

The basin in Lucy's bathroom was bare and there was no toothbrush or toothpaste in the cabinet. Apart from that Geraldine could find nothing of interest and they left, taking Lucy's computer with them.

'Take what you like, Inspector,' was Matthew's response when they told him. 'Just find Lucy.' He looked close to tears.

'She'll be all right, dad,' Ben told his father, but the boy looked as distraught as his father.

'She's just being a drama queen,' Evie said. 'She's run off to a friend to give you a scare, that's all. It's her age, Matthew. She'll be back.'

Geraldine had the hard drive from Lucy's computer sent straight to the Forensic Science Service lab in Lambeth, and followed up her urgent request with a call. The lab assured her they would give the case priority. After that there was nothing more to do but wait.

'Call me as soon as you find anything,' she insisted. 'A teenage girl's life is in danger and we need anything you can come up with to help us trace her urgently. Phone me immediately you find anything. We're particularly interested in any Instant Messenger chats she's been having.'

The next morning a call came through. 'We worked on it through the night,' a voice told her, 'and we've got everything there is. We haven't done a report yet, but your girl was messaging with a kid called Zoe and they arranged for Lucy to go and stay with her.'

'Thank goodness for that. Now all we have to do is find Zoe.'

'In the most recent exchange Zoe said her father would bring her over to pick Lucy up, and they had a code word so they'd recognise each other.'

Geraldine felt a lurch of anxiety. 'You mean Zoe wasn't anyone Lucy knew? They met online?'

'It looks that way.'

'Can you trace Zoe?'

'We should be able to, but it might take a while. There's something not quite right here. It's probably just a glitch. Leave it with us and we'll get back to you as soon as we have something.'

Geraldine called Matthew Kirby straightaway, but neither he nor Ben had ever heard Lucy talking about her friend called Zoe.

'She hasn't got any friends,' was Ben's firm response.

Matthew was predictably vague. 'Abigail used to deal with Lucy.'

'It's lucky Lucy's friend was using her real name,' Peterson said when Geraldine told him. 'That's all we need, really. Now let's see if we can find Zoe.'

Geraldine nodded. 'We'll see what we can find out. In the meantime, the FSS are working on it so if we can't find Zoe, hopefully it shouldn't take them too long to find out where she was sending her messages from.'

55

CONCEALMENT

That evening Geraldine called Lucy's form tutor who agreed to see her straightaway. Miss Abingdon had a low voice and a gentle manner, just the sort of teacher Geraldine would have expected Lucy to turn to in her distress.

'I'm afraid Lucy never opened up to me, Inspector,' the form tutor said sadly. 'She was isolated, even before she lost her mother. It's hard for pupils to join an established social group, but Lucy really made no effort to fit in and the other girls – well, they didn't like her to begin with, and then with the loss of her mother she became even more withdrawn. There isn't really anything more I can tell you. I do my best to get to know all the pupils in my tutor group. We're very strong on pastoral care, but Lucy wasn't receptive to the support we offer here. We did try to help her and, in time, I think she would have come round, but her mother dying obviously disturbed any progress she was making socially.'

'Was she friendly with a girl called Zoe?'

'Zoe Mason? I don't think they were friends. I don't think Lucy had any friends. She was –'

'Zoe Mason?' Geraldine seized on the name. 'Is she in Lucy's class?'

'Yes.'

'How can I contact her?'

Miss Abingdon shook her head. 'She's not in my group, I'm afraid,' she explained.

First thing next morning Geraldine went to school to speak to Zoe Mason only to learn the girl wasn't in school that day.

Geraldine felt her breath quicken. She made a note of Zoe's address and took an IT trained officer with her.

Zoe Mason lived in a neat little house about ten minutes walk from the school. A clematis grew up a trellis at one side of the door, which must have looked attractive when it was in flower although at this time of year it was little more than a long withered twig.

A tubby woman came to the door, wiping her hands on a tea towel. 'Yes?' She scowled apprehensively when Geraldine held out her warrant card, taking a step backwards, her hand on the door. 'Well? What do you want? What's this about?'

'Mrs Mason, your daughter, Zoe –'

'Zoe's feeling poorly. I was just about to call the school to let them know. There's no way she can go to school, the state she's in. I'll give her a letter when she goes back.' She started to close the door.

'Mrs Mason, I'm not here to talk about Zoe's absence from school. I want to ask to her about one of her class mates. Has she mentioned a girl called Lucy?'

'No. She doesn't know anyone called Lucy, and it's got nothing to do with Zoe if some girl from the school is in trouble with you lot.' She sniffed. 'It doesn't surprise me, the way some of them carry on, but Zoe's never been in any trouble and whatever this girl's got herself into, I'm telling you it's nothing to do with Zoe.'

'No one's in trouble with the police, Mrs Mason. One of the girls in Zoe's class has gone missing –'

'Missing?'

'A girl in Zoe's class, Lucy, has gone missing from home and we want to ask Zoe if she can help us to find her.'

'Well, she can't. She doesn't have any friends called Lucy. I'd know if she had.'

'Mrs Mason, Lucy has been in regular contact with a girl called Zoe. They've been sending messages to each other online every day recently. It's quite likely Zoe might have some idea where Lucy's gone, so I'd really like to speak to her. May we come in?'

Zoe's mother led them into a narrow hallway with yellowing wallpaper and a grey carpet. There was a faint musty smell of damp and stale cigarette smoke. Mrs Mason stopped at the foot of a steep staircase and leaned forwards, holding onto the banister.

'Zoe!' she shrieked, her voice suddenly shrill. 'Get down here!' There was no answer. 'She's listening to her music. You'll have to go up.'

A pink sign was displayed on one of the doors: 'Zoe's Room'. There was no response when Geraldine knocked. She banged more loudly on the door. Still no answer. Gingerly she pushed the door open. A strong sweet aroma of joss sticks hit her as she picked her way through piles of magazines which lay inside the door like a barrier: Heat, Closer, Star. In the dim light of a lava lamp she saw an open wardrobe stuffed with clothes, most of which seemed to be black. A girl was lying on the bed, her eyes closed, feet tapping, listening through headphones.

'Zoe,' Geraldine called. The girl didn't move. 'Zoe!' she shouted. The girl's eyes flickered open and she turned her head. Seeing Geraldine in the doorway, she sat up suddenly, yanking her headphones off. 'May we come in and talk to you for a moment?'

'Who are you? What are you doing here?' She was pretty, with dyed blonde hair and blue eyes which looked unnaturally large, outlined in black eyeliner.

Geraldine stepped into the room. 'Hello, Zoe, my name's Geraldine. I'm a police officer and I would like to ask you a couple of questions. This is Roger, and he'd like to take a look at your computer.'

Zoe looked away and fiddled with the headphones that were

lying beside her on the bed. 'I'm sick. I can't go to school. Ask my mum. She'll tell you.' She gave an unconvincing cough.

Geraldine reassured her that they hadn't come round to find out why she wasn't at school. 'It's about a girl we think you may know who's gone missing.'

Zoe looked up with sudden interest. 'Missing? What, you mean like run away? Who is it? Who's missing?'

'Lucy Kirby.'

'Lucy?' Zoe pulled a face. She seemed disappointed. 'Like who's going to notice?'

'Zoe, this is very important. I need you to tell me where Lucy is.'

'How would I know?'

Geraldine took a step nearer. 'We found messages on Lucy's computer –'

'You looked at her computer?' Zoe picked up her headphones again and fiddled with them as she spoke. 'You shouldn't do that. Did you look at her Facebook page?'

'We looked at everything.'

'It wasn't me,' Zoe burst out, suddenly apprehensive.

Geraldine spoke as gently as she could. 'What wasn't you, Zoe?'

'Well, maybe I did join in a bit. But it was mainly the other girls.'

'What other girls?'

'I don't know. I can't remember.'

'What were the other girls doing?' Zoe didn't answer. Geraldine thought about the comments on Facebook. 'Were they bullying Lucy online?' Zoe shrugged and stared at her legs stretched out in front of her on the bed. 'It's very important you tell me the truth, Zoe.'

'We only did it for a laugh,' Zoe said. 'It was only a few things we said. It was just a joke, you know. We all do it, lark about with each other. Only some people have got no sense of humour. She's a dork.'

'Zoe, tell me where Lucy is.'

'I can't.'

'Why not?'

'Because I've got no idea where she is. Why would I? Ask her dad.'

'Zoe,' Geraldine spoke very slowly. 'We know Lucy was sending messages to a friend called Zoe shortly before she left home, and we know she made arrangements to stay with Zoe.'

'Well it wasn't me. My God, she wasn't my friend. She never sent me any messages and I never emailed her. Why would I want to do that? She was weird.'

'How was she weird?'

'You know, weird. No one liked her.'

'And you're sure she never sent you any messages?'

'I told you.'

'Zoe,' Geraldine took a step further into the room. 'Would you allow us to take a look at your computer?'

The girl sat up and glared at Geraldine across the dimly lit room. 'What do you want to do that for? I'm telling you, I never emailed Lucy Kirby. She's so sad.'

Geraldine glanced around. 'May we?' She nodded at a flat screen desktop on a small table. It was switched on.

'Go on then, if it'll make everyone go away and leave me alone. But you won't find any messages from Lucy Kirby there, I can promise you that.'

The SOCO perched on Zoe's chair and began tapping at the keys.

Zoe slipped off the bed and crossed the room to stand at his shoulder. 'My mum got it for me.'

'You don't mind if I take a look then?'

'You can look. You can fix it for me as well while you're at it. It doesn't work properly. It's rubbish.'

'What's wrong with it?'

'I don't know, do I?'

'When did it stop working?'

Zoe shrugged. 'I told my mum to get it fixed but she says we can't afford it. She says there's computers at school I can use, but what use are they to me here? They're crap anyway. Most sites are blocked. It would be different if it was her computer. She'd get it fixed straightaway if it was hers.'

'So you haven't been chatting with Lucy on instant messenger?' Geraldine insisted patiently.

'With that weirdo? Are you joking?'

The SOCO checked and shook his head. 'Nothing here, ma'am. We could send it off to be looked at but I don't think she uses Instant Messenger.'

'I already told you that, didn't I?' Zoe snapped. 'And there's no way you're taking my computer away.'

'Is there another Zoe at school?' Geraldine asked.

'No.' The girl went and lay down on the bed again and picked up her headphones. 'I've no idea where Lucy is, she wasn't my friend, and I never had any messages from her.' She turned her head away and lay staring up at the wall.

Geraldine went back downstairs and found Zoe's mother in the kitchen. After some resistance, she agreed to allow Geraldine and her colleague to look around. They searched every room in the tiny house, the attic and the garden but there was no sign of Lucy Kirby. It seemed Zoe Mason had been telling the truth. Ignoring Zoe's foul mouthed objections, Geraldine instructed the SOCO to take the computer away to be checked, just in case, although she was convinced Zoe was telling her the truth. She had been so sure they had discovered Lucy's friend, Zoe, and now it seemed they were no closer to tracking down the missing girl.

While Geraldine had been away from the station, a report

had been received from the Lambeth Labs, and an emergency meeting was convened on her return to bring everyone up to speed.

'I wonder if Lucy's brother knows of any other friends she had called Zoe. Perhaps someone from York?' the DCI suggested, when Geraldine had told them briefly about the futile visit to Zoe Mason.

'Unlikely,' Peterson said. He had been on the phone to Lambeth Labs discussing their report. 'According to the messages from Zoe, she wasn't far from Faversham. And there's more. The Lab said Zoe's location was too carefully and consistently hidden for it to be accidental.'

'What do you mean?' Geraldine asked, her own anxiety reflected in the DCI's face.

The sergeant looked down at the notes he was holding. 'Zoe's messages to Lucy were sent from a laptop with wireless internet access. The Lab traced the computer but it was bought for cash so there's no way of discovering the identity of the purchaser. The internet connection was pay as you go, so there was no contract, just an initial payment and one subsequent top up of fifty pounds, made with a voucher. We've checked the CCTV in the shop where it was purchased but there's nothing.'

'Keep studying the film. Go through it frame by frame,' the DCI said.

'We have, ma'am.'

'Well go through it again. There must be something. Start checking CCTV records of all recent voucher purchases.'

They all knew it was hopeless.

'What about the location?' Geraldine asked Peterson. 'Haven't they got anywhere with that? Surely the Labs can give us the address the messages were sent from, or at least pin down the area?'

'In theory, yes, but whoever was sending messages to Lucy Kirby was moving around.'

'Moving around? What the hell do you mean?' The DCI sounded angry.

'Unless they catch the user online on the laptop, pinpoint the geographical location and move in straightaway, before the user moves on, they have no way of finding out where the messages are being sent from. They think Zoe – whoever that is – must have been sending messages from a car, driving around to make sure the laptop's whereabouts couldn't be identified while it was in use.' There was a pause while the team registered the implications of what they had just heard. Zoe wasn't a child. 'The chances are Zoe has disposed of the laptop by now,' Peterson added. 'In the final message Zoe told Lucy her father would pick her up.'

'It seems Lucy Kirby has not gone to stay with a friend after all,' the DCI summed up. 'Whoever she met on the internet has deliberately groomed her and carried out a carefully planned abduction.'

Geraldine thought of the lonely, motherless girl and felt sick with fear at the new horrors that she might be facing.

56

JUSTICE

The whole operation was taking far longer than he had originally anticipated but his resolve never flagged. On the contrary, it was the only thing that kept him going. Without it he wouldn't have been able to continue living.

He heard nothing from his ex-wife who had abandoned him a long time ago, swept away into a new life with another partner. He didn't even know whether she had remarried. He didn't know where she lived and had been careful not to let her know his new address or even that he had moved. There must be no possibility of anyone interfering with his plans and her presence in his life could be nothing but a hindrance; he knew what he had to do and she would never have understood. It was strange to think they had ever been close. Thinking back on the time he had spent with her was like remembering the life of a stranger. All he cared about now was his own brief future. As long as he took them all with him it would be worth it and now there was only one left: the doctor who was still alive, prosperous and successful, and completely oblivious of his impending death. It would be soon now. Everything was in place.

It had been easy to arrange revenge on the girl. Dispatching the teacher had taken careful preparation but he'd pulled it off with consummate skill, deriving intense gratification from knowing her family must be suffering as he had suffered. He hoped their distress would persist for the rest of their lives, as raw as the day she died. Anything less would diminish their punishment. He had no desire to be merciful. What compassion had any of them shown? He was concerned only with justice. No one could blame him for that.

He had spent months pursuing the teacher, biding his time when she had been promoted to headmistress. The thought of her triumph had been bearable only because he was arranging her final defeat. There had to be justice and he had become its instrument, reluctantly at first, then joyfully as he discovered the exhilaration of punishing those responsible for an offence against an innocent girl. They might have evaded the flaccid justice system of the law courts but he would not absolve them. There could only be one outcome.

He had no difficulty gaining access to the hospital where the doctor worked and from there it had been easy to find out where he lived. He had been watching the doctor for a while now, making plans and thinking all the time about the girl. Her suffering was behind her now. Soon he'd be joining her and they would be together again at last.

'It won't be long now,' he whispered. 'I'll be with you again very soon, my lovely girl.'

57

ESCAPE

The estate agent had left but Marion and Brian lingered on the pavement.

'It would feel different if someone was living there,' Marion said.

They stood for moment side by side gazing at the empty house, a large semi-detached property. A blue and orange 'For Sale' sign in the front garden stood at an angle, propped against the fence. On the detached side of the house was a narrow alley which led through to the next street, and beyond that a fence ran across the end of the road. The brickwork on the house had been well maintained but the paintwork on the old-fashioned sash windows looked flaky.

'It's overpriced,' Brian replied. 'The outside needs work.'

'We could make them an offer.'

'There's no hurry. We've still got two more to see this week.'

'If it wasn't empty –'

'You like it, don't you?'

She nodded. 'It's nice and quiet here at the end of the cul-de-sac.'

Brian glanced around. 'I'm as keen as you are to get our own place, but the last thing we want to do is make the wrong decision. I think we should at least look at the other two before we make up our minds.'

Marion followed him across the road to their car which was parked outside a detached garage. He had turned the car round so it was facing back the way they had come. Marion walked around the back to the passenger side. As she reached out to open the door she paused and stood, a look of intense concentration on her face.

'Brian.'

'What? Are you getting in?'

'Brian, listen.' Marion turned away from the car to stare at the dingy garage behind her.

'What is it?' Brian called out from the car.

Marion opened the door and leaned down to speak to him in an urgent undertone. 'I think there's an animal or something trapped in that garage.'

'What?'

'There's something in there.'

'Marion, just get in the car, will you?'

'Brian, come here and listen.'

With a sigh Brian took his keys from the ignition, climbed out of the car and walked round the front of the vehicle to join his wife outside the garage. 'It's filthy,' he said. 'Come on.'

'Listen! There's an animal trapped in there. I heard it. We can't just ignore it. I think it's a dog.'

They stood listening for a few seconds then looked at one another in dismay.

Marion spoke first. 'It's not an animal!'

Brian nodded, his eyes fixed on his wife. 'There's someone in there.'

'Help!' The muffled cry came again and something thumped against the door making it rattle violently. Marion jumped.

'It sounds like a child,' Marion whispered. 'Brian, we've got to do something.'

'Hold on!' Brian yelled, suddenly decisive. 'We're going to open the door.'

There was no response from inside the garage. Marion and Brian looked at one another but whoever was on the other side of the door was silent.

'Stand back!' Brian called out. He didn't sound so sure of himself now.

'What are you going to do?' Marion asked.

Brian opened the boot of the car, rummaged through his tool box and pulled out a fine screwdriver.

'Brian, do you think you should?'

'You'd better call the police,' he answered, his face grim. 'But we can't wait for them.'

'But –'

'Just make the call, Marion.'

Brian jiggled the tool around in the lock, screwing up his eyes in concentration. There was a distinct click and the door gave a sudden jolt. With a grunt, Brian tugged it and the door swung open. As he took a step forward to peer inside, he heard someone whimper and a small filthy figure emerged blinking into the daylight. It brushed past Brian and raced away up the road.

'Oy! Stop!' Brian called after it but the ragged figure kept on running, and disappeared round a corner before Brian regained his equilibrium. He turned to Marion. 'What the hell was that? Some drugged up addict. Maybe this area isn't such a great choice.'

'No, I think it was a child locked in there. You were right. I'm calling the police.'

'Let's just go home.'

'We can't, Brian. Someone had a child locked up in that garage. We can't just go home and pretend we didn't see anything.' Brian stepped towards the garage. 'Don't go in. Wait for the police. It could be a crime scene.'

Brain shrugged and went back to the car muttering under his breath. 'This isn't bloody CSI.'

A police car arrived within minutes of Marion's call and two uniformed officers stepped out. They looked very young.

'Marion Chorley?'

'Yes.'

'Can you tell us what happened here?'

While the first policeman questioned Marion, the other one spoke to Brian who climbed reluctantly out of the car again. 'Is this your garage, sir?'

'No it's not. It's nothing to do with us. I'm Brian Chorley. My wife and I were just viewing that property.' He pointed over the road to the empty house.

'You just went in to have a look?'

'Yes. No. That is, we met the estate agent here.'

'Which agency, sir, if you don't mind my asking.'

'Elliott and Parker. The agent who showed us round was called Nicola something.'

'And what happened after you'd seen the house?'

'We'd parked here and my wife heard something –' He hesitated to tell the policeman he'd broken into the garage. 'We called you at once but we could hear someone calling for help, and then it all went quiet, so we thought we'd better get the door open as quickly as possible and when we got it open some kid ran out and hared away off up the road. She looked – crazy.'

'Can you describe her?'

'She was a girl. She looked like a tramp. I think she'd been locked in there for a while, she was so dirty, and the daylight seemed to dazzle her.'

'How old was she?'

'I couldn't say really. A teenager maybe. Thirteen?'

'What was she wearing?'

'Um – it's difficult to say. I opened the door and she just dashed out and ran away up the road. It took me completely by surprise. My wife might remember more. I can't say for sure what she was wearing, it all happened so fast, and she was very dirty.'

'Thank you, sir.'

The two policemen muttered together for a few seconds then one of them began talking rapidly on his phone. He stepped cautiously over the threshold into the garage and shone a bright torch inside. Over the policeman's shoulder Brian glimpsed an upturned chair. Beside it on the filthy floor a length of rope lay twisted. Brian took a step forwards and grimaced in disgust at the stench of excrement and stale sweat. The policeman shone his torch slowly around, pausing at a pile of faeces in one corner. Brian listened to him talking on his phone.

'There was definitely something living here. There's a chair, rope which looks like it's been used recently, and a pile of faeces which could be human.' He moved the torch along the far wall. 'And there's a grey rucksack, sir. It could be the one.' He stepped back and bumped into Brian who was craning his neck to peer into the garage. 'I'm sorry, sir, you can't go in there.'

The police took Brian and Marion's address, asked them to be sure to contact them if they remembered anything else, and said they could go home.

'Who was it, in the garage?' Marion asked but the policeman shook his head.

'I'm afraid we can't say yet, Mrs Chorley.'

58

WHITSTABLE

Lucy had no idea how long she had been sitting in darkness before she finally managed to wriggle free from the rope that tied her arms and legs to the chair. Her wrists and ankles were burning from rubbing against the rough cord. She thought they were bleeding but wasn't able to see, and the skin was too painful to touch. In any case, she knew her hands were dirty and she didn't want the wounds to become infected if she could help it. Her legs trembled as she stood up, accidentally kicking over the chair which fell with a deafening clatter in the silence. She whimpered and shuffled across the garage, hands outstretched, until she came up against a brick wall. She felt her way along the wall into a corner and squatted down to relieve herself. The stench made her gag so she made her way back along the wall, as far from her impromptu toilet as she could go, until her hands met the cold metal of the door. She pushed against it as hard as she could but it wouldn't budge. In desperation, she kicked at it. The clanging reverberated in her ears but the door didn't move.

'Help!' she screamed out suddenly. Once started, she couldn't stop, crying and yelling, until she had to pause to recover her breath. The skin on the back of her neck prickled as she realised there was someone outside. It sounded like a woman's voice. 'Help!' Lucy called out again and she kicked at the door as hard as she could.

A man answered and Lucy recoiled in fear. He had come back. He was shouting about opening the door.

'No,' Lucy sobbed, 'leave me alone.' She drew back from the door and staggered sideways to the wall, pressing herself against it until her shoulder hurt. 'Go away. Please. Go away.'

Someone was fiddling with the lock on the door. The man who had said he was Zoe's father.

'Go away,' she whimpered, shaking and helpless. There was a loud click and a shaft of dazzling sunlight appeared at her feet. Remorselessly the door rose, blinding her with a sudden burst of light. Lucy saw the silhouette of a man standing on the threshold, black against the brilliant background, and adrenaline shot through her. This was her chance. Ignoring the fiery pain in her ankles she charged out of the garage, past the man, and pounded up the street. She could hear him shouting after her but she kept on running, too terrified to look round in case twisting her head slowed her down. She raced left around the first corner, out of sight. Her chest was on fire, her throat burned with the effort of breathing, the muscles in her legs were screaming, but she didn't dare stop. Her only thought was to put as much distance as possible between herself and the man who had locked her in the garage.

She knew he would be following her so she turned again, to the right this time, ran to the end of the road and turned once more, left and then right. She was on another street, exposed to view. At any moment the man might drive around the corner and see her. She couldn't run any more, but hobbled as fast as she could, her legs aching horribly. Across the road she saw an alleyway running alongside a car park and tottered into it. On her right was a one-storey square brick building: WC. The door was open so she darted inside, wrinkling her nose at the smell.

On the periphery of her vision she caught sight of movement and barely managed to hold back a scream. She had to keep quiet. Someone was watching her – a face, blotchy with tears and dirt, red-eyed, with wild hair. With a shock she realised it was her own face, reflected back at her in a cloudy mirror. She looked like a crazed drug addict. In spite of her terror, she almost laughed and fought to control the hysteria bubbling inside her. She had to concentrate and think, or he would find her. Moving away from the horrible vision in the mirror, she splashed her face with cold water. The shock sobered her. She knew it was risky but she couldn't help herself and squeezed her head into the grimy basin to gulp down mouthfuls of icy water. It tasted like metal. When she straightened up she felt nauseous and threw up. The vomit was brown and watery but she told herself it was probably because she had drunk too much too quickly. There was no point worrying now about whether the water was contaminated.

Staring in the mirror, she did her best to comb her hair with her fingers, but it didn't make much difference. Her face was streaked with filth. She held the bottom of her t-shirt under the tap and scrubbed at her face. It wasn't easy to see clearly in the foggy mirror but she thought her cheeks looked cleaner, at least. No one had come in and she couldn't hear anyone outside, so she stole out of the building glancing fearfully around. The alleyway and the car park were deserted. As she limped along the alley the stink from the toilets followed her.

At the other end of the alley was a wide road and beyond that a high metal railing, like the bars of a prison. Lucy crossed the road and went through the open gate. Somehow she felt safer with the railing between her and the man, although she knew he could follow her in. She glanced behind her but there was no sign of him. There were people standing around near the water's edge and she didn't want to draw attention to herself so, taking a deep breath, she slowed down and tried to walk normally, as though nothing was wrong. She passed a sign: Harbour Office. Rounding a bend on the wide walkway, the tarmac underfoot changed to a wide gravel path. To her right, the sea opened out along a channel between platforms supporting large huts and strange grey mechanical constructions surrounded by huge mounds of grey stones. Lucy thought it looked like a quarry, but it was built on the sea.

As she walked on the scene changed, like stepping onto a different planet, full of movement, sound and colour. Overwhelmed, Lucy forced herself to keep walking. She had to put as much distance between herself and the man before she collapsed from exhaustion. She had no idea how long it was since she had last eaten and the exuberance of noise and colour made her feel faint, but she didn't stop. One foot in front of the other, one foot in front of the other, she plodded on. To her right a man was sitting on a deckchair at the water's edge, a bucket of brightly coloured children's windmills by his feet. He saw Lucy looking at the windmills turning in the breeze and began to smile, then dropped his gaze abruptly. Lucy walked on. She passed a craft market on her left, a U-shape of roofed stalls like creosoted beach huts, selling an assortment of knick-knacks: wooden ornaments, toys, hats, jewellery, paintings, bags, dried flowers, meringues and furniture. In the centre of the market a stall with a green and white striped canvas awning displayed fruit and vegetables. Lucy gazed hungrily at the apples and bananas but she didn't stop. Her mouth was watering in anticipation, but she had no money.

Beyond the craft-sellers she passed an indoor fish market. She was watching a crowd of people swarming around a stall, and almost barged into a small child waving a flag.

'Sorry,' Lucy muttered. The child's mother gazed at Lucy in disgust, swept the child up in her arms and hurried away. Lucy glanced down at her jeans, rigid with dirt and dried blood, her hands filthy despite her visit to the toilets, and her damp blood-stained t-shirt. She looked a sight, like she was on drugs or crazy. No wonder the woman had snatched her little child away from contact with her. Lucy raised her eyes and began to notice other people's reactions to her as well. Most of them looked straight through her, as though she was invisible, but a few looked her over with derision. No one came near her. She felt as though she was walking inside a glass bubble, divorced from the rest of humanity who were all going cheerfully about their daily business avoiding her like a diseased rat. She wished she could crawl away and hide.

A group of kids about her own age went past eating chips out of cardboard cartons, and Lucy realised just how ravenous she was. She couldn't remember the last time she had eaten. One of the kids dropped a long fat chip on the ground and she had to restrain herself from lunging forward to seize it. The boy laughed and squashed it flat with his trainer. He saw Lucy watching and glared at her.

'What's your problem, gipsy?'

Lucy hurried on. The harbour path curved round to meet a road and she walked unsteadily along the pavement, aware that people were staring and moving aside to avoid her. She knew she couldn't keep going much longer. As she passed a café, a warm aroma assailed her: bread, sausages, coffee, chocolate, she didn't know exactly what she could smell but she knew it was food. The door was open. The tables were empty. She stumbled across the step and fell against the nearest table.

'We're closing,' a voice called out. 'Bloody hell, what's that?' it added in surprise. Lucy thought it was a man's voice, but he sounded young, nothing like Zoe's father who wasn't Zoe's father. She was as safe here as anywhere and she couldn't walk any further anyway. Unresisting, she allowed herself to sink to the floor where she lay, whimpering and trembling. She no longer cared about what was going to happen to her, aware only of the intolerable hunger and thirst gnawing at her guts.

59

SCHOOL

Geraldine was unable to concentrate on anything while a specially trained officer questioned Ben again, with his father present, but all the boy was able to tell them was that Lucy had said she was going to stay with her best friend. He had never heard her talk about anyone called Zoe, and Matthew was adamant he knew nothing about Zoe either.

'If Lucy did have a best friend called Zoe, she kept very quiet about her,' the sergeant who had spoken to Ben concluded. 'The boy was withdrawn but I'm sure he told me everything he could. He's desperate to get his sister back safely. Matthew Kirby was extremely agitated throughout. It didn't help having him in the room. He kept interrupting, demanding to know who Zoe is, and insisting we set up a nationwide search for Lucy straightaway. I had to explain several times that we haven't yet been able to establish who Zoe is.'

'You didn't tell him what we now know about Zoe?' the DCI asked and the interviewer shook her head.

The only Zoe they had been able to trace was Zoe Mason, and there was no point visiting her again because they now knew that Zoe was a false name Lucy's abductor had been using. It wasn't a lead as such. York Regional Police force was alerted to the situation and they set about contacting all the teachers and children Lucy had known before she moved South as it was possible Lucy had returned to her former home. Meanwhile, Geraldine went back to Harchester Grammar School to question some of the pupils.

'This is Debra. She's in Lucy's class.' The deputy head ushered in a girl with badly dyed blonde hair, heavily made-up eyes, and a skirt rolled over at the top so that it barely covered her thighs when she sat down. Chewing gum with her lips apart, she slumped in the chair and stared at Geraldine, defiant and sullen. As soon as Geraldine mentioned Lucy's name Debra's mouth shut tight and she stared at the floor.

'We're trying to find out where Lucy's gone,' Geraldine explained.

Debra muttered something under her breath which sounded like 'Good riddance.' Geraldine pressed on, the girl consistently responding with unhelpful questions of her own. 'Dunno, do I? What are you asking me for? How am I supposed to know that?'

'Who might know? Who were Lucy's friends?' Geraldine asked and suppressed a flicker of annoyance as Debra snorted with laughter. Geraldine would have liked to tell the blonde girl sitting comfortably in front of her what might be happening to Lucy Kirby at that very moment. 'While you're sitting here, safe and warm, Lucy is probably being raped and tortured, she might be dying right now –' but of course she couldn't say anything of the kind. With luck it might even prove wide of the mark. So she thanked Debra for her time and handed her a card. 'If you can think of anything that might help us find Lucy, or anyone she might have gone to see, please let us know.'

'Do you think she's gone off with a bloke then?' Debra asked, with a first flicker of interest. 'Though she wasn't exactly one to drive boys wild,' she added with a faint smirk. Once again Geraldine had to suppress a flash of anger at the complacent teenager sitting opposite her.

'I'm not able to discuss any details, Debra. Thank you for your time.'

'Is that it then?'

'Unless there's anything you can tell me about Lucy?'

It was the same with all the girls in Lucy's class. Several of them mentioned Lucy's Northern accent in disparaging terms, and they were all interested in the fact that her mother had been murdered and the theory that Lucy had run off with a man. They all told Geraldine that Lucy was 'weird'.

One of the boys claimed he had never even spoken to Lucy, although he called her 'the weird new girl'.

'Weird in what way?' Geraldine asked in exasperation.

'I don't know, do I? I never spoke to her. She was weird.'

One serious looking boy told Geraldine that he believed Lucy was being bullied.

'The head teacher is aware of the issues surrounding Lucy Kirby and is dealing with them,' the deputy cut in quickly.

'Can you tell me who is bullying her?'

The boy glanced nervously at the deputy head and Geraldine held up a hand indicating to the deputy head that she should say nothing. 'Most of the other kids in the class,' he replied earnestly. 'Lucy's a bit –' He struggled to find appropriate words to describe her. 'She's a bit odd.'

'Odd how?'

'Just different, you know. She doesn't fit in. No one likes her.'

'Does she have any friends at school?'

'No.'

'Is she a loner by choice do you think?'

'No I don't think so. I mean no one really wants to be left out, do they? And it's not just that. Some of the others are pretty horrible to her.'

'What do they do?' Out of the corner of her eye Geraldine was aware of the deputy head shifting on her chair. Geraldine was there specifically to enquire about Zoe and was straying off her brief.

'The usual stuff, you know. They tease her about being

ugly. But she doesn't help herself.'

While Geraldine was occupied at Lucy's school, Peterson had been questioning Matthew Kirby and his sister again. On their return to the station they discussed what they had found out. It didn't amount to much but one thing was clear: Lucy had been abducted exactly two weeks after Abigail's murder.

Peterson thought the two must be connected. 'First the mother, then the daughter. What are the chances it's a coincidence?'

'The connection might be tenuous. Lucy was unpopular, neglected, with a mother wrapped up in her work and a father preoccupied with his mistress. The two crimes could be related only by virtue of the fact that her mother's death made Lucy even more vulnerable to the attentions of anyone offering friendship.'

'But it's possible the same person killed Abigail and Lucy.'

'We don't know Lucy's dead.'

'Well, if she is then – and even if he's not planning to kill her – it's still an attack on Matthew's family.'

'I'm not convinced this has anything to do with Matthew. He seems to think all this is happening because Charlotte's ex-boyfriend is out to punish him. But if this Ted character is so insanely possessive of Charlotte it makes no sense for him to want Abigail out of the way. Surely he'd be attacking Matthew, if anyone. No, there's something else going on here.'

'What?'

'I wish I knew.'

60

CAFÉ

'Come on.' Someone was helping Lucy onto a chair. She opened her eyes and blinked until her vision came into focus. A woman with short grey hair was talking briskly. 'That's the way. Sit her down and let her get her breath back. Now make her some tea, with plenty of sugar.' She bent down and spoke to Lucy. 'Are you hurt?'

'For goodness sake, mum, she's filthy,' another voice interrupted. Lucy raised her eyes and saw a young woman staring at her.

'Yes, Irene,' a man was talking to the older woman. 'Not to put too fine a point on it, I wouldn't get too close to her if I was you.'

'That's enough,' the grey haired woman said sharply. 'Cara, make the tea.' The young woman walked off, muttering to herself and Irene turned back to Lucy. 'Now can you tell me what's happened to you? Are you hurt? Don't be scared. I'm going to help you.'

'Mum!' the young woman protested from across the room.

'I said that's enough, Cara. You can see she's frightened. She's only a child.'

'I need a drink,' Lucy mumbled. 'Can I have some water?'

'Here.' Irene handed her a mug, unexpectedly hot. 'It's tea. Drink it.'

Lucy took a sip and pulled a face. 'Yuk. It's got sugar in it.'

'Drink it,' Irene repeated firmly. 'You need it. You've had a nasty shock.' Lucy obediently sipped the tea. It wasn't too bad. As she drank it she looked cautiously around. She was sitting on a black leather armchair at a low table. Three more tables were arranged with similar black chairs. Along the opposite side of the room were two wooden tables with upright chairs and an archway leading into another dining area. On a counter along the back wall brightly coloured salads, rolls, iced buns and cakes were displayed, smelling of coffee and toast, fruit and cakes.

'Would you like something to eat?' Irene asked, following the direction of Lucy's gaze.

'Yes. No. That is, I'm starving but I haven't got any money.'

'Don't worry, we can sort that out later. But first you need to tell me what's happened to you. Has someone hurt you?' Lucy shook her head. 'Where do you live?'

'Nowhere. I don't live anywhere.' She tried to stand up but couldn't summon the energy to move. She just wanted to sit in the warm café feeling safe, and have something to eat. Then she'd leave. The last thing she wanted to do was answer a load of questions.

'How old are you?'

'Fourteen.'

Irene was tall and thin, her eyes bright beneath her grey fringe, and like her two companions she was wearing a white t-shirt and black apron.

'Fourteen,' Irene echoed. She moved away and engaged in a hurried conversation with the younger woman, before coming back to Lucy with a plain white roll and a glass of milk. She sat and watched Lucy wolf it down.

'What's your name?'

'Lucy.'

'Lucy, my name's Irene. What happened to you?'

'I need the toilet.'

Irene led the way and Lucy scrubbed her hands and face as well as she could with the small bar of soap. A printed sign had been pinned beside the sink: Now wash your hands. Beneath it a handwritten notice warned: Caution! Hot Water! Lucy sank down on the toilet seat and cried because someone had cared enough to worry that people might scald themselves on the water from the tap.

When she returned to the café, she saw the sign on the door had been turned around. The café was closed.

'Would you like another roll?' Irene asked her. 'What would you like? Cheese? Ham? Or both?'

Lucy licked her lips and glanced at the door. 'You're closed,' she said. Apart from Irene the café was empty.

'We're closed to customers. You're a guest.'

'Where are the others?'

'They've gone home.'

'Why haven't you gone home? I don't need anyone to take care of me. I can look after myself.' She looked at the door, wondering if it was locked.

'I'm hungry,' Irene replied. 'I'm going to make myself a toasted cheese sandwich. Would you like one?'

Hunger overcame Lucy's resistance and soon she and Irene were drinking tea and tucking into a plate of toasted cheese sandwiches.

'What have you put in these sandwiches?' Lucy asked earnestly, in between bites. 'They're the best thing I've ever tasted, really.'

'That's because you've never been really hungry before.'

'I could work for you,' Lucy suggested hopefully.

Irene just smiled. 'Eat up,' was all she said. 'You look better already. A hot shower and clean clothes and you'll be –' She broke off as someone rapped on the door.

Through the glass door Lucy saw two uniformed police officers. 'You have to hide me,' she stammered, jumping up, but Irene strode to the door and opened it. The two policewomen came in and stood blocking the doorway.

'Lucy Kirby?'

'How did you know I was here?' As she spoke, Lucy realised that Irene had called them. 'I'm not going with you. You can't make me.' She was on her feet, trembling with anger.

Suddenly someone pushed past the police and Lucy saw her father, tears streaming down his face.

'Lucy! Thank God!'

He ran to her and threw his arms around her. He didn't recoil from her filth and foul smell but held her as though he would never let go. 'Lucy, come home with me. We need you. Ben's going crazy without you.' He pulled away and blew his nose. 'I don't know what to say any more. Your mother would have known what to do, but –' He began to sob. 'I'll never see Charlotte again if that's what you want. Lucy, all I care about is you and Ben.' He paused to regain his breath and Lucy waited. 'If I wanted to be with Charlotte I would've left your mother years ago, but I stayed with you and Ben. There's no way I'd risk losing you, not for anyone. The only person I ever loved as much as you and Ben was your mother.' His voice broke and he dropped his face in his hands. His voice was muffled. 'Come home, please!' By now Lucy was sobbing so hard she couldn't speak. 'Will you come home with me, Lucy?' he begged.

'Yes.'

One of the police officers stepped forward. 'Lucy, when you're ready we'd like to ask you a few questions about what happened to you.'

Matthew nodded. 'Yes, Lucy, the police want to know who Zoe is.'

'Zoe –' Lucy hesitated.

'We know Zoe was a false name,' the police officer continued gently. 'Will you help us to find the person who locked you up? I don't need to spell out how important it is that he's found and stopped.' Behind her, Lucy heard Irene mutter a curse under her breath. For a few seconds no one spoke. Lucy looked at her father who nodded at her.

'Yes, alright,' Lucy's voice shook. 'I'll help you. And when you find him, I hope you lock him up somewhere foul and never let him out again. Ever.'

61

ARREST

Geraldine and Peterson spoke very little on the way to Whitstable.

'I'm so relieved she's been found,' Geraldine said as they drove off, and the sergeant grunted his agreement. Neither of them mentioned the man who had groomed Lucy so efficiently over the internet claiming to be a girl her own age called Zoe.

A female officer, trained and experienced in working with young victims had interviewed Lucy who described her abductor as 'gross.'

'He's tall and dark-haired and skinny. He's disgusting.'

'How old was he?'

'I don't know. Old. He's all sweaty and he stinks.'

They had a sketchy description of the man they were looking for: oldish, tall and dark-haired. The broken lock on the garage door had been fixed so that from the outside it was impossible to tell that Lucy was no longer a prisoner inside. As soon as Lucy's abductor opened the door he would be apprehended, but not before. If he was frightened off without unlocking the door and disposed of the key they would only have Lucy's word to rely on for a conviction, and that might not hold up in court. No marked cars entered the street and police activity in the surrounding area was kept to a minimum with sirens strictly off-limits. Nothing was allowed to disturb the normal quiet of the streets and raise suspicion.

Geraldine and Peterson parked round the corner and entered the empty property across the road from the garage through a side door half way along the alley that ran along one side of the house. They found a local detective sergeant and a constable in an upstairs front room watching the garage. There were no curtains at the window so they had to position themselves carefully to ensure they couldn't be seen from the road. Geraldine and Peterson flashed their ID cards without speaking.

'Nothing so far, ma'am,' the local sergeant told them in an undertone. 'We've got uniform out of sight downstairs and in the shed next to the garage, and in the house next door. The neighbours reported seeing a dirty black van parked there recently.'

Geraldine nodded. 'Lucy said he picked her up in a battered old black van.' Everything fitted. Now all they could do was wait for him to turn up.

'What if he doesn't come back?' the local constable asked after an hour had passed.

'Why wouldn't he?' Geraldine replied irritably. She regretted having come. It was uncomfortable hanging around, keeping out of sight of the window. It had seemed like a brilliant idea, to be there at the arrest of the man who had brutally abducted Lucy Kirby, but sitting around in a draughty upstairs room, watching an unfamiliar sergeant pressed up against the wall staring sideways out of the window wasn't an enjoyable way to pass an afternoon. She had forgotten how boring stake-outs were. Peterson was sitting in a far corner, nearest the door, hunched over with an air of suppressed excitement. His optimism raised her spirits. This wasn't helping them to find Abigail Kirby's killer, but it felt as though they were doing something to support the dead woman, by protecting her daughter.

Suddenly the sergeant at the window tensed. His fists clenched, his head craned forward cautiously and he began talking rapidly into his radio. 'Stand by! Stand by! An old black van's drawn up right outside the garage... A tall, dark-haired man's getting out. He's approaching the garage. It looks as though – damn, I can't see. He's behind the van. Right. The garage door is opening. Go! Go!'

A few seconds later the sergeant turned round grinning broadly. 'We've got him. Caught red-handed opening the garage door, and he fits the description the victim gave.' Geraldine returned his smile and they trooped down the stairs and out by the front door.

'His name's Andrew Crozier,' a uniformed constable told them, holding up a driving licence.

Geraldine looked at the man who had been arrested: tall and gaunt, his face flushed and sweaty, an unattractive middle-aged man she might have passed on the street a thousand times without registering his presence. In himself unremarkable, she found him repulsive on account of what she knew about him. Medical examination had confirmed Lucy's statement that she had not been sexually assaulted, but Andrew Crozier could only have abducted her and kept her prisoner for one reason. Overcome with disgust, Geraldine turned away. The garage door was open. She walked around the dirty black van to approach the garage and baulked at the foul stench inside, a combination of vomit, stale sweat and faeces, as though some animal had been incarcerated there.

Behind her a faint commotion kicked off as Andrew Crozier burst out in tearful protest at his arrest. Geraldine smiled grimly as she listened to him incriminate himself.

'I wasn't going to hurt her. Ask Lucy. She'll tell you. I'm her friend.' He was weeping noisily. 'This is all a misunderstanding. I was helping her.' He sniffed loudly and shook his head. When he continued, his voice was stronger. 'Listen, you've got this all wrong. You don't know what happened. She wasn't safe with her father – ask her – and I was looking after her. I was keeping her safe, making sure no one could harm her. I didn't want to hurt her. I wanted to protect her. I'm her friend. Ask her.'

'That's why you locked her up in a garage, is it?' one of the arresting officers said.

'I – I thought she'd be safe here. No one would ever find her.' He gazed around the assembled officers in desperation. 'She asked me to help her. She wanted to come with me. I invited her to – I offered to help but only after she'd told me why she had to leave home. This was all her idea. I've done nothing wrong. I only did what she wanted. I've done nothing wrong and there's nothing you can do to prove otherwise, so just take these off and let me go. I won't speak to her again if that's what you want, only let me go. This isn't fair, I was only trying to help.'

The local sergeant had heard enough and stepped forward. 'Come on, Zoe,' he said briskly. 'It's your turn to be locked up. But don't worry. We'll make sure you have a bucket.' He grinned and a few officers laughed. 'I only hope for your sake your fellow inmates where you're going don't find out about Zoe.'

Andrew Crozier looked terrified. 'Zoe?' he stuttered. 'Who's Zoe?'

'Come on, in the car,' a constable answered. The last Geraldine saw of Andrew Crozier was his face, pale and streaked with tears, staring in despair through the police car window.

'That's the face of a man who's been nicked and is going down for a long time,' Peterson gloated and Geraldine grinned at him, sharing his exultation.

'We've got him, at least.'

'We'll find our killer,' the sergeant told her, buoyed up by the arrest. 'It's only a matter of time.'

Geraldine hoped he was right.

62

REGRET

After the euphoria of finding Lucy, the mood on the team changed when the DCI announced the news about Charlotte Fox's letter writer.

'Ted Burton is out of the frame,' the DCI announced sourly. 'York police traced him and confirmed he was in York the night Abigail Kirby was killed. He works in a camping shop and has never missed a day. He's obsessional, arrives at exactly eight thirty every morning and leaves on the dot of five. The shop manager said they can set their clocks by him. They'd all notice if he was off work for five minutes, let alone a day.'

'Abigail was killed on a Sunday,' someone pointed out.

'Ted Burton was working that weekend. So we're back to square one.'

Geraldine was glad she was meeting her friend, Hannah, after work that evening. Before long she was telling her all about Paul.

'Slow down.'

'Sorry. It's just that I think I like him.' Geraldine took a sip of wine. 'Oh well, it's not exactly important –' She broke off in mid-lie as Hannah raised a sceptical eyebrow.

'I suppose it must be nice to focus on something other than dead bodies for a change.'

'Or my mother's betrayal,' Geraldine thought. She still hadn't told Hannah about her painful visit to the adoption agency, hadn't mentioned it to anyone but Paul... Paul...

'So?' Hannah prompted her. 'He's a doctor...'

'A pathologist. He only works with dead bodies.'

'A marriage made in heaven then.' Hannah smiled, then put her glass down and stared at Geraldine, suddenly serious. 'But is he single?'

Geraldine fiddled with the stem of her wine glass. 'I'm not sure. I mean I know he was married, and he said he doesn't see his wife any more, but he hasn't said if he's actually divorced.'

'Hmm.'

'What's that supposed to mean?'

'Nothing. But you need to find out exactly what you're letting yourself in for before you get involved with him.'

'I don't see it makes any difference. At least he's separated. What matters is whether he likes me.' Their food arrived and the conversation petered out as they sorted out their respective dishes. 'It's difficult,' Geraldine resumed after a few minutes. 'He seemed really interested. He kept asking to see me, and he sent me flowers, and bought champagne, and it all seemed to be going so well. And then I blew it.'

'What happened? It can't be that bad if he sent you flowers.'

Geraldine sighed and poured more wine. 'What makes it worse is that I've got no one to blame but myself. No, actually, that's not true. This is all my bloody sergeant's fault.'

'What is?'

In a low voice, Geraldine explained Peterson's idea about Paul. Hannah was visibly shocked. 'I know it sounds ridiculous – it is ridiculous – but my sergeant went on about it – oh, I don't know why I listened to him.'

Hannah looked worried. 'But did the sergeant have any reason to suspect Paul might have killed someone?'

'No, he was just casting about in desperation, clutching at straws. We all were. A murder case and no leads –'

'You didn't believe it then?'

'Of course not. There's no way Paul could have been

implicated. But then I thought I couldn't just ignore what my sergeant had said.'

'So what did you do?'

Geraldine looked down at her plate. 'I asked him.'

'Paul?'

'Yes.'

'What? You asked him outright if he was a murderer?'

Geraldine nodded miserably. 'Oh, not in so many words but, yes. And he knew exactly what I was asking him and why.'

'What did he say?'

Geraldine sighed. 'He didn't exactly take it very well.'

'I'm not surprised. Honestly, Geraldine, didn't it cross your mind he might have been jealous?'

'What do you mean?'

'The sergeant. Maybe he fancies you and subconsciously he wanted to put you off Paul.'

Geraldine couldn't help smiling. 'This isn't a Mills and Boon story, Hannah. No, my sergeant didn't have any ulterior motives. He's a good officer – or at least I thought he was, until this. No, that's not fair. He simply got it wrong, and I was stupid enough to let him persuade me to question Paul, against my better judgement. Oh, why did I listen to him?' Hannah frowned and Geraldine fidgeted with her fork. The waitress hovered nearby for a couple of seconds and withdrew. 'I knew it was too good to be true. I really thought he was interested in me. And I could talk to him about work and he understood, which made a change.'

Hannah looked surprised. 'You discussed the case with him? I thought it was all so hush hush. You always said –'

'Yes, the investigations are confidential, but Paul did the autopsies. He's part of the investigating team. He knows more about how the victims died than anyone.'

'True. So you questioned him and he didn't take it very well?'

'It's such an insult, isn't it? I can't believe I could have been so stupid. That bloody sergeant.'

'You were only doing your job. Surely Paul understands that.'

'He was really annoyed. I mean, he didn't say much but I could tell.'

Hannah scraped the last crumbs of pizza from her plate. 'I don't blame him.'

'Hannah, you're not helping. I don't know what I can do to put it right. What can I do? I really like Paul. He's different. I haven't felt like this about anyone since Mark and I split up. Craig was just a fling, I never honestly thought that was going anywhere. But I really thought there might possibly be something serious between me and Paul. And I was sure he liked me.'

'He'll understand you were only doing your job. You have to talk to him. That's all you can do now, talk to him and it'll all blow over. After all, what you did wasn't so very terrible, was it?'

'Oh, I don't know. I hope you're right. Anyway, I do have some other news which is potentially even more exciting.'

'What's that?'

'I've applied for a transfer. It was kind of an impulse, although I've been thinking about it for a while. But now I've gone ahead I'm not sure if I want to go –'

'Where?'

Geraldine picked up her glass and took a sip. 'I haven't mentioned it to anyone yet – I haven't even told my sister. She won't like it. I see little enough of them as it is.'

'Where are you thinking of going?' Hannah repeated.

'I put in for a transfer to London.'

'London?'

'Yes, to the Met. It's a good career move, and I need a change. I thought – well, it seemed like a good idea at the time, but now I don't know if I want to leave the area.'

'It's not as if London's on the other side of the world. It's only an hour away.'

'I could be in North London.'

'Well, over an hour then, but even so, it's not that far. We'll just have to meet half way.'

'Anyway, nothing's decided yet. Now, enough about me. What's your news?'

Hannah shrugged but she was smiling. 'Same old, same old. Nothing changes. Only the kids are growing older and more expensive by the minute.'

'And Jeremy?'

'Jeremy's fine.' The waitress brought the bill and they chatted about Hannah's family as they sorted it out.

'Call him,' Hannah said as they were putting on their coats. 'If he likes you, he'll understand.'

'I guess so.'

'And let me know what happens. Call me soon.'

'I will do and – thank you.'

Hannah's lips brushed Geraldine lightly on the cheek and she was gone.

Back in her car, Geraldine checked the time. It was barely nine o'clock. 'Go for it,' she whispered as she dialled Paul's number. There was no answer. Disappointed, she drove home. Sitting on her bed, she tried one last time but Paul still wasn't answering. She opened her bedside drawer, pulled out a small photo and gazed at it trembling in her hand. The colour had faded but the features were clearly recognisable, familiar. As in family. It was almost like looking in a mirror, looking at herself twenty years ago, a young Geraldine, staring at the camera in wide-eyed apprehension. Only she wasn't Geraldine, she was Erin. Erin Blake. And this was her mother, Milly Blake.

Her anger had softened into curiosity. She didn't know

that her mother had discarded her easily. Sometimes women never recovered from losing their babies. For all she knew, Milly Blake had regretted her sacrifice every day for nearly forty years. Perhaps she still felt a tremor of hope every time the phone rang, or there was a knock on the door, a desperate hope that her abandoned child had found her.

The social worker had done her best to quash that hope. 'Milly Blake never contacted us again,' she had explained sadly, as though she cared. It was true that if Geraldine's mother had wanted to be traced she could have written to that effect but there was no letter, not so much as a note, nothing. But a letter could have been lost. Even social workers might misfile documents, or throw them away by accident. Or Milly Blake could be dead. That would be less of a rejection.

Lying in bed, unable to sleep, Geraldine played out various scenes in her head. She imagined knocking on a door which was opened by her mother, bowed, grey haired, but instantly recognisable.

'Geraldine,' she would say, only it wouldn't be Geraldine, it would be Erin. Geraldine smiled. She quite liked her original name. She thought it suited her. She had never liked the name Geraldine, which sounded somehow strident. Erin was much gentler. She wondered, irrationally, if her life might have panned out differently if her name had been Erin.

'Erin,' the woman who bore a striking resemblance to Geraldine would say. 'Erin, I knew you'd find me.' Then she would fling her arms around Geraldine's shoulders…

She switched to a different scenario in her head. 'Erin,' the old woman scolded, 'what are you doing here? Go away!' The door slammed in Geraldine's face. She knocked again and after a moment her mother opened it and peered out. 'I thought I told you to go away.'

'But mother –'

'I'm not your mother. I don't know you. Go away!'

Geraldine woke from an uneasy doze and found her eyes wet with tears. 'I don't care,' she muttered to herself.

She tried to imagine what it must have been like to be pregnant at fifteen in the early 1960s, at the beginning of the sexual revolution, when the pill had only just become available to married women and attitudes were still very conservative. Fifteen was very young, too young. She thought of Lucy Kirby, fourteen years old and still a child, and a wave of pity shook her. Perhaps her mother had withdrawn in shame. Who was Geraldine to judge her? At any rate, she couldn't live with this uncertainty indefinitely.

63

PROPOSAL

On a high after the arrest of Andrew Crozier, the team worked late sorting out reports, checking statements and preparing to interview the suspect. It didn't take them long to identify Crozier as a man who had been questioned less than a year earlier about the abduction and rape of a thirteen-year-old girl he had befriended. They had met in her local park where, according to witness statements, he had used a small dog to lure her into conversation. In the absence of any substantive proof there had been no prosecution when the girl had refused to talk about her experience, or to confirm the identity of her attacker. There was a good chance that apprehending Lucy Kirby's abductor was going to lead to the conviction of a serial paedophile once the DNA test results were completed. The mood in the Incident Room was buoyant.

'Do I really have to remind you all that this is a murder investigation. Let's celebrate when we get a result, and not before,' Kathryn Gordon said, but they had rescued Lucy and even the detective chief inspector's reproach couldn't dampen Geraldine's high spirits.

'The tide's turned,' a constable replied.

'Yes, now we've found Lucy, it's only a matter of time before we solve the Abigail Kirby murder,' Peterson agreed.

'There's no room for complacency on a murder investigation,' Kathryn Gordon reminded them. 'Some of you seem to have forgotten that it was an alert member of the public who heard Lucy Kirby calling for help. Finding her had nothing to do with good police work, so let's not get ahead of ourselves. Now let's sharpen up and concentrate on discovering what happened to Abigail Kirby.'

They all knew they had to return to the main focus of the investigation, but it was a welcome relief to enjoy the respite of a brief feeling of success. Caught up in the general euphoria Geraldine called Paul Hilliard to share the good news about Lucy Kirby, and when he asked to see her the following evening she thought her day couldn't possibly get any better.

Ian Peterson had returned home late on Wednesday evening, after Crozier had been interviewed. His girlfriend, Bev, was already asleep so there was no chance to tell her about the arrest and he left for work the next morning before she was awake. He arrived home on Thursday night in high spirits after finishing his evening in the pub across the road from the police station. He stepped into the living room pumped up and eager to tell Bev what had happened. As soon as he saw her expression he understood that his uplifting day wasn't going to end well.

'What time do you call this?'

Ian glanced at his watch. 'It's nearly ten, but –'

'You're late.'

Ian wanted to throw himself down beside her and fling his arms round her, but hesitated. 'I was kept –'

'And you didn't think to phone? You know we were supposed to be going out with Kirsty this evening. It's her birthday. You promised to be home in time.'

'Oh shit.'

'It's her birthday. You could have called. And why didn't you answer your phone? I could have gone on without you but no, I had to sit here, waiting, in case you deigned to come home.' Bev's voice rose in a childish wail but her eyes remained cold.

Ian shrugged apologetically and launched into an awkward account of Lucy Kirby's disappearance and the subsequent arrest of Crozier. 'We got him straightaway. It had to be wrapped up quickly before anything could alert him to our presence, and it wasn't easy having so much activity in a dead end without being visible, I can tell you. It was brilliantly managed, and we got him.'

'Well, now it's over perhaps you can stop obsessing about your bloody work.'

Ian held out his hands in mute pleading. 'He abducted a thirteen-year-old girl last year but managed to wriggle out of being prosecuted. God knows how many other children he's kidnapped and abused. We've caught a paedophile who goes around abusing young girls. It's a great result, Bev. It's…' He sighed. He would have thought she'd be proud of the work he'd put in, helping to stop this animal. 'He's dangerous, Bev, a monster preying on vulnerable young girls. He had to be stopped. You do see that, don't you? That my work is important.'

Bev turned her face away from him without speaking and Ian gazed down at her short white blonde hair, her narrow shoulders and slim legs, taking in her clothes. Always beautiful, she had made an effort to dress up smartly for her friend's birthday drink.

He sighed, trying to understand where she was coming from, but it was outrageous that she would expect him to prioritise having a birthday drink with a friend over stopping an evil monster like Crozier. 'I'm sorry, Bev,' he lied. 'I was so wrapped up in the case, I completely forgot about the arrangement with Kirsty. But even if I'd remembered, it wouldn't have made any difference. You do understand that, don't you?' She didn't answer. 'And there's still the ongoing investigation into who murdered the teacher. But that's not so pressing. I mean, it was vital we found the girl quickly. He could have killed her – or worse.'

Bev turned to face him and he was surprised to see tears glittering on her cheeks. 'It's all right, love, I get it,' she said gently. 'I'm sorry. Of course finding that poor child and catching the paedophile had to take precedence over Kirsty's drinks. I'm sorry. Come here.' She patted the cushion next to her and Ian dropped down onto the sofa and put his arm round her, pulling her close. Bev rested her head on his shoulder. 'Have you eaten?' she asked.

'I had something.' He didn't add that he'd eaten in the pub. 'So, what have you been up to?'

Bev began to talk but he couldn't focus on what she was saying. After a few minutes she tapped him on the knee. 'Are you listening?'

'Sorry. I was just thinking about the DI.' Talking to Bev often helped Ian to formulate his thoughts and he really needed to work through his suspicions of Paul Hilliard and his concern that Geraldine's judgement had been clouded by her relationship with the pathologist.

Bev pulled away abruptly from his embrace and folded her arms. 'Oh great. Thank you very much. You think so much of your precious DI, why don't you go and live with her? You practically do already. You spend more time with her than you do with me –'

'You know it's not a nine to five job, Bev.' He paused but she didn't answer. 'I don't see how you can be married to a police officer if you can't understand something as basic as that.'

Bev rose to her feet and stood directly in front of him, gazing at him, her eyes wide. 'Married to a police officer?' she repeated. 'Did you say married?'

Ian stared back at her, bowled over. For years he had been planning to marry Bev one day, if she'd have him, but he hadn't intended to propose like this, sweaty and exhausted from a long day at work, with Bev in tears. He'd thought vaguely of a romantic weekend in Paris, a ring passed across the table in an open jewellery box, sparkling on a small velvet cushion, a real corker, like the ring one of his mates had bought for his girlfriend. Bev would love that.

He hesitated, aware that she was waiting for an answer. 'Well, I want to, if you do,' he stammered. 'Of course I do. Don't you?'

'Is this a proposal?'

'Look, I haven't got a ring yet, I mean, I wanted to take you away somewhere romantic… Oh what the hell?' He dropped down on one knee. 'Marry me, Bev. Marry me or I'll be miserable for the rest of my life.'

She laughed, crying again. 'How can I refuse an offer like that?' Ian stood up and wrapped her in his arms, holding her so close that she complained. 'Let go, Ian, I can't breathe.'

'I'll never let you go,' he answered. As he relaxed his grip on her, he was surprised to realise his eyes were watering. 'I should have asked you a long time ago,' he said.

'Why didn't you?'

'I was afraid.'

'Afraid of commitment?'

'Afraid you'd say no.'

'That's the daftest thing I've ever heard.'

He pressed Bev's head against his neck to stop her seeing his tears. He had never felt so happy.

64

JOURNEY

'Fancy an early night?' Ian suggested. 'I've got to be up at six in the morning.'

'I thought you had the day off tomorrow.'

'No such luck. All hands to the pumps I'm afraid.'

Bev groaned and ruffled his hair. 'Oh Ian. And you're so tired.'

'I'm fine.'

'No, you're not. You look absolutely exhausted. Can't they let you have a day off?'

He shook his head, smiling. 'It'll soon be over. Now, how about that early night?'

'Why do you have to be up so early?'

'I need to go in and work,' he replied vaguely. He didn't want to risk anyone finding out what he was planning to do the next day.

The train to York took two hours from Kings Cross. Ian spent the time checking through Paul Hilliard's history once again. His fifteen-year-old daughter had died but Peterson could find no report on the cause of death, which was strange. The records seemed to have vanished. He spent an hour on the telephone to the registrar of births and deaths in York, but they were unable to help him.

'I'm sorry, Sergeant.' The woman on the line, flustered at first, became increasingly belligerent. 'It looks as though someone's taken the file away and not returned it.'

'Don't you keep a copy?'

'We don't have duplicates as a matter of course.' In the end she promised to look into it and Peterson had to be satisfied with that.

Six months after Abigail Kirby had moved to Harchester, Paul Hilliard had been appointed Home Office pathologist for the area. It could have been a coincidence. Abigail Kirby and Paul Hilliard had both been promoted. There was no reason why they shouldn't have moved to the same area, but given the connection through Paul Hilliard's daughter Ian was convinced he was right to investigate, sure too that there was at least a possibility the DI's judgement had been influenced by her friendship with the pathologist. How else could he explain her vehement rejection of his ideas, before she'd even considered what he was saying, and why had she flatly refused to tell the DCI about his suspicions?

Ian stepped off the train at York, crossed the busy station footbridge and made his way out onto the street. He took a taxi into town, choosing not to contact the local police station for transport. He wanted to keep his visit under wraps, at least until he had something concrete to show the DI. If his journey turned out to be a waste of time, she need never find out. He would have spent a long day travelling for nothing, but he had been ferreting around, asking about Paul Hilliard, and he had a feeling something wasn't right. If his suspicions proved to be well founded he would have to face the DI, but at least he'd have some hard facts to show her.

The headmistress of York Girls Grammar School was an austere, grey-haired woman. Ian could imagine her intimidating the pupils in her charge, but she greeted him pleasantly enough.

'Detective Sergeant Peterson, I'm June Melbury. How can I help you?' While her words were urbane, her eyes were guarded. 'May I ask what this is about?'

'I want to ask about a former member of your staff who was here until the end of the last academic year. It's a routine enquiry. Nothing serious. Just a little background information about Abigail Kirby.'

'Oh Abigail.' Mrs Melbury sat down heavily. 'Yes, of course we heard. How terrible.' She shook her head. 'Do you know what happened?'

'We're investigating.'

'And how can I help you?'

'We're not sure yet.'

'You mean, you're here to ask the questions,' she smiled. 'Well, of course, anything I can do to help –'

'Was Abigail Kirby popular with the pupils? Was she good at her job?'

'She was very good with the pupils, especially when they had problems.'

'What sort of problems?'

Mrs Melbury sighed. 'There are so many problems with young girls these days, Sergeant, but it's always best when they come forward so we can help them. It's the ones who don't talk who turn out to be the real worry.' Ian thought of Lucy Kirby, and wondered if she was receiving similar consideration at her school. She was probably one of the girls who kept her problems to herself, although obviously the school knew about her mother's murder. Everyone knew about it.

He realised the headmistress was looking at him, waiting for him to speak. 'Did she ever help a pupil called Emma Hilliard?'

'Emma Hilliard, the suicide? She tried.'

'We know she committed suicide,' Ian lied, looking down to hide his surprise, 'but we need to be clear about the circumstances. Please can you tell me in your own words what happened.'

Mrs Melbury hesitated. 'What has this to do with Abigail Kirby?'

'I'm afraid I can't say. All I can tell you is that we're investigating the death of Abigail Kirby and we need to know about her history with Emma Hilliard. It may just possibly have some bearing on what happened to her. That's what I've been sent here to look into.' He hoped the headmistress wouldn't realise he was winging it. She looked like a shrewd woman, used to penetrating her pupils' fibs.

Mrs Melbury didn't reply straightaway. Instead, she picked up her phone. 'Can you bring me the file for Emma Hilliard?' She listened for a moment. 'Yes, that Emma... Yes, the secure cabinet... Thank you.' She turned to Ian. 'It's all history now. I do hope this isn't going to be raked over in public again. Once the press start up – we barely rode out the storm when it all happened. The school almost didn't survive.' She looked very old and tired suddenly.

'Of course you can rely on our discretion,' Ian reassured her.

A moment later the door opened and a woman scurried in carrying a buff folder which she handed to the headmistress, who nodded her thanks and waited for the secretary to leave the room. She glanced down at the file and spoke slowly. 'Emma Hilliard was fifteen when she fell pregnant. Abigail Kirby supported her.'

'How did she support her, exactly?'

'She helped to arrange an abortion.'

'An abortion?'

'It was what Emma wanted. We advised against it and she had counselling naturally – we insisted as a matter of course – but she was a determined girl who knew her own mind. An intelligent girl. She didn't want her parents to find out.'

'They didn't know?'

'Not at first.'

'Shouldn't you have told them?'

'Her mother was told but not her father. Abigail made the

arrangements with the mother's consent. It was the best we could do, and Emma was very insistent that was what she wanted. Her mother supported her wishes – so she went ahead and had the abortion.'

'Why did she kill herself?'

The headmistress shrugged helplessly. 'Who knows exactly why these things happen? After the abortion she became depressed. She was having help and we thought she was making a good recovery, but one day –' She broke off. After a few seconds she regained her self-control. 'Her father took it very hard. He'd known nothing about the pregnancy, but of course it all came out after her suicide. He was understandably shocked when he learned that his daughter had refused to confide in him and, as he saw it, his wife had colluded in excluding him from supporting his daughter. He seemed to think he could have made a difference, if he had known. And who knows? Maybe he would. Anyway, the marriage broke up after the girl's suicide. They had no other children, only Emma, you see. Her father idolised her. She was a lovely girl, very intelligent, talented, and quite beautiful. I think her father blamed us, but we were only supporting Emma's wishes and her mother knew all about it, so I really don't believe the school can be held responsible for what happened. If we hadn't helped Emma, her mother would have taken her elsewhere and we thought she was better off with people who knew her. Or at least we thought we knew her. It was a terrible tragedy.'

Ian considered. 'How did she actually commit suicide?'

'She hung herself.'

'At school?'

'No. There was that at least. Not that it made any difference to the poor girl. And it was her father who found her… in her bedroom…' She rubbed her bottom lip with the back of a hand that was shaking slightly. 'And then there was another one…'

Ian had to strain to hear her. 'Another one?'

'Another girl – Emma's best friend – she killed herself two weeks later. She threw herself out of Emma's bedroom window. Emma's father said she asked to visit her friend's room to say goodbye, and when he went upstairs, I'm afraid the poor man found her too. It was horrible. She lost an ear –'

Ian started forward in his chair. 'Lost an ear? What do you mean?'

'There was a glass conservatory below the window and she went right through it, shattering the glass and slashing off her ear as she fell.' Mrs Melbury shuddered.

Ian leapt to his feet. 'I need to see the post-mortem report as soon as possible. What was her name?' The headmistress looked surprised at his sudden excitement. 'Her name?' he repeated impatiently.

'Her name was Mary Shelton. She was a sweet girl. You have no idea what an effect all this had on our community here. We're still reeling from it.'

Ian put his notebook away. He didn't have much time before his train back. 'Thank you very much. That's been very helpful.'

She too stood up. 'And all this will be treated in strict confidence?'

'Need to know basis.'

'Thank you. I realise you may not be able to tell me, but do you think this will help your enquiries into Abigail's death?'

'Yes. I think it will.'

'But does that mean Abigail's death was in some way related to Emma Hilliard's suicide?'

'Mrs Melbury, you've been very co-operative. I can't stop you speculating, but please, it's very important you don't mention this to anyone. Don't even mention that I was here. It's vitally important no one knows we've been asking about Emma Hilliard.'

'I can be discreet too, Sergeant.' She held out her hand.

Worried he'd said too much, Ian tried to backtrack. 'We're just making general enquiries into Abigail Kirby's past, trying to find out what sort of person she was. It just happened that Emma Hilliard was the only name we'd come across – that's all –'

She knew he wasn't being strictly truthful. 'There's more to this than you are able to tell me, but don't worry. I won't mention this discussion to anyone. I just hope it helps you to find out who murdered poor Abigail. She helped so many pupils. But a few – like Emma –' She shrugged. 'You can't help everyone, Sergeant.'

'No, you can't.'

Ian reached York station with minutes to spare before his train left, a copy of the post-mortem report on Mary Shelton in his inside pocket. Soon after Paul Hilliard's daughter committed suicide her best friend had fallen from Emma's bedroom window to land on glass which broke, neatly slicing off one of her ears. At the time there had been no reason to suspect that this had been anything other than a terrible accident. That Paul Hilliard had been in the house at the time had been regarded as his misfortune.

Paul Hilliard had subsequently moved to Kent where his daughter's former tutor had been murdered, and her tongue cut out. The only potential witness had been murdered, and his eyes removed.

Ian's elation at the success of his journey faded as the train began to move. He dreaded telling Geraldine, but it had to be done. Reluctantly he reached for his mobile. It seemed to ring interminably before he heard Geraldine's voice, brisk and reassuring. '…I can't come to the phone right now. Please leave a message…'

Ian swore under his breath as he waited. 'Gov, it's Ian. Call me as soon as you get this. I need to speak to you about Paul

Hilliard. I've been to York and –' He faltered. He knew he'd have to tell her but decided it was best dealt with face to face. 'Call me. It's urgent. Don't contact him until we've spoken.' He hung up. There was nothing more he could do. The train hurtled smoothly on its way south.

He waited but the DI didn't return his call.

65

THE TRUTH

As she was washing her hands, Geraldine thought she heard her phone ring. She paused to check her make-up and smooth down her hair, before returning to the living room where Paul was waiting for her.

'Was that my phone?'

Paul looked faintly puzzled. 'Phone?'

'I thought I heard my phone.'

'I didn't hear anything. I was in the kitchen.'

Geraldine checked. 'I thought so. There's a missed call from my sergeant.'

A petulant frown crossed Paul's face. 'You're not on duty now. Ignore it.'

'But –'

'The sergeant would've left a message if it was important.'

'True. But –'

'Come here.' He came very close to her, rested his arms on her shoulders and kissed her on the mouth. His lips felt dry and warm, his tongue probed gently between her teeth. 'Forget about work,' he murmured, kissing her neck. 'It's easier than you think.' Geraldine relaxed into his embrace as he kissed her again. After a few seconds he pulled back slightly, still keeping his arms around her. 'Geraldine, come with me. I want to show you something.'

Smiling, he led her into the hall. She hoped he was taking her up to his bedroom but he took her straight to a bookcase at the foot of the stairs. Geraldine was surprised to see him slide the bookcase sideways across the wall to reveal a small door. He took a key from his pocket. As it turned in the lock, they heard the faint sound of a phone ringing in the living room. She turned.

'Leave it.' Paul looked at her, his face alive with excitement. Geraldine smiled and stepped forward. The door swung open and she followed him across the threshold into darkness. The door clicked shut behind her and she heard the faint scratching of a key turning. There was a brief pause then a sudden light dazzled her. When she opened her eyes, Paul was looking up at her from half way down a narrow staircase.

'Come on.' She had never seen Paul looking so energised, his eyes sparkling in the bright light. He led her down, holding her hand, and Geraldine was astonished to see a white room, bare apart from a large white table and a white cupboard that reached to the ceiling. She wondered how it had been brought down the stairs or if it had been put together down there. The strangeness of the room suddenly made her skin crawl with fear.

'Everything's white,' she said, watching Paul as he unlocked the cupboard. He was smiling to himself. 'Why is everything white?' she asked.

'Beautiful, isn't it?' He had his back to her while he rummaged in the cupboard. She couldn't see what he was doing. Over his shoulder she saw narrow wooden drawers but she couldn't see their contents.

'Why is everything white?' she asked again. Her voice trembled slightly. The whole situation was uncomfortably odd, and she had no idea where it was leading.

A sudden jolt of alarm struck her, a visceral sensation that something was very wrong about this sepulchral cellar, very wrong indeed. On an impulse she turned and darted up the stairs. There was no door handle, only an empty keyhole. She kicked the door. It didn't even quiver.

'Come back down.' Paul spoke quietly.

Geraldine turned on the top step, her shoulders pressed against the unyielding door. 'What did you want to show me?'

'This.' He gestured around the cellar, smiling.

'It's lovely Paul, if you like secret basements,' she answered, keeping her voice under control. 'Now I've seen it, let's go back upstairs.' He didn't answer. 'Why is the door locked?'

He laughed out loud. 'Because I locked it.'

Geraldine smiled back at him. 'I'd like to go back upstairs, Paul. Open the door please.'

'Not yet.'

'But –'

'I want to show you something. Come down here, Geraldine.'

She hesitated but she had no choice. 'I don't want to. It's cold down there.' Paul ignored her and moved across the cellar out of her line of vision. She could only see the top of his head, bowed forward. 'What are you doing, Paul?' Slowly she descended the stairs.

Paul was standing motionless on the other side of the room, the table between them like a barrier. He took a step towards her and as he moved something glinted in his right hand. He was holding a syringe.

'What's in your hand?'

'Don't worry, I don't want to punish you, Geraldine. This will be very quick. I promise you won't feel anything.' Paul met her gaze with an apologetic smile. 'This wasn't part of the plan, Geraldine, it really wasn't. I never wanted to punish you, believe me. If there was another way…' He took a step towards her.

Geraldine stared at him in horror, realising that the man she had been falling in love with was a fantasy; Paul Hilliard was insane. 'No. Wait. I don't understand any of this.'

'I can't let you stop me. Not now.'

'And I won't. Let me go and – we can forget all about this.' He must know she was lying, but she couldn't think what else to say.

'The problem is your young sergeant has been calling, leaving you messages. I can't let you stop me now. You know too much.'

Geraldine shook her head. 'I don't know anything, Paul. No one's told me anything about you.' She paused and took a deep breath. 'I can help you, Paul. Don't you see? If the sergeant knows something – about you – you're going to need my help.'

He raised the syringe. 'I haven't got a choice. The sergeant's next. It's his own fault. He shouldn't have interfered. But you – I'm sorry Geraldine, I never wanted things to end like this.' He raised his right arm and the liquid glistened in the syringe.

'I want to help you. I want to understand. What's going on? Tell me. What's this about?'

'Emma.' He sounded impatient, as though it was obvious. 'This is for Emma.'

'Your daughter?' He nodded. 'She was a beautiful girl.'

'You didn't know her.'

'I saw her photograph. But I still don't understand. What has this,' she looked around the cellar, 'got to do with your daughter?'

'Those responsible had to be punished,' he replied. He sounded so matter-of-fact Geraldine struggled to believe he was really threatening her.

'Responsible for what?'

'For Emma's death. They let her down. All of them.'

'Who?'

'Her friend who never listened, her teacher who gave her terrible advice, and the doctor who killed her.'

Geraldine gulped for air. She felt as though she was

suffocating. 'Teacher? Abigail Kirby was your daughter's teacher? She gave your daughter the wrong advice so you cut out her tongue.' She felt sick. The room was spinning as though she was drunk. Paul raised his hand and a tiny spurt of clear liquid shot into the air catching the light. Geraldine struggled to make sense of it. 'Who else did you kill, Paul? What girl? Why did you kill –'

'That girl was supposed to be Emma's best friend, but she didn't listen when Emma needed help. What kind of a person betrays a friend like that? How could I leave her to carry on, living out her evil life, while Emma...' He shook his head. 'Only the doctor is left now, and he'll be next.'

'What doctor? I don't understand. Why would you want to kill a doctor?'

'The doctor who terminated my daughter's pregnancy, murdered her unborn child –'

'Emma had an abortion?'

'The doctor who killed my unborn grandchild. The doctor who drove my daughter, Emma...' His voice broke.

Geraldine thought she began to understand. 'Are you saying your daughter had an abortion and that's why she killed herself?'

He ignored her question. 'The boy wasn't part of the plan but he saw too much so he had to go. And now I'm afraid you know too much, Geraldine.' He moved round the table towards her.

She edged away from him backwards, never taking her eyes off him. 'What part of my anatomy are you going to remove?'

Paul shook his head impatiently. 'You think too much. That's your problem.'

Geraldine raised her hand to her head, pressing her fingers against her skull in stunned comprehension. 'What part of me, Paul?'

'That's something you don't need to know, and you never will.'

Geraldine glanced frantically around for a weapon of some kind, but apart from the table, the cupboard, and a sink, the room was bare. She couldn't remember if Paul had locked the cupboard when he had closed it and, in any case, if she managed to edge around the table and make a dash for it, he would be on her with the syringe before she could grab hold of anything she could use in self defense.

'Paul –' Geraldine thought she heard footsteps overhead, and felt a tremor of hope. She had to stall him for another few minutes. 'Wait,' she said. 'Let's talk about this. I can help you. Don't jump to conclusions. What makes you think I don't support what you're doing? Your daughter's dead, Paul. What you're doing, you're looking for justice. That's what I believe in too. You can't let the people responsible for Emma's death get away with it. I understand that. Someone has to be punished, it's only right. But there's no reason to kill me. I'm not to blame for what happened to her. And I can help you. What do you think is going to happen to you now the police know what you've done?'

Paul didn't appear to have heard anyone moving around upstairs. 'Save your breath. I don't need your help.'

'You'll go to prison, Paul, for a long time. But I can help you –'

'I told you, I don't need your help.' He smiled grimly. 'I'm almost done. I have to finish what I set out to do. There's only one more – after you and your sergeant – and then it'll be my turn. Come on, we have to hurry. You understand, don't you? I have to finish this. I know it doesn't matter what you think, we'll both be dead soon, but I'd like you to understand.'

Geraldine's mouth felt dry. Her legs were shaking as she tried to circle round the table away from him, aware that he might rush her at any moment.

'I don't understand why you want me to die. This is nothing to do with me. Emma's death wasn't my fault. I didn't even know her. Let me help you, Paul. You need help –'

Paul moved closer. He raised his arm and Geraldine screamed as she edged away from him. Upstairs all was silent. She wondered if she should make a dash for the cupboard where he kept grisly tools of his work, knives, syringes, razor-sharp scalpels, but she knew she would never make it before he reached her. She considered trying to thrust the table at him with a sudden desperate lunge so it would fall on his feet, pinning him to the floor, but there was no way she would be able to shift it by herself.

Suddenly they were startled by a loud thump. Geraldine dithered but Paul wasn't distracted for an instant. In one swift movement he raised his arm and stabbed. The syringe dropped from his hand and she stared, transfixed, as a drop of blood beaded where the needle had penetrated.

66

CELLAR

Sergeant Bell and Constable Letwick were only round the corner when the call came through. The message was garbled but they heard the address quite clearly.

'We're just round the corner,' Bell answered. 'We're on our way.'

'Step on it,' his companion urged. 'We'll be first on the scene.' A constable for nearly two years, Ollie Letwick was fed up with stepping in between brawling drunks, arresting kids who were high and taking statements from shopkeepers who called the station to report shoplifters. There wasn't much point. They were always impossible to identify, hooded, blurred images on CCTV. Ollie longed for some real excitement. 'What exactly is going on?' he asked as they sped along the road.

Bell shook his head without taking his eyes off the road. 'You heard as much as I did. They think DI Steel's in some sort of trouble.'

'Women,' Ollie grinned. The sergeant grunted and put his foot down mumbling about political correctness. 'Just joking,' Ollie said. 'The DI is hardly the sort to need saving. Reckon she can take care of herself.'

'Should be able to,' Bell agreed as they screeched to a halt outside a large detached property. 'This is it.' He hesitated. 'Do you think we should wait for back up?' As he spoke, they heard the wail of a siren. Several police cars raced into view and the pavement was suddenly heaving with uniformed officers.

'Come on!' Ollie leapt out of the car and almost barged into DCI Gordon. He and Bob Bell joined the group of officers following her up the path.

'We had a call from DS Peterson,' the DCI explained to them hurriedly over her shoulder. 'It seems Paul Hilliard could be the man we've been looking for.'

There was a subdued clamour of questions.

'He's the killer?'

'Paul Hilliard? Isn't he the pathologist?'

There was no response to their knocking. They walked around the property but all the doors were locked. At a nod from the DCI one of the constables smashed a small window beside the side door, reached in to undo the bolt and they were in.

'Hello! Police! Is anyone here?' There was no answer. A rapid search of the house revealed it was empty. Constable Letwick and Sergeant Bell were instructed to remain behind until the property was secure, and the posse of police officers withdrew. The house was empty and silent once more as they waited in the front hall for the householder to return home, and for a glazier to arrive to fix the window.

'So much for seeing something exciting,' Ollie grumbled.

'You what?'

'I thought we might see some action here –'

'Action?'

'You know, something happening. A dramatic arrest, or something.'

Bell laughed and was about to reply when they heard a noise, like a muffled yelp. Their eyes met in a puzzled frown. 'Sounded like that came from inside the house,' Bell said in a low voice.

'It came from under the floor,' Ollie agreed.

They looked around. The hall was decorated in cream and pale blue. There was an empty wooden coat stand near the door, a tall bookcase along one wall and three doors leading to the kitchen, the living room and a downstairs cloakroom. They listened, but there was no more noise from under the floorboards.

'There's no access to a basement from here,' Bell said.

'Unless –' Ollie went up to the bookcase and shook it.

'Watch it, you'll have all those books on the floor.'

'That's odd. They're not real books,' Ollie replied as he reached forward to take one off the shelf. 'It's not a proper bookcase. Look, these books are painted on. Come here and give me a hand. I reckon there must be something behind it –' Together they pushed the bookcase which slid sideways to reveal a door. Bell swore softly in surprise and reached for his phone. While he summoned back up, Ollie rapped sharply on the door but there was no response from the other side. The door had no handle, only a keyhole. Ollie pushed the door. It wouldn't budge. He tried again, yelling now for whoever was inside to come and open the door up. There was no answer so he stood back and charged at the door, shoulder first. It flew open with a crash.

Ollie rushed through the door so fast he almost fell headlong down a narrow staircase. Pausing to regain his balance, he stepped forwards.

His companion put his hand on Ollie's arm. 'Do you think we should wait? They'll be here in a few minutes.'

'If she's here, the DI could be in danger,' Ollie whispered back. Bell nodded and Ollie made his way cautiously down the stairs. He had an impression of whiteness and then he heard a woman's voice crying out in alarm.

Ollie leaped down the final few steps and his eyes widened in surprise. On the far side of a table draped in white the DI was crouching on the floor. She glared wildly at him and gestured at a man lying motionless on the floor beside her. Apart from the two figures, everything in the room was perfectly white.

'Over here!' she called out. 'He's unconscious. He's injected himself.' Her voice rose hysterically and she turned away. As Ollie stepped forward he heard feet pounding down the stairs and the room was suddenly crammed with officers. A paramedic hurried forward and knelt on the floor beside the DI.

'This doesn't look good. What did he take?'

The DI was upright now, leaning against the table. 'I don't know, but he's a pathologist. He'd have access to all sorts of drugs – you might find something in the cupboard. That's where he took the syringe from.' Her voice had recovered its strength and she spoke with authority.

'I thought I recognised him,' the paramedic said.

The DI went over to a tall cupboard, opened the door and began rifling through the drawers. The first was full of surgical equipment: scalpels, gloves, syringes, all laid out in neat rows. The contents of the second drawer was the same. The third was stuffed with photographs of a girl.

She picked up one of the photographs. 'That's his daughter.'

'I wonder if she knows he's got a whole drawer of photos of her down here,' Ollie said gazing down at the body.

'She's dead.'

The paramedic looked up. 'So will he be if we don't get him into hospital soon. Where the hell's that ambulance?'

67

MOVING ON

Overwhelmed by memories of Paul, Geraldine barely slept that night. At last she drifted into an uneasy dream where Paul was pursuing her along a dark tunnel that led to a bright white room. She knew that if she didn't reach the end of the corridor she would die, so she kept on running...

The next morning she woke up feeling so mentally drained it made her absurdly calm, as though she was still dreaming. After the shock of discovering Paul's true nature, she felt she would never care about anything again. If someone had rushed in and pointed a gun at her head she would simply have waited for the outcome, unmoved and incurious. After a shower and strong coffee she drove to work very carefully, numb and disorientated, not trusting her reactions. Driving to the station she tried to take a cold hard look at herself and it didn't make comfortable viewing. She had allowed herself to be distracted by her attraction to Paul, who had been playing her all along for his own purposes. Knowing she had been so gullible was even more painful than the loss of what had, after all, been no more than a romantic fantasy. She had not only been deluded about Paul but about herself too.

One thing was certain: she would never trust herself to take anything anyone said at face value ever again.

Her face burned with embarrassment as she walked into the station, wondering what her colleagues must think of her. Paul had stolen more than her romantic ideal, he had shattered her self-confidence. Geraldine had always prided herself on her sharp intuition about people. The intelligence to organise a deluge of information wasn't enough in her profession – after all, a computer could do a more effective job than her. It was her insight into hidden connections that had made her so successful in her career. Since the first day she'd joined the force at eighteen she had loved the job, but if she could misjudge Paul Hilliard so badly how could she ever trust her gut feelings about people again? She felt her self-assurance slipping away as she sat at her desk and began tidying up loose ends, checking her reports and emptying her drawers of sweet wrappers, pens, notebooks, receipts and other scraps of paper.

Kathryn Gordon was surprisingly understanding when she summoned Geraldine to her office to question her again about Paul's attempted suicide. 'Don't be too hard on yourself,' she said as Geraldine turned to leave. 'I know you were close –'

'Paul Hilliard meant nothing to me,' Geraldine replied stiffly.

'There's something else, Geraldine. I have to congratulate you on your successful application for a transfer to the Met.'

Geraldine spun round in surprise and returned Kathryn Gordon's smile. 'Thank you, ma'am. Thank you very much.'

'And now there's work to be done.'

'Yes ma'am.' Reluctantly, Geraldine collected her keys and set off.

She hesitated before she rang the bell to deliver the worst kind of good news, and flinched when Matthew Kirby's expression darkened on seeing her. 'Mr Kirby, I wanted to tell you in person – we've arrested the man who killed your wife.'

He opened the door a fraction wider, his voice urgent. 'Who is he? Why did he do it?'

'His name is Paul Hilliard and he's – he's insane.' Briefly Geraldine explained the reasoning behind Paul Hilliard's killing spree.

'You're telling me he blamed Abigail for his daughter's suicide?'

'Yes. Your wife and his daughter's best friend – another fifteen-year-old girl – were both killed. He was planning the death of the doctor who carried out his daughter's abortion and he also murdered a seventeen-year-old male witness and –' She hesitated to disclose that Paul Hilliard had almost killed her too.

'Oh my God.' There was a pause while Matthew took in what Geraldine had said. 'A fifteen-year-old girl. Well, thank you for coming to let us know.'

'How's Lucy?' Geraldine asked as the door began to close.

'Do you want to come in? But –' Geraldine waited. 'I think it's better if you leave us alone.'

'If you'd like a visit from the family liaison officer, you have the number.'

'Thank you, but I don't think so. I mean, she was very helpful but we need to get back to some sort of semblance of a normal life, if we possibly can. We're moving back to York soon, leaving all this behind us. It's for the best, all things considered. Charlotte's never settled down here either, and her mother's not getting any younger so she wants to be nearby.'

'Charlotte?'

'Yes. She's coming with us. She's been great with Lucy and Ben.'

Geraldine hid her surprise. She hoped Charlotte would be kind to the children, but in any case there was nothing she could do about it. 'And Lucy's alright?' She would have liked to see the motherless girl.

'I think so. As far as we can tell. In a way I think what happened to her kind of helped her to stop thinking about her mother. That sounds terrible, doesn't it? But we're trying to forget. Forget what happened, that is,' he added quickly.

'We're not going to forget Abigail, but we're trying not to remember how she died. If we think of her as though she had an accident it makes it easier to deal with somehow.'

'Of course.' Geraldine certainly sympathised with Matthew Kirby's desperation to shield his children from the horror and agony their mother must have endured, and suspected he'd told them she was unconscious throughout her ordeal. It would have been a kindness to lie about it. Abigail was dead, they had to move on in any way they could. The circumstances in which she'd died might be too terrible for her children to bear.

The truth could be devastating.

His daughter's suicide had crushed Paul. Geraldine wondered how his life might have turned out if he'd never discovered the truth, had somehow believed her death was simply a tragic accident, or whether there was something about him that made his insanity inevitable. He had once functioned as a successful man. He'd qualified as a pathologist, married, had a child. It was impossible to know if the man or the circumstances had triggered his insanity.

Either way, she too had to try and move on, like Matthew Kirby. There was no point in dwelling on how she had been so easily conned by a calculating and devious psychopath who had deliberately set out to exploit her emotions in order to gain inside knowledge of the investigation.

As she drove back to the station she wondered whether Lucy had now genuinely accepted Charlotte into her family, or if she was merely tolerating her presence in exchange for their return to York; an unspoken truce with her father. Either way, Geraldine hoped the girl would resolve her inner conflicts. There was even a chance she might blossom if Charlotte paid her enough attention. Perhaps that too was a tacit deal struck between Matthew and Charlotte, a marriage in exchange for loving Lucy and Ben. Geraldine smiled at her hope that Matthew Kirby and his children might one day achieve happiness through these compromises in spite of everything that had happened.

68

CHANGE

Geraldine steeled herself to hear her colleagues discussing Paul Hilliard, but there was a cheerful air of commotion in the Incident Room on her return. Ian Peterson was standing in the middle of the room surrounded by a group of younger officers who all seemed to be talking at once. Geraldine had missed his announcement, but she soon gathered what was going on.

'The first round's on me,' Ian called out above the hubbub. He grinned as a rowdy cheer greeted his statement.

'When's the happy day?' someone asked.

Peterson shrugged. 'We haven't got that far yet.' He dropped his gaze, suddenly sheepish, and everyone cheered again.

'Another one bites the dust,' a raucous voice sang out. The jeering was drowned in another cheer and several officers clapped the sergeant on the back.

'Come on, first round's on Ian. What are we waiting for? Let's go!' The group of officers surged towards the door, chattering cheerfully.

'You coming, gov?' Ian called out, looking around to see who was following and catching Geraldine's eye.

She smiled. 'You bet. I'll be over the road before you've finished buying that first round. I'll have to come and congratulate you properly.'

'She means commiserate,' someone joked.

'Tell me, gov, how did you know all along that Matthew Kirby was innocent?' Peterson asked her, suddenly serious. 'I was so sure – we were all so sure he'd killed Abigail.'

'Geraldine's intuition is what makes her such a gifted detective,' Kathryn Gordon answered for her.

Geraldine felt her tension lift. Perhaps sometimes it was better to trust her judgement of other people after all. She couldn't give up on herself just because a charming psychopath had successfully misled her. She'd always known the life she'd chosen wouldn't be easy.

'You saw through Paul Hilliard,' she reminded the sergeant.

'True. Maybe I'll be as good as you one day, gov.'

'You might even get to be an inspector, if we're all very unlucky,' someone called out.

'I bloody well hope so,' he answered, turning back to rejoin his colleagues who were milling around in the middle of the incident room, waiting to get to the pub. 'I'll have a wife to support!'

Geraldine turned to Kathryn Gordon who was standing beside her and added under her breath, 'I could do without all this celebrating, I'm knackered. But I'm glad they've sorted themselves out. The relationship's been a bit on and off, but from what I can make out he's crazy about her.'

'Life on the force,' the DCI replied with a wry smile. She turned away and raised her voice to address her colleagues. 'I have a brief announcement to make too.' A hush fell on the bustling room.

'What is it, ma'am?' Geraldine asked, knowing exactly what the DCI was going to say.

The older woman's features relaxed into a smile again. 'I'm leaving.'

'What? Leaving the force?' someone asked in polite surprise.

'Yes, I'm finally retiring and not before time. I'm getting past it.' She waved a hand dismissively at the respectful murmur of dissent. 'It's time to move on.'

'What are your plans?' Geraldine asked.

'Oh, there's so much I want to do, now I'll have the time. I won't be sitting at home knitting.' She gave a forced chuckle that failed to mask a flash of regret and, just for an instant, Geraldine felt a spasm of selfish fear. Kathryn Gordon wasn't all that much older than she was. But Kathryn Gordon had suffered a minor coronary, she reminded herself quickly and, in any case, Kathryn Gordon was nearly old enough to be her mother. In fact, she must be about the same age as Milly Blake. The comparison with her real mother caught Geraldine unawares and she dropped her gaze in consternation.

'Don't be upset,' Kathryn Gordon sounded surprised, but Geraldine could only smile and shake her head; it was hardly possible to explain that it wasn't Kathryn Gordon's impending retirement that had shaken her composure.

'Seriously,' Geraldine went on quietly as the rest of the team gathered around Ian Peterson again, clamouring for a drink, 'what are you going to do?'

The DCI spoke lightly. 'I'm going to travel for a while, see some far away places I've always dreamed about – the Taj Mahal, the Grand Canyon, Istanbul – there's a whole world to be explored out there and then – oh, I don't know. I'll see where life takes me. Footloose and fancy free, that'll be me from now on. No deadlines, no pressure, no problems...'

'Sounds wonderful,' Geraldine lied, 'going off like that.'

'It seems everyone's moving on.'

'Yes, it's exciting, isn't it? But I'll be sorry to leave.'

They both glanced up at Ian Peterson who had come over to join them.

'What's that?' he seized on Geraldine's last words. 'You're leaving the force, gov? But you can't. You –'

Geraldine laughed. 'No, I'm not leaving the force, Ian. I've got a transfer. I'm off to the Met.'

'You're going to London?' For an instant he looked startled, then he reached out and shook her warmly by the hand. 'Well done. That's fantastic. You coming over the road then? Drink to a double celebration.'

'We're on our way, Ian,' Kathryn Gordon told him, and he turned and hurried back to his waiting colleagues.

Unexpectedly, Kathryn put her hand on Geraldine's arm. 'We must stay in touch, Geraldine. Keep me posted on how things go in London. I want to hear all about it.'

'Yes, ma'am.'

'And you can call me Kathryn now,' the Detective Chief Inspector smiled. As they went over the road to the pub, Geraldine hoped the celebrations would focus on Ian Peterson's marriage plans, the DCI's retirement and her own transfer to the Met; anything to avoid picking over the case. It was hard to accept that Paul had cynically encouraged her to fall for a fantasy, a dead end. The real Paul Hilliard was a calculating killer. It would have been far better in many ways if the paramedics hadn't arrived in time to save his life.

She couldn't bear to think about what had happened, or listen to any more speculation about his future, but predictably the other officers were discussing it when she and Kathryn entered the pub.

'He's got to be locked-up in a secure psychiatric unit,' a sergeant was saying. 'He's a complete nut job.'

'Round the bloody twist and then some,' a constable agreed.

Ian Peterson glanced up and saw Geraldine join the circle. 'Hey, gov,' he called out loudly. 'I suppose you'll be too bloody high and mighty to come to my wedding now you're going to London? Oh Jesus,' he added in mock horror, 'I'm getting married, God help me.' He grinned as several of his colleagues began whistling the wedding march. More joined in whilst others began gently ribbing the sergeant, congratulating Geraldine or wishing Kathryn Gordon well in her retirement. With Paul Hilliard's name no longer on everyone's lips, Geraldine relaxed and smiled her thanks to the sergeant who raised his glass to her. Sorry to be losing his company, she wondered if he would miss working with her.

Too worn out to cope with her confused emotions Geraldine left early pleading exhaustion, which wasn't far from the truth. She knew she ought to call Celia and share the news about her transfer to the Met, but didn't feel up to warding off her sister's disappointment. Feeling guilty about not phoning Celia, she called Hannah instead.

'I've heard from the Met and guess what?'

'You got the transfer?'

'Yes.'

'Oh my God, I'm so pleased for you. Well done!'

Geraldine couldn't help being affected by her friend's enthusiasm and began to feel excited herself for the first time. 'To be honest, there's been so much going on, it hasn't really sunk in till now – I'm going to London! Don't say anything to Celia, will you, please? She doesn't know yet.'

'Don't worry, I won't breathe a word, but she's bound to be pleased, it's such a great career move for you. And it'll do you good to have a change of scene after all that's happened.'

'Yes, these last few weeks have been tough. Not that I expect London to be any easier.' Geraldine knew that wasn't what Hannah meant, but Hannah didn't mention Paul's name and Geraldine was grateful for her friend's sensitivity. She would have liked to tell Hannah how much she depended on her friendship, when so little else in her life felt secure. At times it seemed she could rely on nothing but the moral certainty that murder was wrong. She sometimes felt she had constructed her life around that belief.

Only after they rang off did Geraldine remember she hadn't told Hannah about her adoption. Maybe it was better that way. Some things were best forgotten, like Paul Hilliard. However hard she tried to put him firmly out of her mind, whenever she closed her eyes she saw a syringe trembling against a white background and a crazed face glaring at her.

But, like the Kirbys, she was moving on and she had a feeling her memories of Paul Hilliard would soon be eclipsed by the challenges and hazards of life in the capital city.

She couldn't wait.

A LETTER FROM LEIGH

Dear Reader,

I hope you enjoyed reading this book in my Geraldine Steel series. Readers are the key to the writing process, so I'm thrilled that you've joined me on my writing journey.

You might not want to meet some of my characters on a dark night – I know I wouldn't! – but hopefully you want to read about Geraldine's other investigations. Her work is always her priority because she cares deeply about justice, but she also has her own life. Many readers care about what happens to her. I hope you join them, and become a fan of Geraldine Steel, and her colleague Ian Peterson.

If you follow me on Facebook or Twitter, you'll know that I love to hear from readers. I always respond to comments from fans, and hope you will follow me on **@LeighRussell** and **fb.me/leigh.russell.50** or drop me an email via my website **leighrussell.co.uk**.

That way you can be sure to get news of the latest offers on my books. You might also like to sign up for my newsletter on **leighrussell.co.uk/news** to make sure you're one of the first to know when a new book is coming out. We'll be running competitions, and I'll also notify you of any events where I'll be appearing.

Finally, if you enjoyed this story, I'd be really grateful if you would post a brief review on Amazon or Goodreads. A few sentences to say you enjoyed the book would be wonderful. And of course it would be brilliant if you would consider recommending my books to anyone who is a fan of crime fiction.

I hope to meet you at a literary festival or a book signing soon!

Thank you again for choosing to read my book.

With very best wishes,

Leigh Russell

LEIGH RUSSELL *DEAD END*

Author Extended Biography

Leigh Russell studied at the University of Kent at Canterbury where she gained a Masters degree in English and American Literature. In addition to being an experienced secondary English teacher, she has a Diploma in Specific Learning Difficulties and has taught Adult Creative Writing classes. Leigh Russell is married and has two daughters.

Author's Q &A

Do you regret not coming to writing earlier or do you think you need life experience to write well?

It surprises me that I stumbled on my passion for writing so late in life, but it would be churlish to harbour regrets when I've been so lucky in my writing career, attracting the attention of a publisher just two months after I started writing and being offered a three book deal straight away.

Why crime? Did you grow up reading the genre?

There wasn't a conscious decision to write crime, no Grand Plan. About four years ago an idea occurred to me, I began to write, and haven't managed a day without writing since. It was like turning on a tap. Crime stories in particular fascinate me. I enjoy the challenge of devising an intriguing plot and creating a variety of characters, and am interested in the questions raised by murder stories. What is it that drives someone to kill another person? It touches on so many issues - good versus evil, life and death, human relations, all of which are fascinating to explore through the medium of story.

Since the origins of fiction, from Beowulf and the monsters of ancient Greek legend, through Sherlock Holmes' enemy Moriarty, to modern crime fiction, we've been attracted to the detective-hero who combats the forces of evil. Contemporary crime fiction has moved away from the infallible superhero-detective, with elements of a caped crusader – but we still want the comfort of the ultimate restoration of moral order which fiction can offer.

Is there anybody you particularly admire in the crime genre or who inspired you?
Yes, there are so many crime authors I admire – Val McDermid, Ian Rankin, Mark Billingham, Dreda Say Mitchell, Simon Beckett – far too many to list here. I usually read UK authors, but am a huge fan of Jeffery Deaver who has just described me as "*a brilliant talent in the thriller field*". I'm pleased that he's been invited to write the new James Bond novel, Carte Blanche, and can't wait to read it. He seems a perfect choice, not only because he writes so well, but because he is fiendishly clever.

How does it feel to suddenly be a bestselling author? Does it change your way of thinking or the way you write?
I certainly feel more confident about my writing after receiving so many encouraging reviews for my novels so far, but I don't think I've changed much. I'm still hooked on writing. There is an additional pressure in knowing so many readers are following Geraldine's career, but I try to focus on writing as well as I can, and just hope that my fans continue to enjoy my books.

Where do you get your ideas and the material for your stories?
Finding ideas has never been a problem. I wrote in an article once that I can see dead bodies anywhere, which isn't as

ghoulish as it sounds. Writing crime thrillers is like problem solving, fitting the pieces of a jigsaw together. Start with a body and then the questions follow. Who is the victim and what is their story? How much does the reader need to know about the killer and his or her motivation? Finally, the detective enters the story, to investigate the murder. And there you have it — a crime thriller.

Does DI Geraldine Steel represent parts of your own personality and character? If not, where does that protagonist come from?
I write psychological thrillers because people fascinate me endlessly. Although plot drives my narrative, character interests me most. So perhaps it's paradoxical that I have no idea where my characters come from. They must be a composite of people I've met or observed, but they are never based on anyone I know. My plots are worked out carefully in advance, but I tend to give my characters a fairly free rein and watch them develop so sometimes characters say or do something for no apparent reason. Only later do I realise why they behaved in that particular way, because they were preparing for a later scene I hadn't consciously thought about yet. Although they can surprise me, I always try to understand my characters and see the world through their eyes. Geraldine Steel is developing and I feel I'm getting to know her as the books progress. There may be a parallel between the workaholic detective and the obsessive nature of writing, but of course if a writer stops working, people's lives aren't on the line. If you're engaged in a hunt for a serial killer, how do you switch off at the end of the day? And how do you relate to people from other walks of life? If you talked about your work dispassionately you'd sound monstrous, but if you allowed your emotions to become engaged you wouldn't be able to do your job. Writing is compulsive and it can be

very difficult to switch off so I understand the obsessive in Geraldine. As for why my killers are so convincing - that's the magic of imagination!

What do you enjoy about writing a series? What are the challenges?

Writing a series poses several challenges. When I started writing Cut Short I hadn't plotted the arc of my main character all the way through the series as most authors do, since I had no idea this story would turn out to be the first of many, so my protagonist is developing as I'm writing. As the series continues I've tried to achieve a balance between providing my readers with a familiar pattern while at the same time offering something new with each book. I'd hate my books to become 'formulaic', but at the same time don't want to resort to something different and shocking just for effect. In the book which follows Dead End Geraldine relocates, which gives her life a natural shake up, and this adds a new dimension to the narrative.

How does DI Geraldine Steel's character evolve in the first three books?

Geraldine Steel's character has evolved as I've been writing. In Cut Short the reader encountered one aspect of her character. In Road Closed her own personal history is introduced and this is developed in subsequent books. I have introduced a few characters along the way any of whom might figure quite significantly in her life in future books, so her journey is beginning to take shape in my mind, although I'm not quite sure yet how it is going to develop in detail. I suspect Geraldine will continue to have a bumpy ride through her personal life before her issues are resolved in a final scene – which I envisage taking place at the end of Book 20 in the series!

What advice would you give to aspiring writers?

Work hard. The vast majority of submissions are rejected, so it's essential to do everything you can to make your manuscript stand out from the hundreds agents and publishers receive every day. Once you've sent out your manuscript, don't be disappointed if your work is rejected. Publishers and agents will only take on a manuscript if they have enough time to devote to a new author, and their schedules are usually full. If your manuscript reaches them at a time when they are acquiring, there's always a chance your manuscript will be chosen and you'll be offered a publishing contract. After that you just have to hope your book is well reviewed and becomes a bestseller!

What are the ups and downs of being published?

There are lots of advantages to being published. I've met so many interesting people through writing - my publisher, editor, agent, staff in bookshops, librarians, organisers of literary festivals, journalists and broadcasters and of course readers. Then there are my fellow writers like Mark Billingham, Ian Rankin, and Jeffery Deaver who I'm thrilled to list among my fans. And in common with other authors, I have a growing number of anecdotes about people who have helped me with my research. I spent an afternoon at my local fire station researching how domestic fires can start. The firemen couldn't have been more helpful - although they did say that if they were called out to a real fire, they would have to abandon mine! When I interviewed a Borough Commander and a Detective Inspector about life in the Met they insisted I join them for dinner, and continue to answer my queries straight away, as do all my contacts in the police force. I've picked the brains of market traders, human remains experts, a Professor of Forensic Medicine, a furniture historian, IT experts, medical practitioners – the list goes on, a disparate collection of people who share a common enthusiasm about their particular area of expertise, and a willingness to pass on their knowledge. I've been bowled over by how helpful people are. As for the downs to being published... no, I haven't come across any yet. But whatever the benefits, professional and personal, of being published, the real buzz is writing. I absolutely love it.

Where do you see yourself in 5 years' time?
If anyone had told me four years ago I was about to become a bestselling author, I would have laughed. I hadn't even started writing then. So I wouldn't try to predict where I'm going to be five years from now, other than to say that the future is always exciting and mysterious. But whatever else I might do, you can be sure that I'll still be writing. There are enough ideas buzzing about in my head for at least a dozen more investigations, so Geraldine Steel is going to be busy for quite a while, and so am I!

About Us

In addition to No Exit Press, Oldcastle Books has a number of other imprints, including Kamera Books, Creative Essentials, Pulp! The Classics, Pocket Essentials and High Stakes Publishing > oldcastlebooks.co.uk

For more information about Crime Books > crimetime.co.uk

Check out the kamera film salon for independent, arthouse and world cinema > kamera.co.uk

For more information, media enquiries and review copies please contact marketing > marketing@oldcastlebooks.com